who do you love

Center Point
Large Print

Also by Jennifer Weiner and available from Center Point Large Print:

Best Friends Forever
Fly Away Home
Then Came You
The Next Best Thing
All Fall Down

This Large Print Book carries the
Seal of Approval of N.A.V.H.

who do you love

Jennifer Weiner

CENTER POINT LARGE PRINT
THORNDIKE, MAINE

This Center Point Large Print edition is published
in the year 2015 by arrangement with Atria Books,
a division of Simon & Schuster, Inc.

Copyright © 2015 by Jennifer Weiner, Inc.

The text of this Large Print edition is unabridged.
In other aspects, this book may vary
from the original edition.
Printed in the United States of America
on permanent paper.
Set in 16-point Times New Roman type.

ISBN: 978-1-62899-746-0

Library of Congress Cataloging-in-Publication Data

Weiner, Jennifer.
Who do you love / Jennifer Weiner. —
    Center Point Large Print edition.
pages cm
Summary: "In a modern day fairy tale about first romance and lasting
love, a wealthy girl and a poor boy meet late one night in an ER waiting
room. Although only eight at the time, they never stop thinking about
that chance encounter that changed the course of both of their lives"—
Provided by publisher.
ISBN 978-1-62899-746-0 (hardcover : alk. paper)
1. First loves—Fiction. 2. Serendipity—Fiction. 3. Large type books.
    I. Title.
PS3573.E3935W48 2015b
813´.54—dc23
                                                                2015032390

For Bill

I married Isis on the fifth day of May
But I could not hold on to her very long
So I cut off my hair and I rode straight away
For the wild unknown country
where I could not go wrong.

—BOB DYLAN, "ISIS"

who do
you love

PROLOGUE

Rachel

2014

"Rachel?"

I don't answer. I shut my eyes and hold my breath and hope whoever it is will think I'm not here and go home.

Knock knock knock, and then my name again. "Rachel, are you in there?"

I twist myself more deeply into the sheets. The sheets are fancy, linen, part of the wedding haul, and they've gotten silkier with every trip through the washing machine. I pull the pillow over my head, noting that the pillowcase has acquired a not-so-fresh smell. This is possibly related to my not having showered for the last three days, during which I have left the bed only to use the toilet and scoop a handful of water from the bathroom sink into my mouth. On the table next to my bed there's a sleeve of Thin Mint cookies that I retrieved from the freezer, and a bag of Milanos for when I finish the Thin Mints. It's spring, and sunny and mild, but I've pulled my windows shut, drawing the shades so I can't see the members of the mom brigade ostentatiously wheeling their oversized strollers down the street, and the forty-year-old guys with expensive suede sneakers and facial hair as carefully tended as bonsai trees tweeting while they walk, or the tourists snapping selfies in front of the snout-to-tail restaurants where everything's organic and locally sourced. The bedroom is dark; the doors are locked; my daughters are elsewhere. Lying on these soft sheets that smell of our commingled scent, hair and skin and the sex we had two weeks ago, it's almost like not being alive at all.

Knock knock knock . . . and then—fuck me—the sound of a key. I shut my eyes, cringing, a little-girl's game of imagining that if you couldn't see someone, they couldn't see you, either. "Go away," I say.

Instead of going away, my visitor comes and sits on the side of the bed, and touches my shoulder, which must be nothing but a lump underneath the duvet.

"Rachel," says Brenda, the most troubled and troublesome of my clients, whom I'd been scheduled to see on Friday. For a minute I wonder how she got into my house before remembering that I'd given her grandson Marcus a key the year before, so he could water the plants and take in the mail over spring break, a job for which I'd paid him the princely sum of ten bucks. He'd asked me shyly if I could take him to the comic

12

book store to spend it, and we'd walked there together with his hand in mine.

"Sorry I missed you," I mutter. My voice sounds like it's coming from the bottom of a clogged drain. I clear my throat. It hurts. Everything hurts. "Don't worry," says Brenda. She squeezes my shoulder and gets off the bed, and I can hear her moving around the room. Up go the shades and window, and a breeze raises goose bumps on my bare arms. I work one eye open. She's got a white plastic laundry basket in her arms, which she's quickly filling with the discarded clothing on the floor. In the corner are a broom and a mop, and a bucket filled with cleaning supplies: Windex and Endust, Murphy's Oil Soap, one of those foam Magic Erasers, which might be useful for the stain on the wall where I threw the vase full of tulips and stem-scummed water.

I close my eyes, and open them again to the sharp-sweet smell of Pine-Sol. I watch like I'm paralyzed as Brenda first sweeps and then dips her mop, squeezes it, and starts to clean my floors. "Why?" I croak. "You don't have to . . ."

"It isn't for you, it's for me," says Brenda. Her head's down, her brown hair is drawn back in a ponytail, and it turns out she does own a shirt that's not low-cut, pants that aren't skintight, and shoes that do not feature stripper heels or, God help me, a goldfish frozen in five inches of Lucite. Brenda mops. Brenda dusts. She works the

13

foam eraser until my walls are as smooth and unmarked as they were the day we moved in. Through the open window come the sounds of my neighborhood. "The website said Power Vinyasa, but I barely broke a sweat," I hear, and "Are you getting any signal?" and "Sebastian! Bad dog!"

I smell the city in springtime: hot grease from the artisanal doughnut shop that just opened down the block, fresh grass and mud puddles, a whiff of dog shit, possibly from bad Sebastian. I hear a baby wail, and a mother murmur, and a pack of noisy guys, probably on their way to or from the parkour/CrossFit gym. My neighborhood, I decide, is an embarrassment. I live on the Street of Clichés, the Avenue of the Expected. Worse, I'm a cliché myself: almost forty, the baby weight that I could never shed ringing my middle like a deflated inner tube, gray roots and wrinkles and breasts that look good only when they're stringently underwired. They could put my picture on Wikipedia: Abandoned Wife, Brooklyn, 2014.

Brenda's hands are gentle as she eases me up and off the bed and into the chair in the corner—a flea-market find, upholstered in a pale yellow print, the chair where I sat when I nursed my girls, when I read my books, when I wrote my reports. As I watch, she deftly strips the sheets off the bed, shakes the pillows free of their creased cases, and gives each one a brisk whack over her knee before settling it back on the bed. Dust fills the room, motes dancing in the beams of light that push through the dirt-filmed windows I'd been plan-ning to have cleaned.

I huddle in my nightgown, shoulders hunched, knees pulled up to my chest. "Why are you doing this?" I ask.

Brenda looks at me kindly. "I am being of service," she says. She carries her armful of soiled linen out of the bedroom and comes back with a fresh set. When she struggles to get the fitted sheet to stay put, I get up off the chair and help her. Then she goes to the bathroom and turns on the shower. "Come on," she says, and I pull my nightgown off over my head and stand under the showerhead, with my arms hanging by my sides. I tilt my head to feel the warmth beating down on my cheeks, my chin, my eyelids. Tears mix with the water and wash down the drain. When I was a little girl and I'd come home from the hospital with Steri-Strips covering my stitches, my mom would give me a sponge bath, then sit me on the edge of the tub to wash my hair, pouring warm water over my head, rubbing in the shampoo, then rinsing, then conditioning, and rinsing again. She would touch the thick, braided line of pink scar tissue that ran down the center of my chest, then gently pat it dry. *My beautiful girl,* she would say. *My beautiful, beautiful girl.*

My sheets are silky and cool as pond water, but I don't lie down. I prop myself up against the headboard and rasp out the question that I've heard hundreds of times from dozens of clients. "What do I do now?"

Brenda gives a rueful smile. "You start again," she tells me. "Just like the rest of us."

PART I

HALF A HEART

Rachel

1985

I was born with a broken heart. This was a line that got me a lot of sympathy from preschool through sixth grade, when I decided that a congenital heart condition was not what I wanted to be known for, and stopped talking about it at school. My condition was called tricuspid atresia, which meant that on the right side, the valve between the upper and lower chambers of my heart wasn't formed correctly. Blood that should have flowed smoothly from my heart to my lungs moved instead in a sluggish trickle—a lazy schoolkid who'd overslept and couldn't be bothered to run for the bus. Not a good thing if you want to, as the doctors say, survive.

I'd been diagnosed thirty-six hours after my birth, when I'd done the docs the favor of turning a lovely shade of plum. At the local hospital, they didn't know exactly what was wrong, only that they couldn't fix it, so they airlifted me to Miami Children's Hospital, where I received something called a Blalock-Taussig shunt to give the blood an unobstructed path.

Once I'd recovered, my terrified parents took me home, along with an oxygen tank and instructions about what to do if I turned blue or started gasping. For the first year of my life, I slept in a portable crib pushed up next to my mother's side of the bed, with her hand on my chest. Photographs show a tiny, wrinkled raisin of an infant floating in her onesies, with none of the succulent, squeezable plumpness of normal babies. "Failure to thrive" was what they wrote on my charts, and my mother took it like a straight-A student receiving her first failing grade, like she'd been the one who'd been unable to successfully nurture me, instead of me being the one who hadn't grown. Before I was born, she'd been a librarian—just part-time after my brother had come, but it was work she loved. After I was diagnosed, she quit and devoted herself to my care.

"We used to put olive oil in your baby food," she told me—this was when I was a teenager and had embarked on the first of many lose-five-pounds-in-a-weekend schemes, that one involving grape-fruits and cucumbers. She would melt butter in my rice cereal, slather it on bread and crackers, feed me milk shakes where other kids just got milk. Still, it was years before I crept into the very lowest height/weight percentiles for children my age, years before I graduated to my own bedroom, where, all through my childhood and into my teens, I would wake up at least once a week with my mother's hand on my chest and her face twisted in fear that would melt into relief when she was sure that I was still breathing, that my heart was still beating, that I was still alive.

"We thought we would lose you," she told me, over and over. I couldn't blame her. Besides all the surgeries and the risks they involved, when I was six I'd had pleurisy, a lung infection that made my oxygen saturation levels drop dangerously low. My parents brought me to my cardiologist, who sent me straight to the hospital, where the surgeons performed an emergency procedure that night to close off veins that had gotten too big, in a misguided effort to help my body deal with the faulty valve. I'd gone home the next day, even though my mom said she'd begged the doctors to keep me longer, that she didn't think she'd be able to stand it if she found me turning purple again. By my seventh birthday, I'd been hospitalized six times—once after the pleurisy, once with pneumonia, four more times for cardiac catheteri-zations so the doctors could check the shunt.

When I was eight, I went back to Miami Children's for open-heart surgery, a hemi-Fontan procedure that would replace the original shunt and would keep me in the hospital for a month. My mother had been terrified about the operation, of having my chest cracked open again, my poor battered heart exposed to the world. Every Friday for three months before the big day, she would drag me to synagogue and, when the rabbi asked if anyone needed a *misheberach*, a special prayer for healing, she'd march me up to the bimah, the altar in front of the Torah, so he could put his hands on my shoulders and pray. I didn't tell my mom that I was secretly almost looking forward to the surgery. Once I'd had it, maybe she would stop worrying so much, and I could spend my Friday nights watching TV.

The only thing I remembered from the operation was Dr. Bob, the anesthesiologist, telling me to count backward from ten. "Ten . . . nine . . . eight . . ." I said . . . and then I woke up in the recovery room with my mom next to the bed, crying. For the first few days I was on a ventilator. My mom would hold my hand, refusing to let go, eating the sandwiches and apples she'd packed for her lunch one-handed, talking to me constantly. My father would come after work, bringing a stuffed animal every time—a fuzzy yellow duck, a teddy bear, a pink bunny with silky, fur-lined ears. He would tuck each new toy into the crook of my arm and deposit a kiss on my forehead.

"She's a fighter," he would tell my mom, handing her tissues, patting her back. Then he'd sit in the corner, reading magazines, while my mom would comb my hair and fuss with my gown and cry when she thought I was sleeping. "My number-one mom," I would say, and she'd give me a brave, tremulous smile. I spent days, and a few sleepless nights, trying to figure out the right words, something I could say that would comfort her and would also be true. *I promise I won't die* was the obvious choice . . . but I wasn't sure I could promise that, and I didn't think she'd like knowing that I thought death was even a possibility. I stuck with "Number-one mom," which was what it said on the mug I'd painted for her birthday.

At eight o'clock they'd finally leave. My mom would kiss me, her freckled face pale and her curly brown hair, which was usually blown out straight and meticulously styled, pulled back in a careless ponytail. My dad would steer her out the door, one heavy hand between her shoulder blades, rubbing in little circles. Sometimes I'd see her rest her head on his shoulder. Sometimes I'd hear him whisper "I love you" in her ear.

By the second week, I was still in bed, still on a feeding tube and a cannula, with drains sticking out of my chest. "Lookin' good!" said my hospital friend Alice, popping into my room even though I didn't think she was supposed to be leaving hers. When I'd arrived there'd been a big sign reading MASKS AND HAND-WASHING MANDATORY on her door, and I'd heard the nurses scold her for wandering. Alice was twelve and in sixth grade, but she was so small that we were basically the same size. Alice had had leukemia as a baby, and it had affected her growth. She would always be short, even as a grown-up—"That is, if I make it that long," she would say. For a while, the doctors thought she was cured. She'd made it past the five-year mark without a recurrence. Then, when she was ten, she'd started getting sick again. Still, she'd been out in the world long enough to tell me about the roller rink, where my parents never let me go, and about PG-rated movies, and what kind of homework you got in sixth grade. She had kissed two boys playing Seven Minutes in Heaven at a friend's birthday party, and she'd seen *Flashdance*, to which my parents had said, "Absolutely not." They hadn't even wanted to buy me the soundtrack. I'd had to get Nana to buy it for my birthday.

By the third week, the doctors said that I was healing beautifully, and that I was well enough to eat real food. My mother's tears slowed to a trickle. Instead of tucking her hair back into a scrunchie, she'd coax it into ringlets and then do my hair, too. She'd stopped wearing T-shirts and jeans and was back in her usual uniform, crisply ironed cotton blouses and linen pants with narrow leather belts, and I got to swap the hospital gowns that opened in the back for pajamas. We'd play Boggle or checkers, with the games set up on the hinged table that rolled in place above my bed, and she'd let me try on her makeup when she went outside to speak quietly to the nurses and the doctors.

My father would still stop by at night, bringing me things that I could do, not just hold—hundred-piece puzzles, a Walkman with new tapes—Wham! and Madonna, Whitney Houston and Billy Ocean. When my parents weren't there, I would take my new gifts to Alice's room. After I'd scrubbed my hands and slipped on a surgical mask, we could sit on her bed and listen to music, stretching the headphones wide so that she could hear the music in her left ear and I could listen with my right.

"Take that stupid thing off," she'd say, pointing at my mask. "Like that's going to help anything." Alice was terminal. "That means I'm going to die," she'd told me the first day I'd gotten out of bed, when we were in the playroom, together on a couch. It was September in Florida, sunny and warm, and we could see palm trees outside the windows and hear the drone of the mower as a man in a khaki uniform steered it across the lawn. A five-year-old who'd come for a kidney transplant ran around pretending he was a fireman. A little girl with a bald head sat reading *The Cat in the Hat* with her mom. "They don't ever say it in front of me. But I know."

I wanted to know if she was scared, but I didn't want to insult her. "Does it hurt?" I asked instead.

She pointed at the bag of clear fluids dripping into the IV attached to her arm. "They give me dope."

I nodded. After this most recent surgery, I'd

had a button that I could press whenever it hurt.

Alice looked down, adjusting her scarf, so that I couldn't see her face when she said, "I think maybe, by the end, it's going to hurt a lot." Then she raised her head, tossing one of the long, trailing ends of the scarf over her shoulder.

"Elegant?"

"Very." Alice always wore bandanas or fancy fringed scarves in beautiful patterns, turquoise and hot pink and gold. Once, I'd been walking past her room and she'd been cross-legged on her bed with her scarf beside her, and I'd seen her head bare. She had only a thin coating of pale blond fuzz where her hair had been, and there were pink scars crisscrossing her scalp. The night after the playroom I'd had a terrible nightmare, a dream where Alice turned into a cat and came and sat on my chest. Cat-Alice clamped my nose shut with her paws, and when I opened my mouth, she breathed into me, blowing her sickness down my throat so that she'd be healthy again and I'd be the one who had cancer. "It's going to hurt a lot," Cat-Alice hissed, and I woke up sweaty, my heart beating hard enough to scare me.

"Will Alice get better?" I asked Sandra, my favorite of all the nurses. Sandra was sure-handed and gentle when she had to give me a needle or start a line, and she'd always say "Lunch is served, madam!" when she dropped off my tray, lifting the plastic lids off the food like it was

26

something great even when I was just on clear liquids and Jell-O. When the bed next to me was empty, she'd fill it with my swiftly expanding collection of stuffed animals, arranging them in funny displays, the bunny with its long ears spread out against a pillow, the monkey hanging from an IV pole by its tail.

Sandra turned her head from side to side, like she was shaking water out of her ears. "We aren't supposed to talk about other patients." Then she smiled, to show that she hadn't meant to hurt my feelings. She had a pretty accent—her parents had come from Cuba, so she'd learned to speak Spanish before English. Her hair was dark and shiny, her eyes were merry and brown, and she wore a sweet, flowery perfume. I'd take deep breaths whenever she was close, and try to hold the scent in my nose to overpower the smell of the hospital, floor cleaners and chicken soup and pee.

"I hope she'll get better. She's my friend." Sandra didn't answer, but I saw her lips tighten and heard her ponytail whisk against her back as she turned her head away. That, I was learning, was how grown-ups told the truth, not with words, but with what they did. The next night after dinner, I was walking up and down the hall, the only exercise that I could do, and I saw a woman in a skirt and high heels, not scrubs and clogs, talking quietly to Alice's parents outside of her room. I didn't see the name on her tag, but I saw the words HOSPICE CARE. *They spelled* hospital *wrong,* I thought. Alice's mom was pale and silent, but her father was crying, big, heaving sobs that made his shoulders shake while he covered his face with his hands. I walked away fast, pulling my IV pole behind me. I was used to mothers crying—at least, I was used to my mom doing it—but it was unsettling to see a father like that. My father was big, broad-chested, and strong. I couldn't imagine him crying, and I didn't know what I'd do if he ever did.

By the fourth week, I was feeling almost completely better, but Alice was sleeping almost all of the time, and the novelty of hospital life was beginning to wear off. My mom would come every morning, bustling around, rearranging my blankets and books and stuffed animals and the get-well cards that she'd taped to the wall. She'd sit on my bed with me and watch *The Price Is Right.* We'd call out our bets for the Showcase Showdown, keeping track of who won. When dinner arrived at five-thirty, she'd watch me, monitoring every spoonful of soup and cracker that I ate, and if the food wasn't something I liked, she was ready with a tote bag full of jam-and-butter sandwiches, out-of-season cherries, and Fritos ("Don't tell Dad," she'd whisper, passing me the bag). On Friday nights she'd make my brother, Jonah, come with her, and when they left they'd go to Shabbat services, this time to pray for me to get well. In khakis and a button-down, with a yarmulke in his pocket and clean finger-nails that I knew my mom had inspected, Jonah would stand in the doorway, mouthing the words *spoiled brat* when my mom wasn't looking. I didn't mind. At least he still treated me like a normal little sister.

After dinner was more TV, and then story time. I had a big book of *Grimm's Fairy Tales*—not the Disney versions but the original stories, where Cinderella's wicked stepsisters cut off their heels and toes to cram their feet into the glass slipper and the illustrations showed the blood. "Are you sure this won't give you bad dreams?" my mother would ask. I shook my head, not mentioning the dream I'd had about Alice, not asking her any of the questions I had. It would upset her to have to think about a kid dying, even if it was someone else's kid.

Finally, the echoing loudspeakers would deliver the news that visiting hours were over. My mother would stand up and stretch, throwing her arms over her head, twisting from side to side so that her back made popping noises. She'd retuck her shirt, pull out a mirrored compact to put on more lipstick, then bare her teeth in the mirror to make sure they were clean. "Be a good girl," she would say before she'd leave, her heels clicking briskly, the scent of Giorgio trailing behind her.

I'd start out in Alice's room. After dinner was a

good time for her. "Sarah baked cookies," she'd say, pointing at the tin her mom had left, or "Mike brought library books." She called her parents by their first names, which I thought was daring and very adult. She would teach me cat's cradles or we'd play with the Ouija board that Alice had somehow convinced Sarah and Mike to bring her. "Will I ever get married?" she'd asked it, and I'd pushed the planchette, practically shoving it into the YES corner, while Alice shook her head and said, "You're not supposed to do that!"

Shift change was at eight o'clock. If Alice was up to it, she and I would sit quietly on the couch by the intake desk, watching as the nurses hurried to finish their paperwork before they'd pick up their lunch bags and purses and, sometimes, use the staff bathroom to change out of their scrubs, shedding their nurse-skins, turning back into regular ladies. Once, we saw Sandra emerge in a tight black dress and high heels. She'd put on red lipstick and makeup that made her dark eyes look like deep pools. "Hot date tonight?" another nurse had said, and Sandra gave a small, pleased smile as she tucked a flat gold purse under her arm and walked toward the elevator.

With all of the confusion—day nurses leaving, night nurses starting their shifts, different doctors arriving to visit their patients—it was the easiest thing to slip into the elevator and stand close enough to one of the nurses that people would assume she was taking me to another floor, but also near another adult so that the nurses would think I was with a parent. Alice couldn't go, so I was her emissary, the spy she sent out into the world. "Come back and tell me a story," Alice would say, and most nights, that's what I would do. I'd go down to the first floor, find a child-sized wheelchair, clip my IV pole to the hook in back, and wheel myself up and down the halls, slow and steady, like the doctors told me, sometimes peeking into open doors to get a look at the scenes they revealed—an old man sleeping, the wires and IV lines attached to his body making it look like he was being attacked by an octopus; two women whispering at the foot of a bed; two interns taking advantage of an unoccupied room to kiss.

One Wednesday night I stopped by Alice's room, but the door was shut. I heard voices and wondered if her parents were still in there, even though visiting hours were over. A new sign was taped where the one about hand-washing and mask-wearing had been: DNR, said the letters; DO NOT . . . and then there was a long word I couldn't figure out, with a lot of smaller print beneath it. I didn't see Sandra, so I stopped the first nurse who came down the hall, a skinny woman with short gray hair and a wrinkly face.

"Excuse me, what's that say?" I asked, tapping the big word. Her wrinkles got deeper.

"Why are you out here wandering around? It's

31

bedtime." In the harsh overhead light, I could see three silvery hairs glinting from her chin. That was a detail Alice would have loved.

The nurse pointed down the hall. "Bedtime. You don't want to make things harder for the doctors, do you?"

"No, but I just want to know . . ."

She bent down. I spotted another hair, right in the middle of her cheek. I wondered if she didn't have mirrors in her house, or anyone to tell her that she needed some tweezers. "Sweetie, there are very sick kids here, and if the doctors or nurses need to get to their room in a hurry, you don't want to be in their way."

By then I had been in hospitals long enough to know when you could get what you wanted and when it was hopeless. "Good night," I said, smiling sweetly. Back in my room, I decided to go downstairs and see if I could find something interesting to tell Alice about once her parents were gone. I selected a package of chocolate-covered Hostess Donettes from the latest gift basket my mom had sent for the nurses. I wrapped my treats in napkins and bundled up the pink-and-purple afghan my nana had made me. Armed with provisions, the blanket, and my newest stuffed animal, a little teddy bear, I stuck my head out of my door, looked up and down the hallway to make sure that it was empty, then took the elevator down to the emergency room.

I found a wheelchair by the entrance and waited until the receptionist was busy on the phone before wheeling myself into a corner of the waiting room. A TV was playing *Dallas*, and it looked like a slow night. A teenage boy was staring down at his right hand, which was wrapped in gauze, and a lady who looked like his mom sat next to him, reading *Good Housekeeping*. In the next row of chairs, an old man in a short-sleeved button-down shirt and a battered brown hat was breathing heavily. Occasionally he'd suck in his breath and clutch his belly, gasping, "God-DAMN, don't that hurt!" His wife, bundled up in a cardigan and shivering in the air-conditioning, kept repeating, "Monty, I'm sure it's just heart-burn." On the other side of the room, a young mother and father sat with a little girl. "Why did you think putting Barbie's shoe in your nose was a good idea?" I heard the father ask.

I nibbled a Donette, hoping for some excitement. The night before, there'd been a car crash, and I'd seen gurneys speeding through the room, ambulance technicians running alongside them, shouting codes, calling for units of blood, just like I'd seen on TV, except one of the ambulance guys was old and fat and everything was over in ten seconds.

Finally, the doors hissed open, and a boy about my age came in, with a woman in a skirt and a blue blazer trailing behind him. The boy was tall, with skin a few shades darker than mine and thick, curly hair that hung down almost to his collar and looked like it needed a trim. His face was pinched with pain, and he had his right arm folded against his chest, with his left arm holding it there. He and the woman went to the desk, and I overheard her say "Eight years old" to the receptionist before she said "Good luck" to the boy and then walked out the door. The receptionist pointed to an empty row of chairs and said, "Take a seat."

I looked at the boy. He had skinny legs and a dimple in his chin, full lips, and eyes that tilted up at the corners.

I wheeled my chair up beside him. "Hey," I said.

For a minute, he didn't answer. His eyes were wide and shocked, and he had bitten his lower lip so hard that I could see dots of blood. One of his legs was bouncing up and down, like he was nervous or he had to pee. Finally, he looked at me from the corner of his eyes.

"What?"

"What happened?"

"Hurt my arm," he muttered, and glanced down like he was checking to make sure the arm was still there. He had the longest eyelashes I'd ever seen on a boy, thick and curled up at the tips.

"How?"

He paused, staring unhappily into his lap.

"I fell," he finally said.

"Fell where?"

"Off a balcony."

"You fell off a balcony?" I winced, imagining it. "How many floors?"

"Just one," he said. He was talking so quietly that it was hard to hear him. "I was balancing on the railing."

"Why?"

"Circus tricks." He got to his feet, sucking in his breath as his arm jiggled, and crossed the room to talk to the receptionist. He asked her something. She shook her head. He backed away from the desk, looking around the room before choosing the seat farthest away from me and sitting there, slumped, with his head drooping down and his foot bouncing.

I gave a mental shrug and returned my attention to the Ewing family, hoping for something that would make a better story than a kid with a broken arm who didn't even want to talk to me. A minute later, the receptionist called across the room. "Andrew?"

The boy raised his head.

"Can you think of any other place your mom might be? We haven't been able to reach her at the hotel."

Andrew shook his head, and went back to staring at the floor while I stared at him. It was hard for me to believe that a kid my age could be in a hospital all alone.

I wheeled across the room to where he was sitting. Andrew eyed me tiredly, but he didn't tell me to leave. Instead, he said, "How come you're here?"

"I have a congenital heart deformity, and I had a special tube put in so the blood goes where it's supposed to."

"Why are you in a wheelchair? Can't you walk?" he asked.

"Well, I can," I admitted, lowering my voice. "But I get bored, and if I use a wheelchair people just think I'm supposed to be here. Did you come here in an ambulance?" I hoped he had, and that he'd tell me about it. The only time I'd ridden in one I'd been six, and I couldn't really remember my trip. But Andrew shook his head and didn't say anything else. I tried to figure out what else to ask him, some question he wouldn't be able to answer with a nod or a "no."

"Where are your parents?" I asked.

"It's only my mom and I don't know where she is." His voice cracked on the last word, and then he started talking fast, the words tumbling out of his mouth like a spill of stones. "She was the lucky caller on Q102, and we got to come here, and go to a movie premiere and meet the stars. She said she was going down to a party by the pool for just one drink, and that I should stay in my bed and she'd be back by nine, and then it was nine and she wasn't back and I climbed up to see if I could see her and I slipped . . ." His voice

36

broke again, and he turned his face away, looking furious, scrubbing at his eyes with his good hand, first one and then the other, so hard that it had to sting. "Go away," he said, and it sounded like he was still crying. "Just leave me alone."

Instead of leaving I looked out the window, but all I could see was the dark. No ambulances with their lights flashing, no people coming in all bloody, like the man I'd seen two nights ago who had cut his hand when he was slicing a bagel. Alice had giggled a lot when I'd told her that one, probably because, we'd decided, *bagel* was just a funny-sounding word.

"I'm Rachel Blum," I said. "It's spelled B-L-U-M, but it's *bloom* like flowers, not *blum* like *plum*." When he didn't smile or even look at me, I said, "I'm eight, too."

"I'm almost nine. I'll be nine in two weeks," he said.

"Where are you from?"

"Philadelphia," he said . . . and then, after a minute, "The lady told me I'll probably need an X-ray."

"X-rays don't hurt," I said.

"I know that," he said, and looked away again. I could see goose bumps on his arms, underneath the short sleeves of his shirt.

"Do you want to borrow my blanket? My nana made it herself. She knits." Before he could tell me no, I pulled my blanket off my lap, looked around, then sneaked out of my chair to spread it on his lap.

"Thanks."

"Are you hungry?" I handed him one of the little doughnuts, and he took a bite—just to be polite, I thought. I was running out of things to talk about or ask about, so I picked up my bear.

"Hello, Andrew!" I said, in the silly voice I had used for all my stuffed animals when I was a little kid, five or six, and I liked to pretend that they could talk. Sometimes if there were little kids in the playroom I would do it for them, make the stuffed bears and owls and rabbits pretend to meet each other, or go to the first day of school, or get in fights.

He didn't smile, but he did ask, "What's his name?"

I had decided that the bear was a girl and named her Penelope, but didn't want to say so. "He doesn't have a name yet."

Andrew turned the bear over, inspecting its tag. "It says Darwin."

"Yeah, but you don't have to call him that. You can change it. You can keep him if you want to."

"Really?"

"I have a bazillion stuffed animals. My dad brings one every day. I think they sell them in the gift store. All the dads bring them. My mom says it's because it's convenient."

Andrew looked at his lap. "My dad is dead."

I had no idea what to say to that. We sat together silently for a few minutes as *Dallas* gave way to the eleven o'clock news and the man in the hat punctuated the report of an unsolved murder in Little Havana with his groans.

The boy looked at my incision. You could just see the very top of it underneath the collar of my pajama top. "Does it hurt?" he asked.

"It did, a lot, at the beginning." Every time I'd coughed, every time I'd moved, the pain had rolled through me, like something big with lots of sharp teeth was trying to bite through my chest. I was trying hard not to think about how bad it had been, and, if I needed another operation, how bad it would be again. "It's okay now," I told him. "The worst part is that my parents worry. My mom cries when she thinks I'm sleeping. She thinks I'm going to die. My dad just brings me presents and barely even talks to me at all." I touched my scar, feeling the edges of the tape with my fingertips, the bumps of the stitches underneath. "Everyone in my school thinks I'm weird. I have to stay home a lot, or else I'm in the hospital, and when I come back the teachers make a big deal, and everyone stares at me like I'm . . ."

I wasn't sure the boy was listening, but he said, "Like you're what?"

"Like I'm broken. Like I'm a busted toy, or a bike with flat tires. Nobody wants to play with me at recess. At lunch, we eat at our tables, so I don't

39

sit by myself, but at recess they all play Four Square or Princesses and Ninjas, or Red Rover, and no one ever wants me in their game." I didn't tell him the worst part, which was that sometimes I thought that I was broken, too, and that maybe I'd never get better. I'd just keep coming to the hospital and coming to the hospital and finally they wouldn't be able to fix me anymore and I would die.

"Reindeer games," said Andrew. He looked at the bear. "Maybe he should be Rudolph." Then he looked at me. "I don't really have friends, either," he said. He straightened his shoulders, wincing as his arm shifted. "My dad was black and my mom's white, so the black kids think I'm stuck-up and the white kids only play with other white kids."

I didn't know what to say to that, either. There were only two black kids in my entire school, and neither one was in my class. I thought about telling him that he didn't look like he was black, but then I thought that maybe that would be rude. "My mom says to make a friend, you need to be a friend." When my mother had told me that line it had sounded very wise, but when I said the same words they just sounded silly. Certainly it hadn't helped me much. I'd tried to be a friend, but so far it hadn't worked.

"My mom says we keep ourselves to ourselves," said Andrew. "She says it's us against the world."

He pulled my nana's blanket up higher, struggling to do it with just one hand.

"What movie did you get to see?"

He named the film, which had *Blood* in its title and was, I knew, rated R. His leg started to jiggle again, bouncing faster and faster. "The best was when my mom took me to the beach," he said. "I'd never gone swimming in the ocean before."

The beach was just a block away from my house. I'd been to the ocean more times than I could count, but I'd never been swimming. All I could ever do was walk on the sand and dip my feet in the foam, with my mother trailing behind me in a wide-brimmed hat, watching everything I did. Her gaze would bounce back and forth, from my feet to the water, as if a wave might surge up and snatch me away. She'd told me about the undertow, the invisible current that would suck swimmers to their doom . . . but even before I'd learned about the undertow, I was afraid of the ocean, the endlessness of it, how it stretched farther than you could see and was deeper than you could imagine. I preferred swimming pools, and all the houses in our neighborhood had them in the backyard, rectangles or ovals of clear, chlorinated blue. No seaweed, no waves, no chance of getting towed out to Cuba, no strange things lurking down in the depths.

"Did you like it?"

Andy nodded. He had beautifully shaped lips,

full and pink, as if an artist had taken a lot of time to draw them and color them in. I thought he was cuter than Bryan Adams, the singer who Alice said was the cutest boy in the world. "It was so great. The water was really cold at first, and there was seaweed. I didn't like that." I nodded in sympathy. "But I figured out how to bodysurf, and then I went out past the waves, and I flipped on my back, and I just floated." He was almost smiling, and I could picture him, his lean body in the water, his hair billowing out around him, face turned up toward the sun. "It was like being on a roller coaster. I wish I could have stayed forever, but my mom got a sunburn and we had to go back." He gave a great, shuddering sigh and curled more deeply into the blanket.

"She'll be here soon," I promised. Then, to distract him, I asked, "Do you want to hear a story?"

He shrugged, then said, "You can tell me one, if you want to."

"A baby one or a scary one?" I asked. I looked down at my pajamas, which were pink and had Winnie-the-Pooh on them, and wished that I'd put my bathrobe on.

"Scary," he said.

I thought for a minute, flipping through my mental inventory before I made my voice as deep and spooky as I could. "Once upon a time there was a woodcutter and his wife and their two children. They lived in a simple cottage in the deepest, darkest part of the forest, where the sun shone for only one hour every day. And even though the woodcutter worked from morning until night, he could not earn enough money to buy food for his family, and they slowly began to starve."

" 'Hansel and Gretel,' " Andy said . . . but he didn't tell me to stop. As I described the wood-cutter's wife growing so thin that her wedding ring slipped right off her finger, he leaned closer to me, and when I got to the part about how the family had only one potato and one carrot to last them for the entire day, he said, "Wait."

"What?"

"Why couldn't they go hunting and shoot a bird or a rabbit?" he asked.

I thought about it. "The birds and the rabbits were all starving, too, so they left to go to where there was more food," I said in my normal voice. Then I deepened it again. "There was a great famine in the land. A plague of locusts," I added, remembering part of the Passover story we'd learned in Hebrew school.

"What are locusts?"

"Like crickets, but they eat everything."

Andy nodded, satisfied. I continued the story, about how the woodcutter and his wife became so desperate that they decided to leave the children in the woods, thinking, as I spoke, that my story might have been the wrong choice. Abandoned children in the forest sounded an awful lot like an abandoned boy in the emergency room. But it was too late to go back.

"Okay, so, the children were all alone in the woods, except, luckily, Hansel had some bread crumbs in his pocket."

"You know what I always wondered?" Andy said. "If they were starving, why didn't they eat the bread crumbs?"

I'd never thought of that. It occurred to me that Andy might actually know what it was like to be hungry, really hungry, not just-off-the-school-bus, lunch-was-three-hours-ago-and-I'm-ready-for-a-snack hungry.

"The crumbs were so hard that they would have broken his teeth if he'd even tried to eat them. Also, they were moldy. They were green as emeralds with mold!"

The corners of his eyes crinkled when he smiled. "But then if the crumbs were green, they wouldn't be able to see them if they left them on the forest floor."

I groaned and said, "You're kidding me!" the way my dad did on car trips when Jonah asked to stop for a bathroom break ten minutes after we'd gotten on the highway.

"Maybe the forest floor was covered with dead pine needles, which were brown, so the emerald-green bread crumbs showed up."

"Ah." When the sliding doors whooshed open, Andy and I both turned to look, but it was only a gray-haired woman who hurried over to the couple with the little girl and started talking rapidly in Spanish. I caught the word *Barbie* a few times.

"So then what?" Andy asked.

I described Hansel and Gretel's journey back through the forest. How they slept out alone in the dark woods, with all kinds of scary growls and screeches echoing through the night, with only pine needles for beds and leaves for blankets. I told how they caught a single tiny fish and cooked it over a fire they started by banging a rock against a piece of flint that they found in the river.

"Scott Lindsey?" called a nurse. The teenager got up and sauntered through the swinging doors on giant basketball shoes that made his feet look too big for his legs, with his mom, still holding her magazine, behind him. The moaning man watched him go and said, "Shee-it," and his wife looked at me and Andy and said, " 'Scuse his language."

Andy and I looked at each other and started to giggle. "Shee-it," Andy whispered, doing a perfect imitation of the man, and then I said, " 'Scuse his language," and we both laughed even harder, and he said, "Keep going."

"Hansel and Gretel wandered deeper into the forest, trying to find their little cottage . . . but instead they found a hideous witch. She had curly black hair like wires, and a big red wart on her chin." In my retelling, the witch looked like Miss Bonitatibus, my music teacher, who would say, "How honored we are that you could join us," every time I came back to class after being home sick.

"The witch said, 'Come! I will show you a sight such as you have never seen!' And she led them through the forest, to a house made entirely . . . out . . . of . . . candy." I described the walls made of gingerbread, a fireplace filled with peppermint logs, and a roof tiled with Necco Wafers, pale pink and mint green and melon orange.

"Were there any doughnuts on the house?" Andy asked, lifting up the remainder of the one I'd given him.

"The doorknobs were doughnuts, and the floors were milk chocolate, and—"

At that moment, a woman hurried through the emergency-room doors. She stopped and scanned the crowd, her head turning from side to side until she spotted Andy. Her skin, sunburned a painful-looking pink, was much lighter than her son's. She had a tangle of taffy-blond hair and wore high black boots, blue jeans, and a low-cut black top. Black rubber bangles covered one arm from wrist to elbow ("They look cheap," my mother had sniffed when I'd asked her to buy me some), and as she walked over to us, I smelled the nose-wrinkling, sweet-sharp scent of liquor. She looked nothing like my mom or like the other mothers I knew. The moms in my world did not have wild mops of hair, or long fingernails with glittering polish, or four earrings in their ears. I wondered how my mom would look, out of her crisp cotton skirts or linen pants and twinset, and in high heels and a shirt cut low enough to show the tops of her bosoms.

"What happened?" she asked, bending down so that she was looking right into Andy's eyes.

Andy mumbled to her what he'd told me—that he'd waited up for her but she hadn't come, so he'd gotten onto the balcony to try to see down to the pool, and he'd fallen. She touched his shoulder once, briefly. Her colored lids descended, and she stood for a minute with her eyes shut. "Okay," she finally sighed. "Who found you?"

"Lady from the hotel," Andy said.

His mother sighed, then straightened to her tallest—in her heels, she seemed very tall—and said, loud enough for the whole room to hear, "Hello? Is anyone here going to help us?"

"Sorry," said Andy. I heard, but his mom didn't.

The elevator doors slid open, and Sandra walked into the waiting room. Her ponytail was crooked, with strands of hair slipping out of the elastic, and she looked as tired as I'd ever seen her. As soon as she spotted me, she hurried over, just as Andy's mom was saying to no one in particular,

"I bet this is all out of network." She said some of her words in a funny way, *all* stretching into *awl,* and she kept turning her head from left to right, looking, I thought, for someone to yell at.

"Rachel, you need to get upstairs," said Sandra.

Andrew's mom ran her eyes over me briefly— my babyish pajamas, the wheelchair, the IV pole, and the ID bracelet on my wrist. She looked at the moaning man and his wife, the family with the little girl. Everyone was staring at her, but she didn't seem to notice as she turned to Sandra.

"How long has my son been waiting? Why isn't anyone taking care of him? Where's the doctor?" Her accent stretched and shifted vowels, and her voice kept getting louder, and it seemed like with every question she was getting bigger, taller, swelling with rage. "How could you just leave a little boy sitting here?"

The wife of the moaning man turned around. "Where have you been?" she asked, but her voice was quiet, and Andy's mom either didn't hear her or pretended that she didn't. The receptionist came out from behind her desk. "Ma'am. We cannot treat your son, or any minor, without a parent's permission. No one was able to find you. No one at the hotel knew where you were . . ."

"Oh, so this is my fault?" Andy's mother stepped toward the receptionist until they were almost toe to toe. "My son gets hurt, and you leave him sitting here for hours, and it's my fault?"

As his mom spoke, with her hands on her hips and her breasts jiggling, Andy pressed himself into his chair, making himself as small as he could. I reached for his hand and he held mine, squeezing tight before letting go when a doctor, a short man in a white coat with the sleeves pushed up, entered the room. Dark stubble dotted his chin, and his tie had been yanked to one side. "What seems to be the problem?"

"The problem," Andy's mother announced, "is that my son has been sitting here for hours, and not one of you so-called professionals has done anything to help him."

"Mother of the year here," the moaning man's wife said. This time, Andy's mom couldn't pretend she hadn't heard. Her head snapped around and her pink face got even pinker.

"Excuse me, but did anyone ask for your opinion?"

"Where were you?" the woman asked again. "That poor child's been sitting here for over an hour." She shook her head, looking disgusted.

"Ladies," said Sandra, and the doctor offered Andy's mother his hand and bent low when she took it, almost like he was bowing.

"I'm Dr. Diallou." He was round, almost penguin-shaped, with dark skin and a puff of hair over each of his ears. His voice was melodious, like he was singing instead of talking. "May I have the pleasure of your name, madam?"

"Lori Landis." *Lori* sounded like *Lawrey.* I wondered if everyone in Philadelphia talked like that all the time, or only when they were angry. Dr. Diallou put one hand on her forearm and the other, very gently, on Andy's shoulder. "Let's get a look at this handsome young man."

"Finally!" Andy's mom said, cutting her eyes at the woman who'd confronted her. "Finally, someone sees reason!" Tall in her heels, she pushed Andy after the doctor and through the swinging doors. He still had the stuffed bear tucked under one arm.

For a minute, my ears rang with the sound of her voice. My blanket was on the empty chair next to where Andy had been sitting. I reached over and picked it up. Sandra looked down like she'd forgotten I was there. Her face had softened; her usual spark and snap were gone, and her voice was low as she said, "Time for bed."

"I want to stay," I said. "I want to make sure he's all right."

"He's got his mom now." Which was hardly any kind of consolation, and the expression on Sandra's face suggested that she knew it, too.

"I want to stay," I repeated. "I didn't get to tell him the end of 'Hansel and Gretel.' "

"I'll tell him," Sandra said. "I'll tell him that Hansel and Gretel killed the witch, and moved into the house made of candy, and they both lived happily ever after."

That wasn't the ending I remembered. "Don't they go back to their parents?" I asked.

Sandra shook her head. "I think he'd like it better my way."

Upstairs, Alice's door was still closed. Sandra walked me past it and into my room, where I adjusted my cannula under my nose and climbed into a bed made with Care Bears sheets, surrounded by my toys, my books, the lamp with the pink lampshade from my bedroom at home. My get-well-soon cards were lined up on the table, next to my Walkman, my Simon game, my tapes, and my books.

I closed my eyes, listening to the beeping of the heart monitor, the hiss of the oxygen compressor, the low murmur of people in the hallway, the PA system echoing as someone paged Dr. Blair. Normally, those sounds soothed me. That night, though, sleep took a long time to come. I thought about Andy, five floors down, having his broken arm set. I wondered if his mother knew my mom's trick, of having me squeeze her hand as hard as I could whenever I got a needle, passing my pain along to her.

In the middle of the night, I woke up in the dark to a horrible howling sound. For a minute, I thought that I was Gretel, lost in the forest, with animals all around me and no mother or father to keep me safe. The sound went on and on, and I heard footsteps and voices, and then, finally, the noise stopped, like someone had ejected a tape from a player.

I woke up early the next morning, planning on telling Alice all about what had happened in the night. It would be, I decided, my best story yet. I'd describe everything—the nurse with the hairy chin and the girl with the Barbie shoe in her nose and the man who'd been cursing, and about Andy and how he was all alone. Our parents almost never left us alone. Alice would like that part.

When I got to her room, though, the new sign had been taken down, and nothing had been put up in its place. I pushed the door open. The room was empty. The bed was bare, with not even a sheet. Alice's Duran Duran poster wasn't on the wall, and her pink plastic bucket that held her toothbrush and her face towel and washcloths wasn't on the table. The stack of books and puzzles had been removed. Everything except the Ouija board was gone.

I crossed the room and picked it up. A sticky note was attached to the box. *For Rachel,* it read, in handwriting I didn't recognize. Someone had come in and mopped the floor, and the disinfectant smell was strong enough to sting my eyes, but I didn't leave. I sat in the chair with the Ouija board box in my lap. She hadn't said goodbye to me. She hadn't told me enough about what it was like, when you knew you weren't going to get better. She hadn't told me if it had hurt.

"Alice?" I whispered. Maybe her spirit was still nearby. Maybe she was even watching me. But no answer came, and when I closed my eyes and then opened them again, everything in the room was exactly the same.

On the day that I finally got to go home, my mom came early to pack up my things, deliver more treats, and tell the nurses goodbye until next time. She was hurrying around, making sure she'd retrieved my shampoo and conditioner from the shower, when Sandra knocked at the door with a letter in her hand. My name, *Miss Rachel Blum,* was printed on the front of a square pink envelope, in carefully formed letters that were almost too small to read. *Bloom like flowers, not blum like plum,* I thought. Inside was a single sheet of paper, and more of that cramped handwriting, as if my correspondent was being charged for each drop of ink.

Dear Rachel. Thank you for keeping me company the night I broke my arm. And also for Rudolph. I will never forget you. Your friend, Andrew Landis. Beneath his signature was a drawing of a boy with brown hair and something black—my bear, I guessed—under his arm. The other arm was wrapped in white. The cast, I figured. Next to him was a drawing of a girl with curly hair and a big pink smile and, when I looked carefully, a tiny, hash-marked scar on her chest. Around the boy and the girl was a red crayoned heart.

Andy

1987

"Andrew!" Sister Henry's voice echoed down the hallway, but Andy didn't slow down. His eyes were on the door, and the street beyond it; the gray sidewalks and the gray winter sky.

He pounded down the hall and pushed through the glass doors, hearing her heels on the hardwood, hearing her calling—"Andrew, wait!" Like it even mattered. School was letting out at noon anyhow. It was already Friday, and Christmas was on Monday, and break started that afternoon.

One last "Andrew," and he was out on the sidewalk, the cold air stinging his cheeks, head down, arms pumping, running past the row of school buses idling by the curb and racing around the corner. Down Castor, then right onto Kensington Avenue, where the streetlamps were decorated with Christmas wreaths. A train rumbled overhead as Andy ran, arms swinging, knees lifted high, weaving in and out through the people on the sidewalks, the high school kids, the homeless men, the drug dealers. The coat that had started all the trouble was still on his back. Andy ripped it off as he ran and tossed it at a trash can without missing a step.

He knew he was in trouble. Sister would tell his mom about the fight, and he'd be grounded or worse. Maybe his mom wouldn't even give him his Christmas presents . . . but for now, no one could stop him, no one could touch him. For now, he was free.

One of the first things Andy Landis could remember in his entire life was his mom on the phone, his beautiful mom with her red-lipsticked mouth and her hair that fell in ripples down her back, and the gold chain, fine as a thread, that she wore around one ankle. "You know how boys are," she was saying, "you've got to run them like dogs." When he was little, they'd go to a park, a big rectangle of grass in the middle of their neighborhood with a swingset and slide at one of the rectangle's short sides. The edges of the park were studded with broken glass, empty bottles, and sometimes needles, but the middle was a long, unbroken swath of green. Andy would race from one end to the other, faster and faster, finally running back to his mother, running right into her arms, smelling her perfume and cigarette smoke, Camay soap and Jergens lotion, until she patted his back and let him go. The sunshine would sparkle on her gold anklet and in her hair, and he would think that he had the most beautiful mother in the world.

But that was when he was just a baby, not even in kindergarten. Now he was a big kid, tall for his age, already wearing men's-sized shoes. "I don't know what to do," his mother would complain, talking on the phone to Sharon or Beth, her work friends. "Every six months his pants are too short and his shoes don't fit." Sometimes she'd sigh when she looked at him, the same way she'd sigh at the bills that came in the mail, but sometimes she'd smile, pulling him close until his head rested on her shoulder. *My little man,* she would say.

Andy still ran at the park sometimes, but he liked the street best. After school, when his homework was done and the table was set, he would put on his sneakers and his 76ers jersey, the one that had been his father's. In the winter he'd pile on layers, sweatpants and sweatshirt and a hat. In the summer, he'd just wear shorts. The only thing that never changed was the shirt. The 'Sixers had been his dad's team, and now it was Andy's. He'd start off at an easy trot, warming up his muscles, running from Kensington to Somerset, then turning east, past Frankford and Aramingo and Allegheny, racing along the sidewalks, past bodegas and hardware stores, pharmacies and doctors' offices, gas stations and storefront churches and the vacant lot where the vendors were selling Christmas trees, until the street curved into the on-ramp for I-95. That was the three-mile mark, where he'd turn around and head back home.

His gym teacher hadn't believed him when Andy told him how far he could run. He'd taken Andy out to the soccer field and made him do laps until he'd run one mile, then two. "Let's stop now," he'd said, but Andy had said, "I can keep going," and he had, and ever since then Mr. Setzer would let him skip calisthenics and volleyball so that he could go to fields and run.

Swinging his arms in big, high arcs, eating the distance up with each stride, for once not thinking about the nuns hissing at him to stop fidgeting, not worrying about knocking over one of his mother's china figurines, or bumping into the table, or having her glare at him and say, "Jesus, can't you sit still?"

At first his feet were so light it was like they were floating, and the air slipped like cream down his throat. Then he'd start to sweat, and his legs would burn and his breath would come in gasps that tasted like hot pennies. He welcomed the pain, letting it in, then pushing through it, getting past it, savoring the cramps and the fire in his thighs until he was past hurting, until his vision narrowed to just the squares of the sidewalk and every other thought had vanished from his head. Faster and faster, knees lifted to his chest, hands curled into fists, running past the memory of lunchtime at Holy Innocents, when the kids with the free and reduced-price lunch cards like Andy had to get in line ahead of the kids who paid full price; the Winter Concert and the science fair and the Celebration of Learning, when almost every other kid had a parent there and Andy had no one, because his father was dead and his mom had to work, because *money doesn't grow on trees,* because *someone's got to pay for all of this,* even though *all of this* was a crappy one-bedroom apartment where the ceiling dropped chunks of plaster on you when you were sleeping and the windows didn't open because the windowsills had been painted so many times and you had to jiggle the toilet's handle just right if you wanted it to flush.

That afternoon, still in his school uniform of khakis and a blue button-down, Andy ran to the three-mile mark before slowing from a sprint to a jog to a trot to a walk, the sound of his shoes on the pavement softening from slaps to pats. Usually, he would be able to hang on to some of that sensation of rightness, that place past thought. For at least another hour, sometimes for the rest of the afternoon, he would feel good in his body, at home in his skin.

He and his mother lived on the first floor of a row house in Kensington that had been split into three apartments, one on each floor. Andy armed sweat off his forehead and pulled out the house key that hung on a cord around his neck, unlocking the door and stepping inside, releasing the gentle sigh he always gave when he realized that he was alone. A single woman, a widow, lived on the second floor, but Andy hardly saw her, and the landlord kept the third floor mostly empty, using it for cousins and grandchildren when they came to visit. Andy Landis didn't spend much time at other kids' houses when their parents were home, but he was starting to get the idea that not every kid had to be as careful to avoid the lightning flashes of a parent's temper, that other moms were different from his. It wasn't like Lori hit him or ignored him for the few hours between dinner and bedtime when they were together, but sometimes he thought that his mother just didn't like him very much, that if some genie or fairy godmother showed up and promised to take Andy somewhere else, to give him to other parents, Lori would agree without hesitation. But then he would tell himself that Lori worked hard, sometimes six days a week, on her feet for nine, sometimes ten hours, and that he always had enough to eat, and clothes to wear, even if the clothes came from thrift shops or the church donation table, and he was the one who cooked the food and did the dishes afterward.

Three weeks ago he'd been doing his math homework at the kitchen table when his mom had handed him a gray-and-white ski jacket that she'd picked up at church. "It's still got a lot of wear in it," she'd said, sounding proud. Andy had seen the tag with Ryan Peterman's name sewn on the back of the collar right away, but when he'd pointed it out, he'd kept his voice quiet, not wanting to hurt her feelings, not wanting to make her mad.

Lori had sighed, then had looked at him, looked right in his eyes, holding his gaze with her own so that he couldn't turn away. "I can't buy you a new one, and you're too tall for last year's," she'd said. "This one's almost good as new."

You can buy me a new one, Andy thought. *You can, but you won't.* He knew about what she called her "mad money," how there was a chipped mug all the way in the back of the kitchen cabinet that was full of quarters and bills, ones and fives and tens and twenties. Every few months she'd ask the Strattons if Andy could sleep over and she'd take a bus to Atlantic City with her girlfriends. Sometimes she'd come back laughing, her wallet full of crisp new bills, but mostly she'd walk right past him into her bedroom and shut the door without a word.

Andy had stuffed the jacket in the darkest corner of the coat closet, but that morning, finally, it had started to snow, and Lori had insisted that he wear it, had even walked with him to school to make sure he didn't take it off.

Ryan Peterman hadn't wasted a second. "Hey, asswipe, that's my old jacket!" he'd shouted, loud enough for the rest of the fifth grade to hear.

"Fuck off," said Andy—that being, of course, the only acceptable response. Ryan had yanked down the collar to show the other kids his name. Andy felt the world narrowing, the way it did when he ran, only this time, instead of just the street or the grass or the sidewalk, all he could see was Ryan Peterman's big, stupid pale face as he drew his arm back and started pounding Ryan, on his cheek, his head, his shoulders and chest and sides, hitting and hitting until Ryan's nose was dripping blood and he was crouching down with his arms over his head, screeching "Get him off me! Get him off me!" and the Sisters had come with their habits belling out behind them, rulers at the ready.

Andy went to the kitchen, cracked ice cubes out of their battered metal tray, wrapped them in a dish towel, and held them against his knuckles. When the ice melted, he helped himself to a bowl of Cheerios with cut-up banana while he watched cartoons. They didn't have cable like the Strattons, who lived down the street in a row house that looked just like theirs, except it wasn't apartments and the family rented the whole thing, all three floors just for them. Miles Stratton was in his class at Holy Innocents, not exactly a friend, but friendly. Sometimes Andy would go over in the afternoons and they'd watch *The Dukes of Hazzard* and *Three's Company*. Here, he was stuck with a choice between Looney Tunes and soap operas. He watched the Road Runner chase Wile E. Coyote off cliffs and under trucks filled with dynamite while he slurped the last of the milk, rinsed the bowl and spoon, and put them in the dishwasher. He made sure he returned the milk to the fridge and the cereal to the cupboard, checked to see that the tiny square of their table was wiped off and the rickety wooden chair was pushed in, before he went back outside.

"You're so considerate!" Miles's mom always said when he came over. "My mom always says it's the maid's day off," Andy would tell her. It was one of Lori's refrains, one that she'd repeat if she ever saw Andy's dirty clothes on the bath-room floor or if he'd forgotten to put the seat down. Mrs. Stratton was always nice to Andy. She'd ask him to stay for dinner and she'd always bake something for dessert and give him some of it, a big chunk of cake or a slice of pie, to bring home. "Tell your mother hello," she would say, but Andy never would, and he'd throw the sweets in the trash can by the bus shelter before he got home. The Strattons were black, like Andy's father; like Mr. Sills, the handyman who came around every week or two, tightening dripping faucets and oiling squeaky doors; like most of the people in the neighborhood. They were black, and Lori was white, and he was pretty sure that Mrs. Stratton didn't really like her. Once, when he'd left Miles's bedroom to use the bathroom, he'd heard Mr. Stratton, who worked for the gas company, talking down in the kitchen. *How come she moved here? How come she's not back with her own?* Mrs. Stratton had murmured something—Andy had heard his own name and nothing more—but then Mr. Stratton had said, "Well, how sure are we about that? She wouldn't be the first bird to try to slip an egg into another man's nest." "Stop," his wife said in a cold voice Andy had never heard her use. After that, Andy had never felt like just a regular friend of Miles's, a normal kid from school. Instead, he'd thought that they looked at him as the kid with the white mother and a black father, half one and half the other, a kid who didn't belong.

Mrs. Stratton was a stay-at-home mom, but Andy's mom worked at a beauty salon called Roll of the Dye in Rittenhouse Square, which was Philadelphia's fanciest neighborhood. She left the house at nine-thirty Tuesday through Sunday and came home at seven, smelling like perm solution and cigarette smoke, with sneakers on her feet and her high heels in her purse. Andy had to have the stoop swept, the floors vacuumed, the couch pillows smoothed, the table set, and dinner—boiled noodles with canned spaghetti sauce, or frozen pizza or pot pies or a Swanson Hungry-Man for him, a Lean Cuisine for her— heated up and ready. By second grade, he knew how to use the microwave and the oven, and Lori had taught him to run the dishwasher and the washer and dryer. *Most kids aren't responsible enough for this, but I think you are,* she'd said, and Andy had been glad to learn, proud that he knew something other kids didn't. It wasn't until that fall, when he'd read the part in *Tom Sawyer* where Tom tricks the other kids into white-washing the fence, that Andy realized, with a feeling that made his face and ears get hot, how his mom had fooled him.

He looked over the kitchen again, the linoleum in front of the sink worn to translucence, the sputtering olive-green refrigerator, the stick-on pine paneling that was peeling off in strips from the walls. Mr. Sills had said he could fix it, could make it look like new and it wouldn't take more than a day, but Lori had told him thanks but no thanks. "You do enough as it is," she'd said, and Mr. Sills, looking sad, had shrugged, then packed up his toolbox. "Call me if you need anything," he'd said, and then looked at Andy. "That goes for you, too, young man," he'd said. Andy knew that he would never call. *We don't take charity,* Lori always said. Andy thought that maybe she paid Mr. Sills, when he wasn't looking, to change the lightbulbs that she couldn't reach and fix the basement window after it had cracked, which made it okay.

Andy counted each ring of the church bell and was surprised that it was only three o'clock. He walked to the closet, planning to put on his shoes and go outside again, when he heard a key in the door. He froze, head down, as his mother stormed into the room, home from work four hours early. Her blond hair, which had been gathered into a high ponytail that morning, was falling down, tendrils hanging against her cheeks, and her hands moved in angry jerks as she unzipped her coat, fake shearling, with the white lining already turning yellow, and tossed it on the couch.

Andy hurried to hang it up. Lori stood there, unmoving, just looking at him. All the stylists at Roll of the Dye had to wear black, which for Lori meant black jeans and either a black blouse or a black jersey top, always tight, always unbuttoned or cut low enough to show the smooth skin of her chest and the tops of her breasts. *Aspirational,* Andy had heard her call it, which meant that she had to look pretty so the women who came to the salon would want to look like her and that even the old ones or the fat ones would think that they could if they let Lori do their hair.

"I got a call from Sister Henry," she began, her voice deceptively soft. He saw how her hands gripped the edge of the couch and how her skin had gone pale with red splotches underneath her makeup. "What happened with Ryan Peterman?"

From his spot in front of the closet, Andy said nothing.

"This is the second time this year," his mom said. "One more fight and they'll expel you."

Andy didn't answer. In September, Darryl Patrick had called Andy an Oreo, black on the outside, white on the inside, "except you don't even look black." That wasn't exactly an insult, but he'd fought Darryl anyway, in the playground after lunch, and when his mom had asked what had happened Andy had just said, "He started it," and had refused to tell her anything else.

"Andy?" Lori asked. "Andy, what are we going to do about this?"

Andy put his hand in his pocket and crossed his fingers, hoping that if he kept quiet she'd let it go, but Lori kept on.

"What were you fighting about?" Andy didn't answer. His mom kept right on going. "Because you didn't want to wear his old coat," she said. Andy gave a tiny nod. She sighed, lifting her hair off her face, then letting it drop. "Honey, I told you. If I could buy you a brand-new coat, I would. I'd buy you a hundred coats if I had the money."

No, you wouldn't, he thought. The pit of his stomach felt cramped, and his face felt like it was on fire. *If you had the money you'd go to Atlantic City and play roulette with your friends.*

"And now," she said, "I've got to call the Petermans and apologize." She stomped into the bedroom, locking the door behind her, except the door was a cheap, sad thing, like everything in this cheap, sad place, and Andy could hear what she was saying. *That shouldn't have mattered,* and *A jacket is a jacket, Andy wears hand-me-downs all the time, this wasn't any different.* Then there was a pause, and then Lori said, *Oh, no, I couldn't . . . No, really, it's not necessary . . . No, Andy can't be rewarded for this, he needs to understand that what he did was wrong.* Then a lot of *uh-huh*s and *I see*s and then, finally, a *thank-you.* He stood behind the kitchen table, waiting, one leg jiggling until he pressed down hard to make it stop. Finally his mother emerged.

"What happened?" he asked. He'd gotten a scraped cheek and a black eye in the fight. Lori reached across the table and touched his face.

"The Petermans understood why you were embarrassed," she said. "Ryan wants to use some of his allowance money to get a coat for you."

"Oh, no," Andy said. He was horrified. The only thing worse than wearing Ryan's old coat would be wearing a new coat that Ryan had bought especially for Andy. That was when Lori put her hands against her eyes and started to cry; not the big, showy sobs she sometimes did, but just sitting there silently while tears rolled down her face.

Andy hated when she cried. It made him want

to run out of the house and onto the street and sprint, all-out, until he was as far away from her as he could get. He made himself stand up and pat her shoulder. "It's okay," he said. When he tried to hug her, it was like trying to put his arms around a bundle of sticks. She didn't move to help him, didn't do anything except sit there and cry. He leaned down, resting his cheek on her head, smelling shampoo and hair spray and Jergens lotion, the cigarette that she'd smoked on the walk from the train to the house and the Tic Tac she'd sucked to cover it up. "I'm sorry," he said. "I promise I won't get in any more fights." He patted her shoulder some more, and brought her a glass of water that she didn't touch. Outside, he heard a bus wheeze by, and voices, two ladies talking about getting their Christmas shopping done.

"Are you hungry?" he asked. Lori shook her head.

"But you get something," she said. "There's money in my wallet." She moved her hands away from his face, trying to smile. "You're a growing boy."

He wouldn't take her money. Not on that night. Instead, he took down the envelope on the top shelf of the closet where he kept his own savings, the two dollars he got for feeding Mrs. Green's cats on weekends when she went to visit her mother in Virginia and the five that Mrs. Cleary had given him for teaching Dylan Cleary how to ride a bike, the quarters and fifty-cent pieces that he'd collected for shoveling neighbors' steps and sidewalks in the winter. The money was supposed to be for a bike. He'd been saving up since Miles had gotten a mountain bike the year before. He took out ten dollars, ordered a pizza with mushrooms, his mother's favorite, and gave the guy a dollar tip when he came.

"Thank you," she said, when he set the box on the table. Her voice was low and toneless. Her hair was down, hanging in her face. When he was little he'd thought that his mom was as pretty as a movie star, or as any of the models from the hair magazines that she'd bring home from work, but now he could see how much of her beauty depended on makeup—pencils that made her eyes look farther apart than they were, liners that made her lips not look so thin. Her hair wasn't even blond, not really. She colored it because it was really what she called "mouse brown." He didn't care. Even with her face washed clean and her roots showing and her eyelashes wispy and pale without mascara, even though her eyes were a little close together and her lips were too thin, he still thought that she was beautiful.

He put out plates and napkins, but Lori only nibbled half a slice of pizza before going to her bedroom, leaving Andy alone with the TV.

He watched Jim Gardner on the local news, then Peter Jennings. He solved two puzzles on *Wheel of Fortune* and a whole row of sports questions on *Jeopardy*. At eight o'clock, *The Cosby Show* was on. Theo was getting bad grades in school. Andy ate four slices of pizza while Cliff and Clair talked it over. He imagined living in a big house with nice furniture and colorful art on the walls and a mom and a dad who worried about your grades (his own mom barely glanced at his report card, never noticed his A in math or the *Needs Improvement* he'd received for Conduct). Theo Huxtable would never have to wear a coat that some other kid had paid for. Theo's mom would understand, without having to be told, why he would rather not have any coat at all.

That night, on the pullout couch, Andy thought about how sometimes his mom would call a "love you" over her shoulder before she went to her bedroom and he took the cushions, still warm from her body, off the couch to make up his bed, or she'd say it in the morning before he left for school, and she'd kiss him, leaving lipstick on his cheek. A few times he could remember her telling him that he was her baby, her one and only.

But if she loved him, why didn't she ever get him new things? Why did she let him spend three months wearing sneakers that were held together with duct tape? Why didn't she listen when she brought home Toughskins from the church clothing swap and he tried to tell her that none of the kids wore Toughskins, they all wore Levi's?

He'd explain, and then she'd say the thing she always said: "If wishes were horses, then beggars would ride."

Andy rolled over, flipping his pillow to the cool side. One of his feet was jiggling, making the bed's frame squeak. Miles Stratton's mother put notes in Miles's lunch. Sometimes Miles would read them out loud in a shrill falsetto while the other kids in the lunchroom laughed. *I am so glad to be your mother,* he'd said. *You make me proud every day.* Once, when Miles wasn't looking, Andy had pulled one of the notes out of the trash. There was a little bit of tuna fish on its corner. He'd cleaned it off as best he could, then folded it up in his own backpack. Sometimes he would read it and pretend his own mom had put it there. *I love that you are an enthusiastic reader,* Mrs. Stratton had written. It was funny, because Miles wasn't really an enthusiastic reader. Neither was Andy. Still, he kept the note, and imagined that it was from his mom.

On Saturday, the day after the jacket fight, Andy got up early, put on his heaviest sweatshirt, and went running. Then he walked home, with his hood up and his hands in the kangaroo pocket, wishing he had money for hot chocolate and a doughnut. It was a chilly day, the slate-gray sky spitting snow, but everyone he saw seemed happy, bundled up in hats and mittens, carrying shopping bags. Tiny white lights twinkled from windows, green wreaths with red bows hung on doors. The Strattons had a Christmas tree that Andy could see through the window, topped with a papier-mâché angel that Miles's sister, Melissa, had made. The angel had a gold tinsel crown, and Andy knew that under her white dress, between her legs, there was some gold tinsel pubic hair that Miles had snipped from the crown and glued there. Lori never bought a tree. "Too messy," she'd said, even though last year Mr. Sills had dragged one to their door, a pine tree, all bundled up in plastic netting and smelling like a forest, and said he'd set it up for them and, after New Year's, haul it away.

Back at home, he cleaned the bathroom, even though it wasn't his turn. He was sprawled on the couch, flipping through the Batman comics that Miles had lent him, when he heard a knock on the door.

Andy grabbed the cordless phone so he could call 911 if he had to. Making sure the safety chain was in place, he cracked the door open a few inches and peeked out. A heavyset woman whose short hair was dyed a flat shade of brown was standing on the front step, with an anxious expression on her face and snowflakes melting on her cheeks. A tall, red-faced man in a shiny green satin Eagles jacket was beside her. These were his grandparents, Lori's mom and dad. He hadn't seen them in almost exactly a year.

Now here they were, with their arms full of gifts.

"Andy?" said his grandma, in a high, trembling voice. Andy's stomach clenched.

"Merry Christmas," said his grandfather. "How about letting us come out of the cold?"

"We brought you cocoa," said his grandma, and held up a cup from Wawa for Andy to see. "And some little things for you and your mom."

"I can't," said Andy, pushing the words through numb lips, and even though he felt sad, the words came out sounding angry. *My house, my rules,* Lori had told him, over and over. *I never want them to darken my door again.* The last time her parents had come over was for dinner on Christmas Eve the year before, and there had been a terrible fight, with his mom shrieking *Get out of my house,* and Grandma dragging Andy into the bedroom, putting her hands over his ears. But of course he'd heard all of it, the sound of the turkey platter crashing into the wall and her father saying the n-word, and saying that Lori should learn to keep her legs shut, saying *You made your bed, now see how you like lying in it.*

When he was little, like in nursery school, his grandparents were around a lot. His grandma would spend a Saturday with him while his mother worked, or sometimes he would stay at their house in Haddonfield for a whole weekend. His grandma would take him to her favorite bakery in South Philadelphia, where the ladies behind the counter, all dressed in white like nurses, would give him cookies with sprinkles and say things like "What a cutie!" and "Look at those lashes."

"Is he yours?" one of the ladies had once asked, and his grandma's face had tightened as she pulled Andy against her and said in a cold voice, "Of course he's mine."

Once, she'd brought him to Center City, to see the light show at Wanamaker's and to sit on Santa's lap. Another Christmas his grandfather gave him hockey skates, then took him to a rink. Andy had watched the other skaters, then wobbled around the rink once, going slowly, getting a feel for the ice, and before long he'd been zipping around the rink, his arms swinging easily and his blades crisscrossing in long, smooth strokes, with his grandfather waving every time he whizzed past. But then they'd stopped coming as often, and Lori's face would get that scary, masklike look when he asked about Grandma and Grandpa. The skates had gone into the closet and stayed there until one day they'd disappeared.

The only time he could count on seeing his grandparents was at Christmas. Every year they would go to their house in Haddonfield for a feast: turkey and ham and lasagna, sweet potatoes and mashed potatoes and green bean casserole with crunchy fried onions on top, rolls and biscuits and corn bread and three kinds of pie and cannoli from the bakery: *the old neighborhood,* his grandma called it. Andy would get to see Uncle Paul, his mother's brother, and his wife, Aunt Denise, and their little girls, Jessica and Heather, who'd be wearing matching party dresses with sashes and poufy skirts, and his mom would bring home a shopping bag filled with leftovers that they'd eat for a week.

A year ago, his mom had invited her parents over on Christmas Eve. She'd taken the day off from work and stayed up in the kitchen until two in the morning, squinting at cookbooks and muttering curses and kicking the oven door shut. She burned her first pan of lasagna, and when the turkey didn't fit into the oven she'd had Andy hold it, his palms pressed against its pimpled white skin, while she'd hacked it in half and put it into two separate roasting pans. The pies had come from Acme, and the whipped cream came from a can, and there weren't any cannoli. Andy had helped his mother carry a folding table from the Clearys' basement and set it up in the living room. There were red and green carnations in a vase, a borrowed tablecloth on the table with the white plastic Chinet, and his mother, sweaty and pale, hurrying around and saying things like *God help me* and *This better work* and *If she says one word about the plates I don't know what I'll do.*

An hour before her parents were supposed to arrive she'd gone to shower and dress, telling

Andy to vacuum the floors and do the rest of the dishes and for God's sake make sure the bathroom was clean. The Lori who emerged from the bedroom wasn't a Lori that Andy had ever seen before. Instead of her usual clothing, she wore a loose red sweater with long sleeves, baggy black slacks, and black shoes with barely any heel at all. Her hair was pulled back from her face, neatly braided. She'd hardly put on any makeup, and instead of dangly earrings she wore tiny gold ones in the shape of the cross.

The dinner had been fine, even though there was so little room in their apartment that when Andy's grandpa sat on the couch his knees bumped the folding chairs around the table. His grandma had praised the food, saying again and again that she couldn't have done better herself, even though the turkey was pink on the inside and the green bean casserole was burned on top. Grandpa had been silent, drinking beers right from the bottle after Lori told him she didn't have mugs. Finally, after she'd served dessert and poured coffee, his mother had said, "There's something I wanted to discuss."

"What's that, honey?" Andy's grandma had asked. Lori fiddled with her necklace, another gold cross. With her head bent, and no eye shadow or mascara, she looked as young as she must have looked in high school, except her nails were still long and red and filed into sharp-tipped ovals, and when she clasped her hands her sweater gaped open, showing the top of the tattoo on her breast. He thought it was a flower, or maybe it was a name, spelled out in fancy script, but that was one of the many, many things that Andy knew not to ask about. He could see the creases on her forehead, and he could hear her breathing, deep and slow, the way she did when she was angry but trying not to be.

"Thank you for coming," she began.

"It was lovely," said Andy's grandma. His grandfather didn't say a word. Andy thought that he was staring at the tattoo, like maybe he hadn't known that it was there.

"You know how important it is to me to keep Andy in Catholic school. To make sure he has a good education."

His grandma murmured, "Of course." His grandfather was still silent. *Pull up your sweater,* Andy thought, as hard as he could, but his mom didn't hear.

"I work five, sometimes six days a week at the salon. I'm on my feet for sometimes ten hours a day." Andy's grandfather gave a noisy sniff. His mother flinched but kept talking, her eyes on her lap and her hands pressed together, like she'd rehearsed the speech and was going to say it straight through to the end, no matter what. "I hate to ask. You know I do. I just need a little help right now. My car won't pass inspection, and Andy's tuition is due . . ."

His grandfather, who'd been sitting so still, finally spoke. "Why don't you ask Andrew's father's family for help?"

Lori's hands twisted against each other. "Dad, you know that's not going to happen."

"I can't say that surprises me," said her father. "No, I can't say that at all."

Lori cut her eyes toward Andy. "Honey, go into the bedroom," she said, in the tone he knew never to argue with. He walked down the hallway, hearing her say, "Either tell me yes or tell me no. But don't insult me."

"If you're asking for my money, don't tell me how to behave," her father said. Andy stopped before he reached the bedroom door, knowing that no one was thinking about him anymore. As far as the three of them were concerned, he might not even be there at all.

"Your mother and I wanted better than this for you," his grandfather was saying. "We tried to raise you right. We thought you'd meet a boy, a nice boy, and marry him, and live somewhere decent, maybe near us, in a house, with a yard, good schools for your kids. Now look at you." His voice was full of disgust. "Look at this." Andy could imagine him sweeping his arm across his heavy body, indicating the shabby apartment, the frayed carpet and peeling walls, the folding table with its metal legs visible beneath the tablecloth. "We did our best. Scrimped and saved to send you to Hallahan, and what do you do? Spread your legs for the first black boy who smiled at you."

Andy heard his grandmother then, her voice high and shaky and shocked. "Lonnie, that's enough."

Grandpa ignored her. Then he must have turned back to Lori. "If you had any sense you'd let Andy come live with us."

"I am never giving up my son," Lori said, her voice icy. Andy's face was burning, his stomach twisting in a way that made him think he was going to throw up, and he was rocking back and forth, he was glad, glad that his mother wouldn't give him away like a pet she didn't want anymore, except he was also thinking about his grandparents' house in Haddonfield, the basketball hoop over the garage door and how there was a room there, just for him, with a bed with a blue-and-green-plaid bedspread, and a guest bathroom that only he used because he was the only guest. It would be nice—and then he shut that thought down, clamped it off like stepping on a hose to stop the flow of water. How could he even think that way?

His grandmother came down the hall, hurrying him into the bedroom, pressing his face into her middle. Her sweater smelled of roast turkey and Tide. "You made your bed," his grandfather was yelling, "see how you like lying in it," and his mother was saying, "Get out of my house and don't ever come back," and "You're dead to me, both of you, dead to me," and—the worst thing—"You can forget about ever seeing Andy again." His grandmother had stood there, squeezing Andy tight, squashing him against her, saying "Oh, sweetheart" over and over. And he must have been scared because he'd been holding on to her, his arms around her waist, until his grandfather came into the room.

"Get your coat, Bernice. We're going."

"Oh, no, Lonnie. Not like this."

"Get your coat," he repeated, and Grandma let Andy go with one last squeeze. His grandfather had knelt down with a grunt. Andy heard his knees pop. His face was red and his eyes were watery as he put his arms on Andy's shoulders. "Andrew," he began. Then Lori had been in the room, throwing the door open so hard that it slammed into the wall with a sound like a gunshot.

"Get away from him," she'd said. "You don't get to speak to my son ever again."

When they were gone, his mother had stood with her hands braced against the front door, red nails vivid against the white paint, as if they might come back and try to push their way back through. Finally, she'd turned to Andy and in that terrible, low voice had said, *If they call, hang up the phone. If they ever come, you shut the door in their faces. As far as I'm concerned, you don't have any grandparents. We don't need them. We have each other. That's enough.*

But now Lori was gone and they were here. Andy could see the wrapped and ribboned boxes in their hands.

"Honey, please," his grandma said. The heavy gold earrings that she wore had stretched out her earlobes, and her red lipstick was smeared on her front teeth. He remembered how she always smelled good, and her soft sweaters, and cookies with sprinkles, and how he'd felt when she'd said, "Of course he's mine."

Andy's throat felt thick and his eyes were burning. "I can't," he said again.

His grandfather stepped forward until his chest was almost brushing the door, and Andy could smell him, Old Spice and cigars. He was a heavy man with iron-gray hair combed straight back from his deeply grooved forehead. He'd been a pipe fitter and worked in the Navy Yard, but now he was retired.

"Andrew," he said, in his deep voice. "We know we're not welcome here. But please, son. Whatever's going on between the two of us and your mother isn't your fault. You haven't done anything wrong. We just want to give you some Christmas presents. We love you very much."

Andy felt like something was ripping at his insides. "I can't," he repeated, his voice cracking. He shut the door and locked it, and walked, as fast as he could, all the way through the apartment until he was in his mother's bedroom, with the bedroom door shut behind him. He rested his burning forehead against the wall, ignoring the knocking, and made himself take deep slow breaths and count to one hundred before he opened his eyes.

His grandparents were gone, but they'd left the presents on the steps, wrapped in red paper that showed reindeers pulling a ho-ho-hoing Santa's sleigh through the starry sky. Andy looked left, then right, before scooping them up and bringing them inside. He locked himself in the bathroom, even though Lori wasn't due home for an hour, and tore through the paper. There was a bottle of perfume for his mom, and a hardcover *Guinness Book of World Records* that he'd asked for on his list to Santa, and a package of new socks for him. The biggest box was from Strawbridge's. In it was a winter coat, a blue-and-red one, exactly what Andy would have picked out himself.

He looked at it for a long time. Maybe if he left it in his locker at school, and wore it only at recess? Or if he told Lori that one of the neighbors, maybe Mrs. Cleary, had given it to him because it didn't fit Dylan? Or that it was the gift coat from Ryan Peterman?

Except his mother would thank Mrs. Cleary, who wouldn't know what she was talking about, and the Petermans would probably have Ryan bring the coat over and make a big show of his generosity, his Christian charity. Andy could tell the truth, could stand in front of his mom and say, "My grandparents gave it to me and I don't want to give it back." Except then her face would get still and pale and she'd turn away, propping her hands against the back of a chair like she couldn't even stand up on her own. Maybe she'd even start crying again, and Andy didn't think that he could take it. *We're a team,* she always said. *It's us against the world.*

His mom kept the garbage bags underneath the sink. Andy pulled one out and put everything inside, the coat and the book, the socks and the perfume, the boxes and the wrapping paper and the ribbons. He inspected the bathroom to make sure he hadn't left a scrap of tape or wrapping paper behind, and then ran out the door. We love you very much, he heard his grandfather saying. "No, you don't," he muttered. "No, you don't."

Outside, more snow was swirling down, and an icy wind was scouring the streets, stirring up grit and trash. Andy pulled up the hood of his sweatshirt and started walking fast, head down, with the bag in his arms. Mr. Sills's rattling pale-blue pickup truck pulled to the curb, and Mr. Sills climbed out, dressed in khakis and a plaid shirt, with his big belly pushing at his belt, his white curls under a gray knitted cap. He, too, had a wrapped box in his hands.

"Merry Christmas!" he called. Andy ignored him, tucking his chin down into his chest and hurrying past before Mr. Sills could give him the present or start asking him questions. There was a Dumpster behind the Spanish restaurant on Kensington Avenue. He heaved the lid open, threw the bag deep inside, and let the lid fall down, with an echoing clang that he could feel in his teeth.

Next to the Dumpster was restaurant trash—newspaper, plastic bags, coffee grinds and eggshells, a rotted half of a head of lettuce, and a chunk of a broken brick about the size of a baseball. Andy picked up the brick. The roughness felt good against his skin. He stepped onto the street and then, before he could think about it, before he even knew what he was going to do, he lifted his arm and threw the piece of brick, as hard as he could, through the windshield of a car that was parked at the meter in front of the restaurant.

The glass rained down in jagged shards. A lady on the sidewalk screamed, and the man beside her pointed, yelling, "Hey, kid!" Andy ran, and at first the man who'd yelled was chasing him, except he was old and slow and Andy left him behind, his long legs eating up the pavement, weaving down one-way streets and cobbled alleys too small for a car, not feeling the cold, not thinking about the jacket or his grandparents or his mom, thinking of nothing, feeling nothing, hearing nothing, not even the shriek of sirens, until a policeman's hand grabbed the hood of his sweat-shirt, yanking Andy backward. The cop was soft and jiggly underneath his blue uniform shirt, and his belt, with a walkie-talkie on one side and a gun on the other, dragged down his pants. "Merry Christmas, asshole," he said.

Andy twisted violently. "Fuck you, fatso," he said. Then the cop grabbed his hood again and slammed Andy into the brick wall of the row house beside him. The air went rushing out of Andy's lungs as the cop pulled his arms back and up behind him, twisting them hard, and the pain pushed everything out of his mind, and he barely felt the snow in his hair, on his cheeks, melting and mixing with his tears.

Rachel

1990

I ran into the bridal room feeling sick with shame, my eyes burning and my heart galloping in my chest. My party clothes, a gray miniskirt with flounced tiers and a pink-and-gray top, with pink tights and pink Mary Janes, were arranged neatly on the hanger on the back of a chair, and I shoved it over so that the clothes spilled to the ground and lay there in a sad little heap. I had never been so ashamed, never imagined that such shame was even possible, in my entire life.

My bat mitzvah had started off perfectly. I'd studied for weeks, practicing until I could chant every line of Hebrew along with the tape that Cantor Krugman had made for me to play on my Walkman. Nana had taken me shopping and we'd picked out the navy-blue dress that I'd worn for the service ("Sophisticated," Nana had said approvingly) and the outfit I'd wear to the party. My mother had finally let me get my ears pierced —not at the Piercing Pagoda at the mall, where all my friends had gone, even though I'd begged her, but at my pediatrician's office, "just to be on the safe side," she'd said. Even though I'd been doing well for the last year and a half, I still had to be careful about infections. The morning of the service, she'd brought me to her beauty parlor, where Annette, who did her hair, had done mine, using a round brush to blow it out perfectly straight. I'd gotten a manicure, my first, and my mom had even let Annette curl my lashes and put on a little mascara and some pink lip gloss. The whole time, she'd sat in the waiting area, watching me in the mirrors, sometimes with her hands pressed together over her heart, sometimes sniffling a little bit, which should have been a warning, if I'd only paid attention.

The service had started at ten o'clock. The sanctuary wasn't packed the way it was on High Holidays, when every seat, even the ones in the balcony, would be taken, but the first ten rows were full, with aunts and uncles and cousins, my nana's sister, my great-aunt Florence, and her husband, Si, my father's two brothers and their wives and all of their kids. My friends sat together, Kara and Marissa and Kelsey and Britt and Josh S. and Josh M. and Derek and Ross, plus every kid in my Hebrew-school class. My parents were in the front row. My mom wore a rose-colored suit, a pleated silk skirt that fell to her knees, and a jacket that buttoned up tightly enough to show her shape, and high heels that matched, and my father and Jonah both wore dark suits and ties. Up on the bimah, holding the heavy sterling-silver pointer, moving the finger over each Hebrew word, I'd been so nervous that my knees had almost been knocking together, but once I'd made it through the first blessings I started to calm down, and I sang the prayers and chanted my portion and read my speech almost perfectly. The subject of my Torah portion was sex offenses—which, as Rabbi Silver said, did not lend itself naturally to a bat mitzvah speech. Together, we'd decided that I could talk about rules in general—which ones we should follow, which ones we should question, which biblical injunctions made sense in the 1990s and which could stand what Rabbi Silver called "some interrogation."

By the time I'd finished my legs felt wobbly, but from relief instead of nerves, and I was excited for the party, which would be held in the social hall as soon as the service was over. Twenty round tables for ten were waiting, draped in pink and silver cloths, with pink and white hydrangeas in silver bowls at each of the adult tables and dozens of pink and silver balloons at the kids' tables. There would be passed appetizers and then the grown-ups would get chicken or salmon and the kids would have a taco bar, and there'd be a disc jockey and six dancers, three boys and three girls, to lead us in the line dances and the games.

Rabbi Silver had given a speech, and then Mrs. Nussbaum from the Sisterhood had presented me with gold candlesticks and a copy of the *Gates of Prayer.* My parents and Jonah and I had stood together, huddled underneath my father's prayer shawl, as the rabbi read a special blessing. "And now," he'd said, "if Rachel's parents, Bernard and Helen, would like to say a few words?"

I had expected my father to make the speech. When my parents had come up for their *aliyah*, my mom had been crying, and her voice was so faint when she sang the blessings over the Torah that finally the cantor had just shifted the microphone toward my dad. But then, as I'd watched, my dad had put his hand on the small of my mother's back and given her a little push, propelling her forward so that she almost bumped into the fringed blue velvet that covered the bimah. She pulled a piece of paper out of her pocket, unfolded it, adjusted the microphone, and cleared her throat.

"When Rachel was born . . ." she began.

"Can't hear you!" hollered my great-uncle Si, who had plumes of white hair protruding from his ears and smelled like Luden's cherry cough drops.

My mother gave a trembling smile. She pulled a handkerchief out of her sleeve and started again, pressing her hands down on the page that she'd smoothed out on the podium. "When Rachel was born it was a difficult time for our family. As many of you know, Rachel was born with a con-genital heart deformity that required immediate surgery. For a few days . . ." And here, she made a horrible gasping noise, like she wanted to sob and was trying to swallow it instead. Her next sentence came out in a rush. "For a few days we didn't know if our sweet little girl would survive."

I felt an iciness come over me, first numbing my toes, then my ankles, then freezing my belly, turning my arms to chunks of wood. *This isn't happening,* I thought. *She isn't doing this.* But she was.

"When Rachel was six . . ." She swallowed hard and sniffled, and then clamped her hand down on my upper arm, grabbing me like she thought I'd try to run. "We found her in her room, and she wasn't breathing. I thank God every day for the paramedics who got there so quickly, who revived her and started her heart again, but you never forget . . ." She gave another awful gulp. "You never forget how it feels to see your child like that. For years, Rachel slept with a heart monitor, next to our bed. Every year, it seemed, there was another hospitalization, another surgery, or a trip to the emergency room, something that would make me think all over again, God is going to take her. And I asked myself why this had happened. Why it had happened to me, and my husband, and our son; why God was testing us this way, why he would have given us such a treasure, only to take her away."

"Can't hear you!" yelled Uncle Si again. I'd been staring down at my shoes, with my hands clenched, praying sincerely for the first time during the entire service, praying for this speech to end. I made myself look into the audience. Britt Weinstein was staring, her eyes wide and shocked, and both Joshes looked like they were laughing. I'd been to about ten bar and bat mitzvahs by then, and I knew that it wasn't unusual for a parent to get emotional or even weepy giving the speech, talking about how their little boy or little girl was now a man or a woman; only this wasn't just a regular mom having a normal reaction. This was my mother telling the secrets that I'd spent the last nine months trying so hard to hide.

That September, I'd started at a junior high that drew students from five different elementary schools in our town of Clearview, Florida. There would be lots of kids I didn't know there, kids who didn't know me as the girl with the broken heart; poor Rachel, who'd missed all those days of school, who had to sit on the bleachers during gym class while the other kids played flag football; Rachel, for whom they were always making get-well cards in art and who once had to carry an oxygen tank with her to class.

I had spent the summer figuring out how I would remake myself, turn myself into a different kind of girl, a laughing, breezy girl, a girl to whom the worst thing that had ever happened was waking up and finding that her favorite jeans were still in the wash.

Clothes were part of it, and my mother was more than happy to take me shopping, to buy me everything I'd seen in *Mademoiselle* and *Seventeen* and *Sassy*: high-waisted acid-washed jeans, Henley shirts, a pair of shortalls with suspenders that crisscrossed in the back, and even cropped T-shirts that showed a few inches of my belly when I stretched. "Don't show your father these," she'd said, wearing her usual worried look as she paid, and I'd hugged her and promised that I wouldn't and told her that she was the best mom in the world. When I started school, the new kids saw a confident, smiling girl with tanned arms and legs and shiny, curly hair; a girl who, as far as they knew, had never been sick. Every morning, I spent half an hour on my hair, using anti-frizz serum and mousse and a curling iron to make it look like Elizabeth Berkley's on *Saved by the Bell*. I wore it down, or in ponytails, with pink high-tops on my feet and my shirts always buttoned, or with collars that came up high, so that nobody saw my scar.

By Halloween I had a whole new group of friends, the popular girls and the boys who hung around them. Marissa was funny, with a dirty mouth, and she'd already kissed three boys and gone to second base with one of them. Kara's parents were divorced and her mother had a boyfriend and Kara had the house to herself every afternoon. Kelsey was quiet and smart, but so pretty that she was a member of the popular crowd without even trying, and Britt had been Kelsey's best friend since first grade, even though I wondered whether Kelsey had picked her because she was so ordinary-looking that she made Kelsey look even better, like a plain gold band showing off a diamond. There were boys in our orbit, not boyfriends, but boys who liked us, Derek and Marcus and Josh S. and Josh M., and now all of them were sitting there, staring at my mother, who was sobbing so hard that she couldn't even get out the words she'd written down.

My dad stepped up beside her and put his arm around her waist. He whispered something that I couldn't hear, but my mother shook her head and leaned so close to the microphone that her voice boomed out, making people flinch. I could hear the high-pitched whine from Uncle Si's hearing aid as she said, "I don't know why God chose for our daughter to be sick and to struggle, to have a condition she'll be dealing with all of her life, but I think it's made Rachel not just beautiful but strong, and appreciative of every day that's been given to her, and I know . . ." She pulled back, shoulders shaking. I shot Jonah a desperate look, and he rolled his eyes back at me, as if to say *I can't believe this, either.* It felt good to have my brother on my side, even though he'd been furious at me that morning, probably remembering his bar mitzvah, and how I'd been in the hospital the week before his big day and my mom had been so distracted that she'd forgotten to bring in his suit for alterations and Nana had ended up pinning his cuffs the morning of the service while Jonah had stood with his lips pressed together trying to act like it didn't bother him and like he wasn't going to cry.

"I know it's not for us to question God," said my mother in her wobbly voice. "And I know that every day with Rachel has been a gift, and I pray that we all have many, many more." And then, when I was convinced that it couldn't get any worse, now that she'd made my friends think that I was basically one of those bald, scrawny kids on the Make-A-Wish Foundation's commercials, or like Alice, my hospital friend, my mother threw her arms around me and buried her face in my hair, holding me so tightly that I couldn't move, could barely even breathe until Rabbi Silver and my father together had gently pried her away and led her, still crying, back to her seat.

Music was blaring through the walls of the bridal room, Kool & the Gang's "Celebration." My friends were probably all dancing, their shoes off, wearing the monogrammed RACHEL socks that we'd bought as one of the party favors. I sat on the couch, still in my blue dress, thinking that I could just stay in here until the party was over. I'd say I didn't feel good. After my mother's speech, it was a guarantee that everyone would believe me.

"Rachel?" The door opened and Nana came inside, stepping carefully over the pile of my clothes.

"Well," she said, "that was quite a performance!" I made a noise that wasn't quite a giggle without uncovering my eyes. Nana came and sat beside me and I let myself lean into her, smelling dusting powder and Ivoire perfume.

Nana was my mother's mother, but so different from my mom that sometimes I couldn't believe they were even related. Nana lived in an over-fifty-five community just fifteen minutes away from us, a development full of man-made lakes and identical houses clustered around a golf course, but she was hardly ever there. She used her home like a changing room where she'd stop between trips to do her laundry and spend a week or two visiting friends. Then she'd repack her bags and take off again. "I have wanderlust," she'd say, and she went everywhere, sometimes with tour groups from the synagogue, sometimes by herself. She'd take cruises to Alaska, tours through Israel and Europe and Japan. Once, she'd gone on safari in Africa, dressed in crisp khaki pants and ballet flats. She'd send postcards of the Wailing Wall and the Eiffel Tower and Big Ben, and bring home pictures of jaguars and lions, and laugh as she told us how every shadow through the canvas wall of her tent looked like a big cat but would turn out to be just a tour guide or one of her fellow travelers. She'd promised me that when I finished high school, I could choose a destination and she'd take me with her, anywhere I wanted to go.

In the bridal room, as the music changed to Whitney Houston's "I Wanna Dance with Somebody," Nana squeezed me against her. Her skin was pale and soft, with rouged pink cheeks, and she'd let her hair go white and cut it short, so that now it was a nest of curls on her head. I'd never seen her without makeup, or when she wasn't dressed in what I thought of as an outfit, usually in shades of cream and rose and pink. For my bat mitzvah, she wore a tweed skirt and matching jacket made of tiny squares of pink and white with darker-pink trim around the lapels and the pockets, with a cream-colored silk blouse underneath, and she wore a hat, the way she always did in synagogue, a jaunty disc of pale-pink wool with the tiniest bit of netting peeking out from under the brim.

"Aren't you going to put your party clothes on?" Her voice was so gentle, and, suddenly, I wasn't angry anymore. I only wanted to cry.

"Why'd she have to do that?" I asked. I sounded like a little kid, like I was six and not thirteen, not officially an adult. "Why'd she have to make me sound like such a freak? I'm okay now, I haven't even been in the hospital since sixth grade, and now all my friends are going to think I'm a huge weirdo." My voice was wobbling just like my mother's had, but there was no way I was going to cry.

"I'm not going to argue with you. That was not ideal." Nana's voice was dry. "Your friends will still be your friends, if they're good friends. But I think that maybe your first act of Jewish womanhood is going to be forgiving your mother."

That made me finally sit up and look at her. In my experience, parents were the ones who forgave kids—for leaving wet towels on the floor or leaving lunchboxes in our backpacks over the weekend, for forgetting to take in our homework or bring home permission slips, for the hundred ways, large and small, that we messed up and disappointed them. Children did not forgive their parents. But Nana was looking at me, her expression serious. "Parents aren't perfect," said Nana. "I wasn't, and your mother isn't, and if you have children you probably won't be, either." I liked her a lot then, for saying *if,* not *when,* the way my other grandmother, my father's mother, always did. "Your mother loves you very much, and it hasn't been easy for her. I know you don't like thinking about it, and I certainly can understand that you don't want to make a big deal about it, but, Rachel, she really did suffer."

I shut my eyes again. I knew that Nana was right and that my mother had suffered, but all I could think about was how she'd give this exact speech, this exact same performance, at my graduation, and my wedding, and when—if—I had my first kid, and how everywhere I'd go and with everyone I'd meet, my mother would be there to remind them about how I might look normal but I wasn't; how I was really sick and fragile, how I almost died and could almost die, that I would never be like them.

Outside the door, I heard people laughing, the sound of running feet, probably girls on their way to the bathroom. The appetizers were probably being served by now, the little hot dogs wrapped in pastry that were my favorites, and the egg rolls with the apricot dipping sauce.

"Did you hear what the rabbi said about being a woman of valor?" Nana asked.

I shrugged. I didn't want to admit that I hadn't exactly been listening to the rabbi, that I'd been thinking about the party, and how great it was that I had new friends who were pretty and popular and had never known me as sick or strange or broken.

Nana shook her head, smiling. "That man does love the sound of his own voice. But he wasn't bad today. *Eshet chayil*," she said in Hebrew. "There's a poem about it, from Proverbs. I used to know the whole thing, but the part I remember best—the part that made me think of you—says, 'She opens her hand to those in need, and offers her help to the poor.' "

"My mom isn't poor," I mumbled.

Nana sighed. "No, but she's needy. She needs to believe that you're going to be all right, and that's something no doctor can tell her for sure. Can you imagine how hard that's been?"

I couldn't. But I thought that I could at least be kind to my mother, even if I didn't understand her, even if she embarrassed me.

Nana pulled herself up straighter, adjusting her hat, then recited, " 'Charm is deceptive and beauty short-lived, but a woman loyal to God has truly earned praise.' "

"I don't know if I believe in God," I blurted. I'd been thinking about that a lot, but I hadn't planned on saying anything, especially not on the day of my bat mitzvah. But what kind of god would let six million people die in ovens in the Holocaust? What god would let little kids get kidnapped, or die in their car seats on hot days after their parents forgot that they were in the car? What god would let a baby be born with a defective heart, or let her mother embarrass her to death at her bat mitzvah? Why would God have let Alice die?

Nana surprised me. "I'm not sure I do, either," she said. "But I do believe in people being good to each other." She squeezed me again. The top of my head rested against the softness of her cheek. "That's what I've always loved best about you, Rachel," she said. "You have a kind heart."

"Yeah, a kind, messed-up heart that doesn't work right and is probably going to kill me, like, tomorrow, so my mom better wrap me up in bubble wrap and never let me out of the house."

Nana pulled me close and kissed my forehead. "You make me proud," she said, which, as far as I was concerned, was a lot better than *I love you.* "Now get dressed. You're missing your own party." I went to the changing room, slipped into my miniskirt, and ran down the hallway, feeling, still, not like a woman but like a little girl.

Andy

1990

"Hey there, Flash!" called Mr. Sills. His front tires bumped up over the curb onto the sidewalk. He muttered something, threw the truck into reverse, and succeeded in backing it into the spot, then opened the passenger's-side door so that Andy could climb inside. It was a steamy August morning, eighty degrees already with highs in the nineties. Andy wore shorts, sneakers, his lucky 'Sixers jersey, and carried a soda bottle that he'd filled with water and left in the freezer overnight.

"You ready?" asked Mr. Sills, putting the truck back into gear. Andy nodded. "Nervous?"

Andy shrugged.

"Talkative as ever," Mr. Sills observed, and drove them off toward the freeway, which would take them eventually to Franklin Field.

On that terrible day before Christmas when Andy had thrown the new coat away and had smashed someone's windshield and gotten picked up by the police, Mr. Sills had been the one to come down to the station and called Andy's mom. For the second day in a row, Lori had left work early and had come down to get him. In her tight black shirt and bright-red lipstick and a

Santa hat perched on her head, she'd charmed the desk sergeant and even the cop who'd picked Andy up. As soon as that guy, Officer Nash, had learned that Andy was just ten—a lie that Lori told while she'd rested her hand on his forearm and let her breasts just brush his shoulder—he'd agreed to let Andy off with a warning. "But he can't get in trouble again," he'd said, and Lori had smiled sweetly and promised that he wouldn't.

Sitting in the passenger's seat of her old Nissan, Andy had been ready for anger or even for her terrible, silent, helpless tears. But Lori had surprised him.

"This can go one of two ways," she'd said. Her voice was very calm, and her hands were steady on the wheel. "Either you keep getting angry and you keep getting in trouble and you end up in juvenile detention or reform school or jail, or you figure out something to do so you don't keep getting in trouble. My suggestion is that you run."

He wanted to ask her how that was supposed to work, how running was going to keep him from fighting, when she said, "If you want to hit someone or you want to throw something, I want you to run first. I want you to run until you can hardly lift your legs and your arms. Run until you're exhausted, and then, if you still want to hit someone or throw something, you just wait 'til you've caught your breath again and then go for it. Try it," she'd said, holding up her hand and stopping his "But, Mom" before it had gotten out of his mouth. "Try it for one month, and if it doesn't work we'll think of something else."

Maybe it was her advice that had helped him, or maybe it had been the paper route he got that spring, the one he'd taken so he could pay back his mother, who'd paid for the windshield's repairs.

Mr. Sills had been there the first Sunday morning that spring when the *Examiner* truck had dropped four bundles of papers on the sidewalk in front of Andy's house. Andy was leaning over the bundles when Mr. Sills emerged from his house on the corner, puffing fragrant smoke from his pipe. Andy wondered if the noise from the rumbling delivery truck had woken him up.

"Lot of papers there," Mr. Sills said, crossing the street.

Andy nodded.

"Don't suppose you've got a bike?"

Andy shook his head. He was still saving, even though some days he didn't think he'd ever get enough money for even a used tricycle.

"Talkative fella." Mr. Sills reached into the pocket of his loose khaki pants, pulled out a short, curving knife, and popped the twine that held one of the bundles of papers. "So you're just gonna what, exactly?" he asked.

Andy indicated his backpack, emptied of schoolbooks, plus the two canvas totes the

Examiner had given him. He'd worked it all out, in bed the night before, how he'd do two runs, carrying a dozen papers in the bag on his left, keeping as many more as he could fit in his backpack and the bag on his right, so that he'd be able to reach across his body to grab and throw the papers while he was on the move. "I'm going to run."

As Mr. Sills puffed his pipe, looking amused and a little worried, Andy loaded up. After memorizing his first three stops, he tucked his route map in his front pocket, then started running up the street to the house two up from his own, then across the street to hit three houses in a row, and that was it for Rand Street. He hooked right on Ontario, dropping off two more papers, then turned on Argyle with his wrist cocked. A stray cat hissed and scrambled out of his way. An old car belched greasy gray smoke. The ground was clotted with trash, cat shit and crumpled news-papers, shreds of the wax-paper stamp bags that dope came bundled in, even, sometimes, a needle or syringe. There were runners on every corner, some of them no older than he was, keeping their eyes open for customers or cops.

Andy ran down Argyle Street, then two left turns and he was on Malta, and his right-hand bag was empty. He reached into his backpack for another bundle, moved it into his left-hand bag, did Malta Street, then raced back up Ontario to his house. In his head, he heard the voice of Jim McKay, the *ABC's Wide World of Sports* announcer. *Young Andy Landis is in position to shatter the world record for the mile . . . I've never seen anything like this kind of speed and determination. This young man is surely one to watch.*

He sprinted across Kensington, where the sidewalks were still mostly empty and the stores still hid behind metal grates. Past the Spanish restaurant with the Dumpster, the one where he'd found the chunk of brick, but they didn't take a paper, so Andy didn't have to look. Down Willard. Up Madison. Down Jasper Street to East Hilton, up Kensington again to Allegheny, then Wishart. Even here, where everything was asphalt and concrete, with a damp breeze blowing from the Delaware River. He could smell spring and see patches of green grass growing in the abandoned lots, weeds pushing up through the cracks in the sidewalks, and he felt like he'd found what he was meant to do with his life—to run along streets, throwing the elastic-banded rectangles of news-print so they landed in the center of the stoops, moving faster than the guys on bikes, faster than the cops cruising by in their cop car. This was the thing he'd been born for, meant for, made for. Sweat streamed down his cheeks; his blood hummed in his veins; his heart beat hard, steady, and strong. He wanted to run forever.

"Easy there!" called Mr. Sills, who was sitting

in his truck with the windows open, sipping from a coffee cup, when Andy came back for the last bundle. "Don't want to give yourself a rupture!"

Andy waved, grinning, and then he was off again, the air warm on his cheeks, past a bunch of girls whose bare legs flashed in their denim shorts, feeling like with every step he was slipping out from underneath something—his fight with Ryan Peterman, who hadn't spoken to him since what Andy had come to think of as the Day of the Coat; his mother not letting him see his grandparents; the way the lunch ladies would look when they gave him an extra scoop of spaghetti or mashed potatoes; the fact that his Toughskin corduroys were already too short, exposing a few inches of ankle. The way it felt on the playground, where the kids had started splitting into groups, black on one side, white on the other, and Andy wasn't ever sure where he should be. The way it felt when every other kid at the father-son Sunday-morning Mass and pancake breakfast had a father except him.

Up Allegheny, over on F Street, down Westmoreland, almost bumping into an old guy walking a poodle. "Sorry!" he called over his shoulder, and the guy said, "Watch it, Roger Bannister," and Andy knew without being told that Roger Bannister was a runner, just like him.

He was almost sorry when he delivered his last paper, on Clearfield Street, near McPherson

Square, which was allegedly a park but actually an open-air drug market where his mom had warned him to never ever go. He saw more dope-trash and needles on the street, plastic bags blowing by, bundled-up homeless people lying on the benches or in the round concrete tunnel that was meant for little kids to climb through. He stood with his head down, hands on his knees, sweat pattering onto the pavement, catching his breath, and then he heard a car behind him toot its horn, and it was Mr. Sills in his blue truck. "Come on, Flash," he said. "How about I treat a working man to breakfast?"

Normally Andy would have just shaken his head. Even though Mr. Sills was allowed in their house—he'd actually been the one who'd found them their new place, a row house in a different part of Kensington, right down the street from where he lived—Andy spoke to him as little as possible. Once, at school, a teacher had asked if he'd be interested in the Big Brother program, where he'd be paired with a man who would take him places, movies and museums, things like that. Andy had said, "No, thank you"—he knew what Lori would have to say about him spending time with, and maybe telling their business to, a stranger. But he thought sometimes that his mom let Mr. Sills hang around to be a kind of Big Brother, a man he was supposed to respect and look up to, a role model, quote-unquote. He didn't want that, didn't want some strange man telling him what to do or, worse, acting as if he was Andy's father, so he was polite to Mr. Sills and never anything more than that.

But that morning he was starving, and he knew they were out of both cereal and bread for toast. "Let me check," he said, and before he could lose his nerve he raced back to the row house with Mr. Sills's truck rumbling behind him.

"Hey, Mom!" he called.

"Hey is for horses," she called back, the way she always did.

"Can I go get breakfast with Mr. Sills?"

He heard her sigh and got ready for her refusal, but she said, "If you aren't back in an hour I'm calling the police."

He washed his hands and face and changed his shirt. Mr. Sills was parked out front in his old blue truck, and Andy climbed into the passenger's seat, which had been cleared off. There were four or five mugs rattling around underneath his feet, along with old copies of *National Geographic.*

He'd been worried about conversation, but Mr. Sills talked enough for both of them—about why the new washing machines broke down so often, about his niece, who'd just had a baby. "Nine pounds, nine ounces. A bruiser!" Andy didn't say much, but he didn't mind listening. The cab of the truck was fragrant with tobacco and coffee. The empty mugs on the floor rolled around and clinked softly whenever they came to a red light.

At the Country Club Diner, they settled into a booth. "I'll have the usual, sweetheart," Mr. Sills said to the waitress, who seemed to know him and filled his coffee cup without being asked.

"How about you, hon?" she asked Andy, her hip cocked and her pen hovering over her pad.

"Just some toast." Andy swallowed hard. He could smell eggs and bacon, and he could see a pile of French toast as a waiter carried a platter to the next table.

"That's it? Anything to drink?"

Andy looked at the menu. Orange juice was $1.25 for a small cup, which was ridiculous when an entire half gallon only cost $1.99. "Just some water," he said.

"He'll have the Hungry Man," Mr. Sills said, then looked at Andy. "How do you like your eggs?"

The Hungry Man was so much food that it came on two plates, with a dish of grits on the side: a stack of pancakes, two eggs over easy, bacon and sausage, and crisp white toast cut in triangles. Andy dumped syrup on his pancakes, slathered butter and jam on his toast, sprinkled hot sauce on his eggs, and ate all of it, remembering to say "Thank you" when Mr. Sills added a large orange juice and a hot chocolate to the order. He ate and ate and ate, and when he stopped he thought he'd never been so full, not even after Christmas dinners at his grandparents' house.

Mr. Sills, who'd had only poached eggs and rye toast, had kept up his steady patter throughout the meal. Andy was happy to learn that he, too, liked the 76ers, especially Charles Barkley. "The Round Mound of Rebound," said Mr. Sills, patting his belly. Mr. Sills was round himself—round face, round stomach, and big, thick fingers. He wore gold-rimmed glasses, and his skin was medium-brown, not as dark as Mr. Stratton's, but not as light as Andy's. Andy's dad had been medium-brown, too, and sometimes Andy wondered how he'd ended up looking so much like his mother, at least in terms of color. Lots of times, when he was with his mother, white people thought he was white. Sometimes they'd even say bad things about black people to his face, like once when Andy had said where he lived to a lady who worked at the shoe store, and she'd crinkled her face and said, "Why would you want to live in that neighborhood with all of them? You aren't black."

"No," Lori had said, smiling sweetly, pulling Andy close, "but his father was," and the woman had backed away, looking shocked.

"You like basketball?" Mr. Sills asked him.

"It's okay," he said, and used his napkin to make sure he'd gotten all the syrup off his chin. Mr. Sills was looking at him carefully, in a way that made Andy think that there was still some left, when Mr. Sills said, "Your dad played, you know."

Andy was too shocked to say anything. Nobody ever talked about his father. Nobody even said the words *your dad* to him. Lori had hardly told him anything. "He went into the army and he died. End of story," she would say, the handful of times Andy had gotten brave enough to ask. He knew that his father's name had been the same as his, and that his father was black, and had gone to Catholic school, and that he'd gone into the army after Andy was born and he couldn't find a job. He'd been stationed in Germany, and he'd said he would send for Lori and baby Andy, but then he'd been killed in an accident. Where in Germany? What kind of accident? Where were his parents, and had they ever met Andy? He would ask, and Lori would shake her head, looking so sorrowful it was almost as if she was shrinking, disappearing into her black clothes right before his eyes. They didn't approve of me, she said, in a way that made Andy think that they didn't approve of him, either.

"My dad played basketball?" Andy's voice was husky, and both of his toes were tapping, bouncing against the diner's carpeted floor.

"Yessir," said Mr. Sills. "Center. Played with my son, as a matter of fact. In high school."

It took Andy a minute of rummaging to remember that he knew where his dad had gone to high school, because Lori had told him once. His parents had met at a high school dance and gotten married right after they'd both graduated, his mom from Hallahan and his dad from . . .

"Father Judge?"

Mr. Sills nodded.

"Did you know him?" Andy asked. "Did you know my dad?" Those words, *my dad,* felt so good to say that he wanted to say them as often as he could.

"I knew of him," said Mr. Sills. "Saw him on the court a time or two." When Mr. Sills smiled his cheeks crinkled, sending his glasses up toward his eyebrows. "Your daddy was probably the best high school basketball player in the Catholic League. Maybe even the best in the city."

All of this was news to Andy. His heart was pounding hard, the way it did when he was running. "He was?"

Mr. Sills opened the leather folder, glanced at the bill, and put down a twenty and a ten. Andy did some math and realized that was probably why the waitress had been so happy to see him.

Once, he'd gone out for pizza with the Strattons, and the lady taking people to their tables had stiffened when they'd walked in, and asked "Are you picking up takeout?" when she hadn't asked any of the other families that question. She was white, and most of the people in the restaurant were, too, and Mr. Stratton had been scowling by the time they were finally seated. "Typical," Andy had heard him say.

"Come on," said Mr. Sills. They climbed into the blue truck and drove back toward the new apartment . . . but instead of dropping Andy off at his house, Mr. Sills led him to the row house halfway up the block where he lived. Andy hesitated as Mr. Sills unlocked the door. Lori had approved breakfast, not a home visit, but he was so desperate to hear anything about his father, from someone else who'd known him, that he would have gone in even if Lori had been standing right there in front of the doorway, her arms crossed, saying *I don't think so.*

Mr. Sills led Andy into the first-floor apartment and walked toward what Andy assumed was the kitchen as Andy stood, stunned and staring. It looked like every bit of space in the small room —every inch of the wall, every scrap of the floor —was crammed, was covered, was occupied. Pictures, paintings, pages cut from magazines, all in frames a dozen shades of copper and brass and gold, lined the walls, almost obscuring the trellised green-and-cream-patterned wallpaper. One section of the wall was covered entirely in mirrors. He saw stacks of books and magazines, standing lamps, a strange brass thing Andy would later learn was a cuspidor, tables with delicate legs edged up against a couch, and two slip-covered armchairs. Layered over the floor were carpets in patterns of red and gold, blue and emerald green.

As he looked more closely, the room began to resolve itself. Andy saw a narrow pathway that led from the door to the kitchen and branched off to allow passage to a grouping of armchairs on one side, a couch on the other. The framed art was arranged by subject—one section of the wall featured paintings and drawings and photographs of flowers; another spot held landscapes; and a third was devoted to representations of dogs, some in human poses, others just doing regular dog stuff. One painting depicted a bunch of dogs in human clothing playing cards. The mirrors were of all different sizes, from as small as the one in his mother's compact to as big as a television screen. A few of them were hand mirrors in fancy gold frames that had been shaped to look like vines and flowers. There was no fireplace, but there was a marble mantelpiece against one wall. On it, alone, was a gold-framed photograph of a slender black woman in a wedding dress. She stood in profile, with a bouquet in her clasped hands and a long veil drifting down on her back.

"That was Mrs. Sills," said Mr. Sills. He was carrying a tray with a teapot and a plate filled with half-moon-shaped butter cookies with scalloped edges and a sprinkling of sugar on top, and Andy, who fifteen minutes ago had thought he wouldn't eat again for a week, found that he was hungry again. "Go on, help yourself," said Mr. Sills. Andy took a cookie, and Mr. Sills poured them tea.

"She's been gone eight years now. I miss her so." He said this all matter-of-factly, like it was nothing special, to acknowledge that someone had died, to say that you missed her. What if Lori had a picture of his father in their place, somewhere that he could see it every day? Andy couldn't imagine it. When he was little, she'd shown him a single shot, of her and his father on their wedding day. Lori had worn a big white dress, and her hair had been like an explosion on top of her head, barely held in place with a glittering white band. Standing beside her, lanky and tall, was his father, looking uncomfortable in his tuxedo, with his wrists sticking out from the sleeves. His father had big, dark eyes and close-cropped hair, his lips the same shape that Andy saw in the mirror in the mornings. "Do you have other pictures?" he'd asked his mom, as recently as September, but her face had gotten tight as she'd shaken her head.

Andy followed Mr. Sills along the narrow pathway that led to two armchairs with a table between them. Under the table was a waist-high stack of old *Sports Illustrated* magazines, and Andy gazed at them with naked longing while Mr. Sills continued on. The room reminded Andy of a picture in his illustrated version of *The Hobbit* that showed Bilbo Baggins's burrow. He looked around at the framed posters of old boxing matches, the piles of *National Geographic*s and old *Life* magazines, and the china figurines that, even to his unpracticed eye, looked much more expensive than his mother's. There was a chess set on the low table in front of the couch, and a grouping of what Andy thought were hatboxes, some deep and some shallow, stretching almost as tall as he was, against the wall.

"Where'd all this stuff come from?" Andy asked as Mr. Sills came back with a big photo album in his hands.

"Here, there, and everywhere," said Mr. Sills. He sat down in the chair next to Andy, sipped from his cup, then opened the book. "Here we go," he said. "Mrs. Sills put these together. One for every year DeVaughn was in high school."

Andy flipped through the pages slowly. There was DeVaughn's class picture, which depicted a round-faced boy with Mr. Sills's smile. Then came a shot of the freshman basketball team, three rows of boys in red-and-blue uniforms, with a list of names underneath them. Andy found DeVaughn Sills in the front row. And in the row behind him was a familiar smile and his own name. Big hands cradled a basketball, the wrists and fingers the same shape as his own.

Astonishment washed over him, pebbling his skin with goose bumps, making his mouth go dry. He skimmed through pages of DeVaughn's report cards, a written report on the Geneva Conventions, and finally stopped on a yellowed article clipped from the *Examiner*. " 'Father Judge

Falls in Semifinals,' " he read. " 'Despite the best efforts of standout sophomore center Andrew Landis, whose 28 points tied for a school record, the Crusaders were defeated by the Knights in the semifinals of the Catholic League's basketball tournament.' "

With the story was a black-and-white shot of a man—a kid, really—caught midjump, with the basketball balanced on his fingertips, poised at the rim of the hoop. Andy bent until his nose was almost touching the photo-album plastic, studying every detail. His father, Andrew Sr., had the same long face, full lips, and wide-set eyes, but his nose was broader, and his hair more tightly curled. Andy saw his father's legs, revealed in the brief shorts that players wore back then, long legs with visibly muscled calves and thighs. His father had the same ropy muscles in his arms, the same build as Andy, narrow but strong.

There you are, thought Andy, with astonishment and joy. There was his other half, the rest of him, the man who'd contributed his mouth, his eyes, his long, strong legs to his son. Andy could tell that the wedding picture showed him frozen in a moment where he'd been told what to wear and how to stand, but here he was himself, leaping into the air like gravity no longer applied, so vivid and alive it seemed as if he could continue the motion, ascending and turning his hand until the ball slid through the hoop in a perfect whoosh, nothing but net. His dad must have felt the same way about the basketball court that he did about the track or any stretch of open road. That was where he lived. That was where things made sense. That was where he belonged.

Andy flipped through the pages rapidly, scanning each clipping for more mentions of his father, finding a few. *Center Andrew Landis contributed 22 points to the Crusaders' victory over West Catholic Prep. Andrew Landis scored a record-beating 32 points.* No more pictures.

"Standout center Andrew Landis," Andy whispered . . . and then, so softly that Mr. Sills couldn't hear him, "Dad."

"That's him," said Mr. Sills. "He had that sense that the good ones have, that way of getting to the place where you need him. And was he fast!" Mr. Sills gave an admiring whistle. "When he got the ball on a breakaway, no one could catch him. But he wasn't showy, you know? When he'd dunk he wouldn't hang off the rim, waving his legs around, acting a fool. He'd just get the job done, run back down the court, look for the next shot."

Andy didn't know what to say. He still couldn't quite believe that Mr. Sills had known his dad, that he was finally getting some information. What was his father like? Was he funny or quiet? Did he get good grades? Did he like cars or comic books or music? Did he have a lot of friends, or just a few? Had he had any girlfriends before

Lori, and why had he picked a white girl to love?

"Did you ever meet my dad's parents?" he asked.

Mr. Sills shook his head.

"Or any of his friends?"

Another headshake.

"How about your son?" He struggled for the name. "DeSean? Were he and my dad friends?"

"DeVaughn," said Mr. Sills, and then he went quiet, lacing his hands over his belly, staring at the wall. Finally he said, "I don't mean to pry, but what has your mom told you about your father?"

"Nothing!" The word came out so loud that it seemed to bounce off the mirrors. "She hasn't told me anything. Just that he went to the army, to Germany, and he died in an accident."

Mr. Sills nodded and put down his cup and got to his feet. "It's yours, if you want it," he said to Andy, pointing at the photo album.

"Thank you," he said, remembering his manners. "Thank you for breakfast. Thank you for everything."

Mr. Sills waved one big hand. "It's nice to know you actually can talk," he said. "Don't be a stranger now."

I am a stranger to everyone, Andy thought. *That's what my mom wants.* He clutched the album to his chest as he ran home. His plan was to ask his mother questions, ask her if she'd seen his dad play basketball, ask her what she remembered, and how they'd met, and what he'd said to introduce himself. What he'd said the very first time they'd met. But the door was locked, the lights were off, and Lori's car was gone.

Andy let himself in, turned on the lights, and went to the kitchen. He spotted a note on the table, next to a surprise—a little stack of pictures. *Andy,* the note began. Lori never bothered with *Dear. I found these when I was cleaning out my closet.*

Then there was a space, as if his mom had stopped to think, or maybe to gather her strength.

It's hard for me to talk about so please don't ask questions. No signature. No *Love.* No mention of where she'd gone or when she'd be back, either.

Anger rose inside of Andy, squeezing up from his belly, burning in his throat, making his hands clench. *Please don't ask questions.* But this was his father, the man who'd given him half of what he was, and she'd never told him anything, except sometimes, accidentally. A Marvin Gaye song would come on the radio and she'd say, *Andrew used to love that one.* Or, once, Andy had found a busted clock radio in the corner of their closet, and she'd sigh, *Oh, your father always said he'd fix that.* Things would slip out, then she'd press her lips together tight and sometimes cross her arms on her chest so her whole body said, *Don't even ask.*

Andy sat down and looked through the sad little stack of pictures, faded square snapshots, some of them yellowed and sticky, like they'd been stuck in an album, then pulled out. There was the one from their wedding that he remembered, and a picture of what must have been high school graduation, with Andrew in a cap and gown, grinning at the camera. There was a recklessness in his smile, a tightly coiled energy that Andy could sense in the set of his shoulders, the way his arms were raised. If the picture had shown his feet, Andy bet that his father would have been on his tiptoes, bouncing the way that Andy bounced, barely able to hold still, like if he didn't move he'd burst out of his skin. *There you are,* he thought again, and wasn't sure if the *you* meant his father or himself.

Next came a Polaroid that someone had taken of Lori, with her belly bulging under a blue-and-white-checked top: *9 mos,* someone had written —his grandmother, Andy thought. At the very bottom were a few pictures of little Andy, a squinting bald bundle swimming in a blue one-piece thing with a little lamb printed on the chest . . . and, finally, baby Andy in his father's arms. His dad was holding him, one big hand, with its bulging knuckles, cupping Andy's head, touching his nose against Andy's. His white undershirt showed his corded forearms, and his biceps made the sleeves bulge. He imagined that he could hear his father's voice. *Don't worry,* he was saying. *Your mom loves you, even if she doesn't do a good job of showing it. You're a fine young man. I'm proud of you.*

Andy fanned out the photographs like a hand of cards. He arranged them in a square, then a row, then picked up each one again for careful review. Finally, he slipped them under the plastic of the two empty pages in Mr. Sills's album and put the album in his closet, where he kept his clothes and comic books in boxes, and his bedding folded up during the day.

Slowly, over the spring, he and Mr. Sills became friends. When summer came and Miles's parents sent him to camp, and the weather got so hot that most people just stayed in the air-conditioning, Andy would accompany Mr. Sills on jobs. He'd hear the rattling blue truck with CARETAKING & REPAIRS painted on its side pulling up to the curb and sometimes driving over it, and he'd come out of the house or run down the street, so that when the truck was parked he could open the passenger's-side door and either take out the heavy toolbox or climb in for the ride. He learned to do a dozen different things—unclogging toilets, rewiring blown fuses, scooping dead leaf-goop out of gutters, patching up roofs when they leaked. "My assistant," Mr. Sills would announce, leading Andy into each new house.

Andy didn't talk much on these forays into people's places, their bathrooms and roofs and backyards, but he didn't have to. He liked to listen to Mr. Sills talking about basketball—big plays, memorable shots, a best-of-seven playoff series that had come down to the final seconds of the last game. Mr. Sills would show Andy what he was doing while he worked, his big fingers deft and precise: "This is a Phillips-head screwdriver. That's what we need here—see how the screw's got a cross on top, not a straight line?" Andy loved the names of the tools—*levels* and *hex keys, needle-nose pliers* and *socket wrenches.* He liked how carefully Mr. Sills kept them, wiping them down with a clean, oiled cloth after each use, putting each wrench and screwdriver into its own compartment in his toolbox. He liked being able to do little jobs around his own house, unsticking a window or tightening a drawer pull. "That's a man's job," Mr. Sills had told him when Andy had first started following him around. "A man takes care of his house, and a man takes care of his tools."

On his days off, Mr. Sills went antiquing, which, he'd told Andy, he used to do with Mrs. Sills before she'd passed. He made the rounds of different thrift shops and consignment stores, driving his truck all over Philadelphia and South Jersey, talking back to the guys on sports radio. All the salespeople knew him and would put things aside for him—the magazines he liked, antique silver forks and spoons, Spode china in the Blue Italian pattern that he collected. In the shops that smelled like must and mothballs, yellowed paper and old clothes, Andy would page through comic books while Mr. Sills chatted with one of the old ladies who always seemed to be behind the cash registers. They would spend the morning shop-ping, then have a late-afternoon lunch of thick, juicy sandwiches from John's Roast Pork, a cinder-block shack next to the train tracks where men in suits and ladies in high heels waited with construction workers and truck drivers. Lots of times, people thought Mr. Sills was Andy's grandfather, Mr. Sills's grandson, which made him feel like he'd swallowed something warm and sweet on a cold day. Sometimes Mr. Sills would call him *son,* and the word would catch in his heart like a hook.

For Christmas when he was twelve, he used some of his paper-route money to buy Mr. Sills the brass elephant bookends that he'd seen him admiring in a shop called Time and Again on South Street in Center City. At the same place, he bought his mother a necklace, a real pearl on a gold chain. It cost forty dollars (actually fifty, but the old lady behind the counter had said, "Forty for you"), and it was worth it to see his mother's expression when he woke her up on Christmas and gave her the small square box, wrapped in red paper with a gold ribbon.

"It's too much," she'd said, and tilted her head up toward the ceiling, blinking, the way she did when she was trying not to cry, even though it was so early that she hadn't put on her foundation yet, or the mascara that turned her lashes into stiff, bristly spider legs. Her hair, uncombed and unteased, hung in soft waves over her cheeks. She looked as young as a teenager in her plaid pajamas and chenille robe as she got out of bed and went to her closet. "Here," she said, sounding shy, handing him a rectangular package wrapped in Sunday's comics. "I hope I got the right kind."

Andy's hopes weren't high. Most years, Lori got him useful stuff—shirts for school, a new blanket, and bars of soap and toothbrushes for stocking stuffers. When he found the Nike Air Flight sneakers, white with a blue swoosh, he shouted with delight. "I hope they're the right size," Lori said, and Andy had hugged her and said, "They're perfect."

Since the big fight, Andy and his mother had made their own Christmas traditions. They'd open their presents first thing in the morning. Then Lori would bake the one thing she made from scratch, cinnamon rolls with yeast and honey and flour that made a dough that had to rise twice. They'd have cinnamon rolls and sliced ham for lunch. Then Lori would put a prestuffed chicken into the oven, and they would watch *A Christmas Carol* and *It's a Wonderful Life* on TV. Lori would drink eggnog and Andy would drink hot chocolate, topped with whipped cream, and every time the whipped cream was gone, he'd take the canister out of the refrigerator and spray another white ruffle on top. "Only on Christmas," his mother would say, and kiss the top of his head. In the warm little row house, with his belly full of good food and the living room full of the blue glow from the television set and the lights from the Christmas tree that he and Mr. Sills had carried in together, Andy felt warm and safe. For the last two years they'd gotten a white Christmas. The plows would push high drifts up against the cars still parked on the street, and the wind would send silvery gusts of flakes twirling and spinning down the empty sidewalks, but inside, all was calm and all was bright. Lori would wear Andy's necklace, and she'd put on a Santa hat in the morning, and by the end of the day it would be cockeyed, one side slipping down over her penciled-in eyebrow, her lip-sticked mouth curved into a pretty smile, and Andy would think that no boy had ever loved his mother as much as he loved Lori.

In his new sneakers, Andy ran through the spring and the summer, timing himself as he did laps around the park, getting ready for high school track-team tryouts in August. Because Lori was working, Mr. Sills had agreed to drive him. Stopped at a light, about to get onto the highway, his friend had patted his shoulder and said, "You're going to do just fine."

Andy didn't answer. He rolled down the window,

letting the hot air and the city sounds come through, and pushed the door lock down, then pulled it up, then pushed it down again, rolling his water bottle back and forth in his free hand.

Roman Catholic, Andy's new school, was downtown, right in Center City, at the corner of Broad and Vine, and it didn't have a track of its own. All of its meets were away meets, and most of its practices were held at the Penn campus. Mr. Sills dropped Andy off at Franklin Field, said "Good luck" one more time, then drove off to go fix an air conditioner.

It had been warm the week before, but that afternoon in August the temperature had soared into the nineties. Andy counted thirty boys sweating on the infield, some of them doing stretches, others standing in groups, talking. A man in a Roman Catholic T-shirt with a whistle around his neck introduced himself as Coach Maxwell. He had a blunt face like a clenched fist and a short, stocky body that seemed to be made entirely of muscle. His khaki pants were crisply pressed; his plain black sneakers were as pristine as if they'd just come out of the box.

Coach Maxwell reached into his pocket and removed a stopwatch. The two men beside him, Andy saw, both had pads of paper and pens. "Okay, fellas," he said, and lined them up and told them what to do.

At his direction, the boys ran sprints, then

hurdles, the quarter-mile, the half-mile. They did standing long jumps and running long jumps. Coach Maxwell would watch, occasionally saying something to one of his assistants. At the starting line for the mile, with eight other guys, some of them in fancy running cleats, Andy thought coolly, *I'm better than you are.* He had put in more time, all those mornings on his paper route, all those afternoons in the park. He'd worked harder, and he could suffer more.

There was no pistol, just the coach yelling, "Go!" At the sound of his voice, Andy sprinted to the front of the pack, pushing himself until his lungs burned, grabbing the lead and holding it, fighting off every challenge, leaving the second-place finisher at least ten lengths behind him.

When they were done, Coach Maxwell sent the boys to the bleachers. Andy could feel their eyes on him, could catch snatches of their conversation, could hear his name repeated. Then the coach called Andy down, and put his hand on his shoulder, the same way Andy had seen Ryan Peterman's father do. "You've got something special," he said. That blunt face relaxed long enough for a brief smile. "Too early to tell how much. Too early to tell how special. But you've got something," he said. "Did your mom or dad ever run?"

"Basketball," he told Coach Maxwell. His heart was swelling. *You've got something special.* He wondered if his dad had felt this, this kind of pure happiness, like he'd swallowed the sun, sinking a game-winning three-pointer, or stripping an opponent of the ball. "My dad played basketball."

Coach Maxwell clapped his hands once, calling the boys together. They sat on the first two rows of bleachers, shoulder to shoulder, listening. "You're gonna work harder than you ever imagined," he said. "We will run sprints. We will run laps. We will run suicides. We will lift weights. We will do burpees and squats and lunges and jumping jacks until you wish you were never born. There's no *game*," he said, thin lips curling, blunt face contracting even more tightly as he let the distasteful word out of his mouth. "No game, no ball, no points, no substitutions. No cheerleaders shaking their ta-tas. No band. No homecoming. It's just you and the track and the clock. It's the most elemental thing there is—the simplest and the hardest. Not every boy's cut out for it. Boys get bored. Boys get tired. They don't want to put in the time it takes to build the FOUNDATION that is the KEY to SUCCESS."

Andy had nodded. He didn't care that there was no band or cheerleaders at track meets, that football and basketball players got all the glory. Scores and goals, ribbons and medals, all of that took a distant second place to the joy that he felt when he ran, the sensation of being entirely in his body, every worry and concern left behind, feeling the ground beneath his feet, the air against his skin, moving so fast it was almost like time itself had to hurry to catch up.

"You put in the EFFORT, you get the RESULTS," Coach Maxwell roared that August, his red face getting even redder, a thin mist of saliva surrounding his mouth, and when he asked, "Are you ready to work hard?" all the boys, Andy included, shouted some version of assent.

Indoor track was in the winter; outdoor was in the spring. Andy did both. By the end of freshman year he held the statewide record for the 1600 meters, for Catholic and secular schools, and was named to his first all-regional team. He kept his paper route in the mornings, eventually applying for a longer route that paid better. He started a lifelong habit of meticulously recording his workouts—every lunge, every squat, every turn around the track. After school, he would go to the Central Library at Nineteenth and Vine, check out every book about running that he could find, and read and reread them until he could recite passages from memory. He learned about Roger Bannister, who'd done what scientists said was impossible and run a mile in less than four minutes, and Jim Ryun, who in 1964 became the first schoolboy to duplicate that feat; about Paavo Nurmi, the Flying Finn, who'd gone undefeated for 121 races. He read about Bill Rodgers, who won four Boston Marathons, and Frank Shorter, whose 1972 gold in the Olympic marathon had started the running boom in the United States, and Alberto Salazar, who'd run so hard as a twenty-year-old in the Falmouth Road Race that his body's temperature soared to 107 degrees, and a priest was called to the finish line to read him his last rites. Salazar was his favorite, Salazar and Steve Prefontaine, a front-runner, like Andy, who'd been a schoolboy star and once held the American record in seven different distance track events, from the 2000 meters to the 10,000 meters, and never lost a collegiate race in his distances.

By the time he was sixteen Andy had set three goals for himself: He would go to the University of Oregon, like Steve Prefontaine. He would run in the Olympics. He would make money, enough for anything he and his mother ever wanted, so that they'd never have to worry again.

Rachel
1993

"This is going to be amazing," I said to my best friend, Marissa Feldman. I capped my bubblegum-flavored Bonne Bell Lip Smacker, put it back in my Bermuda bag, and snapped the wooden handles shut. We were riding in a tricked-out bus that was taking us and twenty other members of Beth Am synagogue's youth group to Atlanta for the first week of our summer vacation, where we'd sleep in dorms, eat in a dining hall, and build houses in a low-income neighborhood for an organization called Home Free.

This was the first time my parents had let me leave home for longer than a single night's sleepover, and it had taken months of pleading, plus a phone call from Rabbi Silver and a special check-in with my cardiologist.

"Good to go," said Dr. Karen, whose hair had started to show strands of silver in the years she'd been treating me. My parents and I were sitting in her office, and Dr. Karen was behind her antique desk, piled high with charts, and her binoculars and birding journal. *Most doctors play golf,* she'd told me once. *I collect birds. Much less stressful.*

"She'll need to be careful," she'd told my parents, who'd sat side by side, holding hands. "As you know, this is a chronic condition, and she'll be managing it all her life, just like diabetes. But the surgeries worked as well as we hoped they would. For all intents and purposes, she's got a normal heart now." She leaned forward, looking at them with a smile. "Let her be a normal teenager," she said. "I know that's not easy for any parents to do, but try to let her spread her wings."

Of course, me spreading my wings was the last thing my mother wanted, but I'd cajoled and bullied and finally threatened to stow away on the bus if they didn't sign the permission slip, and now here I was, watching the scenery through the window get greener as we headed east, up through Georgia.

I adjusted the angle of the reclining seat and touched my hair, making sure my hairband was still in place and that the face-framing waves were still framing my face, not curling up in revolt. After the disaster of my bat mitzvah, I'd been convinced that unless I did some serious damage control, my social life was over and my friends would abandon me. I'd spent the whole party, and the whole rest of the month, not exactly saying that my mother was crazy, but strongly hinting that she was prone to exaggeration; that I really hadn't been that sick, and now, of course, I was completely fine. "She just feels bad that she gave up her job, I think," I'd said, and Marissa and Kelsey and Kara and Britt had nodded, maybe thinking of their own mothers. Marissa's mom was a lawyer who was never home. Kelsey's mom was an art teacher who did that job only because she hadn't found a gallery to sell the wire sculptures she made in the spare bedroom she called her studio, and Britt's mom, like mine, had once worked but was now home full-time, over-managing her children's lives.

Marissa raised her quart of Gatorade, the one she'd spiked with vodka before we left town. "To new cuties!" she said, and swallowed, then passed me the bottle. Marissa had an older brother at the University of Florida who, for the extortionate rate of ten dollars a trip, would buy us peach schnapps and wine coolers in such adventurous flavors as Racy Raspberry and Whatta Water-melon, but lately we'd moved on to vodka, reasoning that it was more sophisticated than the sweet, babyish drinks that I suspected we both secretly preferred.

I took a sip, trying not to wince at the burn, or to worry when it felt like my heart had hic-cupped when the booze went down. Acting like a careless, laughing girl who hadn't come any closer to mortality than the death of a grand-parent or a beloved pet was only part of it. Proving it mattered more. For that, there were boys.

First there'd been Jason Friedlander, who'd asked me to dance at my bat mitzvah and then, before the candle-lighting ceremony, had taken my hand, led me into an empty classroom, and kissed me. It was shocking, to feel his hands on my shoulders, his face against mine, his breath in my mouth. When Jason tried to sneak one of his hands up my top to explore the recently brassiered terrain, I pushed him away, not wanting his fingers to find the raised, bumpy line of my scar.

"What?" he blurted. He was breathing hard, and his brown hair, which turned out to be remarkably soft, was flopping over his eyes. "Don't you like me?"

The truth was that until that day I'd never given Jason any thought, and didn't have an opinion about him one way or the other. After that day, though, he became all I could think about. His face, which had once struck me as unremarkable and maybe even a little goofy, was suddenly handsome. His hands, his lips, the confident way he touched me—all of it combined made me dizzy, like I would swoon right onto the floor. Best of all, his desire, the way he'd chosen me, made it clear to the whole seventh grade that I was a normal girl.

By the time my parents drove me home—my mother, still teary, apologizing for embarrassing me; my father, gruff and a little stern, saying, "Now, Helen, just calm down"; and my brother, Jonah, rolling his eyes with a rolled-up joint barely hidden in his suit pocket—all I could think about was Jason. Had he liked me for a long time? What had caught his attention—my hair, my eyes, my laugh? Did he think I was pretty? Was he my boyfriend now?

The questions left me feeling like someone had adjusted my skin, taken nips and tucks and tiny tapers, and now it fitted me perfectly, and every inch of it was tingling with a new awareness. I felt unbroken, whole. Late that night, inspecting myself naked in the bathroom's full-length mirror, with a towel pressed against my chest to cover my scar, I thought about Jason looking at me this way, seeing my flat belly, my narrow, high-arched feet, my long neck, the shape of my breasts. Maybe I could never be the prettiest girl or the one with the least-complicated history, but if I was a good girlfriend, if boys liked me, it meant that I was normal, just like Kelsey and Britt and the rest of them.

Tell me more, I'd said to Jason when he'd talked about making it to the state quarterfinals in Little League the night his mom drove us to see *Edward Scissorhands* at the six-plex. *Tell me more,* I'd said the next year to Scott, whose parents were getting divorced and whose dad had moved into a one-room conch shack on Casey Key near Sarasota. After Scott had been Derek, who'd starred as Captain Hook in our school's spring musical. When the show's run ended, I talked him into keeping the hook so we could park in handicapped spots when we went out for pizza. People would start to yell at us, to tell us we were inconsiderate and rude, until Derek flashed his hook and gave them a smile at once woebegone and brave, and they'd swallow hard and start to apologize.

After Derek was Anand, who had run lights during the show and comforted me after Derek hooked up—no pun intended, I'd told Marissa—with Jill Pappano, who'd played Tiger Lily. By my sophomore spring, Anand was replaced by Troy, a tennis player with beautifully molded calves and forearms and, it soon emerged, nothing much to say, although he was the most persistent of my boyfriends, always trying to slide his hands up one article of clothing or down another, or pushing my hand between his legs and saying things like, "Feel what you do to me."

I knew what he wanted. By then girls were starting to get serious with their boyfriends. Marissa had gone all the way, except she and her boyfriend had both been drunk at the time, so she claimed it didn't count, and Britt had given a guy a blow job, except none of us had met the guy, a sophomore at Duke whom Britt said she'd met during spring break on the beach. The truth was that sex scared me. My whole life, I'd had to be careful with my body, never running too fast, never getting too hot, taking vitamins and staying hydrated and washing my hands until my skin chapped, knowing that, with my weakened immune system, I'd catch any cold that was going around, and a cold could turn into the flu, which could turn into pneumonia, which could send me to the hospital again.

Sex was the absence of control, the opposite of caution. It meant letting go entirely. What if I couldn't? Or worse, what if I could and did, and got hurt?

It wasn't something I could discuss with my cardiologist, kind Dr. Karen with the mono-grammed handkerchiefs that she kept in her pocket for crying parents and the curly hair she kept cut short and never bothered styling. She had been taking care of me since I was a baby, so there was no way I could ask her what would happen to my heart if I did it, and it certainly wasn't something I could talk about with my mom. After my sixteenth birthday, she'd knocked on my bedroom door. I'd opened it to find her standing there, still wearing the nametag from the library, where she'd started volunteering three days a week, dressed in pale-gray linen pants and a peach silk blouse. My mom wasn't beautiful, but she was pretty, with her pale, freckled skin and soft, light-brown hair and round brown eyes that always looked a little surprised, like someone had just snuck up behind her and pinched her bottom.

"What's up?" I asked. It was Friday night and I had plans to meet up with my friends on the beach.

Without answering, she came and perched on the very edge of my bed, like she didn't want to get comfortable. She crossed her legs, fiddled with her rings, and then gave me a stiff little speech about how I was now, "in some senses," a woman; that I'd be making my own choices about my body and she and my father hoped that I'd make good ones. "I don't have to tell you how much it matters," she'd said with a sad smile, which was true. The year before, Jonah had gotten his girlfriend pregnant. There'd been a weekend of phone calls, worried looks, and fights conducted in whisper-shouts in my parents' bedroom. I could hear my dad saying, "Helen, forget it," and could hear her saying, "Bernie, calm down." All of this had culminated in a Sunday-night sit-down: Jonah and my parents, his girlfriend, Greta, and her mom and dad in the living room, and me, hiding just out of sight on the second-floor landing, where I could hear every word. On Monday morning, Greta had gone to the doctor's. Jonah declined to accompany her, and by the end of the week they were broken up. That was what I knew about sex—that it could feel good, but it could also get you in trouble, could ruin relationships, shame your parents, end in all kinds of disaster.

I'd tried masturbation. Marissa had been doing it since she was twelve, had described it enthusiastically, and had even, one night when we'd each had three wine coolers, offered to do a show-and-tell. But my attempts had been halfhearted failures. Even though I'd read dozens of sex scenes and seen at least as many in the movies, I had a hard time imagining what it would actually feel like, and my solo efforts just left me with a sore wrist and the same vague, crampy feeling I'd have the day before my period arrived. *A whole lot of nothing,* I would think, rolling onto my side. Maybe it was all a lie, something people made up to sell books and movies.

Still, I was as romantic as any teenage girl. I'd play UB40's "(I Can't Help) Falling in Love with You" on repeat until my dad yelled "Enough!" down the hall. I wanted love, the big love, the kind people wrote songs and made movies about. I wanted to be the center of some guy's universe, the only thing he could think about. I wanted to matter that way.

"Hey!" Marissa elbowed me, then passed me the bottle again. I glanced at the chaperones at the front of the bus, then drank, savoring the glow in my belly, and with it, the knowledge that I was breaking the rules, being a bad girl . . . which was to say, a normal girl. The bus driver had put on *Back to the Future*, which almost everyone was ignoring. Kids were talking, or were sneaking sips from water bottles filled with liquids that were not water, or were smoking cigarettes in the bath-room, in spite of the NO SMOKING sign. Rabbi Silver was up front deep in conversation with Melissa Nasser's mom—something about Israel, I guessed, which was Rabbi Silver's number-one topic. In the very back of the bus, a few couples were making out. As I watched, Patti Cohen positioned herself on Larry Mendelsohn's lap, and Larry slipped his hand up the back of her blouse. I watched him work his tongue in and out of her mouth for a moment, then said, "I bet I know how he looks when he's plunging a toilet."

"That's disgusting," squeaked a high, childish voice from the seat behind us.

Marissa shoved the Gatorade bottle into her Gap tote, then glanced over her shoulder. Bethie Botts gave her a wide, empty smile.

"Another planet heard from," I whispered, and we both rolled our eyes.

Every high school has its hierarchy. Every totem pole has its girl or guy at the bottom, the kid who even the most acne-plagued nerds or socially inept grinds or unhappily closeted homosexuals can look at and think, *There, but for the grace of God.* For as far back as my memories of school went, our low girl was Bethie Botts. Aka Big Bethie. Aka Beth the Blob. Bethie was enormously fat, which was one of the reasons no one was sitting next to her—there wasn't room. Her thighs bulged against the seams of her nylon slacks (no jeans or pants for Bethie, what she wore could only be called slacks); the flesh of her belly and breasts and upper arm wobbled over the dividers to jiggle against the velour of the empty seat.

Bethie's face was wide and round as a pie, greasy and studded with clusters of whiteheads, blackheads, and cysts in various stages of eruption. Her hair was lank and brown and hung limply on her shoulders. She wore argyle sweaters in unflattering pastels, and old-lady sneakers, wide and white, without the desirable Nike swoosh or the less popular but still acceptable

Adidas stripes. Bethie met the world with a flat, incurious stare, and when she spoke, it was in an off-putting simper. Her nails were ragged, her cuticles frequently bloody. She'd waddle along the hall-ways of Clearview High School, her nylon pants swishing, her eyes fixed on nothing, a smirky smile plastered on her face.

Then there was her smell—awful, enveloping, and seemingly permanent, surrounding her like her own personal weather system. In elementary school, there'd been notes of urine mixed in with the scent of unclean flesh and unwashed clothing. As she'd gotten older, the pee had been replaced with eye-watering body odor, a stink that was like what Mark Twain said about the weather—everyone complains about it, but nobody does anything. In Bethie's case, people had tried. Well-meaning teachers had pulled her aside, suggesting antiperspirant or deodorant or soap. Less kind classmates like Mikey Henderson or Joel Marx would say, "Jesus, Botts, take a shower! You fuckin' reek!" One December, Rabbi Silver had given us all little Chanukah gifts, and Bethie's was a collection of soaps and sample-size perfumes. None of it worked—not the gifts, not the insults. Bethie's smile never wavered. She never looked hurt. But she never smelled any better.

"What's her story?" Marissa had asked after her first week of junior high. Marissa had gone to a different elementary school than I had. We'd been assigned seats next to each other in homeroom on our first day of school, and we'd quickly become friends. "Is she retarded or something?"

I shook my head. "She's not retarded. Just weird. And she's always been like that," I told Marissa. "She's like Stonehenge, only stinkier. She never changes."

Things might have been different if Bethie had been nice, if she'd made an effort with her appearance or her manner. Certainly there were other fat kids in Clearview, even a few other kids with bad skin or cheap clothes, but they had friends, a circle, a place to sit at lunch. Not Bethie, who was actively unpleasant. If you tried to start a conversation with her, she'd ignore you or answer your questions with non sequiturs or snotty replies.

"What are you reading?" Marissa asked Bethie that first morning in class.

Bethie looked up, that dumb smile in place, as always. "A book," she said, in her incongruously sweet, girlish voice.

Marissa looked at me, to see if she was being mocked. I shrugged. With Bethie, you never knew.

At six o'clock, the bus pulled into KFC. The kids from Beth Am sat in groups of threes and fours, except for Bethie, who sat by herself until Rabbi Silver took the seat across from her. Back on the bus, Marissa and I polished off the spiked Gatorade. I leaned my head against the window. Marissa flipped open *The Bridges of Madison*

County, which everyone was reading that spring. "Listen to this," she said, and read, " 'The leopard swept over her, again and again and yet again, like a long prairie wind, and rolling beneath him, she rode on that wind like some temple virgin toward the sweet, compliant fires marking the soft curve of oblivion.' "

"Oh, puh-leeze," I groaned. "How can a leopard be like a wind? Aren't leopards, like, furry and heavy? And how can a fire be compliant? And—"

"Hush," said Marissa, and continued. " 'This is why I'm here on this planet, at this time, Francesca. Not to travel or make pictures, but to love you. I know that now. I have been falling from the rim of a great high place, somewhere back in time, for many more years than I have lived in this life. And through all of those years, I have been falling toward you.' "

I pursed my lips and made the whistling noise of a bomb plummeting to earth. "Falling for years. It's going to hurt when he lands."

"Have you considered the possibility that instead of fixing your heart, the doctors accidentally removed it?" Marissa asked, pulling out her lip gloss from her own Bermuda bag and using the wand to slide another coat of shiny pink over her lips. The bus groaned and lurched around a corner, then up a steep drive toward the plush green lawns and white-brick buildings of Emory University. We climbed off the bus, collected our duffels and suitcases and sleeping bags from the sidewalk where the driver had arranged them, and followed Rabbi Silver into the auditorium.

"They'd better not make us wear hard hats," said Marissa, giving her permed curls a pat. "Finding cute overalls was bad enough."

"Safety first," I said, feeling a pang of worry. When they'd signed the permission slip, my parents had included an entire page about my medical history, but what if whoever was in charge hadn't read it and had me on a crew that was doing heavy lifting? I patted my own hair, thinking that I'd do what I always did in situations like this: say I had my period, then sit on the bleachers or in the shade. I'd packed my Walkman and my copy of *Wuthering Heights*, as well as the latest issue of *People*, which I'd swiped from our mailbox, with "Mariah Carey's All-Star Wedding" on the cover. If I ended up on the sidelines, I'd be fine.

Marissa pitched the empty Gatorade bottle toward a trash can. It bounced off the rim and fell to the ground, but she was halfway up the path and didn't notice. Sighing, I picked up the bottle and threw it away. When I turned around, a guy was looking at me, a guy with broad shoulders and very white teeth and brown hair cut short. He wasn't doing that overt checking-me-out thing. Instead, he was staring like he recognized me, and the weird thing was, I felt like I recognized him, too.

Rabbi Silver called, "Rachel! Come on!" I hurried into the auditorium just as a middle-aged woman with shiny platinum hair pulled back like a ballerina stepped to the front of the crowd and held up a hand for silence. "My name's Darcy Edelman. I'm the director of the local chapter of Home Free, and I want to thank you all for your service," she said. "If you'll head up here to find your nametags, please. The color of the tag is the color of your group."

I found my tag, which had a blue border. The guy who'd been looking at me had a blue tag, too. He was tall but not too tall, thin but not too skinny, with the contours of muscles in his arms and chest visible underneath his plain blue T-shirt. He had a narrow face, a high forehead, brown eyes, straight, thick eyebrows, and a dimple in his chin. Even though it was cut very short, I could tell his hair was curly, and his lips were beautiful, full and almost pursed, like he was waiting to give someone a kiss. No braces, I noticed . . . then I saw that he was looking at my nametag.

"Rachel?" he said. He had a nice, deep voice.

"Don't tell me that's your name, too," I said, smiling up at him, thinking of how proud Marissa would be that I'd already caught the eye of a cute guy.

"Rachel Blum," he said. His eyes moved from the tag to my face. "Were you ever in the Miami Children's Hospital?"

145

I studied him more closely. "Yes. Only half my life. Why?"

He smiled, just a brief flash of his teeth. "You told me a story."

I stared up at him, feeling my heart give another hiccup, feeling like the lights had dimmed and the auditorium had gone silent. "You wrote me a note," I said, trying to connect this handsome guy with the kid I'd met in the emergency room. "I sent you a letter, but it came back." This was true. I'd written to Andy to ask if his arm had indeed been broken, and if he'd gotten to go back to the ocean before he and his mom had gone home, and if his friends had signed his cast, but the letter I'd worked on so carefully had come back a week after I'd mailed it, stamped UNDELIVERABLE and NO FORWARDING ADDRESS.

His eyebrows drew together, and he looked down at his sneakers, plain blue-and-white Nikes; running shoes, not the puffy white schooners that came with their own inflation system that the boys in my school favored, whether or not they'd ever held a basketball. "My mom and I moved right after we got back from that trip."

"I can't believe it!" I said, still looking for traces of the hurt eight-year-old in this cute boy, and noticing that he was taking as careful inventory of me as I was of him. "Isn't this crazy?" I could feel my heart pound, and I felt breathless, the way I remembered feeling when I was six and had pleurisy, only this time it felt wonderful.

"Crazy," he confirmed, looking me over like he couldn't believe I was there, like I'd disappear at any moment, as the Home Free woman clapped her hands.

"In the morning after breakfast you'll all find your team leaders and be directed to your work sites. For now, get a good night's sleep."

"I guess I'll see you in the morning," I said.

Andy smiled at me. "See you in the morning."

"Okay. Great." The back of his hand brushed my arm as he walked away, and I felt his touch echo inside me as I stared after him, his broad shoulders and narrow hips, tanned skin and close-cropped hair, feeling like a girl in a movie or a book, a girl who'd been through all kinds of adventures and trials, and had finally glimpsed her reward.

The next morning Andy nodded at me as he boarded the bus with a bunch of other guys, the ones from his school that he'd sat with at breakfast. I thought he was going to walk right past me, but at the last minute he dropped into the seat next to mine. I thought I looked good. I'd woken up early, even before the alarm I'd set, which gave me time to take a long shower, spritz on peach-scented body mist, and put my hair in hot rollers. Back in the room, I'd spent fifteen minutes rifling through everything I'd packed to find the right long-sleeved white shirt to go underneath my distressed denim overalls (even in the summer heat, the Home Free people had insisted on long sleeves to keep us safe from I wasn't sure what). I wondered if he'd put any thought into his clothes—a purple T-shirt with the words HOLY CROSS on the front in gold, and a pair of jeans that fit him just right.

"Good morning," I said.

He turned to me. "Rachel Blum. *Bloom* like flower, even though it's spelled *blum* like *plum*." The corners of his eyes crinkled when he smiled.

Pleasure flooded through me. He'd remembered! "Well, clearly, you've spent the last eight years thinking of me nonstop."

"I did take a break every once in a while. For the PSATs. Stuff like that."

His teasing gave me an excuse to ball my hand into a fist and punch him playfully on his upper arm, which felt as solid as it looked.

"Don't lie. I'll bet you were even thinking of me during the PSATs. I'll bet no other girl you've ever met could tell 'Hansel and Gretel' as well as I did."

He shook his head, with the smallest smile on his lips and his thick brows drawn together. "You have a very high opinion of yourself."

"Not really. I can just tell when a man is obsessed."

He stretched his long legs into the aisle. I pulled

out the tube of sunscreen I'd stuck in the front pocket of my overalls.

"Sunscreen?" I asked. He took it and sniffed.

"Is this peach scented?" He turned the tube around in his hands, frowning at the price tag. "Eleven dollars?"

"Ten ninety-nine."

He shook his head in mock incredulity, thick eyebrows drawing down, the corners of his eyes crinkling again.

"What, you don't think I'm worth it?" I grabbed the tube back and squirted some lotion in my palm. "It's got restorative nutrients. Vitamin E. That's an important one."

"Of course." He watched as I dabbed my finger in the gel and spread it on my cheeks and nose. If I'd known him a little better I would have smoothed the leftover sunscreen on his face, but instead I used it on the backs of my hands. When we reached the work site Andy stood up.

"Time to work, Ten Ninety-Nine." He took the tube out of my hand and tucked it back into my overalls pocket, and I followed him off the bus.

Our "house leader," a young woman named Alex, who was taking a year off between college and law school to work for Home Free, gave us an orientation, telling us about the neighborhood, showing pictures of the family who would be living in the house, and then explaining that we wouldn't actually be building a house in a week. "The majority of the work's going to be done by actual trained construction workers, which, believe me, is for the best," she said. "What we're going to do is get everything ready so that they can come in and do the job fast."

Getting everything ready meant clearing the lot of trash and debris, sorting screws and bolts into their proper piles, carrying lumber and sacks of concrete from a truck onto the work site, and culling piles of donated clothes and kitchen tools. I was hoping Andy and I would be assigned to the bolt-sorting station, but instead, Alex gave each of us a contractor-sized trash bag and a pair of canvas gloves, signaling that I'd be spending my first day of summer vacation as a trash-picker. When Alex gave us the go-ahead to start, I was careful to position myself right near Andy, so it was natural when we headed off in the same direction.

I was used to Florida heat and humidity, but at least at home everything smelled clean, and you could usually catch a salty breeze from the ocean. On this windless morning the sky was a washed-out blue so pale it was almost white, and the air seemed to hunker down, squatting on your skin, stinking of exhaust. The weedy dirt was full of broken glass, fast-food Styrofoam clamshells, and the occasional clump of dog poop.

Andy leaned down, scooping up handfuls of newspaper in his gloved hands. I daintily plucked a coffee cup between my thumb and finger and said, "Tell me everything that's happened between the last time I saw you and today."

"Everything?" He grabbed a broken bottle. "That could take a while."

"We have time."

He watched as I pinched a scrap of newspaper in my fingers. "If that's how you pick up trash, we do."

"What happened with your arm?" I asked.

He shrugged. "I don't remember much. They did an X-ray, and they splinted it. I had to go back for the cast." With one hand carrying his rake and the other full of trash bag, he had to use his forearm to wipe his forehead. "My mom wasn't happy."

I remembered his mom, her cloud of hair, her booze perfume, the way she'd talked to Andy, like he was an adult who should have known better. "So what else?" I asked. "Where do you live? Any brothers or sisters? Or pets?" *Or girlfriend,* I thought, and decided I'd figure out a way to get that question in the mix.

"It's just me and my mom in Philadelphia," he said.

Alex clapped her hands and, at her instructions, Andy and I started raking the lumpy ground. I edged myself closer until I felt his shoulder brush mine. Heat bloomed on my skin, and my heartbeat quickened. I was trying to think of what else I could ask him when he said, "Do you do sports?"

I shook my head and touched my chest, the ridge of scar invisible underneath my shirt. I wanted to see if he'd remember. I wanted him to look at me—at my waist, my legs, and my hair, my best feature, the one thing everyone noticed and praised.

"I like reading," I said. Andy made a face, his heavy brows coming to a V over his eyes.

"Not my favorite."

"I can guess," I said, smiling.

"What do you mean?"

"That letter you sent. You had the unhappiest handwriting I've ever seen."

"Unhappy handwriting?" His mouth twitched upward. When he bent down to scoop up the weeds, I could see the bulges of his vertebrae against his shirt, and I could smell soap and clean cotton. "What are you talking about?"

"You had these tiny little letters, like it hurt you to write them. Like you were being charged for every drop of ink." I followed along as Andy put his rake against the wall, picked up a pile of lumber, and at Alex's instruction, carried it to a spot on the dirt. I grabbed a piece myself and followed along. "Have you done this before?"

"What, volunteered?" Andy asked.

"No. Built a house. You look like you know what you're doing." It was true. His movements were quick and assured, graceful and practiced, which made him a contrast to the boys and men in my life. My father's household skills started and ended with replacing the batteries in the garage door opener. Jonah was so lazy that even if he'd had any kind of innate abilities to deal with broken lamps or grumbly garbage disposals, he'd choose to stay stoned in his bedroom instead.

"I've got a friend who's a repairman. I help him out sometimes."

"I think our repairman is a pervert," I said. This was true. The guy my parents called for home repairs was named Norman. He had a droopy, hangdog face and seemed to always have his hands in his pockets, and once, I'd seen him staring when Marissa and I were in the pool.

"My friend isn't a pervert," Andy said, and started taking longer steps, so that I had to hurry to keep up with him.

"I didn't say he was! Not all handymen are perverts!" I set my piece of wood down. "Although actually the guy who cleans our pool is kind of creepy, too."

"You have your own pool?" He sounded impressed. I wanted to tell him that everyone on my street had a pool, that a pool was no big deal, but I thought that maybe, for him, it was.

Andy scooped another armload of wood, and made a face when I picked up another single piece. "You can't carry any more?"

"Sorry, I'm a delicate flower."

"You were carrying that big duffel bag last

night. What was in there, anyhow? Your entire wardrobe?"

I tried to remember when Andy could have seen me with my bag. He must have been watching me, I thought, feeling giddy, watching when I hadn't noticed.

"How do you know about my luggage? Were you spying on me?"

"No."

"Oh, you were," I said. I'd teased boys before, gotten them to laugh, but I thought that if I could get a smile out of Andy it would be better than all of their laughter combined. "You have that look. You're obviously working for the CIA."

His lips twitched into an almost-smile. "How about this time you try two sticks of wood, princess?"

"As much as I'd like to contribute more of an effort, the thing is, with wood I could get a splinter, and that could get infected, and then I could get really sick," I said. I liked when he called me *princess,* especially because *Jewish American* wasn't in front of it.

"That's why they gave us gloves." He lifted a hand to show me. "And make us wear long sleeves."

"Splinters can get through long sleeves," I told him. "Splinters can go anywhere." I dropped my voice to an ominous whisper. *"Anywhere."*

"You're crazy," he said, shaking his head. Back

at the woodpile, I made a show of adjusting my gloves, and Andy gravely piled not one but two pieces into my arms.

"Think you can handle all of that?"

"I'll try," I said, and took a deep breath, trying to stop my heart from beating so hard. "Do you have any hobbies outside of construction?"

"I run," said Andy. His face was sober, his eyes were intent. "I'm going to go to the Olympics one day."

"Really?" I said. "I hear the tickets are pretty expensive."

"Oh, you," he said, in a funny, scolding tone. He wasn't smiling, though. He wasn't kidding.

"What is your . . . event?" My school had a track team, the same way we had teams for everything else, but none of my friends were on it, and I'd never been to a meet or a match or whatever they had.

"I'm a distance runner. I run cross-country in the fall—the course is just over three miles. Then I do the sixteen hundred meters, the thirty-two hundred meters, and the eight-hundred-meter relay in the spring, but in college I'm probably going to do the five and the ten thousand meters."

"So that's how far?"

"Three and six miles."

"I think I'd pass out if I had to run a mile." I wasn't lying. The most running I'd ever done was in junior high, when the bus came at seven-fifty in the morning and I'd have to dash down the street to meet it.

"They don't make you run in gym?"

I touched my chest again. "Remember, I'm a delicate flower. The most I do in gym class is square dancing."

"Square dancing," he repeated, shaking his head.

"How does it work? You go to college . . ." I said, and let my voice trail off. Even if he won the entire Olympics and then went off and won a war, I knew there was no way I could date him if he wasn't going to college. His religion, I guessed, might also be a problem. When my cousin Abby, my mother's sister's daughter, had married a guy named Tim whom she'd met in college, I'd overheard my mom on the phone, saying things like "At least the children will be Jewish," and "Maybe he'll convert." Then there was the race thing. My parents had certainly never said that they'd wanted me with a white guy, probably because it had never occurred to them that I would date—or even meet—a teenage guy who wasn't white. They weren't racist—they'd never used the n-word, and they frowned when Great-Uncle Si talked about why the *schvartzes* were best at sports, but I didn't think they knew too many black people, and I guessed that maybe they wouldn't be thrilled if I wanted to take Andy to the prom . . . which I was already considering.

"I'll run in college," Andy confirmed. "Oregon,

I hope. They've got the best facilities, and that's where the best coach is right now. Then, if I'm good enough, I'll go to a development camp. Those have sponsors, like Nike, and they'll pay me to live there, and train and compete. I'll be twenty-three for the 2000 games, which is just about right, although guys at my distance can compete into their thirties. So, 2004, 2008, maybe even 2012."

An Olympic runner. I tried to picture it. I saw myself in the stands, dressed tastefully and patriotically in blue jeans, a lacy white blouse, sheer but not too revealing, with a red band in my hair. The cameras would cut to me as Andy burst past the finish line. I'd jump out of my seat and throw my hands in the air. Cut to Andy, down on the track, with one hand shading his eyes, searching the stands, looking for me.

"So you train, and you go to this camp, then to the Olympics, and you bring home the gold, and your picture's on the Wheaties box . . ." He smiled at me. "Then what?"

His smile got bigger. "Coach, maybe. Or find something else I like."

"People!" Alex hollered, clapping her hands. "Lunch break!"

Andy reached over, took one of my curls between his thumb and forefinger, and gave it the gentlest tug, so that it sprang back, bouncing against my cheek.

I was too surprised to say anything. I'd been kissed, I'd been groped, I'd had boys unhook my bra and try to put their hands down my pants, but I had never been the recipient of any gesture as intimate and assured as what Andy had just done. I wondered if he'd done it before, if it was a move he'd perfected on dozens of different girls. That wasn't how it felt. It had felt spontaneous, specific to me. *He likes me,* I thought. But maybe not. Maybe he was just playing around, amusing himself. We hadn't kissed yet, and that would be the thing that would seal it and tell me for sure whether he was just being friendly to someone he'd known a long time ago or whether he felt what I did.

Lunch came in brown paper bags, sandwiches and fruit, packaged cookies and bottled water. Andy took two, then handed me one and led me to a scant patch of shade underneath a scabby-looking tree.

"Wish this house had a swimming pool," he said, pulling his T-shirt away from his chest, where sweat had darkened the fabric until it was almost black. Normally I hated sweaty guys. When Troy would try to hug me after his matches I'd endure it, then hand him a towel. I found that I didn't mind Andy's sweat at all. "What's your father do?"

"Commercial real estate," I said, hoping Andy wouldn't ask too many questions and reveal how little I knew about how my dad made a living. I was eating my apple, daydreaming about Andy and me swimming together, how I'd float in the water with his hands underneath me.

"Do you wear jewelry?" he asked.

"Huh?"

He leaned over and brushed the skin at the base of my neck with his fingertips, then touched the bump of the scar through my shirt. My skin flushed. I felt color rise in my cheeks as I leaned toward him, the way the faces of flowers follow the sun. "You should have something pretty, right there." He looked me right in the eyes, and I held his gaze, not smiling, not making a joke or a funny face, just seeing him and letting him look at me.

I spent the night and the next day in a daze, pulling weeds, carrying boards, sorting through secondhand dishes and silverware, always aware of precisely where Andy was, feeling his eyes on me, or imagining that I did. On the bus to and from the work site he sat next to me. He told me about his paper route, his mom, his friend Mr. Sills. "I got in a few fights when I was little." He shook his head. "Almost got kicked out of my elementary school."

"Why were you fighting?"

He stretched his legs out into the aisle. "Ah, you know."

"No, I don't. Girls don't fight. We just spread rumors and steal each other's boyfriends." I wondered if he thought I was using the word *boyfriend* a lot as a hint.

"Like, someone would say something about my clothes. It was kids' stuff. I grew out of it."

"Did you win your fights?"

His teeth flashed white against his skin. "Every one of 'em."

"The winner!" I said, and took his hand, lifting his arm in the air, like a referee would do to a victorious boxer, while I wondered about his clothes and why kids had laughed at them.

On the ride home, the air-conditioning felt wonderful after a day in the sticky sunshine, and we'd sit, sometimes not talking. The silence felt easy, not weird, as the neighborhood out the window changed from vacant lots and boarded-up businesses to the tended lawns of the houses around Emory. At dinner, he would sit with his friends and I would sit with mine, listening to my classmates complain about the boring work and the stifling heat, wishing they'd be quiet so I could replay the conversations I'd had with Andy, or think about how his leg had felt, pressed up next to me.

With a boy from home, I might have made the first move, especially if we'd been at a party together and he'd had a few beers and maybe I'd been drinking, too. I would sit on his lap or squeeze in next to him on a couch, or put myself in a position where he'd be more or less forced to kiss me. Here in Atlanta, there were no parties, and if there was booze, I hadn't heard about it. And I still didn't know how Andy felt about me —if he liked me or liked me–liked me ("I don't know what's up with Andy, but you should definitely not be an English major," Marissa had counseled when I'd described my dilemma in those terms).

The fourth day of work was brutally hot. "Drink lots of water!" Alex told us in the morning, and there were extra thermoses full of ice water set up for us as we measured and marked lengths of lumber in the sun. Andy brought me a cup of water and reminded me to put on sunscreen, and I concentrated as hard on not sweating in front of him as I did on my job.

The workday ended early, at three o'clock, when it was almost ninety-five degrees. Gratefully, we piled on the cool bus. Once Andy and I had taken our usual seats, I closed my eyes, and as we began the drive back to campus, I found myself half-asleep, drowsy from the heat. My head came to rest on his shoulder, not because I'd planned it, but because that was where it landed. I woke up when my cheek hit his shoulder, and froze, holding my breath, feeling the heat of his skin through the cotton, wondering if he'd move me back. Instead, he shifted his body so that I was resting more comfortably next to him and then, so gently that at first I thought I was imagining it, he began to stroke my cheek, just rubbing the side of his thumb against it, so gently that I could hardly feel it.

"Your skin is so soft," he whispered. I thought about whispering back, something about my moisturizer, but instead I just made another noise, a pleased little coo, and reached across his body, and he tucked my small hand in his big one.

That night, after dinner, he came to my table and stood there quietly until Marissa and I looked up. "Do you want to go for a walk?" he asked. Wordlessly, I got to my feet, and he took my hand and led me out the door. There were trees on campus, dotting the grassy lawns, places I imagined the college students probably sat to do their homework, and that was where he took me. We sat side by side, leaning against a tree trunk, looking up at the sky.

"In Philadelphia, you can't see the stars like this," he said.

"I went to Cape Cod once, and it was so dark there that you could see everything, hundreds of stars." I didn't want to talk about the stars, or the city versus the country. I turned toward him, seeing the shape of his face in the darkness, feeling the warmth of his hand around mine, thinking *If he doesn't kiss me, I'll die.*

"Will you save me a seat at breakfast tomorrow?" he asked, as the campanile rang ten o'clock and kids started streaming back to their dorms.

"Unless I meet someone I like better," I said. A hurt look flickered across his face. For the second it took him to realize I was teasing, he looked like he was eight years old again, his lips pressed together and his brown eyes sad. I remembered how alone he'd been that night in the hospital, how his mom seemed more interested in embarrassing the nurses than in making sure Andy was okay. A boy who'd grown up the way he had probably had less tolerance for teasing than someone like me.

Then he slipped one hand behind my neck, the other around my waist, pulling me so close that I could see the long lashes I remembered, curling up at the tips. His hand was so big and warm at the base of my skull, cradling me with ease. "Good night, Rachel," he said. I shut my eyes and tilted my face toward his and then I felt his lips on mine, warm and gentle and unhurried, sweeter than any kiss I'd ever had before.

I drifted into the dorm room, barely seeing the bunk beds, the desks, the closet made of honey-colored wood, with a handful of empty metal hangers dangling from the rods. I pulled my nightgown out of my monogrammed pink-and-orange duffel bag. Lyrics from a dozen love songs were running through my head, and every single one of them, every word about longing and desire and not being able to live if living was without you, felt like it had been written specifically for me. *Don't stop believin'*, I hummed. *Hold on to that feeling*.

I was still humming Journey when Marissa came charging through the door, with Bethie galumphing along behind her.

"What's going on?" Marissa demanded.

Bethie pulled out a book from one of the two plastic Piggly Wiggly bags in which she'd packed her stuff.

"He kissed me," I said.

"Oh my God! Finally!" I grabbed her hands, and we bounced on the bed, squealing, barely noticing when Bethie, carrying a tiny tube of Crest, a toothbrush, and a threadbare white towel, went waddling out of the room, then came waddling back, with her damp hair staining the back of her nightshirt. We talked—"tell me everything," Marissa kept saying, and I was happy to oblige—while Bethie read a library copy of *A Wrinkle in Time*, which I remembered fondly from sixth grade, lying on her side underneath the skimpy brown blanket that she'd brought from home. Her evening finery was an oversized baseball-style shirt with a glittery unicorn cavorting across the rolls of her belly and chest, and a pair of pale-blue sweatpants so tight that it looked like they'd been spray-painted on her thighs.

I thought that I would never fall asleep, especially because Bethie insisted on leaving her desk light on. I didn't care. I wanted to stay awake all night, remembering everything about Andy—his warm hand on my waist, his long legs in his jeans, what he'd said, what I'd said, the low rumble of his voice, the way he'd smelled. The way his lips had felt against mine.

I woke up the next morning on the bottom bunk bed, dust motes dancing in the bright morning light, already feeling the humidity through the brick walls. *It's a dream,* I thought. Then Bethie Botts pushed her way through the door.

"Something for you!" she said in her high, toneless voice. She dropped a plain white envelope on my sleeping bag. I saw my name, written in the tiny, crabbed black letters that I remembered from all those years ago. I slit the flap open with my thumb and found a single sheet of paper. "Rachel," said the note. It was folded around a red paper clip that had been bent into the shape of a heart.

I leaned against the wall, feeling faint, holding the heart tight in my hand, while my own heart hammered in my chest, until Marissa came back from the bathroom and climbed onto my bed. I smelled Finesse shampoo and the apricot scrub that she used as she leaned close. "What is it? Let me see? Oh my GOD," she squealed, when I opened my hand to show her.

"I know." I couldn't believe he'd done something so romantic and sweet, something that made me want to jump, and run, and cry with happiness. I took a record-breakingly short shower and practically waltzed back to the room. I dried and styled my hair, applied my makeup, pulled on a pair of light-blue jeans, a long-sleeved red shirt with tiny buttons at the collar. Then I rummaged in my bags until I found the Star of David pendant my nana had given me for my bat mitzvah. Carefully, I worked the charm off the gold chain and replaced it with Andy's heart, adjusting it so it hung against the hollow of my throat.

Too soon, there were only two days of the week remaining. I carried pieces of lumber, and watched Andy's face and his arms as he sawed. He was nothing like the boys I'd known, with his dedication to his running, and his single mom in the city, and his friend Mr. Sills, and his stories about how he'd won the Catholic League's cross-country championship, and how his buddy Miles was supposed to be on the trip but had gotten suspended for throwing another kid's backpack out the school bus window.

"What's it like, being biracial?" I'd asked him once, shyly, during one of our lunch breaks under the tree. He'd been peeling the slices of turkey from the bread, rolling them up and eating them first, the way he always did.

Andy shrugged. "I've never been anything else. I only know what it's like being me."

I thought I understood. When people asked me what it had been like to grow up with my heart thing, to have had all those operations, I could talk about missing school and birthdays, but the truth was that I couldn't say what it was like because I'd never known anything different.

I wasn't expecting Andy to expound on the topic, but he surprised me. Looking down at the ground, where there was nothing to see but dirt and twigs, he said, "It's like being two people."

"What do you mean?"

"When I'm with my mom or my . . ." I heard his throat click when he swallowed. "My grandma, I was going to say, but I haven't seen her in a long time. They're white, and when I'm with them, people think that I am, too, so sometimes I get to hear what they really think about black people." He gave me a rueful look. "Which is pretty rough. I usually think the black guys on my track team don't think I'm black enough, or they think I'm trying to be white, or trying to sound white . . ." He plucked a blade of grass from a patchy clump and rolled it between his thumbs. "And then there's all the questions. People ask what you are, where you're from, and you can't ever just say America or Philadelphia. Then you catch them looking at you sometimes, trying to figure it out." He tied the piece of grass in a knot, flicked it into the dirt with his index finger, and pulled out another piece. "You don't ever just get to be . . ." More grass-twiddling. "Normal, I guess. Just a normal person where people look at you and they know what you are. You always have to decide—who you're going to be with, who you want to be that day. That hour, even. The people who know me don't think of me like that. But other kids . . ." He shifted his weight, rocking side to side like he was getting ready to stand up and walk away. "I wish sometimes I knew more kids like me." Then, in a voice so quiet I almost couldn't hear, he said, "I wish I knew my dad."

I wanted to tell him that I understood about wanting to feel normal, about wishing that there was someone like you in the world, someone who'd been there, in the place where you were, and could talk about it, and would tell you the truth. But I'd never told anyone about Alice—not my parents, not Nana, not anyone. I didn't have the words. I thought that maybe I'd kiss him— he looked so sad, with his eyes half shut as he looked at the ground. What I did was touch his arm, then slip my hand in his. *I know,* I thought, and he looked up like he'd heard me. *I know.*

Then it was Saturday, our last night in Atlanta. "You did good," said Alex as we crowded into the framed-out house. It was still unfinished, all rough plywood and bare walls, with stacks of

PVC pipes for the plumbing piled up high, but it was undeniably on its way to being a real house, with rooms and walls and staircases and doors. And bedrooms. I wondered if Andy and I could miss the bus on purpose and find a blanket to spread across the splintery floorboards, that we could be there together when the sun went down. When the evening sky was pansy-purple, and all you could hear was a symphony of birdsong and crickets.

Maybe he was thinking what I was thinking, because he took my hand, holding me back as the rest of our crew filed out of the house and into the yard. It was dim in the house, and it smelled like fresh lumber. Andy pulled me against him, slipping his hands around my waist. *I love you,* I thought . . . but I didn't say it. Girls should never say it first.

"What if this were our house?" he said.

I joked about how it wouldn't be ideal, with no indoor plumbing or electricity. I could hear the other kids laughing as they got on the bus, and Alex grumbling as she gathered discarded canvas gloves. Andy hugged me, and I rested my head on his chest, remembering a cartoon I'd seen, a Lynda Barry comic where a girl, grotesque and freckled, sat in her bedroom and watched the boys play basketball in the twilight, how she stared at the boy she loved and thought, *We are married, secretly we are married now.*

We are married now, I thought, and Andy took my hand and squeezed it, and we walked slowly, side by side, out of the doorway and into the twilight.

To celebrate our last night, there was pizza for dinner, and they showed a movie in the gym, *The Princess Bride,* one of my favorites. If there hadn't been chaperones stationed at all of the doors, Andy and I would have found a way to get out of there and be alone. As it was, we found a spot in the deep shadows in the corner and sat together, Andy with his back against the wall and me leaning against him, my back to his chest, pressed so close it would have been hard to slip a piece of paper between us, kissing and kissing until the taste of his mouth was as familiar to me as the taste of my own.

When the movie ended, Andy walked me to my dorm. "Can you stay awake?"

I nodded. I'd never felt less like sleeping. I would stay awake all night, all week, if that was what it took.

"I'll come get you," he said. I nodded again and kissed him, standing on my tiptoes, not caring when kids walked past us, calling, "Get a room!" *Maybe he'll take me back to the house,* I thought. There was no way that could happen, of course—the site was twenty minutes away, there were no cars, no cabs, no buses. But that was what I imagined, Andy carrying me in his arms, the two of us alone together in the empty rooms.

"Are you sure?"

I touched his cheek, then squeezed his hand. "Yes."

I hurried back into my room, stripped off my clothes and jewelry, wrapped myself in a towel, and trotted to the showers, where I scrubbed everywhere I could reach, washed my hair twice, then stood in front of the mirror with my mousse and blow-dryer, wondering where we would go, wondering if we'd go all the way, and if it would hurt, feeling my heart gallop like a pony. I was so glad that I'd waited, that this hadn't happened with Derek or Scott or Jason or Troy, that I had held out for true love.

When I came back to the room, my heart necklace wasn't next to my clothes on the dresser. I looked on the floor to make sure it hadn't fallen. I shook out my sleeping bag and each piece of clothing that I'd worn. I searched the drawers and the floors, checked my overall pockets, then ran back to the bathroom to make sure it wasn't there, on the shower floor or the edge of a sink. Marissa was still out—she'd been spending a lot of time with a guy from Baltimore named Pete. Bethie Botts was lying on her bed, in a cloud of misery and funk, paging through Cynthia Voigt's *Homecoming*, another one of junior high's greatest hits.

"Bethie," I said, still out of breath from running back and forth, "have you seen my necklace?"

"What necklace?" asked Marissa as she loped into the room. Her cheeks were pink, and there was a single dogwood blossom stuck in her hair.

"My heart," I said, feeling frantic and a little sick. "I left it on the dresser and I went to take a shower and now it's gone." I went over to my duffel and emptied it onto my sleeping bag, jamming my hand into the front pocket, praying that my fingers would find the heart. Marissa, meanwhile, had walked over to the edge of Bethie's bed. She held out her hand.

"Give it up."

"Go away," said Bethie, without raising her eyes from her book.

"Bethie, do you have it?" I asked. My voice cracked. "Or do you know where it is?"

"Oh, she knows," said Marissa. A coolness was slipping over her face, making her look very adult and very frightening. "Bethie," said Marissa. "Beth-eeee. Come out, come out, wherever you are, and give Rachel her necklace."

Bethie didn't answer, but her greasy moon-face looked flushed. Her knees were propped up under the covers, and she started to move her thighs back and forth, in, then out. In a single swift motion, Marissa grabbed the top of her blanket and yanked it toward the bottom of the bed, exposing Bethie's unicorn nightshirt and powder-blue sweatpants. The pants had no pockets that I could see.

"Leave me alone!" squeaked Bethie. She was cringing, pulling her legs toward her chest, and all I could think of was a worm whose rock had just been kicked over, squirming away from the sun.

"I'll leave you alone when you give Rachel her necklace back, you fucking thief."

I held my breath. I'd never heard Marissa say the word *fucking* to someone's face.

"It's just a stupid paper clip!" Bethie said, in her high, babyish voice. "Maybe it got lost."

"It did not just get lost, Jabba the Hutt. What'd you do, eat it?"

"Marissa," I murmured. It was one thing to call Bethie Jabba the Hutt in private. Saying it out loud was taking things to a place where I didn't think I wanted to go.

"Give it back," Marissa said. She grabbed the shoulders of Bethie's nightshirt and pulled her upright.

Bethie scowled at Marissa. "Let me go or I'll tell Mrs. Nasser."

"I'll tell Mrs. Nasser," Marissa repeated, in a savage falsetto. "What are you, in kindergarten, you fucking tattletale? Give it back!" She punctuated her words by giving Bethie a hard shake. Bethie jerked away and glared at me.

"Probably you just lost it," she said. "No big

deal. Your parents will just buy you a new one."

"It was a present," I said. "And it was hand-made. My parents can't buy me a new one." My face was flaming, and I was close to going to her bed and shaking her myself. I knew that she'd taken it. I was positive. Seeing me this happy was more than miserable Bethie Botts could stand. "I didn't lose it. It was right there," I said, pointing to the dresser. "If you know where it is, please just tell me."

She gave me that same smug look and opened her book again. I walked over to her bed and looked down at the top of her head, her greasy hair, the strip of white skin where she'd parted it.

"Did you throw it out? Did you flush it? Did you eat it?" I had never talked to anyone that way, but I was furious. That heart meant more to me than anything else I had, even the diamond earrings my parents had given me as a bat mitzvah gift, or the afghan that Nana had knitted that I'd taken to the hospital for every operation.

Bethie didn't say a word. Marissa stalked over to the corner where Bethie had put her plastic bags and grabbed them both.

"Hey," Bethie whined, "hey, don't!"

Ignoring her, Marissa tore the bags open and dumped them out on Bethie's bed. Two giant pairs of white cotton briefs. A pair of stretchy black leggings with a hole in the knee. Tiny sample-sized bottles, clearly swiped from a hotel, of shampoo and mouthwash. A sliver of something—soap, I guessed—wrapped in toilet paper. A raggedy gray stuffed elephant that was missing one eye. Marissa picked it up.

"Is this, like, your spirit animal?" Marissa asked.

"Put it down," said Bethie, who was starting to look scared. "I didn't take your stupid heart, so don't you touch my stuff!"

"Like I want to be touching it," said Marissa. "I'm going to need to disinfect my hands after going through your mess." She gave the sad little pile a derisive poke.

"Tell me where my heart is." I snatched the stuffed toy from Marissa. "Give it back or I'm flushing this."

"Don't!" Bethie said. "He's special!"

I used my thumbnail to pop out the elephant's remaining eye. It pinged against the floor, and lay there, a brown glass circle that seemed to gaze at me accusingly. My heart was pounding so hard I could feel my chest heaving, and I was shaking all over, from fury and shame and from a strange kind of excitement, the thrill of going all the way over to the dark side, where my worst, most hurtful impulses reigned.

"Cut it out!" Bethie cried. "Don't hurt him!"

"Give it back," I said.

"I don't know where your heart is!" Bethie shrieked at me.

175

The words *neither do I* zipped across my consciousness, and were gone in an instant.

"Give him back," Bethie said, and held out her hand.

"Why do you care?" I asked. "Your parents'll buy you a new one."

"I don't live with my parents," said Bethie. "I'm in a foster home."

"Boohoo, poor you," said Marissa. Her eyes were shining; her color was high. Was she enjoying this like I was? She certainly seemed to be having some strange kind of fun. "Did your parents kick you out because you stole their stuff, too?"

Bethie bent her head so that her chin touched her chest. She was crying now, big, gaspy, unlovely sobs. I threw the elephant at her, as hard as I could. "Next time, steal some deodorant," I said. "Steal some clothes that don't look like they came from the clearance aisle at Goodwill." I was going to go on, to tell her to steal some shampoo, steal some Clearasil, when a voice behind me said my name.

I turned. Andy was standing in the doorway of our dorm room. He had my necklace dangling from one hand. "It was in the hall," he said.

I slumped against the wall, trying to calm down, wondering how much he'd heard, feeling my face flame as I remembered. "Oh, thank God," I said.

Bethie was still crying. I felt dizzy, almost sick with shame, worse than the time my dad had caught me sneaking a look at the *Penthouse* I'd found under his mattress, worse than when I was six and my mom had refused to buy me a candy bar at the grocery store, so I'd slipped one in my pocket, and the cashier had seen. I picked the stuffed elephant's eye off the floor and walked to Bethie's bed. "I can fix it for you," I said.

"You can't," she said. She had her knees pulled up tight against her chest. One hand was yanking her hair, hard enough that it had to hurt. "You can't, you can't, you can't," she said, pulling her hair with each repetition.

"Sure I can," I said, and made myself touch her shoulder. Her flesh felt hot and loose under the nightshirt. "And I can give you some other ones, too. I've got a million Beanie Babies, from when I was in the hospital."

Bethie kept rocking and pulling. "You don't even get it," she said. "I don't want new ones. I want Tyler. He's the only thing left."

Left from what? I wondered. Left from her parents, probably. I felt so small then, as small and low as I'd ever felt. The happiness that had filled me when I was in the shower was gone, along with that odd, savage joy that had animated me when I was calling Bethie names and hurting her things. I wanted to climb under my covers or shut my eyes like a little kid.

"Bethie," I said, keeping my voice soft. "I'm sorry I was mean."

"Everyone's mean to me," she snarled. "You're not special. You think you're special but you're not."

"I'm sorry," I said again. She flung my hand off and turned her face toward the wall.

Andy was still in the doorway. I looked at him, and he looked down, his face expressionless. Without a word, he put the heart back on my dresser, then turned and walked away. The three of us were silent until the door had closed behind him.

"Good work, Bethie," said Marissa. "Way to ruin other people's love lives."

Bethie didn't answer, didn't even turn her head to look at us.

Slowly, feeling stunned and embarrassed and completely miserable, I took off my cute outfit and put on my pajamas. Without a word to Marissa, without even brushing my teeth, I climbed into my sleeping bag and turned toward the wall. I was shivering, with an ache in the pit of my stomach, too sad to cry. Whatever Andy and I had had, whatever had started between us, it was dead now. I wasn't the girl he wanted . . . and I didn't have anyone to blame but myself.

I got to breakfast early the next morning and left my duffel bag by the door in the pile labeled "Beth Am." Rabbi Silver had told us we needed to get everything out by nine, to make room for the incoming volleyball players. In the dining hall, Andy was sitting with his classmates, with his eyes on his plate, not looking at me, not looking at anyone. I sat between Marissa and Sarah Ackerman, not eating a bite, not saying a word. I'd put my hair up into a bun, the way I did around the house when no one I cared about would see me. My face was scrubbed, and I was wearing cuffed jeans and my single remaining clean T-shirt, a plain white one. That morning, when Bethie was in the bathroom, I'd taken my Walkman and my tapes and left hem on her bed with a note that said, "I'm sorry." I had no idea if she liked the kind of music I did, but they were all I had, and it was all that I could think to do.

When breakfast was over, we filed into the auditorium for the farewell session. There were speeches from various rabbis and priests and teachers about how we'd done great work, how giving back was important, and how we'd formed friendships that could last a lifetime. After the final "goodbye and Godspeed," Andy was one of the first people to leave the auditorium. I jumped out of my seat, stepped over a few of my friends, and ran to catch him.

"Hey!"

He was walking toward the buses, moving fast, with his hands in his pockets and his head down. "Andy!" I reached for his hand, and he let me take it, but his fingers were cool and limp, and when I squeezed, he didn't squeeze back.

"Can I . . ." I swallowed hard. "Will you talk to me?"

He let go of my hand and picked up the pace. "We're supposed to be on our buses."

"Please." He kept walking. "Andy." I grabbed his sleeve, like a little kid.

"Lovers' quarrel?" Marni Marmelstein sing-songed as she walked by. I pulled Andy around a corner where no one could see us.

His face was serious; his dark eyes were sad. "I should get on my bus."

"I need to say something." I was desperate to defend myself, to not have him look at me that way, with disappointment, with disdain, like he didn't want to know me anymore. "You don't know Bethie. She's awful. She walks around with that dumb smile on her face, and she smells bad, and she's mean. She's rude if you try to talk to her. It's not like people haven't tried to be nice to her, to be her friend. I've tried," I said, which was technically true, even if the real truth was that the last time I'd extended any kindness to Bethie had been at my bat mitzvah, when my parents had insisted I invite her.

"What happened to her? What happened to make her that way?"

"I don't know." The truth was, I'd barely spared Bethie Botts much thought in all the years I'd known her, except to wonder how she could care so little about the things that worried me so much—how to look pretty, how to smell good, how to wear the right clothes, be friends with the right girls, never say anything or do anything that would mark you as different.

"She's poor," said Andy. His voice was low and toneless. "She doesn't dress like you and your snotty friends because she can't afford it."

"I'm not snotty!" The words burst out of me. After all the years of pretending that I was the same as my classmates, here I was, desperate to claim my status as different. "You don't know what I'm like!"

"I know what I see," said Andy. I hung my head. I knew what he saw when he looked at me. A girl with designer jeans and fancy sneakers, a big house with a pool out back. A girl with her own bedroom, her own car and phone and phone number, a girl whose parents had told her they'd send her to whatever college she wanted to attend and whose grandmother had promised her a graduation trip to wherever she wanted to go. How did that look to a guy who'd gotten free lunch and wore secondhand clothes?

"I was awful last night. I know I was. But I've never done anything like that before. I just wanted my heart . . ." My voice caught.

Andy's voice was so quiet I had to strain to hear it. "I thought you were different."

I looked up at him, fist clenched, waiting until he met my eyes. "I am different. I'm the girl who missed six weeks of school for three years in a row because I was in the hospital, and when I came back I had to carry an oxygen tank around. I'm the girl who's had so many operations that the anesthesiologist sends me a birthday card, and I still wake up with my mom standing over my bed and crying because she thinks . . . she thinks . . ." Words were spilling out of my mouth, unplanned and unstoppable. I'd never told anyone this, never talked about it, hardly even to myself. "I had a friend in the hospital once, her name was Alice, she was the only one who ever told me the truth about stuff, about what it's like to be that sick, to get that close to dying, and then she died, she died, she died when I was eight, the time in the hospital when I met you, and she was the only one who understood and I never even got to say goodbye to her, so I know, I know what it's like to feel . . ." I stopped, gasping, trying to catch my breath. Tears were sliding down my face, my nose was running, I was sure that I looked awful, but I didn't care and I couldn't stop. I wiped my eyes and lifted my head. "To feel like you're the only one."

He made a noise then, a sort of angry sigh, and closed his eyes. I saw his lashes resting on his cheeks, and his scalp peeking through his cropped curls. His hands were balled into fists, hanging at his sides, but he didn't push me away when I hugged him.

"Andy," I whispered. It was like his whole body was a fist, hard and unyielding. I pressed against him, pushing my chest against his chest, fitting my head beneath his chin, until I heard that same angry sigh, like he didn't want to be near me but he couldn't make me leave.

I kissed the spot underneath his ear, kissed the hollow at the base of his neck, kissed his cheek, and pressed my cheek against his. "Please," I whispered, and he made a sound like a nail being pulled out of wood, and bent his head down and kissed me. His lips were cool at first, but I cradled the back of his head, holding him close, opening my mouth to let his tongue touch mine. He groaned again, this time more softly, squeezing me hard, pulling me up against him until my feet left the ground. "I wish," he whispered in my ear, and I knew what he was wishing for—to turn back time, to have it be last night, to be in a room by our-selves, a room with a bed and a door that locked.

"I'll come see you," I promised. "I'll write."

I felt him nod as he held me.

"You have to write back," I said. I was crying again, as overwhelmed with happiness and hope as I'd been with sorrow. "Real letters, okay? With your tiny little handwriting."

He set me down on my feet. "You know that

bear you gave me?" When I nodded, he said, "I've still got it. I kept it, every time we moved, every-where we went."

My heart felt like it was overflowing, like it would burst out of my chest.

"I love you," I said, not caring that I'd said it first. He kissed my lips, kissed my cheek, and then, so low that I could barely hear it, said, "I love you too."

PART II

SOMEBODY'S
BABY

Rachel

1995

Even barefoot in her kitchen, in the loose-fitting clothes that she never wore out of the house, Nana looked stylish. Her fingernails were polished, her loose linen pants were crisp, and around her left wrist she wore a silver bracelet with a black pearl set in the center, a souvenir from a long-ago trip to Tahiti.

"I'm not saying no," she told me from her perch on the step stool. "I'm saying that it's a big decision. Your first love is important. It's part of your story. The story you'll tell yourself, the one you'll tell about yourself, for the rest of your life." Nana had just returned from her latest trip, a three-week sojourn on a slow-moving barge that took her from Bruges to Paris, with stops at castles and vineyards, tulip fields and the formal Keukenhof garden. She'd come back with painted wooden clogs and a snow-filled glass globe with a miniature windmill inside. I had a snow globe from every place she'd been, from every trip she'd taken since I was born.

"I know," I said. My face felt hot and my throat was constricted. After two years of phone calls and letters, I couldn't believe that there was a chance that Andy and I would finally see each other . . . and I was pretty sure of what would happen when we did. "He's wonderful. I'll introduce you. You'll like him. I know you will."

"Whether I like him isn't what matters." Her feet were bare, her toenails, as always, neatly shaped and painted. She was vain about her tiny, narrow feet with their high arches.

"His name is Andy," I began.

"I know his name," said Nana as she stretched to hang one of the densely patterned blue-and-white Delft plates on the wall above her stove. While she was barging, she'd had her kitchen redone. The floors were squares of creamy white marble, with matching marble countertops and a stainless-steel stove and refrigerator. It had sounded sterile and chilly when she'd described it—the white paint on the cabinets, all that gleaming metal—but there were touches of color that warmed the space. A seaglass-green vase on the table held a bunch of bright daffodils. Hanging on the walls were plates from her travels to Portugal and Italy and Greece, inlaid ceramics and glazed pottery.

"And you know where I met him, and you know we've been talking for two years." Nana also knew that I had begged my parents to let me see him. I'd told them I would take a plane or a train, or even a bus, that I would pay for the trip with my own money, that if I stayed with Andy his mother would be there and nothing bad would happen. Finally, in utter desperation, I'd told them that they could take me to Philly themselves and chaperone us around the city, watching as we dutifully inspected the Liberty Bell and Constitution Hall. They'd turned me down every time, no matter how insistently I'd asked, no matter how good I'd been. No matter how hard I'd worked to bring my math grade from a B to an A-minus, or that I was volunteering at the Playtime Project, where homeless children came to the JCC once a week to swim and play.

Senior year, I'd started campaigning for Andy to be my prom date. He had enough money to come down by bus and even stay in a hotel, but my parents refused that, too.

"There are plenty of nice boys right here in Clearview," my mother would say from her seat at the dinner table, and my father, from his place at the head, would nod and say, "Helen's right," before reaching for the platter of chicken or grilled fish. Nana was my last chance, my only hope. Graduation was a month away and she was taking me on what she called the Grand Tour—Rome and Florence, Paris and London. It had been Andy's suggestion that I ask if we could stop in Philadelphia first. *It's a big airport,* he'd told me. *Lots of international flights leave from here.*

"He's very mature," I told Nana. "He's got two jobs—a paper route in the morning, and then he

189

works in a bowling alley three nights a week. He's going to Oregon on a full athletic scholarship." None of which impressed my parents. They cared about grades and SAT scores, not about sports. When I'd asked if I could apply to Oregon, they'd told me absolutely not on that front, too. "There are plenty of good schools on this side of the country," said my mother, without adding that not only did she want me close to home, she also wanted me close to the doctors who'd been caring for me all my life. "Helen's right," my father would echo, from his spot at the card table in the corner, where he did crossword puzzles and Sudoku.

Just after my eighteenth birthday, I'd threatened to go to Philadelphia on my own. I had money, all of those birthday and bat mitzvah checks adding up to more than enough for plane tickets. I was legally an adult and there was nothing they could do to stop me.

My father had called my bluff. It was the first time I could ever remember him being angry at me, truly angry, not just annoyed. Annoyance made him raise his voice. Anger, I learned, made him speak quietly and deliberately. *If you want to be independent and make your own choices,* he had told me, *then you can pay your way through college, too.* Had he meant it? I wasn't sure. But after our talk, I'd overheard him with my mother in the kitchen. She'd asked him something—I couldn't hear the words, just her voice rising at the end of the sentence—and he'd said, in a maddeningly indulgent tone, *puppy love*. I'd been so angry that I'd had to dig my nails into the flesh of my palms.

Nimbly, Nana climbed off the stool, folded it up, put it away, then sat at the table, studying me. I held my breath, enduring her scrutiny, until she gave a single, brisk nod. "We can fly through Philadelphia."

"Oh my God, thank you," I said, and skipped around the table to hug her, excited and a little scared that, after all this time and all this trying, it was finally going to happen, and I was finally going to see him again.

On the morning of our flight, I set my alarm for 4:00 a.m., so that I'd have an hour to do my hair and makeup before the car Nana had booked pulled into our driveway. The skies were a clear, cloudless blue, my suitcase was already waiting by the front door; all that was left was for me to pile my makeup and hot rollers and the Judy Blume novel that I'd bought for the plane—*Smart Women*, not one of her kids' books—into my carry-on, the purple backpack I used for school. We were booked on an early-morning flight out of Miami International, which was full of people, mothers comforting crying babies, businessmen and flight attendants towing wheeled suitcases, and the slow-moving elderly, making their way tentatively through the security check. Dressed again in linen, black pants and a black jacket with a white top underneath, Nana moved through the airport with confidence, knowing exactly where to take our bags and who to tip, and how much. She had platinum and preferred status on all of the airlines, thanks to all the frequent-flier miles she'd amassed, so we'd be flying first class to Philadelphia, then business class to London. In our seats at the front of the plane, Nana requested water and tomato juice, declined the flight attendant's offer of a cheese omelette or fruit plate, but asked if we could both have napkins, silverware, and a plate. I watched as she unzipped her carry-on tote and removed a baguette, a small jar of honey, a chunk of soft cheese, and a bunch of green grapes.

"Never trust airline food," she said, dividing the cheese and the bread. We ate, then Nana closed her eyes while I reread the last letter I'd received from Andy, the one I'd already folded and unfolded so many times that the paper had softened to the consistency of cotton.

Dear Rachel,

I can't believe that I'm going to get to see you, after all this time. There's so much I want you to see. I hope my neighborhood doesn't scare you. I hope you get to meet my friend, Mr. Sills, who has heard so much about you that he says he feels like he knows you already.

I have missed you so much, for so long. All I want to do is hold you, but I think I should show you the city, too.

I will see you soon.

Andy.

I always signed my letters *love*. He usually just wrote his name. He was as stinting with that word as he was with the rest of them. My letters were long and detailed, almost like diary entries. I'd tell him what I did all day, and who had said what in English or chemistry or calculus, about the fight my brother was having with my parents over the car that he wanted that they refused to buy, and how I knew he was sneaking girls into the house when they were out and I was at school. I'd learned to expect just a handful of sentences from Andy, but I trusted that he loved me; that every Friday night he'd be on the phone to talk and to listen.

After we'd landed and collected our luggage, Nana led me to the cab line and directed the driver to the Rittenhouse Hotel, which overlooked a lush green park full of manicured shrubs and thickly leafed trees, fountains and sculptures and beds of flowers. The park was crisscrossed with stone paths, and the paths were lined with benches. Businessmen sat eating drippy sand-wiches, with their ties tossed over their shoulders, and young mothers supervised their children as they dipped their hands in the water of a long, rectangular reflecting pool.

After we'd freshened up, Nana gave me a map of the city and told me her plans. She was meeting old friends for a late lunch, then accompanying them to see the Barnes collection, out on the Main Line. Then she'd return to the room for her afternoon siesta—a custom she strongly believed Americans should adopt—and at eight o'clock we'd have dinner in the hotel.

"I want you to be careful," she told me, winding a scarf around her neck. "You're a beautiful young lady, and you're old enough to know your own mind, but you haven't seen this boy in years. You might find that you don't feel the same way about him that you did two summers ago."

"I do," I said . . . but the truth was, I'd wondered about that myself. What if he didn't look good or smell good, the way he had in Atlanta? What if I looked at him and just saw an ordinary guy?

Nana kissed my cheek and squeezed my hand. I checked myself in the mirror—the long white eyelet sundress with the tiered skirt that I'd bought, and my new boots, ankle high with a low heel, pale-blue leather with embroidered birds and flowers in turquoise and silver and pink.

Cowgirl boots had been the fad at my school, and I'd asked for and received my pair for Chanukah. I glossed my lips, gave my hair a final spritz of spray, then took the elevator to the lobby and stepped out the door.

There was a fountain in front of the hotel. At its center was a bronze sculpture of a slender girl in an ankle-length dress, balanced on one foot like she was running. Andy was waiting in front of the fountain, in a plain blue T-shirt and jeans. His hair was still short, but he looked bigger, more solid and adult than I'd remembered, as he raised a hand in greeting and his lips formed my name.

I had imagined a scene where I'd throw myself into his arms, where he'd lift me up, holding me against him, raining kisses down on my face. The reality was more awkward, with the two of us looking but not touching, not quite meeting each other's eyes. Even with all the letters, all the calls, so much time had gone by. His shoulders had filled out; his back looked broader; his face looked even less like a boy's face, more like a man's. "You look pretty," he said shyly. He started to reach for my hand, then stopped and reached up to tug gently at a curl. I was the one who took his hand and pulled him close, playfully bumping my hip against his, feeling something inside of me start to unclench as I thought, *This will be fine.*

"Are you hungry?" he asked. Up in the hotel room, I had been, but now the logistics of having a meal—finding a place, ordering the food, chewing, swallowing, paying the bill—seemed overwhelming and endless, fraught with dozens of possibilities for potential shame. What if I spilled something, or he made dumb jokes with the waitress, the way my great-uncle Si sometimes did? ("It's too bad a nice place like this doesn't allow tipping" was one of his favorites.)

"Are you? Hungry?" I asked Andy.

"I'm kind of always hungry," he said, and I smiled, remembering the way my brother used to come home from school, take a mixing bowl, fill it with cereal, dump in a quart of milk, and eat the whole thing, and then follow it up with an enormous dinner an hour and a half later. "Come on," he said.

We walked down Walnut Street, past blocks of fancy shops, and crossed Broad, which, Andy explained, was the city's major thoroughfare. "Every May they shut down the street and there's a race, the Broad Street Run. It's ten miles long."

"Have you ever done it?"

He smiled at me. "I won the eighteen-and-under age division last year."

"Of course that's only because I didn't enter."

"Oh, you," he said, the way he'd said it in Atlanta, before the horrible fight with Bethie. I pulled him close and stood on my tiptoes to kiss him, feeling beautiful as the wind swirled my dress around my ankles.

The Reading Terminal was filled with hundreds of people, dozens of stands, and all kinds of mouthwatering smells—cinnamon rolls and doughnuts, pork sandwiches and roast turkey, falafel and gyros and dumplings. Andy and I walked past the places that sold Greek food and Mexican food, deli and sushi. Then he found us a table and asked what I wanted. "I don't know," I said. "It all looks so good."

"I'll surprise you," he said, and came back in ten minutes with a roast pork sandwich with greens and sharp provolone, two warm pretzels, glistening with butter, and a quart of soup filled with noodles and dumplings. "A little of everything," he said, and even though I thought I would be nervous or feel awkward, the sandwich was so delicious that I devoured half of it, then wiped my mouth and daintily dipped a chunk of pretzel into the cup of honey mustard that had come with it. "Better than the Home Free stuff," he said, and I said, "Oh, God, remember those sandwiches?"

"I don't think they would have been so bad if they hadn't been warm."

"Yeah, sitting in a bus for four hours in July doesn't do much to improve turkey and cheese."

He'd bought bottled water to drink, and on our way out we stopped at Bassetts for ice-cream cones, chocolate for me, strawberry for Andy. "What now?" he asked. "Want to see the Liberty Bell?"

"Nothing against our founding fathers, but I want to see where you live."

His face clouded, but all he said was "Okay." When we'd finished our cones he took my hand, and we walked down Market Street and followed a pack of people down the stairs to a subway station. Andy gave me a token and we passed through the turnstiles and boarded a northbound train. I'd ridden the subway in New York and the Metro in Washington, but always with my parents, never alone. Sitting next to Andy, with my leg pressed along his, feeling his warmth, the way he smelled like sunshine, like springtime, I felt very grown-up, nervous and excited.

After six stops, we got off at Kensington and Somerset, descended a flight of metal stairs, and started to walk. Kensington Avenue couldn't have been more than ten miles from Walnut Street, with its Tiffany's and its fancy boutiques, but it was completely different. There were five-and-dimes, with broken neon signs and flyblown, age-warped posters—BUY ONE GET ONE LADIES SLIPPERS; CHILDREN'S COATS 30 PERCENT OFF. Even the chain stores and restaurants, places I knew, looked different. The Burger King in Clearview was freestanding, on a neatly mowed patch of lawn with a parking lot that got repaved every summer. This Burger King was in a storefront, its broken windows patched with cardboard and tape. The sidewalks were stained and dirty, marked by blackened clumps of stepped-on chewing gum and glistening puddles that I didn't recognize until I saw a man hawk and spit onto the street, as casually as if he'd been dropping an empty cup into a trash can.

"Not much like Clearview, is it?" Andy asked without looking at me. He had never been to my town, but I'd described it and sent pictures—the pastel-painted Spanish-style houses, with red tile roofs, the lawns, the pools, the beach. It was true, this wasn't much like the placid, quiet, safe place where I'd grown up—it was dirty, noisy, crowded —but it had a kind of thrumming pulse, an energy and vigor that I'd never seen before. Everyone walked faster here, like they had somewhere to be, and there were all different kinds of people—a girl with elaborate braids and big, rectangular gold earrings singing to herself, in a voice just as good as anything I'd heard on the radio; two women in black robes and headdresses that covered everything but their eyes pushing strollers containing regularly dressed babies, one a girl, one a boy; and a man leaning against a telephone pole, on legs that looked like they were about to collapse underneath him, wobbling back and forth. He had on dirty blue jeans and no shoes and no shirt, and he looked like he was drooling as he stood there.

Andy kept one hand on the small of my back, steering me past the homeless people, past the medical-supply stores with unsettling displays of canes and walkers and portable toilets, and past an off-track betting parlor. The air felt like it was leaving a thin film of grime on my skin as he led me around a corner, up a short block, then to a brick building that I recognized from the pictures he'd sent, three stories high with the door painted green. "This is it," he said, and unlocked the door to the row house where he lived with his mom.

I held my breath as I stepped inside. Andy had described the place, had said that it was small, that it didn't get much light, that the ceilings were so low his mother told him if he grew any more he'd start bumping his head. What I'd imagined wasn't anything close to how sad, how poor the little rooms looked, especially after the luxurious Rittenhouse Hotel, where the heavy drapes were held back with tasseled gold ropes, where the carpet was thick and deep and the pillowcases smooth and white and cool. Andy stood in the center of the living room, not meeting my eyes. A television set dominated the room; a coffee table in front of the couch held a few out-of-date copies of *People* and *Vogue*. There weren't any book-cases or books, no pictures on the walls except one that I recognized—Andy's graduation picture, a shot of him in a red cap and gown. He'd sent me the wallet-sized version. The one on the wall was blown up much bigger. Looking around, I saw a few other pictures, all of either Andy or his mother or the two of them together, one from what must have been his eighth-grade graduation, because he was, once more, in a cap and gown. He'd explained to me once why graduations were such a big deal—because not everyone in his school made it through high school, much less college. I wanted to stay longer, to study a younger Andy, but he took my hand and walked me to the kitchen.

"Do you want anything to drink?"

I wasn't thirsty, but I was nervous and curious. The kitchen smelled like bacon grease, even though every surface was scrupulously neat, the white and gold-flecked Formica counters wiped down spotlessly, the stainless-steel sink empty, and the drainboard filled with bowls and silverware. Andy reached into the cupboard, took down two plastic glasses, then looked at me.

"Just some water," I said, and he filled both glasses from the tap. I sipped, and he drank deeply, his throat moving as he swallowed. I was overwhelmed with an urge to kiss him there, where I knew the skin would be so soft.

"Philadelphia's so pretty," I said, and then immediately realized how stupid that sounded, given what I'd seen on our walk to his house. "Do you go there a lot? To the Reading Terminal?"

He nodded, with a look of amusement on his face. The kitchen was so small that I felt especially aware of him, as if every time he moved he disrupted the atmosphere and I could feel the air moving against me.

"Are there parks around here?"

The expression on his face was hard to read, amused and a little exasperated. "They sell drugs in the parks around here."

I didn't know what to say about that. I'd tried pot, and more than once, at parties I'd seen cocaine, laid out in lines on a mirror. A boy in my class named Seth Riccardi was the one who seemed to have it. Marissa had told me that Seth's dad used it, and had so much that he didn't notice when Seth borrowed from his stash. I'd seen it, but I'd never tried it—pot and beer were one thing, but cocaine was something else.

"Have you ever?" I asked. "Tried anything?"

"Just beer," he said. "And not much. I've got to be careful. If Coach finds out you've been drinking or anything else, you're off the team." He picked up his glass again, and I watched him drink.

"Where's your room?" I asked.

"Upstairs," he said, pointing to a staircase so narrow that I imagined his shoulders brushing the wall as he walked up or down.

"Can I see it?" My throat was dry, and there was an upswelling of feelings surging through me, fear and nervousness that I'd say the wrong thing or do the wrong thing, a feeling that if I could just hold him everything would be all right.

His room calmed me a little, maybe because it felt like Jonah's room, like the rooms of the boys that I'd dated before, although it was by far the neatest boy's room I'd ever seen. Books were piled against the wall in a careful stack, some school-books, books about running or about runners or by them. Posters covered the wall, one from *Scarface* and one from *The Godfather*, one of the rapper Tupac Shakur, with his bandana and his old-looking eyes. There were also half a dozen different runners. I recognized Steve Prefontaine from his long hair, and Bruce Jenner from the Wheaties box. His room smelled like he did, a little bit like sweat and the inside of sneakers, like soap and clean clothes and cologne. On the dresser I saw a bottle of Old Spice and a stick of Mennen deodorant, next to a bowl full of loose change and a rolled-up necktie, red and blue, and a picture in a wooden frame. I stepped up close. A black man in profile held a baby in his arms, gazing down into the baby's face with a delighted smile.

"Your dad," I said.

"My dad," said Andy. Beside the picture were a candle, a short, fat white one, and in a frame, a picture of the two of us in Atlanta that Marissa had taken. He was standing behind me, with his chin resting on my head, and I was giving the camera a goofy smile. "Oh, you kept it!" I said, and clapped my hands, imagining that I could feel my heart swell.

"I just moved the one of Heather Locklear," he said, so I punched his arm, like he probably expected. One wall was filled with newspaper clippings, stuck up with plain silver tacks. Andy had sent me copies of a few of these, the ones that featured pictures of him breaking through a finish-line tape, his arms lifted in triumph, mouth open in a shout. His acceptance letter from Oregon and a typed note from the coach were both on the wall. I walked over to look at them, and Andy walked with me, his hands on my shoulders as I read out loud.

"Congratulations. I am looking forward to welcoming you to Oregon in September."

The bed was just a mattress on the floor, but it was a big one, queen-size, I thought, the same as my bed at home. It was covered with a plain dark-blue comforter, and there were two pillows on top, in light-blue pillowcases. I wondered if he'd cleaned his room for me, if he'd changed the sheets and pillowcases, and the thought sent blood rushing to my face and between my legs. There was just one window, and I could hear street noises through it, radios and cars and conver-sation and the rumble of the train. I thought about my bedroom, the flowered wall-paper, the canopied bed and the corkboard covered with pictures of my friends, the full-length mirror beside my dresser. I would lie on the bed with the windows open, hearing the ocean, but nothing else—no cars, no people, sometimes not even a lawn mower. It was a lonely feeling, and I thought that living in a city, even if you were all by yourself you would never be lonely; you'd always be reminded of how close you were to other people.

"Not real romantic," said Andy. His eyebrows were drawn down, his big hands hanging by his side, and there was a faint frown on his face, and a tiny nick on his jawline where, I thought, he'd cut himself shaving. I wondered if he was nervous, too, embarrassed by his bedroom or his house or his neighborhood.

"It's perfect," I said. I was the one who took the two steps across the distance that separated us and pressed myself against him, feeling his chest, his strong legs, the heat of his body through his clothes. I put my arms around him and he bent down, holding the back of my head and kissing me, gently and carefully, like my mouth was a fruit he was trying for the first time.

He tasted like strawberries—from the ice cream we'd eaten, I thought—and he sighed when the tip of my tongue brushed against his, shivering and pulling me closer. "Is this okay?" he whispered.

"Okay," I whispered back . . . and then, to prove it, I slipped one hand up the back of his shirt, gliding it over the smooth, warm flesh underneath, and I nibbled his earlobe, then the side of his neck. He sighed, pulling me closer, and it was as if the sound had gone straight to the slim span of flesh between my legs. I could feel myself swelling, becoming more tender, an insistent, tickling itch.

His hands fumbled with the clasp of my bra. "Here," I said, and unhooked it. Then his shirt was off, and my shirt was off, and we were pressed together, my breasts, my scar, all bare in the dusty afternoon light.

"Hang on," he said, and pulled away. I could see his erection, pressing against his jeans, and watched as he casually slid one hand down his pants to adjust himself. *Boys,* I thought, and felt an overwhelming tenderness toward him, affection at that unself-conscious gesture, at the way he could live in his own body and be completely at ease in a way that I didn't think girls ever could.

Reaching into his back pocket, he pulled out a book of matches and lit one, and touched the flame to the plain white candle on his dresser. Painted metal blinds covered his window. He twisted a plastic rod, rolling them closed, and the room got darker, full of flickering shadows and candlelight.

He kicked off his shoes and lay down on the bed, and then I tried to kick my boots off, except they were too tight and I ended up having to sit on the edge of the bed, pulling.

"Everything okay up there?" I could hear the smile in his voice.

"Just fine," I said, pulling harder, finally working my feet free so that I could lie down beside him. I felt anticipation and a little fear, and a wish to slow down time, to notice everything, so I would be able to replay the whole scene perfectly in my head. Turning on his side, Andy slid one arm underneath me, pulling me close. But he didn't kiss me, didn't touch my breasts, even though my nipples were puckered and hard. With one finger, he traced the raised and knotted flesh of my scar, and when I shut my eyes, he whispered, "Look at me." When I kept my eyes shut, he said my name—"Rachel."

I made myself relax, made myself look into his eyes, and for the first time since I'd seen him on the train platform, I felt the ease of our Atlanta days returning. *My Andy,* I thought, leaning toward him just as he was lowering his face toward mine. Our noses collided.

"Ow!" I said as tears filled my eyes.

"Oh, jeez," Andy muttered. "Are you okay?"

"No, no, I'm fine." Was my nose too big? I worried that it was, sometimes. Then Andy was cupping my head in his hands.

"Maybe just hold still," he said, and then he kissed me, slowly at first, then harder. He touched my scar, then my breast, a tentative brush, and I arched my back, pressing myself into his palm.

"Okay?" he asked again, and instead of answering I pulled him close, gripping his shoulders, feeling the heat of his skin, the muscles beneath it, smelling him, feeling his mouth against mine.

We kissed and kissed, and then he bent his head to take my nipple in his mouth, circling it with his tongue. I felt the muscles in my thighs and belly clench, felt my hips lift toward him without knowing that they would. I wanted so badly for him to touch me between my legs, where I was slippery wet, as aroused as I'd ever been, and for the first time I felt an absence there, a new understanding that this was a part of my body that could be filled . . . and I wanted him there, wanted him inside of me so badly I thought that if I didn't get it I wouldn't be able to stand it.

Finally, I grabbed his hand and drew it down, inside my pants, outside of my panties, a black lacy pair I'd bought at Victoria's Secret. Andy gave a harsh, almost pained gasp as he touched me, feeling the wetness that had soaked the cotton. "Wait," he whispered. He yanked down my pants hard enough to let me feel how strong he was and how impatient, and I pulled my panties off myself. He pushed my legs apart, his big hands moving me easily. For a minute he just looked. I squeezed my eyes shut. I'd shaved all the hair that would have shown when I wore my swim-suits, but there was still a lot there, a few shades darker than my brown hair, coiled in tight curls,

and I wondered what he thought, if I was supposed to look that way. He stroked the hair,
tugging at one of the little curls the way he'd
pulled the one on my head. Then he slipped one
finger inside me, parting the outer lips, dipping
into the wetness, caressing upward until he found
the tiny little bump.

"Ooh!" I hadn't meant to say it so loud, but
when he put his finger on that spot it was like
when we'd learned about circuits in science class,
when you touched a live wire to another and
electricity flowed through. Andy moved his
finger gently, leaning forward to kiss me, and it
was like nothing I'd ever felt, nothing I'd ever
imagined. How had he known how to do this?
Had he done this with other girls? I wondered, and
then I pushed the thought away, because I was
feeling too good to care about that or anything.

Andy moved one finger gently, rubbing me, and
slipped another finger inside, moving it until he
was right up against the barrier. My arms were
spread wide, my hands were gripping the sheets,
and I was breathing hard, and my heart was
pounding, but I barely felt it, barely cared. Finally,
he lifted himself onto his elbows and looked at
me, his face serious in the shadowy light.

"Okay?"

"Yes," I said. "Yes. Please."

He had a condom. I watched him pull it out of
the pocket of his discarded jeans and open it with

his teeth. Together we rolled it down, smoothing it over his hard penis. I didn't feel any anxiety or any shame, even though I'd never seen a penis up close.

"Tell me if I'm hurting you," he said. I lay back, spread my legs, shut my eyes, and sucked in my breath when I felt the tip brushing me. Then his mouth was on my breast, and my hands were on his shoulders, and he was pushing his way inside of me, rocking back and forth, inching himself forward in the tiniest increments, until I couldn't stand it anymore, until I grabbed him and whispered, "Oh, God, go deeper, put it in deeper." With a groan, he pushed himself all the way inside of me, and there was pain, an instant of searing pain that made me gasp . . . and then his face was buried in my neck, and he was shuddering, his hips jerking, whispering, *I'm sorry, I'm sorry, I couldn't wait.*

I cradled his head in my hands. I stroked his hair. My hips were still rocking in a faint up-and-down motion. I wanted to put my hand between my legs or have him put his hand back . . . and then he did just that, cupping me, covering me possessively.

"Am I bleeding?" I whispered.

He didn't even look at his fingers. "Did it hurt?" he asked instead.

"Just a little."

"And did you . . ."

"I don't know," I whispered, with my face against his chest. He had some hair there, and he smelled so good, that specific Andy smell, soap and cotton and his skin. "I don't think so."

"What do you mean?"

"I'm not sure I ever have."

He looked down at me, his expression a familiar mix of amusement and doubt. "How can you not be sure?"

I squirmed, feeling embarrassed. "I don't know! It's not like with boys, you know."

He held still, like he was considering this . . . and then he was touching me again, with just one finger, moving lightly, almost teasingly against me. The fluttering ache intensified, and my hips rocked faster, and I felt his penis, slick with whatever they'd put on the condom, begin to stiffen against my leg. He was propped on one elbow, watching my face as he moved his finger, higher, then lower, slowly, then more quickly. I sighed and wriggled, and then, when he was touching me in the spot he'd found the first time, I whispered, "There."

"Like this?" he whispered back, and then, because it was Andy, because my body was moving without my direction, because something was building inside of me, something wonderful and unstoppable, I grabbed his wrist and moved his hand the necessary fraction of an inch. My hips rose and fell, rose and fell, and my breath was coming in pants, and then my hips snapped up, and I froze as an unbelievably pleasurable feeling burst through me, radiating out from where Andy was touching down toward my feet and up through my chest as I felt myself, my whole body, clenching and releasing.

"Oh," I whispered, "oh my God."

Andy bent down and kissed my cheek. "Did you?"

I caught my breath and opened my eyes. When I could speak, I said, "If there's anything else I don't think I could stand it," I said, and laughed, a little shakily.

"Pretty girl," he said. His hands were moving in my hair, big, warm hands. I put my head on his chest and closed my eyes as contentment rose and swelled and filled me, until there was no room left for any doubt. He'd been lonely, and I'd been lonely, but if we were together, we'd never have to be lonely again.

We must have fallen asleep, and when we woke up, the candle had gone out. Outside the window, the sky was almost dark.

"What time is it?" I asked, and then, before he could answer, I looked up at the digital clock on his dresser that was flashing 7:12.

"Are you late?"

"Oh, God," I said, pulling my dress over my head, looking around for my panties. "I have to be back at the hotel at eight. Can we make it?"

"I guess we'll see." He found his own clothes as I put on my boots and we ran down the stairs, leaving the bed unmade, the blankets tangled, the sheets stained.

Andy took the stairs up to the train tracks two at a time, then turned around and ran back down, holding my hand and helping me to the top. On the train, he offered his seat to a pregnant lady. "God bless you," she said, and sank down with a sigh, putting her grocery bags between her legs. Andy held on to a steel pole, and I held on to Andy, pressing against him every time the train sped up around a curve or lurched to a stop. There was a little bit of pain still, an unfamiliar soreness between my legs, and I welcomed it as a reminder of how we'd been together.

At almost eight o'clock, it was completely dark, the air soft and warm, and Rittenhouse Square Park was as crowded as it had been in the afternoon when I'd left. We ran past a violinist, a beautiful girl in a black dress that showed most of her back, playing something sweet and sad, her bow dancing over the strings, her velvet-lined case open in front of her, half full of coins and bills. Beside her, a homeless man slept on a bench. On the bench next to him, a young couple sat, holding hands, the girl with her head resting against the guy's shoulder.

The cool air and the hushed stillness of the Rittenhouse Hotel's lobby were a shock after the crowded bustle of the park. The air smelled like lilies, from the enormous arrangement on an octagonal-shaped table in the center of the room. I turned my head when I heard my voice, and there was Nana, dressed for dinner in black pants and a beaded jacket.

She pressed her cool, powdered cheek against my heated one and looked at me, smiling. "Introduce me to your friend."

"Nana, this is Andrew Landis. Andy, this is my nana Faye."

Andy shook her hand gently. "It's nice to meet you."

"The pleasure is mine." Nana was looking at him, taking his measure. "Did you two have a nice day?" She looked at me, then put a finger under my chin and turned my face toward hers. "It looks like you got some sun."

I felt myself flush even more deeply. "We had lunch at the Reading Terminal, and then we walked around for a while. Andy showed me where he lived."

"Sounds perfect," Nana pronounced. "Young man, would you like to join us for dinner?"

Andy shifted from foot to foot. "Are you sure I'm dressed all right?"

Nana studied his T-shirt and jeans. "If you aren't, I'm sure they'll be happy to give you a jacket. I should warn you, it will most likely be an awful jacket."

I clapped my hands. "Oh, yes! Yes, please!"

Andy gave me a mock-angry look, then smiled and took my hand. I felt like I was melting as I leaned against him. When Nana wasn't looking, he leaned down and gave me a kiss.

The maître d' at the restaurant did make Andy wear a jacket, and it was hideous, a blue-and-yellow plaid thing made for someone much shorter and wider than Andy was, but he put it on without complaining, and followed the hostess to a table by the window that looked over the park. I was worried that he'd never been in a place like this—not that I'd spent much time in fancy French restaurants, either—but when the waiter asked what we wanted to drink, Andy said that water would be fine, and then when he came back to take our orders, I asked for the sea bass, and Andy said, very politely, "I'd like the burger, please," which was the least-expensive thing on the menu.

"And how would you like that prepared?" the waiter asked.

Nana lifted her hand. "Young man, are you sure you wouldn't rather have the steak?"

When he smiled, his white teeth flashed. "I never say no to steak."

"French fries?" asked the waiter, his pen hovering over his pad.

"Can I just have steamed spinach?"

"Of course."

"Watching your weight?" asked Nana, looking surprised.

"No, ma'am. I just try to eat healthy. Not a lot of fried stuff. Coach wouldn't approve."

"Disciplined," Nana said, and smiled.

I sat there, glowing, feeling pretty and content, with my tanned shoulders beneath the thin white straps of my sundress and my handsome guy beside me, as Andy and my nana talked—about her childhood in Newark and his in Philadelphia, how they'd both lived in row houses and both had jobs as teenagers, she in a candy store, Andy with his paper route and part-time job at the bowling alley. She told him all about her travels, and how, in 1960, her husband had taken her to the Olympics in Rome, where she'd seen Wilma Rudolph win the one-hundred-meter and two-hundred-meter races, and her team take the four-by-one-hundred relay. When the bottle of wine she'd ordered came, she asked the sommelier to pour each of us a taste, and Andy swished it around in his mouth the way she did, before swallowing and saying, "Not bad."

We had profiteroles for dessert, and even Andy had a bite. When the check came, Nana said, "Rachel, I'll see you in the room, if you want to say goodnight downstairs."

We held hands in the elevator, and I leaned against him, trying not to cry. The next morning I'd be on a plane, and when he was going to sleep in Philadelphia I'd be halfway around the world.

Andy walked me to the fountain where I'd first seen him again. The drive was busy, with valets in uniforms running with car keys, and fancy cars pulling up for the doorman to open the doors and help the ladies out.

"This was so nice," I said, hating how inadequate the words sounded.

Instead of answering, he bundled me into his arms, pulling me close. His kiss triggered a jolt of pure longing in my body. "How am I going to stand it?" I asked when he let me go. I was starting to cry. I'd been so worried, and it had been so perfect, and now we'd be apart again. "I don't want to go."

"We'll have time," he told me.

"I have your heart," I said, and reached into my pocket, and showed him the red paper clip on a chain. I wiped my eyes and hoped my nose wasn't running. "I have it with me every day."

"You have my heart," he said, and hugged me again, and whispered *I love you*. He gave me one last kiss and then, without looking back, he walked toward the park, out into the vibrant, fragrant night.

Andy

1996

Andy saw her as soon as the bus pulled up to the newsstand in the center of town, thinner than the last time, dressed in jeans and a sweatshirt with Greek letters, jumping up and down and waving at him. She grabbed him, kissed his cheek, took his hand, and started chattering before he'd had time to pull his duffel out from the storage compart-ment. "Did you win?"

In the clear late-autumn sunshine Rachel looked like a flower, her pretty face peeking out from her curls, eyes shining. She looked very young, and very sweet, even though, during their phone call Friday, before he'd left for the meet at UVA, she'd been delightfully explicit about what she planned to do when they were in bed.

"Don't I always?" Andy lifted her in his arms, kissed her nose, her cheeks, her lips, first quickly, then longer.

"Always," she confirmed, lacing her fingers with his, swinging his arm up and down as she led him toward campus.

As soon as he'd gotten his schedule of meets in September, he'd gone to the map that he'd tacked up over his desk, using his ruler to figure out how many miles each meet was from Beaumont, Virginia, where Rachel was earning a degree in history at Beaumont College. With an eye toward travel, Andy had set up his classes so that the last one finished on noon at Friday, and the first one of the week didn't begin until four o'clock on Monday. Coach had agreed to let him change his plane ticket, which gave him forty-eight hours to spend with his girl.

"Are they calling you Streak?" Rachel asked.

He shook his head.

"Can I call you Streak?" she asked, then said, "You know what? I'd better not. What if people think I'm talking about your underwear?" She swung their joined hands up and down, let go long enough to wave hello to a pair of girls dressed like she was, then grabbed his hand again.

Andy had gone undefeated in college so far, enough of a feat for the papers to take notice. Lori had sent him the clippings from home: *Local Runner Triumphs Out West.* A sticky note had been attached to the page. *I'm proud of you,* she'd written, the way he'd always wanted her to write when he'd been in elementary school, pulling notes from Miles Stratton's mom out of the trash. When he'd started track in high school his mom had never made it to his meets. It wasn't until he'd started winning, breaking records, and collecting medals and accolades, All-State honors, and recruiting letters from coaches that Lori had started getting her friend Marie to switch shifts so that she could be there to watch him run.

At first she'd sat by herself, high in the bleachers, maybe feeling awkward in the company of all the moms she'd barely met, the ones who knew to wear the school colors to meets and when to call their sons' names. Slowly, as the weeks went by and the weather got warmer, Lori had drifted toward the other mothers, joining them as they cheered. Sometimes Mr. Sills would sit with her in the stands, both of them cheering for him, Lori in her high voice, Mr. Sills in his deep one. Eventually, his mother had started sitting right by the track. She'd hand him his warm-ups, tell him she was proud. She'd even called her parents to tell them the news after he'd won States his senior year, and had let them come to his graduation. Where his grandpa had said, "I'm proud of you," and his grandmother had cried.

"My little man," Lori had said in the car at the airport, the morning he'd left for Oregon. "I can't believe you're so grown-up." In the early-morning light in jeans and the Oregon sweatshirt he'd bought her, she looked so young, with her smooth skin and her long hair, now colored a more natural shade of blond, artfully highlighted and curled into soft waves. She was only thirty-six, years younger than most of the other boys' moms. Maybe now that he was gone she'd have a boy-friend. If she met a nice guy he'd be fine with it.

He worried, picturing Lori coming home from work, smelling like bleach and perm chemicals, to find the kitchen cold and dark, the couch empty.

He'd climbed out of the car, pulled out his duffel bag, one of a dozen donated to the team by a sneaker company, and tightened the laces of his shoes, which had been donated by another. His days of hand-me-down coats were over— between his paper route and the bowling alley and the giveaway T-shirts and warm-ups he got, he had plenty to wear.

"I'll miss you," said his mom, and swiped almost angrily under her eyes with the sides of her thumbs. "I should've done better."

Surprised, he'd asked, "What do you mean?"

She'd brushed away more tears. "I should have encouraged you more. I should have come to more of your meets." She'd sniffled, then said, "I should have bought you that goddamned coat in fifth grade."

"Oh, Mom." He pulled her into his arms, surprised at her smallness. When he'd been little he thought she was as tall as a giantess, big and scary, but now he could see her clearly, a petite, still-pretty woman who'd tried her best for him. Maybe she hadn't done everything right, telling him that they were a team, that it was the two of them against the world and that they could never let anyone else in . . . but she'd worked hard to support them. She'd never had a boyfriend, never once, in all their years together, brought a man home, the way most of his friends' single mothers would do. If she hadn't given him everything he'd wanted, at least he wasn't spoiled, and he'd learned, on his own, how to push himself hard, how to work for the things that he wanted.

"Go on," she said. "Can't miss your plane." Carefully, she used the pads of her thumbs to pat concealer beneath her eyes. Her nails were long, shaped into ovals, perfectly painted, as always.

"Mom," he'd said again, and she'd waved him away, a brief, dismissive gesture, turning her face so that he couldn't see if she was still crying.

"I know," she'd said. "I know."

He'd picked up his bag, put his backpack on his shoulders, and walked through the airport's automatic doors, to the gate, and to college, the next step in the future he'd mapped out for himself years ago. Oregon was the best place in the country for college runners. He'd train and race and impress the coaches with his skills and speed and, most of all, his attitude, his capacity to work hard, to push through the pain, to take whatever they gave him and keep coming back for more. He'd win the NCAAs and the Nationals and the Olympics; he'd get paid to endorse things, to give speeches and lead clinics and coach; he'd buy Lori a house someplace warm, so that she could relax, enjoy herself, not have to wait on other people all day long. He wondered how she'd look when he gave her a gold medal, or the keys to a house that he'd bought; how it would be to have his mom completely happy, entirely approving, glad that he was her son. *Work hard* —he heard Coach Maxwell's voice in his head. *Do your training, run your laps, and maybe some-day you'll find out.*

The Beaumont campus looked like a small village; a rich little village made of old brick and marble buildings crawling with ivy, of plush green lawns and weathered wood benches, wide stone walkways, and students who looked like they could all be Abercrombie & Fitch models. Rachel had lived in the dorms for her first year. Sophomores were allowed to live off-campus, or in their fraternities or sororities, and that was where she had moved. "Here we go," she said, leading Andy down a street lined with stately mansions, all with Greek letters hanging over their doors and wide, carefully tended lawns, and tall trees that had been planted to shade the paths to the front doors. The Gammas were housed in a three-story white building with marble steps that looked like a smaller version of Scarlett O'Hara's plantation house in *Gone with the Wind*, with its pillars and its deep front porch. Inside, it was cool and smelled like furniture polish and roasting chicken. Rachel's room was on the third floor, and the first thing Andy noticed was that it wasn't just one room but a suite of rooms, a bedroom and a sitting room with a desk and a couch and a little refrigerator and a fireplace, an actual, working, wood-burning fireplace, with a neat stack of logs in a round iron holder beside it.

A fancy dress in dry-cleaner's plastic hung on the back of her closet door. A pair of shorter dresses were draped over the back of her chair, and her tops and pants and shoes were folded in stacks, all of them in cream and teal, the sorority's colors.

"It's Pledge Week," she had warned him back in early September, when they'd gone over his schedule on the phone.

"Which means what?" he'd asked.

"Formals," she'd said, as if it was the most obvious thing in the world. "I'll be crazy busy." Rachel had been elected the pledge cochair, in charge of recruiting PNMs, which Andy had come to learn meant potential new members. Disappointed and trying not to sound that way, he'd said, "We can try another time," but immediately she'd said "No," and "Please come," and "Don't be silly," and "I want you to come to the dance." Then, before he could ask for specifics about what Pledge Week would involve, she'd said, in her creamiest whisper, "Guess what I'm wearing right now." The words, the tone, just the whisper all had their usual effect, sending every drop of blood from the waist up racing down south.

"Hey," she murmured, looking up at him from underneath her lashes. Andy noticed that while there were clothes on almost every available surface, hanging from every hook and covering all the furniture, the bed—queen-size, thank God, a welcome change from the singles they'd been grappling on for freshman year—was pristine and bare. "Come," she said, throwing herself down on the mattress. "Let's burn this one off."

He shook his head, trying to look disapproving, but she pulled him down, kissing his neck, then his ear, and he knew that she was right—they'd been apart for so long that the first time probably wouldn't last long enough to be any good for her. She was just as eager as he was, shucking off her sweatshirt and her jeans until she was naked against him. He could feel her ribs and clavicles when he touched her—she'd gotten thinner since going to college. Every morning she and her sisters would gather in the living room and put some step aerobics video on and all exercise together. It had sounded like hell to him, working out indoors, without the air and the sunshine, without going anywhere, and he didn't think she'd needed to lose any weight. "Come on," Rachel had groaned when he'd made his case. "My butt was enormous." It had been bigger, but he'd liked it like that, liked stroking it and squeezing it, filling his hands.

Rachel was squirming against him, one leg

thrown over his so that he could feel her against him, the wetness and the heat. "Oh, I can't wait," she whispered. He put his hand over her mouth, knowing that if she kept talking like that it would put him right over the edge. Parting her lips, she sucked at the pad of his index fingertip. He used his knees to wrench her legs apart. "Ow!" she squealed as he jabbed at her, too hard, desperate to be inside. Then she rolled her hips and he slid forward, up and in, and could almost hear the click as they fitted themselves together.

When they were finished, and lying side by side, still breathing hard, she said, "Okay, let me see 'em."

"They're fine," Andy protested. Rachel gave him a stern look as she sat up and beckoned until he swung his legs into her lap. Every time, after they'd been apart for a while, she'd ask to inspect his feet, then act horrified by what she saw, and every time he'd demur, but he thought that she was secretly pleased—or at least impressed—by their condition, and he knew that he enjoyed her careful attention.

Rachel gasped, and frowned, and ran one fingernail lightly up the sole of his right foot. "Can you feel that?"

Andy shook his head—the calluses were too thick. "God, you're like a mountain goat or something. These aren't feet, they're hooves." She cooed over his battered toes, saying, "This little piggy went to market, this little piggy stayed home, this little piggy has no toenail, and this little piggy has no toenail either . . ."

Pulling his feet out of her lap, he gathered her into his arms. "Ooh, am I about to be ravished?" Rachel asked as she started kissing his chest. She'd twisted her hair into a coil on top of her head, so that he could see the shape of her skull, her sweet little ears, slightly pointed at the top. He ran his hands over her shoulders, down to the small of her back, then stroked his way slowly back up, listening to the throaty noises she made, feeling her breath quicken. They had probably made love dozens of times since the first night in Philadelphia, and it was never less than wonderful. Not that there weren't missteps—times he finished too quickly, or when they'd be in the throes of it, Rachel on her hands and knees and Andy, slick with sweat, behind her, when she'd get embarrassed about the noises they made, and the more he tried to assure her that he hadn't noticed them, the more ashamed she'd get. She'd elbowed him in the eye once, in her haste to climb on top of him. He'd given a startled yelp and she'd said, "Quiet down, you've got two of those," and then she'd gripped him, stroking him slowly, rolling her thumb over the head, and added, "but only one of these," and he'd forgotten all about his eye, forgotten all about everything as he'd grabbed her and pulled her down.

"Rachel?"

"Hang on," she said, and hopped out of bed, pulling on a robe and walking to the sitting room. Andy half dozed as he heard Rachel and another woman talking. "Everything okay?" Andy asked when Rachel came back to the bedroom, and Rachel, rolling her eyes, said, "I don't know what part of 'French manicure or a short, neutral nail' they don't understand."

"Are you kidding?" he asked, but she shook her head. She was adorable, with her soft brown eyes, her pert little chin, the sprinkling of freckles on her nose and cheeks. Andy even loved her little white teeth. *My little honey, my little sweetheart,* he would call her, and she'd stand on her tiptoes and say, "I'm full-grown!" Now she was looking at him, trying to look authoritative, not adorable.

"It's important that people really commit to this. If the sisters don't take it seriously, the potentials won't take it seriously, and we won't get the best girls."

"The best girls," Andy repeated. He'd known that was a mistake even before Rachel raised her eyebrows and opened her mouth, then shut it, turning calmly toward the makeup mirror at her desk.

"How is wanting the best girls for our sorority any different than a track team having cuts?"

"But what does the best mean?" He had wondered, ever since she'd rushed the year before, how his funny, merry Rachel who could make a joke about everything could take all of this, all the rules and guidelines, so seriously. Not to mention how thin she'd gotten, and how he never saw her anymore without a full face of makeup. He could picture the evening yawning ahead of him, all those long, empty hours to fill, Rachel off at the rush party downstairs while he stayed hidden in the bedroom like some kind of male Anne Frank. Guys weren't invited tonight, not until Saturday's formal. He saw himself trying to get some homework done in this frilly, scented girl-den, trying to make a meal of the yogurts and SlimFast shakes that were all Rachel ever kept in her fridge. ("What would happen if you put a beer and a burger in there?" he'd asked her once and she'd said, completely deadpan, "They'd take me out back and shoot me.")

But now her feathers were ruffled. "We do charity work," she'd said, spacing her words out, speaking each one distinctly. "We volunteer. We tutor. While you're off running laps . . ." She paused and made her index and second finger take a little jog around the edge of her desk, "we're trying to improve the community. We want girls who are committed to what being a Gamma means, to what it stands for."

As far as Andy could tell, being a Gamma stood for being one of the pretty, popular girls at Beaumont, a girl more interested in having the right clothes and dating the right guy than she was in tutoring inner-city kids or raising money for the battered women's shelter, but he knew better than to say so. It wasn't an officially Jewish sorority, but plenty of its members were Jewish, and almost all of them were white.

Once, he'd asked why the sororities were so segregated, and Rachel had acted like he'd accused her of something awful. "The black girls have their own sororities," she'd said. "They don't even want to join, but if they did, of course we'd treat them the same as anyone else." Andy had nodded, but he'd wondered. A few times he'd started asking Rachel whether she'd told people that he had a black father, and every time he'd stopped himself. *Of course she did,* he'd think. *It doesn't matter to her.* Still, he thought about it, when he walked through Beaumont by himself and felt strangers looking at him; when he saw, or imagined that he saw, the security guards watching him with special interest when he went into the coffee shop or the convenience store at the center of town; when the guys who joined Rachel and her friends in the dining hall always wanted to talk about rap music, assuming he'd bought every CD and knew every song; when in fact, in his experience, it was the nerdy Jewish guys who could quote every N.W.A. lyric perfectly.

Maybe his race didn't matter to Rachel, like she'd told him every time the topic came up, but he was sure there were girls in the sorority to whom it mattered a great deal. Even if Rachel had never lied about it, she could have used a little strategic silence here and there, let people think that Andy was Hispanic or Israeli or Greek. She'd told her parents, and they'd been nothing but polite and nice to him when he'd been visiting during Parents' Weekend last spring, but he wondered about them, too, and whether they wouldn't be happy if Rachel ditched him in favor of one of those Dr. Dre–quoting Jewish guys.

Even if he'd never asked her specifically about race, he had asked lots of questions about the girls she hung around with at Beaumont. They all dressed the same way, the same brands of jeans and shirts and shoes. "It's like they got a memo," he'd once said to Rachel. He'd meant it as a joke, but then Rachel explained that a version of such a memo actually existed.

"It's just suggestions, really," she'd said, looking embarrassed, which meant she at least knew how ridiculous it was, and Andy didn't want to fight, but he wondered sometimes about whether he could actually have a future with a woman who handed other girls instructions about Girbaud versus Guess jeans, and how many buttons' worth of cleavage they could show.

"You look nice," he told her as she sat in front of her light-up makeup mirror and assaulted her eyebrows with her tweezers. The year before, she'd cut her hair in that face-framing, short-in-front, long-in-back style that the *Friends* actress had somehow convinced every woman in America to get, but now it was long and curly again, the way it had been when they met in Atlanta, the way he liked it best. She pulled on a short white skirt, a blue silk blouse, a scarf at her throat in the sorority colors, and a pair of beigey high heels that matched the color of her skin and made her legs look impossibly long.

Her kiss was brisk, almost impersonal. "See you at midnight," she said, and then, in a swirl of hair spray and perfume, she was gone.

Andy sneaked into the bathroom, marveling at the array of stuff, enough scrubs and lotions and masks to stock a drugstore. He spent a long time in the shower, enjoying the water pressure—the showers at Oregon usually felt more like a trickle. He used exfoliating cream for his legs and deep conditioner for his hair, and considered a leave-in olive oil treatment before deciding that it might be missed. Back in his jeans and sweatshirt, he slipped down the back staircase, which Rachel told him had once been for servants to use, and roamed around the campus, buying a few slices of pizza for dinner, then sitting on one of the benches to eat them and watch the people go by. Ten black girls in blue suits and black shoes, all in a line, were balancing potted plants on their gloved hands as they marched by him. They were followed by half a dozen guys, each pledge carrying his own books and a second backpack, no doubt laden with a senior brother's texts. Andy decided, again, that fraternities and sororities were the stupidest thing in the world.

Finally it was midnight. Andy lay in bed while Rachel paced around the room, shoes off, hair loose, telling him the story about some potential getting drunk and puking in the ladies' room— "She told us she was on antibiotics, which, I'm sorry, but shouldn't she have remembered that before she, like, drank three glasses of punch?"— and how she'd heard that some other sorority was ripping off the theme for their formal, which was One Thousand and One Arabian Nights. "They're doing Midnight at the Oasis, which is basically the same thing. And I heard they rented an elephant," she fretted.

"That's—" *Awful,* he'd been going to say, but Rachel jumped in with "I know! God, I could kill myself for not thinking of it!"

"Maybe you could just get a fat person."

Rachel paused, halfway through unhooking her bra. "Huh?" Even though she'd gotten thinner, her breasts, in profile, were round and heavy as some kind of fruit. Melons were the cliché, of course, but hers reminded him of peaches, from the tawny pink-gold color of her skin to the sweetness when he kissed her.

"A fat person," he said, mostly kidding. "You

know, so a fat person could come to your parties."

He could see her making up her mind, deciding whether to be amused or combative. "We have fat people," she finally said.

"Who?"

"Missy Sanders."

"Missy Sanders isn't fat," he said, hoping they were talking about the same person, a bosomy, rosy-cheeked blond whose thick legs were more muscle than flab and who was an all-conference field hockey player.

"She isn't thin," said Rachel.

"And isn't her father a senator?" Andy asked.

Rachel slipped on her pajama top, a stretchy cotton button-down imprinted with red hearts. Freshman year, she'd bought out Victoria's Secret, and had worn some kind of weird new outfit every time he visited, lacy bras and panties, sheer, short nightgowns, garments made with hooks and wires to pull her waist in and push her breasts up. Finally he'd told her that his favorite outfit was a plain white tank top and pajama bottoms loose enough that he could slip his hands inside of them.

Rachel made a face as she pulled on her bottoms. "State representative," she said.

"So if her dad was a senator, could she be actually fat?"

Rachel shook her head. "Nope. If her dad was president, maybe. And that would only be if she had a gorgeous face and a four-point-oh, and her mom was a legacy." She crossed the room, went to her closet, slipped her gown out of the plastic and held it up against her, frowning at her reflection in the full-length mirror. The dress was turquoise and strapless, with gold embroidery. "Are you getting 'Princess Jasmine,' or just 'slutty'?" she asked.

Andy didn't answer; wouldn't answer, wouldn't pretend that this was an actual problem. Rachel frowned, and then her face brightened. "Oh, and look! Look what I found for you!" She rehung the dress and stretched to reach the top shelf of the closet, letting Andy enjoy the view of her rear in the snug pajama pants. Then she handed him a little round beanie with a tassel on top. "Um, yeah," he said, getting out of bed and setting it back on her desk. "No."

She pouted in a way he normally found adorable. "It's a fez," she said. "It's authentic."

"Not wearing it."

"But . . ."

"Rach," he said, feeling the familiar itch, like he was going to jump out of his skin if he didn't find a way to start moving. He loved her. She was sweeter than any girl he'd ever met. She made him laugh, took him out of himself, made him feel light when he could feel so weighted down sometimes, being angry about old grievances and insults, real and imagined. He'd thought about her constantly during the two years after they met again in Atlanta, when he'd get letters that told him everything about what she was doing, what she was thinking, how she was feeling. He knew his letters were less revealing—she'd always teased him about writing like he was being charged for every drop of ink—but on the phone, he'd talk about practices and track meets, which of his teammates were working hard and which were goofing off, and she would listen to him, asking questions, recalling things he'd said weeks or even months before, indulging him with a patience he'd never imagined and certainly never experienced from anyone except Mr. Sills.

He and Rachel still wrote, and they still talked, but he thought that not only had the sorority sucked up most of her time but it had encouraged her worst impulses, turned her into a girl who cared too much about manicures and formal gowns and hardly had time to listen to him or any interest in the future beyond the next rush or the next dance.

Andy shifted from foot to foot. The night was cool and crisp, the air smelled like apples and the smoke from all those fireplaces, and there was a towpath that ran in a two-mile loop around the man-made lake that some wealthy Beaumont alum had had dredged so the crew team would have a place to practice. He could run a quick lap, maybe two. Rachel was looking at him, waiting for him to finish. He forced himself to hold still, drumming his fingers on the desk, next to the stupid hat. "You wanted me to rent a tux, so I rented a tux. Which, by the way, was not cheap. I came because I wanted to see you. I know you're busy and I don't want to be in your way, but I'm not your dress-up doll."

She stepped close to him with her hair down and her face gleaming and her breath smelling like toothpaste. In spite of himself, he felt his body react. His hands slipped around her waist, cupping her bottom, pulling her close. "There's a prize for best-dressed couple," she whispered, rolling her hips against him, then pulling back, then coming in again until he grabbed her, holding her still. She looked up at him, her eyes big, lashes fluttering. "My sorority gets points."

Jesus. He let his hands drop. "Okay, okay," she said, and laughed, and nuzzled against him, grabbing his hands and putting them back on her bottom. "Not that you wouldn't have looked adorable in the fez, but I get it. You're a man, not a Ken doll. Free will. Learned about it in philosophy class." She walked to the door, stuck her head into the hallway, then grabbed a towel and grabbed his hand and pulled him back to the bathroom. "I already took a shower," he said.

"Cleanliness is next to godliness." There were three stalls, all in a row, with only curtains separating them. Rachel turned on all three showers and pulled the curtains aside, and then pulled him in with her, with all that hot water drumming down. For twenty minutes, as the room filled with steam, he whispered to her, making her laugh, before she filled her palm with bath gel, then took him in her hand, sliding with delicious slowness up to the tip and back down again. "Honey," she said, with the water washing her face clean, slicking her hair back so that he could see her face without its frame of curls. "I love you."

The next morning, he woke up ready to go again, but Rachel was out of bed before he could reach for her, giving him the kind of kiss he imagined long-married wives gave their husbands when they left for work. Andy made the bed, did his workout, showered and changed, and got one of Rachel's friends to wave him into the dining hall, which had a vaulted ceiling, marble floors, and long, heavy wooden tables where the students ate, or didn't eat (he'd once dined with some of Rachel's sisters and had spent thirty minutes watching them shift salad around their plates).

Andy had pancakes and turkey bacon, then sneaked into the library, which was lovely, like an old mansion full of books, all carved dark wood, gleaming brass lamps, and rows and rows of carrels. Andy found himself a nook with a big chair that overlooked the quad, and did his homework: Sociology of the Family, Abnormal

Psychology, and a grueling plod through twenty pages of Aristotle for his philosophy seminar. Most of his teammates were educational foundation majors—gym teachers in training, in other words. A few of the even less academically inclined studied geology, commonly known as Rocks for Jocks, where the professors would pass you as long as you didn't fall asleep and snore too disruptively in their classrooms. Andy hadn't decided yet between comp lit and political science. He liked reading about how the world worked, about why people did what they did.

Homework took him until one in the afternoon. Beaumont had a two-block downtown with a cheese shop that sold sandwiches, a Chinese restaurant, and a fancy French place, where parents took their kids when they came for graduation. Counting his pocket change to pay for two bagels with cream cheese, Andy saw some smooth-looking, wide-bodied guy in a leather jacket smirking at him before paying for his own lunch with a credit card—probably, Andy thought, one where parents got the bills. He stood at a narrow counter, munching his bagel, as the wide boy climbed into a BMW with a Beaumont sticker on the back window.

Beaumont kids were assholes. He and Rachel had been fighting about it for a year, and had finally reached a kind of détente, where he agreed to acknowledge, at least privately, that it was impossible for every single kid who went there to be a jerk, and Rachel admitted—again, only in private—that plenty of them, including her beloved sorors, were the kind of blinkered, privileged, entitled assholes who'd go sailing through life, assuming that their hard work, not their privilege, was what ensured them their good jobs, good schools, nice houses, and pricy vacations. *Born on third base and think they hit a triple,* his mom used to say, and Andy found himself thinking that almost constantly when he walked around Beaumont, where Rachel tried so hard to fit in. He knew, because he'd asked her, that she'd never told anyone at college about her heart condition or all of her hospitalizations. The scar she'd explained away by saying she'd had an operation—operation, singular—to correct a birth defect. She kept her portable oxygen tank in a suitcase in the back of her closet; she kept her nails painted so no one could see her finger-tips' bluish tinge, and the one time he'd heard someone ask her to go running, she'd made an excuse about cramps.

"Isn't it pretty here?" Rachel would ask . . . and it was; like a postcard, like the picture you'd get in your head when you thought *college,* the kind of place made to appear on brochures. In the fall, students would gather on the quad for class, sitting underneath oak and maple trees with their leaves glowing gold and scarlet, and in the spring the kids who looked like they'd been selected for their good looks would play Frisbee on the beautifully tended grass.

Twice a week, Rachel and her sorority sisters took a van downtown to tutor kids who went to the public elementary school. Rachel had been working with Keila, a soft-spoken sixth-grader with bright brown eyes who called Rachel *Miss Rachel* and looked at her like she'd invented MTV. At least once a month, they'd go to the zoo or the park or the movies or to the fancy restaurant in town for tea. "I wish I could do more," Rachel would say, and would daydream out loud about adopting Keila once she graduated, as if Keila didn't have a mother already.

"I just don't get it," Rachel would say when Keila would casually mention that Mommy's new boyfriend had borrowed her duffel bag, the pink, monogrammed one that Rachel had bought her for her birthday, and hadn't ever brought it back. "Why would she let a guy like that anywhere near her children?" Andy wanted to tell her that it was easy to make good choices when you had a web of people supporting you, not to mention money as a safety net when everyone else in your family did the right thing, went to college, held down a job. "She's doing the best she can," he'd say, and Rachel would sigh, and repeat, "I just don't understand." Andy understood, even if he could never quite make Rachel get it.

Sometimes—more often than not—he thought that Rachel and her classmates were just playing at being caring and open-minded, at noticing that there was a world wider than them, their college, their peers. They'd experience poverty in two-hour chunks twice a month, like it was a movie they were going to see or a TV show they were watching, something they'd click off or walk out of when it was done, something they sat through just so they could talk about it with everyone else who'd seen it and had something to say.

That night, Andy hung around the dining hall, hoping that another one of Rachel's friends would let him through. No luck, which was a shame. Not only was the dining hall lovely, with its soaring ceilings and stained-glass windows, but the food was incredible. Different flavors of frozen yogurt every night, a once-a-week sundae bar with all the toppings, vegetarian options, and cold cereal, if you didn't like what was for dinner. On his campus, there were choices, but not that many, and the dining hall was modern, all sharp angles and glass; not ugly, but not anything like this. Once a month, there'd be a formal night. The chefs and servers (all African American, Andy had noted) would dress up in tuxes, or black dresses and frilly white aprons, and serve crab Newburg, steamship round of beef, surf and turf with lobster tail and filet mignon. At his first formal dinner, Andy had eaten until his stomach stretched his waistband, and was wondering if he could slip a few filets into his backpack for the trip back home, when one of the servers, a middle-aged woman with a round face, had shyly slipped him a foil-wrapped package filled with steaks. Was it that she hadn't recognized him and knew he went to a different school . . . or was it that she'd recognized that he was half black (which not everyone did) and wanted to do something nice for him? He'd wondered about it.

By seven o'clock he was back in Rachel's room, showered and shaved and in his rented tuxedo, watching Rachel do her makeup again. The Smiths played on her stereo—Andy had thought it was a blessing when she'd finally moved on from Whitney Houston and Mariah Carey, except Morrissey's moaning was even worse. The house smelled like perfume and sweet, fruity drinks, like cigarette smoke and a little bit like vomit when he passed an open bathroom door. The Gammas hadn't been able to come up with an Arabian cocktail, so they were serving Zombies, made with pineapple juice and maraschino cherries and three different kinds of booze. Because he was bored, Andy started flipping through the Gamma handbook, which was on Rachel's bedside table. He read from the text out loud. " 'For recruitment, your hair has to be curly or straight. No waves.' Why no waves?" he asked, and Rachel said, "Looks sloppy."

Andy kept reading. " 'You will either need to have a curling iron (for our curly gals) or a flat iron (or a blow-dryer if you have pin-straight, flat hair and you're super good with hair so you can blow your hair out). Don't count on other girls letting you borrow theirs or doing your hair for you because then your friend won't have time for herself. Note: if you have straight hair and you want to wear it curly, don't. Your hair needs to be able to hold for fifteen-hour days and hair-spray-crunchy or limp hair is not acceptable. Also, get some heat protectant and shine spray.' "

At her vanity, Rachel lifted a bottle of each of the substances in question and waved them triumphantly. Her breasts shivered with the motion. Andy wondered if they'd have time for a quickie before the dance, then resigned himself, knowing that Rachel would refuse, on the grounds that it would ruin her makeup.

"This is crazy," said Andy. "You know that, right?"

"Keep reading," said Rachel.

" 'If you have bangs, they need to be styled correctly. If they're long and you're afraid they're going to be in your face the whole time, get some bobby pins that match your hair color . . .' Can I ask you a question?"

"You just did," Rachel said, through a mouth filled with bobby pins.

"My mom could make a fortune here," Andy said. "I mean, do the girls really need someone to explain to them how to use hair spray?"

Rachel sighed. "I know that you don't see it this way, but we're helping them. Because, whether you want to admit it or not, looks matter. What if you were applying for a job, and no one told you that your hair looked bad, or that your lipstick was all wrong?"

"They'd hire you anyway, if you were the most qualified?" Andy ventured. In an ideal world, anyhow. In the real world he wasn't so sure. How would he be treated at Oregon, for example, if he weren't a runner, if he didn't have a ready-made group of friends, built-in status?

Rachel had given her head a shake, half in anger, half in sorrow. "It's not like that for girls."

He wanted to ask more questions—like what straight versus curly versus wavy hair had to do with job interviews or with giving back to the community; whether Keila cared if Rachel had red or pale pink polish on her nails—when someone knocked on Rachel's door. "Hey there, Andrew Landis," said Pamela Boudreaux, who was Rachel's co-vice-president, a legacy whose mom had attended Beaumont, an Atlanta native with a syrupy drawl and a wry sense of humor. In her room once, Andy had picked up a framed photograph of Pamela in a white dress. "Were you in a wedding?" he'd asked, and she'd chuckled and said, "Honey, that was my debut."

"We've got a situation," Pamela said, pulling Rachel over to the window seat. Andy listened closely enough to learn that the situation involved a sister whose dress was "inappropriately revealing."

"I see London, I see France, I see Stacey Saperstein's underpants. Or I would, if she was wearing any."

"Oh, dear," Rachel murmured.

"She said it's Dolce & Gabbana, thank you very much, and she's not changing."

Andy closed his eyes, listening to the two of them try to solve the problem of Stacey Saperstein's ass crack, and imagined the next day's run around Beaumont's track: ten minutes at an easy jog; hundred-yard sprints times four, each followed by a thirty-second recovery, then four two-hundred-yards, two four-hundred-yards, and two race-pace miles with a five-minute break in between. He imagined kneeling, setting his feet in the blocks, fingers tented on the pebbled surface of the track, crouched and waiting, imagining the starter's pistol . . . Then Rachel was shaking his shoulder, saying, "Hey, Prince Charming, it's time for the ball."

Even he had to admit that the room was lovely. Rachel and her sisters had strung up tiny, twinkling white lights, and stapled billowing clouds of white tulle across the ceiling to look like clouds. Yards of fabric with tiny mirrors sewn on draped the walls, making it look like the guests were dancing inside a tent. Two bands took turns onstage, playing three fast songs for every slow one (Rachel had explained, very seriously, how they'd come up with that ratio). In his tuxedo, among a throng of similarly dressed guys, Andy didn't feel awkward. Maybe, indeed probably, those guys, all of whom were white, owned their tuxes, didn't have to rent them, especially didn't have to rent them using a coupon their girlfriend had sent—but it didn't matter. He took Rachel in his arms, holding her close, as the second band's lead singer crooned, "I knew I loved you before I met you, I think I dreamed you into life."

"You did a good job," he whispered, and her face lit up, so pretty, even though part of him wanted to soak a napkin in water and wipe off all the foundation and blush and concealer and eyeliner ("ladies, please, ONLY black or brown!") and eye shadow ("neutrals, blended very well, and do I even have to say no pastels or vivid colors?") that the checklist mandated, until she looked like the girl he'd met in the hospital again. "Tell me a story," he'd say, and she'd smile and take his hand, and for a minute they'd both marvel at how long they'd known each other, and talk about how they would be together forever.

"Hey, watch it!" A red-faced guy holding two red plastic Solo cups bumped into Andy. Beer surged over the edge of a cup and slopped onto Rachel's gown.

"Oh!" Rachel stared at the stain in horror, then dashed away, leaving Andy and Beer Guy looking at each other. Beer Guy was a beefy fellow who looked like he'd been force-fed into his tuxedo. His gut swelled against his buttons; his neck bulged over his collar.

"Jesus, didn't you see me?" Beer Guy whined. Andy held his hands up, quickly recognizing that this guy was drunk, drunk enough to not care about anything.

"Sorry."

"You're goddamn right you're sorry. Sorry piece of shit." The guy's tiny, mean eyes, shoved deep in the glistening, sweaty flesh of his face, did a fast flick up and down, taking in Andy's face, his tux, his feet. A predatory grin stretched his fat, drunk face, showing off the kind of straight teeth you got only after a few years of expensive orthodontia. "Nice shoes, ass-face."

Andy felt himself blush. The guy at the tuxedo store had wanted to rent him formal shoes, for an extra eight bucks. Andy didn't have an extra eight bucks, due to the expense of the bus tickets and the new undershirts he'd had to buy (Rachel had run her finger over the frayed collar of the one he'd worn on his last visit, and she hadn't said anything but he'd known what she was thinking). He had worn his blue Nikes, thinking it was ultimately kind of a cool look, an I'm-too-hip-to-be-bothered-to-match look. But maybe not.

"Lookin' good, Duckie," Beer Guy sneered.

"You too, my man," said Andy, turning away. That would have been the end of it; should have been the end of it, except Beer Guy said, "What, no dress shoes in the church donation box?"

If he'd accused Andy of stealing his tuxedo, Andy would have ignored him. If he'd gone racist, Andy would have simply walked away, or gone out, in his sneakers, and run until the urge to hit the asshole went away. But those three words, *church donation box,* made Andy remember just that. At his church it hadn't been a box, it was a table, a folding table with a scarred plastic top where the donations would be arrayed by size and by gender. The boys' stuff was always in the middle. He remembered his mom angling for a seat on the aisle so that as soon as the priest started to say *Peace be with you* she could be the first one there, picking over the donations, grabbing fistfuls of stuff that wouldn't even fit him, giving a triumphant shriek when she spied something good, something quality, with a name brand she recognized, like Ryan Peterman's old winter coat.

Andy looked over the guy's shoulder, his eyes widening like he'd seen something important. "Check it out!" he said. Ponderous as a hippo in a mud wallow, the guy had started to turn, exposing a lovely, immense span of jowl. Andy drew back his fist and hit the guy hard, and the guy went down, taking both beers with him. He was getting ready to kick the guy in his ribs with his Nikes, which, in retrospect, would have hurt Andy more than the guy, who was well padded, when two of Beer Guy's buddies grabbed his arms, and a third one started pounding on him. Andy saw the fist approaching just as Rachel came running over in her gown, her lipsticked mouth open in a perfect O of dismay.

Beer Guy's name was Kyle Davenport, because of course it was, and he was president of the Alphas, because of course he was, and the Alphas were the brother fraternity to Rachel's Gammas. Because obviously, that, too. Rachel told him all of this, sitting on the edge of her bed, holding a wet washcloth full of ice against the side of Andy's face, where one of Davenport's fraternity brothers had pasted him.

"This is not ideal," Rachel said. She'd changed into her pajamas, and most of her makeup had been wiped or cried away, but her hair was still in its updo, which made her look like a little girl playing dress-up, wearing a strange kind of hat.

"I'm sorry," Andy said for what felt like the hundredth time since Rachel had come running to him, skidding through the beer puddle, saying, *Oh my God, Andy!*

He took the washcloth out of her hand. "So what happened?" he asked.

She sighed, looking deflated. "The cops came."

He nodded. He'd caught some of that while Rachel had been hustling him out the door. "The good news is, we were checking IDs, so we're not going to get in trouble for serving anyone under-age." Another sigh. "Kyle didn't know your name, and he didn't say much about how it all started, so nobody's going to be charged. The bad news is, having cops show up at your rush party isn't going to impress potentials." Another sigh. "Or the alums. This just doesn't reflect very well on us." *Me,* Andy thought. *I don't reflect very well on you.*

"I should go," he said, without realizing he was going to say it out loud.

Rachel lifted her hands to her eyes and rubbed them like a tired toddler. "Maybe that's a good idea," she said. Andy sat back, startled. This wasn't part of the script. He'd apologize, and she'd forgive him. He'd say that he should leave and she'd insist that he stay, telling him that she understood why he'd hit that asshole, and how, given the situation, she would have done the same thing, and that whatever trouble she was in, however mad her fellow officers were, none of that mattered, because she loved him.

Except that didn't seem to be happening. Her face was unreadable, her back and shoulders stiff. He reached for her hands. She pulled them away and got off the bed to face him. "You don't think we're good people," she began.

"That isn't true," he said. His lip was already puffing up. He wondered if he'd get a black eye, too, and whether Coach would notice, and what he'd say to explain it.

She held up her hand. "No, just listen, okay?" She huffed out air, balled her hands into fists, said, "God, I'm so sick of this."

"Sick of what?"

"Sick of being talked over! Even in my women's studies class, it's always guys doing the talking, so how about you just be quiet and listen for five minutes?"

"I listen," Andy protested, thinking that he definitely didn't need to enlarge the argument to include Rachel's imagined oppression. One look at her face, at the scorching glance she threw him, and he closed his mouth.

"You think we're bad people. No, don't deny it," she said, holding up her hand like he'd tried to argue. "You think we're shallow and frivolous and we only care about our hair and makeup, and maybe some of that's true. Maybe a lot of it's true. But that's not all we are. And, Jesus, Andy, even if it was, that doesn't mean that it's okay for you to get into fights at our formals, to embarrass me or put my position at risk."

Put my position at risk. She sounded like a boss, giving the new hire a bad performance review. He stared at his sneakers, trying to keep his leg from jiggling, forcing himself to hold still and take it.

"I'm sorry," he said again. "I don't know what else to tell you. It was dumb, and I shouldn't have done it."

With her back to him, he could see a blurry reflection of her face in the window. He thought she was crying, but he wasn't sure.

"You know, I could have a boyfriend here. I could," she said in a thin, high voice. "It's not like guys don't ask."

Andy felt like he was trying to swallow a ball of steel wool.

"My friends ask me all the time what I see in you," she said. "They think you're stuck-up."

"I'm stuck-up?" He couldn't keep from sounding incredulous. These girls, with the cars they drove and their clothes and their credit cards, they thought he was stuck-up?

"You barely even talk to them. You act like you're better than they are. You judge them . . ."

"I don't—"

"You do," Rachel said. She was definitely crying now. "Maybe you don't do it on purpose, but they can tell." She paused. "I can tell. You're always examining me, trying to see if I'm good enough, if I've stopped being so shallow and snobby. And I never quite get there, do I?"

He wanted to go to her, put his hands on her shoulders, turn her toward him. He wanted to kiss the tears off her cheek, pull off her pajamas, take her to bed, where everything was always right between them. But her body was stiff under his hands, and when he tried to get her to turn around and look at him, she wouldn't move.

"I think you should go," she said. Her voice was dull; her eyes were aimed at the floor.

"I've already got a ticket for the bus. It leaves at seven. I don't . . ."

"I don't want you here." Rachel raised her head and stared out onto the darkened quad, looking angry and fierce, like one of those carved figure-heads on the front of ships. He was furious, but he wasn't sure where to direct his anger—at Rachel? At Beer Guy? At himself, for losing his temper? At his mom, for dressing him from the church's donation table in the first place?

"Okay," he said, and Rachel left the room without a look, without another word.

It took him five minutes to pack up his stuff—his toothbrush, his books, his boxer shorts, the stupid tux. He walked down the sorority house hall, head bent, hearing girls whispering behind the closed doors. At two in the morning, the campus was deserted, and he knew he had to find somewhere to be, unless he wanted to endure a second go-round with campus security.

At the all-night convenience store he bought three hot dogs and a big bag of pretzels, and paid another quarter for a cup full of ice. For a while, he sat on the bench in front of the shop, eating, then wrapping chunks of ice in paper napkins and holding them against his cheek. By three he was at the bus station, trying to read Sociology of the Family under the dim glow of the streetlights. He dozed for a while—probably not safe, but whatever, he'd already been beaten up. At sunrise, he came awake to the feeling of someone's hand on his shoulder.

Startled, he jumped to his feet, ready to run, ready to fight, ready for anything. Rachel was standing there, with a cup of coffee in one hand. Her hair was pulled back in a bun, with curls escaping around her face. Her eyes were red; her skin was blotchy. She looked beautiful.

"I love you, you know," she said.

He wanted to tell her that he was sorry. That he was stupid. That he didn't think she was dumb or shallow, that he knew she had a good, true heart. But everything got tangled on its way from his brain to his tongue, twisted up with the memory of the beefy Beer Guy with his mean, glittering eyes, the disdainful twist of his lip, the way he'd made Andy feel like nothing, like less than nothing, like something a guy like that would flick off his cuff on his way to his good, clean, well-lighted life. So he kept quiet, just held Rachel's hand, tracing the shape of a heart on her palm until the bus pulled up to the station and it was time for him to go.

Rachel
2001

I tucked my subway map into my bag, pulled out my notebook, and squinted at what I'd written, making sure I had the address right. It was early, just after seven on a gorgeous fall morning, and I was way uptown, doing drop-ins on families who had open cases with the Office of Children and Family Services. My master of social work program at NYU required a twenty-one-week internship, and I was doing mine with the Family Aid Society, which helped families dealing with housing issues, and all of the concerns that went along with that—unemployment, absences from school, the inability to buy and store nutritious food, and not knowing how to cook it when you had it.

Some days, my boss had told me, my job would be nothing but paperwork, filling out forms and faxing them to the appropriate agencies, and then refaxing them when they got lost . . . but most of the time my work was on the ground, meeting with families—mostly single mothers and their kids—helping them get what they needed, whether it was an impromptu lesson in what to do with the kale from the farmers' market, or taking little kids off a mom's hands while she filled out a job application or spent a few hours at a community college.

I looked up at the door, then down at my notebook, then back to the door again. I was in the right place, even if I'd gotten slightly lost on my way here. I banged again. "Flora?" I yelled. No answer.

"She ain' here," called a lanky guy reclining on the stoop next to where Flora and her two daughters lived. He wore a white ribbed cotton tank top, loose-fitting jeans that he'd belted below his hips, and the newest Air Jordans (in my time as an intern, I'd learned to recognize brand-name sneakers—lots of my clients either wanted them or spent way too much money to get them).

I put my notebook in my pocket and smoothed my skirt. "Do you know where she is?"

Lanky gave a lazy grin, exposing a gold tooth, and adjusted the angle of his baseball cap. "She left up outta here with her man."

"Which man is that?" Flora had gotten on FAS's radar—and eventually mine—because she'd brought her three-year-old daughter Ariel to the ER with a greenstick wrist fracture, the kind frequently caused by the twisting of large adult hands. When the social worker on call had interviewed her, she'd admitted that her boyfriend could "get a little rough," especially when the kids interrupted his appointment with televised professional wrestling on Monday nights. We'd gotten Flora's boyfriend into anger management counseling, signed them both up for a parenting class that neither one was attending with any degree of regularity, and planned visits, both scheduled and unscheduled, to check in on the girls. If Flora had found a new fellow, that was good news. If she'd pulled her daughters out of school to run off with him, that was less than ideal.

The guy on the stoop shrugged. "Don't know his name. He hit the numbers. Took 'em all back to the DR."

"Got it." I knocked one last time, more for show than anything else, then stuck one of my new business cards into the crack between the door and the jamb, and then, trying to look purposeful in my stride, with my unruly hair pulled back into a bun, I walked toward my next appointment, enjoying the sunshine. It was a gorgeous day, clear and sunny without being savagely hot; and a light breeze seemed to have scoured the sky. Fall was coming—there was a crisp edge to the wind that let you know it was September and not May. *A perfect morning,* I thought, and pulled out my newly issued cell phone to call my boss, Amy Ung, to tell her that Flora was gone.

"Back to the motherland, huh?" Amy was tiny, with glossy, blunt-cut black hair that fell to her shoulders and in bangs across her forehead. She was in her thirties, always impeccably dressed in crisp pinstriped pants and a man's-style white cotton button-down that she'd probably purchased in the boys' section of some upscale department store.

Amy and her sisters were all native New Yorkers, raised by parents who had emigrated from China and ran a restaurant in Queens. (When I'd asked what kind, Amy had stared at me in silence, then said, "Chinese.") Despite thirty-eight years in America, her parents still barely spoke English, although they understood it, which meant that, from a young age, Amy, their eldest, had been their liaison to the white-people world. Watching the way her parents had been treated by the officials from the health board who inspected their kitchen to the principal at Amy's school had left her with a desire to keep other families from being mistreated. Amy was married to a Jewish guy named Leonard, a surgeon doing his intern-ship at Lenox Hill, and she and I had become friends in part, I think, because she had so many of her nights free while Leonard worked thirty-six-hour shifts and napped in a bunkroom in the hospital.

"No boyfriend?" she'd asked, the first night we'd gone out for drinks.

"No one special right now," I'd said, and given her the abbreviated version of Andy and me, and how that had all ended in my junior year. I thought we'd been fine after the disastrous formal, but whenever I called his dorm room, Andy was out or busy, more often than not, and when he was around, he didn't have much to say—he was either exhausted from a workout or preparing for a meet or on his way out with his teammates. After he didn't return my calls for two weeks straight, I got the message. He didn't want me anymore.

I had dropped out of the Gammas that spring—or, rather, I'd gone inactive, telling my puzzled parents that it had been too hard to study with all the parties, hinting that the rampant disordered eating was also a factor. All I had to do was say the words *not the healthiest environment* and my mother was on a plane to help me find a new place. I should have felt guilty—the environment in the Gamma house was no more or less healthy than the atmosphere anyplace else on campus—but I didn't. After the formal, I'd started to see the sorority, and all of Beaumont, through Andy's eyes—its whiteness, its richness, its manicured, almost stagy perfection, and even though I'd tried, I couldn't un-see any of it. It was irritating, as if I'd been wearing a pair of proverbial rose-tinted glasses, and Andy, who was supposed to love me, slapped them off my face.

The apartment my mother and I had found off-campus wasn't all that different from my suite in the sorority house—it had been carved out of the upper floors of a Tudor-style mansion made of cream-colored stucco and dark wooden beams. My suite had a fireplace, in addition to a black-and-white-tiled bathroom with a big old bathtub, a small but functional kitchen, and a little balcony.

Even though Andy and I hadn't officially broken up, it seemed like all the guys on campus had gotten word of my single status over the summer. When Charlie Corman asked me out in October, I didn't feel guilty about saying yes. I dated Charlie and a few other guys my senior year, a few more since I moved to Manhattan. I still felt Andy's presence, hovering over my life, informing my decisions, always there, like background music, faint but discernible, and none of the guys could banish his voice from my head.

When I applied to NYU my senior year to get a master's degree in social work, my parents had been dubious—about New York, about social work, about me spending my life with the poor, the homeless, the addicted, and the mentally unwell. I'd never told them about what had happened in Atlanta with Bethie Botts, or with Andy at the formal. What I'd said was that the world was a hard place, much harder for most people than it was for us, and that I wanted to help if I could. "You sent me to all of that Hebrew schooling, and they kept talking about *tikkun olam*—how it's our job to heal the broken world. I want to do that." My mother had gotten weepy, and even my dad, who I suspected would have been happier to see me as a teacher or a librarian or, best of all, a stay-at-home mom, had said gruffly, "I'm proud of you," and pulled me in close for a kiss.

My next visit that morning was with Brenda Perrone. Mother of three, ex-wife of two, Brenda had been the first case I'd handled completely on my own, after she'd shown up at our office in July, frantic and furious and dragging her children behind her, complaining that she'd come home to her apartment in Red Hook to find the door padlocked and an eviction notice stuck above the padlock.

"You knew this was coming," Amy had said as she handed me Brenda's file. "Rachel will be handling your case now." Ostensibly the office had gone to a computerized system years ago, but the reality was that there were still paper files, stuffed full of disturbance-of-the-peace citations that looked almost exactly like parking tickets; mimeographed copies of the inventories the corrections officers took when you went to jail. *One nail clipper, one wallet, brown leather, containing one five-dollar bill, three one-dollar bills, two quarters, a nickel, and two pennies.* I flipped through Brenda's file until I found the eviction notice and copies of the three follow-up letters that had been sent via certified mail.

"You signed for these," I said. "Did you even read them?"

Brenda tossed her long black hair and tugged at her short leather jacket before looking down at the pile, then up at me. She was thirty-three and improbably pretty, given the hard life she'd led. Her own father had been abusive, her mom had died young, and she'd dropped out of high school, moved in with her boyfriend, and had her first baby at fifteen. "My girlfriend Celinda, the same thing happened to her, only it never happened. Nobody locked the door to her apartment."

I flipped some more. "Your ex-husband told you six months ago that he lost his job and couldn't afford the rent and that you and the kids would have to find a less expensive place."

"When was I supposed to do that?" Brenda asked. She was working long days in a bakery, which left her no time to set up appointments and check out possible housing. I had encouraged her to keep her job; I'd found a short-term shelter where the family could stay together, and a kennel that would board their dog, and city-funded summer programs for her children, including one where her oldest boy, Nicky, got to spend July with a wealthy and well-meaning family at their summer cottage on Nantucket. In August, she'd moved into a new place in Harlem, on a quickly gentrifying block filling up with young couples who wanted more space than they could afford in trendier neighborhoods but weren't ready to abandon the borough.

That morning I found Brenda sitting on the couch of her still mostly empty apartment, on the twelfth floor of a fifteen-story building. Her eyebrows were plucked into thin arches; her eyes were heavily lined with black pencil. Her thin hair clung to her scalp and face in sticky clumps, her breath smelled like stale coffee, and her two-bedroom apartment had already acquired its signature scent of cigarette smoke and unflushed toilet, with accent notes of fast food and dog. Brenda's pride and joy was a Siberian husky, a dog she'd told me she'd paid a breeder a thousand dollars for, whose breath made you think that a small rodent had crawled inside her mouth and died there. The dog, who was large and white and named Whitey, spent most of her time curled up asleep at Brenda's feet, and at least once every ten minutes she'd let loose a long, mellow-sounding fart, like a low note on a clarinet.

"Who pays a breeder a thousand bucks for a dog when you can go to any shelter and get a dog for free?" I'd asked Amy during one of our dinners. We'd go out together, once a week, and were methodically working our way through all the cuisines in New York City. By then we'd sampled Ethiopian, Italian, Thai, and Korean. We were eating Indian that night, samosas and saag paneer and tandoori chicken. Amy had given me an indulgent smile and said, "Oh, grasshopper, you have much to learn."

I shifted on the couch. Brenda pinched the sleeve of my jacket between two long-nailed fingers. "This is real nice," she said.

"Thank you." The jacket wasn't anything special, but it would, I hoped, look formal enough to command some respect from the women I worked with, most of whom were older than I was. Lucky for me, my parents had bought me a leather tote when I'd graduated from Beaumont, and it was still in good shape, big enough to hold a day's worth of case files, my wallet and keys, and the tape recorder and camera I needed to do my interviews or document conditions at a client's home.

Brenda let go of my jacket and toyed with her hair.

"How have things been?" I inquired, keeping my voice intentionally mild. I'd learned, from shadowing Amy for three months, how to keep judgment off my face and out of my voice, and to try not to ask a question unless I knew the answer. When I'd arrived, I'd used the bathroom, where I had spied with my little eye a man's razor and a can of Barbasol next to the sink, and whiskers in the bowl. Her oldest son was eighteen, small for his age, with no beard that I could see.

Brenda slid her gaze sideways. She knew she wasn't supposed to have another adult with a paycheck sharing the apartment that had been approved for just her and her children. She also knew, or at least I guessed she did, that the amount of work and red tape it would require to evict the boyfriend was such that the agencies involved would probably decide to look the other way, in the event I decided to blow the whistle.

"What's the story, morning glory?"

She shifted on the couch. "It's just a friend who's visiting. A guy I knew from my old job."

I didn't speak and kept looking at her. Another thing Amy had taught me was that strategic silence could be a social worker's best friend. And it worked. Brenda kept talking.

"I just thought he could help out. With the bills. I've got electric, water, gas, cable . . ." She raised a finger for each utility, as if I was unfamiliar with what it cost to live in an apartment. Fresh paint on her nails, I noticed with annoyance. Brenda couldn't get it together to feed her kids breakfast most mornings or to make sure they got to school half the time, and her phone was constantly being turned off—not safe, I told her; if there was an emergency, she'd need to be able to call 911— but she always found time and cash for a manicure. A manicure and a man, and she usually got pissy when I called her on it.

"Is this friend Brian that we talked about last time?"

Brenda chewed on her lower lip. Brian-that-we-talked-about-last-time, Brenda's latest gentle-man caller, had been crashing on his brother's couch, technically homeless. "He just needs a place to stay until he's back on his feet," she'd told me. Back at the office, I'd learned that Poor Brian had a lengthy criminal record, including burglary, larceny, and violation of a Protection from Abuse order, and that he owed thousands of dollars in child support.

"Brenda," I said.

She raised her chin and said, "I'm a grown-ass woman. I can see whoever I want, and you need to respect my choices."

Deep breath, Rachel.

"Do you understand why it's not a good idea to have Brian move in?"

"Because I don't know him very well," she muttered.

"Because he has a criminal record," I said. "Because his last girlfriend said he'd beaten her children."

She straightened her neck. "Brian and I talked about that," she said. "He said that was just his ex making trouble for him, because she's crazy."

"Isn't that what every guy says about his ex-girlfriend? 'She's crazy'? Isn't that what your ex is probably telling his new girlfriend about you?" I wondered if that was what Andy, somewhere, was saying about me.

She nodded, but she didn't look happy. "Fine, I'll tell him he has to move out." Almost immediately she winced, realizing her mistake. "I mean,

I'll tell him he can't move in." Which meant, of course, that Brian had already moved in, and that she probably had no real intention of telling him to go.

If it had just been a guy, I might not have cared. But this was a potentially dangerous guy. *That* I cared about.

"You know you're not supposed to have another adult here. And I know how much you love your kids, how you'd never put them at risk or do anything to hurt them. Brian might seem terrific, and he might have turned his life around, but we don't know that. You wouldn't want to have to find out the hard way that you were wrong. You're too good a mom for that."

She sighed and stared at her hands, and finally managed a small and reluctant nod. I wasn't sure she meant it, but for now it was the best that I could do. The hell of it was that the system didn't operate on possibilities and potentials. You couldn't pull kids out of a house because you thought they might get hurt. You'd have to wait until they did.

I flipped to a fresh page on my clipboard. "Let's talk about Dante. He was absent twice last week."

Brenda cast her gaze down toward the rip in her couch. "He had an ear infection."

"Middle ear or outer ear?"

Brenda fiddled with her own lobe. "Uh . . ."

"Did you take him to the doctor?"

Eyes down. Nod.

"Do you have a receipt? We can probably get you reimbursed for the copay."

"Somewhere," she mumbled. "Unless I put it out with the recycling."

"If I call the doctor's office, are they going to tell me you were there?"

Mumble.

"Sorry, what was that?"

She raised her chin and met my eyes. "I didn't take him in. I called, I talked to a nurse, she said we'd just be sitting there for four hours like we did last time, and Jim at the bakery said I couldn't leave again or he'd fire me, and besides, I knew what was wrong. Even if I did go and we sat there, they'd just give us antibiotics."

This was probably true, but sick kids needed to go to the doctor, and Brenda needed frequent reminders.

"So what happened?"

She squirmed. "I gave him antibiotics."

"Where'd you get them?"

"Leftovers."

"From the last time he had an ear infection?"

Mumble mutter mumble.

"Brenda, I'm sitting right here and I can't hear you."

She raised her face, eyes flashing. I must have sounded like every teacher she'd ever had, every boss who'd said, "Speak up, I can't hear you."

"I had some left over."

"So you gave Dante your old medication? Did you have an ear infection?"

"Yeast infection. But what's the difference? An infection's an infection."

Oh my God. I tried to keep my face still while I scribbled a note and pulled out my phone. Brenda took advantage of my distraction to flip on her TV.

"About Dante," Brenda said after I'd gotten him an appointment at the clinic to have his ear looked at the next afternoon. I gave her a look and she turned the TV off. "You think I can get him tested for ADHD?"

"Why? What's up? Did one of his teachers say something?" Of Brenda's three kids, Dante was my favorite. A grave, polite little boy who, on the day Brenda had moved in, had held the door open for me and then plodded along next to me on a walk to the playground, his pace and posture those of a little old man. Twice he'd asked how much farther it was, and one time, he'd stopped to catch his breath. He wasn't as heavy as some of the kids I'd seen—he was carrying perhaps ten extra pounds, most of it on his belly—but my guess was that the only exercise he got involved his thumbs on his handheld videogame.

"Nooooo." Brenda stretched the word like chewing gum. "But, I dunno. His grades aren't great. I think he has a hard time focusing."

"Do you have the TV on when he's doing his

homework? Does he have a quiet place to sit and work? Remember we talked about that?" She nodded. My guess was that in this house the television was always on. My further guess was that Brenda wasn't interested in Dante's lack of focus or poor grades as much as the additional three hundred bucks she'd get every month for a child who'd been diagnosed with a disability, the way Nicky, her oldest, had been years before. The money was supposed to go for educational support—a classroom aide, an after-school tutor, visits to a psychologist. But the system was so stretched that there was no structure in place to check on how parents actually used the money. I suspected that the extra cash she'd gotten for her oldest son's diagnosis was sitting right in front of us, with a sixty-inch screen and surround sound.

"I just wish Dante had a shot," I'd told Amy the week before. It was Friday afternoon, the end of the day and the workweek, but she was lingering over a pile of paperwork. Leonard was at the hospital that weekend, and Amy was in no hurry to go home.

"Brenda dropped out of school when she was fifteen because she was pregnant. Her mom had her when she was eighteen. She's got three different kids from two different guys, and the only thing she cares about is finding a new boy-friend."

"Forget her." Amy ran her hands over her hair,

which was perfectly smooth, then straightened her stack of files. "Sorry to be blunt, but she's not going to, you know, take classes at CCNY and then go to Harvard. And realistically, her kids might end up making the same choices she did."

I thought about quiet, serious Dante, with his choppy at-home haircuts and his round glasses; the way he had used the Model Magic I'd bought him to make a mobile of the solar system, with the planets strung up on fishing line. His big brother's plan to join the army had been foiled by his arrest record, as had his ability to get a job, so Nicky still lived at home, along with Dante's sister, sixteen-year-old Laurel, who reminded me, in a way that tore at my heart, of Bethie Botts. Laurel had the same untended skin and greasy hair, the same cold gaze and resentful expression, combined with body language that telegraphed "Leave me alone."

"You can't ever let yourself get stuck on one kid or one family." Amy flipped open a compact and touched up her perfectly lipsticked mouth. Amy always came to work with lipstick on, that ruby-red slash the only makeup she wore. Dispassionate, cynical Amy, who underneath the guarded exterior was as tender as anyone I'd met. "Write 'em off." I tried . . . but something about Dante had lodged in my heart. Browsing in a bookstore, I'd look at a children's book and think *Dante would like that*. While I was watching TV, a commercial for a movie would come on the air, and I'd imagine taking him to the show, buying him popcorn, taking him out to eat after and asking if he'd liked the movie, and which star had been his favorite. Everything echoed: Dante reminded me of Keila, my little sister from college. Laurel reminded me of Bethie, with whom I'd had no contact since high school. Everyone and everything reminded me of Andy; eight-year-old Andy alone in the hospital, the first time I'd recognized the possibility of being the helper instead of being helped.

"So can I get him tested?" Brenda asked.

"I'll ask my supervisor," I said. Brenda's face arranged itself into a pout. "You're a wonderful mother," I told her again, "and I know you and the kids are going to do well here." She was smiling faintly when I shut the door.

It was eight thirty in the morning. If I caught an express train I could be home at my sublet in the West Village in twenty minutes, take an hour to have breakfast, grab the yoga mat that I was forever leaving at my studio or the supermarket, and then go to the office.

We were at Astor Place, just ahead of my normal stop at Bleecker, when the subway stopped. Something came over the static-clogged public address system, as fuzzy as the one in the hospital had been, but all I could make out was "this train will not be proceeding." Sighing, I joined my fellow passengers streaming onto the platform.

"Are they sending another train?" a young, perfectly barbered man in a tailored gray suit asked. There was impatience in the tone of his voice and the set of his shoulders: a swaggering Master of the Universe who couldn't be detained in his quest for the buck. I watched a woman raise her cell phone to her ear, her eyes squeezed shut, lips moving, before she flipped it shut and shoved it back into her bag.

By then, people were pushing toward the exits, some of them on phones, all of them hurrying. I joined the line, climbed the stairs, and stood in the street, in the eerie silence, and saw the pillar of smoke.

"Oh my God."

"They're saying a plane hit the Twin Towers," a woman called.

"Like, a little plane?"

"A commuter jet."

"Where are you getting this?" asked the Master of the Universe.

"My son's an intern at CNN. He says eye-witnesses saw the plane hit. They're evacuating both buildings."

"My husband's there." A woman, maybe a few years older than me, similarly dressed for business, looked around, wide-eyed. "My husband's there," she said again, as if someone had contradicted her, before pulling out a cell phone of her own.

Then the street started shaking, a slow, low rumble that rose to a deafening pitch. I thought I felt the ground tilt. In my good Coach bag, my phone was ringing, and, without thinking, I reached for it, flipping it open and raising it to my ear.

"Rachel? Rachel, honey, where are you?" My mom sounded the way she had when I was six, and she'd come into my bedroom to find me blue and gasping for breath.

"Astor Place," I said. "I was going back home on the subway. Do you know what's going on?"

"Daddy and I were watching the *Today* show." As they did, every morning of their lives. "Two planes hit the Twin Towers. They're saying it might be terrorists."

"Who's saying that? If it's Mr. Lifshitz, please don't listen." Mr. Lifshitz was the neighborhood conspiracy theorist.

"CNN," said my mother. "They're saying that terrorists hijacked planes and they flew them into the World Trade Center; they don't know how many people are dead . . ."

I heard her voice start wobbling. "I'm fine, Mom. I'm okay."

"You need to get out of there right now, Rachel Nicole, right this very minute." She was talking to me like I was six and she'd caught me picking my nose in front of company. The crowd in the street was frozen, still staring south, when we heard what we'd quickly find out was the first tower falling.

"We need to get out of here," someone said.

Amy, I thought. Amy lived in Park Slope. I could cross the bridge, go to her house, wait until the trains were running again . . . and if she was already in the office, I would find someplace, a coffee shop or a bookstore, and stay there until either she came back or I was free to go.

Thank God I have sneakers in my bag, I thought as I started walking. Policemen with bullhorns were directing us toward the Williamsburg Bridge. Everyone seemed to be talking on cell phones. Some of them were crying. *Thank God I have a bottle of water. Thank God none of the families that I know live down that way.* I'd tucked my cell phone into my bra—a bad habit, Amy had lectured, and one that would probably either ruin the phone or give me breast cancer. Now I felt it trill against my breast.

"Hello?"

"Rachel?" I recognized his voice, even though I'd never heard it like this. Andy Landis sounded scared . . . and that, more than anything, made what was happening real to me.

"Andy?" I started to cry. It didn't occur to me to ask how he'd gotten my number. "Do you know what's happening?"

"Where are you? Are you somewhere safe?"

"I was on the subway, but they stopped it,

and we all got out, and I saw all the smoke, and then we felt it, and we heard. Is it true?" I was starting to shake, my whole body quivering. "Is it terrorists?"

"Where are you?" he asked me again.

"I'm going toward the Williamsburg Bridge. I was going to try to go home, but they aren't letting anyone through."

"I was in the gym. The TV was on." He paused. "They're saying there were two planes. Passenger jets. They're saying people are jumping out of the buildings."

"Oh my God," I said, and looked up at the sky, like I was expecting a plane to come swooping down on us. I'd been to the World Trade Center. I'd shopped at the Borders in the concourse; I'd been, with one of my New York City beaus, to Windows on the World at the top of the North Tower.

"Don't be scared," Andy told me. "I can stay on the phone with you until you get somewhere safe. Just keep breathing. Keep walking. I'm right here."

"They're telling us to go to the Williamsburg Bridge," I repeated.

"Where are you now?"

I checked the street signs. "We're going east on Eighth Street."

He covered the phone and I heard him ask someone a question. Then he was back. "Two miles and you're on the bridge. You can do that."

"I've never walked two miles in my entire life."

"Not true. Remember our picnics by Lake Carlisle?" That was the lake back at Beaumont. We'd had lots of picnics there, lazy Saturday afternoons where either I'd rest my head on his chest or he'd put his feet in my lap and we would talk about our classes and our parents and the dreams we'd had the night before. "We walked around the lake and that was a two-mile loop. You're going to be fine. You can do this. I know you can."

I looked toward the plume of smoke, rising into the air, obscuring the beautiful blue sky.

"Talk to me," I said in a hoarse voice that hardly sounded like my own. "Tell me where you are."

He did. As I made my way down the FDR Drive and, eventually, all the way over the bridge, Andy told me that he'd graduated from college but was still living in Oregon, that he'd been recruited into a training program that housed and fed athletes, gave them coaching and plane tickets and shoes and clothes and got them ready for the Olympics. I walked along with people just as shocked as I was, some covered in soot, some of them crying. Sometimes I'd listen to Andy, and other times I'd catch bits of conversations—a girl whose fiancé worked for a trading company with offices in the North Tower, a mother whose kids were home with their grandmother, probably watching on TV, worrying about her, and she couldn't reach them on the phone.

"What did you have for breakfast?" I asked Andy, and he told me about the pancakes he'd made with protein powder, how his roommate, Mitch, thought that they tasted like feet but ate them anyhow because he hated to cook.

"How about you?" he asked, and I told him about the bagel and coffee cart on the corner, how different New York City was from anyplace else I'd ever lived, how Philadelphia had made me want to find a city of my own. I walked, and he talked to me—about his workout that day, the case of foot fungus that had spread through the team, his coach and how he was different from his college coaches, and Mr. Sills, who'd come all the way to Oregon for Andy's final college meet.

I was almost over the bridge, my phone's battery beeping, signaling its imminent death, when Andy asked, "How is your heart?"

You broke it, I thought about telling him. "Fine," I said instead. "It's been fine."

"You should come here," Andy said.

I switched the phone to my other ear. I was in Brooklyn now, with no sense of how to find Amy's place, or of what I'd do when I got there. People filled the streets, but there were no cars, no music, no honking horns, no crying babies. It was as if real life had been canceled for the day. I felt the way I once had lying on the operating table: the narrowness of the bed, the chill of the room, the terror I felt every time they put the mask over my face and made me start counting backward, and the certainty that the lights overhead, the mask, the doctors, were all the last things I'd ever see.

"Rachel?" The phone was beeping ever more loudly . . . and Andy was still there.

"Oregon?" I said. "Why?"

"Because it's safe."

"Safe," I repeated. Safe sounded good to me.

Andy paused then, but not for long. "And because I love you."

Andy
2001

It had been more than five years since he'd seen Rachel; almost three years since he'd called her at the sorority house and one of the girls had said, "Sorry, she's out with Kyle." Since then his world had narrowed to include just running, eating, sleeping, then running again; a stringent cycle of train, recover, repeat; race, recover, repeat; then train some more. She'd sent him a note when she'd graduated, telling him about her plans for graduate school, wishing him well, and he'd wanted to send a note in return, telling himself that he hardly thought about her at all, but that wasn't exactly true. What was true, Andy decided, was that he was not thinking of her with the painful, burning urgency he remembered from the nights when she was all he could think of, when he'd spend days with his roommate's car keys in his pocket, carrying on conversations with her in his head, waiting for her to call, ready to go. He came to consider Rachel calmly and with kindness as his first love, the one who'd showed him that love was possible. He hoped that she'd be happy.

All that had been revealed as the flimsiest kind of lie when Mitch O'Connell, a runner from North Carolina State, had come sprinting into the weight room, going all-out even though it was an easy day, saying "Something's happening in New York City." He knew that Rachel was there, and he'd been desperate to reach her, desperate to know that she was okay. Her parents had given him her number—they'd been, he thought, too terrified to tell him no—and she'd picked up on the first ring, and he'd talked her over the bridge, into safety, and realized he'd never stopped loving her at all.

For a week, she'd stayed in the Park Slope neighborhood of Brooklyn, at her boss's house, and she and Andy had talked every night for hours, the way they had as teenagers, or in college, when they'd stay up all night in her bed. When she went back to Manhattan they'd kept talking, with Rachel describing how the air was full of ash and how it stunk of burned plastic, how the streetlamps and walls were plastered with signs for the missing, photographs of loved ones who'd worked in the towers, and how the newspapers were full of stories of husbands and wives, parents and children, all praying that there'd been survivors; that somewhere, in some hospital bed, lay their husband or their mother, suffering from amnesia, not even knowing his or her name, but alive. She described scenes of people weeping on the streets, strangers hugging each other; of five-star restaurants sending pans of food to the fire-houses and police stations and people starting college funds for the children of the men and women who'd died. "Everyone wants to do some-thing," she'd told him, "but nobody knows what to do."

"Come here," he told her over and over, until finally, in the middle of October, she'd decided that maybe a vacation would be a good thing. Andy had started counting the days, wondering what she looked like now, what he'd look like to her, whether things could still feel the same.

At last he stood by the baggage carousel in the Eugene airport. He'd wanted to go to the gate, but after what people were calling 9/11 there were new rules about airports. He was holding a dozen roses—not red ones, which she'd never liked, but apricot-colored, the petals tipped with orange. He'd been watching travelers coming down the escalator when he felt a hand on his shoulder and smelled coconut-scented shampoo and familiar perfume. He turned, and Rachel stood there, smiling. Her cheeks were rosy, like she'd been spending time outside, and he could see freckles dotting the bridge of her nose. She wore jeans, a light-blue button-down shirt, a colorful embroidered belt, and boots like the ones he remembered from her trip to Philadelphia. Diamond studs, also familiar, twinkled from her earlobes. Her hands were tanned and strong, and she looked not older, exactly, but more confident, not looking all around at the new place where she'd landed, but looking right at him with a smile.

"Hey, stranger," she said. "Do I get a hug?"

He took her in his arms, feeling the gentle swell of her breasts and belly against him, in a far more intimate embrace than she'd probably planned. Before he could enjoy it, she stepped away. She pointed out her suitcase and her duffel bag on the carousel. He scooped them both up and walked her to the car he'd borrowed from one of the trainers in order to go get his girl.

After she'd remarked on the beauty of the Willamette Valley, the cool air and the pine trees, and how clean it all smelled after New York, she settled into the passenger seat, smiling at him. "I've seen your name in the papers."

"Oh, yeah?" he asked, suddenly shy and at the

same time eager to know what she'd read, which pictures she'd seen.

"My mom and my brother keep up with you. You almost made the Olympic team last year, right?"

He nodded. "It was always a long shot."

"But you can try again in 2004?"

"That's the plan." She was wearing dark-red lipstick, which was different. When he'd known her she'd worn lighter colors. He wasn't sure whether or not he liked it. Then he asked himself why it mattered what he thought about her makeup. She lived in New York City; he lived in Oregon. She probably had a boyfriend and had just been too polite to tell him, and even if she didn't, it wasn't like there was the possibility of this being anything besides a friendly visit. Still, his brain conjured up his bedroom. Specifically, his bed, with its fresh sheets and freshly laundered comforter. He imagined Rachel's hand in his, Rachel's voice in his ear, saying *Hurry. Hurry.*

He squirmed in his seat, giving his nylon warm-up pants a quick tug. Rachel ducked her head. *Do you think it'll always be like this when we see each other?* she'd asked him once, during one of his Beaumont visits, maybe the time when he'd driven for almost two days with only a three-hour nap to see her, all the way to Virginia in his teammate's cousin's old Tercel. It had been five in the morning when he'd gotten to the

Gamma house, too early to ring the bell, and he'd thought he'd look like a stalker or a vagrant if he fell asleep in the car. He'd been sitting behind the wheel trying to figure out where to go when he heard a tapping on the window, and there was Rachel in her bathrobe, one finger pressed to her lips. *Shh.* When Rachel started talking it took him a few seconds to realize that she was actually there; that this was real Rachel and not dream Rachel, the one who apparently had lived in his head since college, and maybe even since Atlanta.

"I was thinking about this the other day. You know I've known you longer than I've known almost anyone in my life?"

He was prepared to argue the point—they'd known each other over a long time, but not continuously—but then he was pulling into the camp's parking lot, and Rachel was looking around, wide-eyed, at the gyms, the tracks (there were three), and the people. A group of women ran by them, sleek as whippets in their briefs and singlets. "I think between the six of them they've got a breast and a half," she said. She held her purse against her midriff. Andy gently tugged it away.

"You look fine," he said. He wanted to tell her that she looked better than fine, that she was so pretty, that her body looked as lush as a bowl of fruit, all juiciness and curves. He had been to bed with a few of the women runners. Their legs

285

were limber but all sinew and bone, and they were indeed flat-chested. Worse, some of them treated sex like it was a bonus workout their coach had assigned, pumping their hips like they were trying to get their heart rates up instead of having fun.

He drove her to the residences, which were nothing special, a ten-year-old collection of two-story brick buildings, with a freshly paved parking lot and a few extremely fit people carrying groceries out of their cars or laundry bags into them.

"Hey, Landis, you coming?"

Andy waved at Mitch. "I've got to go," he told Rachel. He pointed out the hiking trail at the base of the mountain, handed her the keys to his place, and kissed her, the kind of kiss a husband might give his wife of ten years as she dropped him off at the train station. "Have fun," he said.

"Hurry home," she told him . . . and then she said, "I'll want to see those feet later." She turned toward the steps of his building, walking with an extra sway to her hips, the heels of her boots thrusting her bottom out in a provocative way. *I hate to see you go, but I love to watch you leave,* he thought—a lyric from one of the rap songs Mitch liked to play. He watched her and found himself enjoying the image of Rachel in his kitchen, Rachel in his bedroom, Rachel at the mirror, holding up shirts, putting on lipstick, playing with her hair.

Andy jogged from the lot to meet the rest of his team. "You just get laid?" Mitch asked, and when Andy shook his head no he said, "I hope you're going to, because you're grinning like a fool."

Andy only smiled more widely, gave his laces a tug, and stepped onto the pebbled-rubber surface of Track 3, where he started to run.

"What happened to us?" Rachel asked. They were having dinner at a French place that she'd picked, after grilling a few of his teammates for recommendations and then asking, in a half-serious, half-teasing way whether Andy's training diet permitted something as wild and decadent as roast chicken. "Do they have salmon?" he'd asked, and she'd rolled her eyes, but then hugged him and said, "Never change." He was remembering how they'd gone out when they were in college. He'd order grilled fish or a salad while Rachel would request a burger or pasta, and the servers would always bring her his food. "No, he's got the dainty plate," she'd say. *Daintyplate,* like it was all one word. "He has to watch his girlish figure."

That night, she ordered roast chicken, and he had a turkey burger, not salmon, but still, and she laughed when he asked for steamed spinach instead of fries. "I'm not letting you have any of my mashed potatoes," she said. "Just FYI."

"I'm fine," he said . . . but, of course, she tried to feed him a bite of her potatoes, which were creamy in the way that only a few sticks of butter could account for. They decided to share a bottle of wine. He had a single glass, and she had two, a glass more than usual, he thought—because of her heart she'd always had to be careful about alcohol. After a few lurches and stumbles, or instances where they'd both ask a question at the same time, they were talking as easily as they had back when he would visit her in college and they'd stay up all night. She'd told him about Alice, and how she thought she would never get the smell of the hospital out of her nose, and he'd tell her about how one of the ladies at an antiques shop in Voorhees thought that Mr. Sills was his father, and he'd never bothered to correct her. Rachel was a wonderful storyteller. With her voice and her face she could turn into anyone— Brenda, the truculent single-mom client who gave her little boy her yeast infection medication even though there was nothing wrong with his plumbing; Amy, her brassy-sounding boss; Jonah, who was, as she put it, limping through law school after obtaining his college degree on the six-year plan.

Over dinner, Andy told her how, on his last visit home, there'd been another little boy trailing behind his friend, holding Mr. Sills's toolbox and handing him the nails.

"Were you jealous?" Rachel asked.

Andy shook his head, smiling. "Maybe a little. Mostly I was glad another little boy got what he gave me."

Rachel said she understood, and could remember feeling the same way going back to see Dr. Karen, her pediatric cardiologist, after she'd aged out of her practice and finding a line of other little boys and girls in the waiting room. "I guess I wanted to think I was her star patient, her one and only . . . but there are always more kids."

"That's very mature," he told her.

"I've grown up a lot," she said, and attempted to look mature, folding her neck down and furrowing her forehead. Maturity lasted for about three minutes, and then she told him the story of how she'd been at a playground, picking up one of her clients' kids because the client was stuck in a meeting with her parole officer, and how the little girl had come racing across the yard, clutching a plastic bag and shouting, "Miss Rachel! Miss Rachel! Guess what I have in my bag?"

"I thought it was, you know, an art project or cookies or something, and she says, 'No, it is my UNDERPANTS, because I accidentally got some POOP ON THEM!' "

Andy told her about Mitch, who could be counted on to miss almost every flight he was booked on. "Even if he's at the airport, in the waiting area, he'll be in the men's room when they do the final boarding call." She asked him about a meet in Jamaica (hot) and the half-marathon in New Mexico (also hot) and the marathon he'd run in Rome (hot, humid, and the hands-down worst course he'd ever run, with miles of cobblestones that made his knees ache just remembering them). The conversation slowed, the silences stretching, until they were just staring at each other. Vaguely, Andy realized that the restaurant was emptying out, that there were servers clustered around the host's stand, that the candle in the center of their table had almost burned down to nothing.

"Any dessert or coffee?" the waiter asked, his pen hovering.

"Nothing for me," Andy said automatically.

"He will be enjoying the apple pie," said Rachel, smiling sweetly. She'd piled her curls on top of her head, and he could see the pale curve of her neck, glimmering in the dim candlelight. "And I will have a fork and a glass of port."

"Port?" asked Andy, when the waiter was gone.

"Yeah, I know, it sounds like I'm the Grey Poupon guy, but I had a . . ." She looked down. She'd changed her clothes during the afternoon and was wearing a black skirt and a fancy white shirt with lace around the collar. "I knew this guy. He liked port. At first I was like, do you drink it before or after you polish your monocle? But it's really good, especially with walnuts."

Boyfriend, Andy thought. That was what she'd

been about to say—*I had a boyfriend who liked port.* He felt his heart speed up and made himself breathe deeply, thinking, *Be realistic, it's been years, you know she hasn't just been sitting around waiting for you, right?* He realized that a part of him had hoped just that. When the port came, she lifted the glass and raised her eyebrows, but he refused to taste it, not wanting anything to do with Rachel's other guys.

"So," she said. They'd abandoned the pie—he'd had a single bite, and she'd pushed it away after a few of her own, saying, "Not hungry, I guess." The waiters were gone; the hostess in her black dress was yawning at her podium. "We should get going before they kick us out."

He wanted to ask her about the port-sipping boyfriend, about anyone else she'd dated, about Kyle Davenport, back at Beaumont. But was that fair? Hadn't he dated other girls? The female runner, in her thin red-and-white shorts; the sweet-faced girl from his Gender and Globalization class senior year; one of his neighbors, a woman in her forties with a deeply tanned face and a tight, almost boyish body, who'd done her laundry the same night that he did and had invited him to stop by if he wanted a beer? If he and Rachel were meant to be together, it would happen. Meanwhile, he'd told himself, it was only sensible that they explore. Date other people. Be free. He'd told himself all of this, and he believed it, and then he pictured Kyle with his arms around Rachel's waist, Kyle with his muscley tongue in her mouth, Kyle, naked and neckless, in bed with Rachel, his Rachel, and he'd punched his wall hard enough to pound a hole through it, the first thing he'd hit since Kyle's face.

"How was your last year at Beaumont?" he asked as they walked back to his car. In his phone calls to Brooklyn she'd told him about her life in New York City, her supervisor, her clients, the apartment her parents had helped her to rent in the West Village, but they'd never touched on her senior year, or spoken about how she'd ended up with Kyle Davenport.

"I moved out of the sorority house." Andy, surprised, said nothing. "It was different, living on my own. But I was glad I did it. I think I was more ready to live in the real world than if I'd stayed in the Gamma house and had all my meals cooked and my laundry done. And then I graduated, and then I moved to New York."

"When did you dump Kyle?"

"When did I what?"

"Kyle Davenport," he said.

She turned to him, her eyes wide, her face scrunched up in horror. "As if," she said.

Andy felt a great lightness rising through him. "I called one night, and I asked for you, and whoever answered the phone said you were out with Kyle Davenport."

"Andy," said Rachel. She'd turned to face him, and she looked completely serious. "If Kyle Davenport was the last man on earth, I'd date women."

He felt like he was drowning, only the water was made of light. It was the strangest mix of emotions—anger, for having wasted so much time, joy that he'd been so wrong, that Rachel had always been the Rachel that he'd loved, who would never have even considered Kyle.

"So why would someone tell me that?"

Rachel, who'd been staring at him just as intently as he'd been looking at her, shook her head. "Some of the girls were pretty pissed about the thing at the formal. We ended up on probation . . . oh, whatever. It's not a big deal."

Andy reached for her hand, and Rachel let him take it. She twined her fingers through his.

"So no Kyle," he said, still feeling overwhelmed. Rachel shook her head and smoothed her hair with her free hand, a familiar, endearing gesture. He squeezed her fingers, tugging at her until they were hip to hip as they walked. "Every morning for six months I'd wake up thinking, *Screw it, I'm going to go see her. If she's going to dump me, I can at least make her do it in person.* And by the end of the day I'd have talked myself out of it again. I'd think, *She'll probably laugh at you.*"

"I would never have laughed," she said.

They walked in silence through the parking lot. When they got to his car, he hugged her, holding her tightly against him, an embrace still on the right side of propriety, one that could still be considered friendly, but only just. When they broke apart, her face was flushed, her eyes shining. "I hope it won't be another five years before we see each other again."

Instead of answering, Rachel reached for him, putting her small, warm hand on the back of his neck, lifting her lips to his. They kissed, first lightly, then more urgently, his tongue in her mouth, her hips tilted against his, her breasts against his chest, her whole body sending a message that was undeniable. "Want to come up?" he asked. She'd left her bags in his apartment, with the understanding that they'd pick them up after dinner and he'd take her to the hotel she'd booked. More than once, when they'd been talking, he'd offered her his bed, saying he'd sleep on the couch, and Rachel had turned him down, politely but firmly.

Without a word, she climbed into the passenger seat, smiling at him, saying, "Yes."

As soon as his front door was shut they started kissing again. Her tongue fluttered against his, and his hands were deep in the softness of her hair, and it was like time unspooled, carrying them right back to when they were teenagers. He pulled her against him, thinking that he'd never get her close enough, that if he could fold her inside of him, like a mother tucking a baby into her coat, he'd do it. He'd keep her warm, he'd keep her safe, he'd keep her with him always.

Taking her hand, Andy led her to his bedroom, which looked like every room he'd ever lived in —a bed, a dresser, the posters on the wall—except for a machine humming softly in the corner. Rachel stopped kissing him long enough to point. "What's that?"

"Oxygen simulator," he murmured, his hands busy with the buttons on her blouse. "It's supposed to simulate altitude."

Rachel said something that sounded like *For fuck's sake.* Andy felt relieved she hadn't seen the back porch, where a tank with a submerged treadmill allowed injured runners to run under-water, and then they tumbled onto his bed. She nibbled at his chin, his ear, touching his face with her fingertips, sighing, whispering "You feel so good." Once, she pushed him back, propped herself onto her elbows, and asked, "How long has it been?"

Andy knew what she was asking, and it wasn't how long it had been since he'd seen her. He thought back to his last romance, if you could even call it that, ten minutes of undignified fumbling in the bathroom of a bar downtown. "It's been a little while," he said. That girl—God, he wasn't even sure what her name was—had scribbled her phone number on his hand in eyeliner, if he remembered right, after neither one of them could find paper or a pen. The next week, when they'd met for drinks, Andy realized that they had absolutely nothing to say to each other and that, when he didn't have four beers inside him, she looked like an eel, with a narrow body and a big, horsey mouth.

Not many of the runners had serious girlfriends. Hookups were more common, a night or a weekend with another athlete who understood the deal, or a woman who'd attach herself to you at a meet, or in a bar. Andy remembered the time he'd spent with a television reporter who'd been covering the Olympic trials in Atlanta. She'd worn a girdle and had gotten annoyed when he'd laughed. "It's a foundation garment," she'd said, her pretty face looking less pretty when she scowled. After they'd finished, he'd been starving, but all she had in the refrigerator of her chrome-and-stainless-steel loft was seltzer and a jar of pickles.

Not Rachel, he realized, now that he had Rachel in his arms again, her lush curves and her soft skin, her beautiful hair, her beautiful scar. That was the problem with the reporter. That was the problem with all of them. None of them were Rachel.

He felt her slip down the bed. She unfastened

his pants, eased his briefs over his hips, and brushed the length of his cock with her palm before taking him in her mouth. He sighed, eyes shut, thinking about how unbelievably good it felt when Rachel gave a throaty moan, then rolled her mouth from base to tip and whispered, "Look at me."

He looked and saw that she had her eyes open, locked on his, as she opened her mouth, hollowed her cheeks, and slid all the way down. He wondered if some other guy had asked for that— *I want you to look at me when you do it*—or if she'd seen it in a movie, or read it in some magazine. *Ten Secrets to Turn Your Guy On.* Rachel's expression went from ardor to confusion as she felt him start to soften.

"What?" she asked.

"Shh," he said, pulling her up so they were face-to-face again. He slid his hands between her legs, positioning fingers and thumb the way she'd taught him. Except that wasn't right. She hadn't taught him. They'd figured it out together, how to make her come. He nuzzled against her, his lips on her neck, nibbling and kissing his way up to her earlobe, where she'd always been ticklish. "Ooh," she whispered. "Ooh! Oh, oh, oh," she sighed as he worked his fingers against the slick seam . . . and then she forgot to pose, forgot about trying to look good, and lost herself inside her own pleasure. Andy watched her squeeze her eyes shut as she clamped her thighs against his wrist and snapped her hips up, once, twice, three times before she froze, all the muscles in her thighs and belly and bottom tense and quivering, and he felt her contract against his fingers.

Before she could recover, he'd rolled her onto her back and slipped inside her. After the first thrust he had to hold still, knowing that if he kept moving, if he gave himself up to the exquisite tightness, the heat, he would explode. He wanted her to come at least once more, with him, and he didn't want her to tease him, the way she some-times used to if they hadn't seen each other in a while and he finished before she'd had a chance to get started.

"It's not a race," she would say. "You're not trying to beat your personal record here." He'd always taken care of her . . . or, sometimes, when he was sleepy, he would just curl around her, holding her close, with his fingers inside her and her fingers working at her clitoris, and they'd taken care of her together. But he wanted it to be good that night. He wanted everything to be perfect.

He reached down and stroked her cheek, then her hair. "Oh, God," she whispered, swiveling her hips in a way he knew would send him right over the edge. "Oh, wait. Do you have a condom?" she whispered.

Andy opened his nightstand drawer and ripped open a Trojan. Rachel watched, frowning. "Tell me they sell those as singles," she said.

He kissed her, pleased that she was jealous, thinking that he'd tell her anything she wanted to hear, and, finally, he slipped inside her again. She gasped and shut her eyes, and then neither of them spoke. She had one hand on his shoulder, the other slowly stroking his back, from the nape of his neck to the base of his spine.

"You feel so good," she whispered . . . and then Andy couldn't hold back any longer. He plunged inside her, deep into that maddening clutch, that heat. Rachel moaned, her hands locked onto his shoulders, her breath against his face, her voice in his ear, urging him on.

"Oh, baby," he gasped as she put her lips against his ear, whispering his name over and over, like a chant or a song or a prayer.

If there was going to be awkwardness, it would come when they'd finished; when they looked down and saw that he was still wearing his socks and she still had her panties hooked around one ankle. There would be the condom to dispose of, the strangeness of a woman in his bed for the first time in months, and Rachel would surely have something to say about his decorating skills, how his bedroom was as austere and empty as a cheap hotel room, with no bookshelves, no dining-room table, a secondhand couch in the living room, and the posters he'd had since college on the walls. But as soon as they were done, Rachel rolled into his arms, curling herself against his chest, and said, "I missed you!" in the friendly, happily surprised voice of a woman who'd bumped into an old best friend at the grocery store. With her hands balled into fists, she punched lightly at his chest, like it was his fault they'd been apart.

"I missed you, too," Andy said. He'd been smiling for so long he was sure that his face would ache in the morning. "I feel like . . ."

"What?" she asked. "How do you feel?" He remembered how she'd always been interrogating him, quizzing him about his emotions, pushing him to give her more than just a "fine" or "happy" or "tired."

"Like nothing's changed," he said. "Like you went out to get bagels or something, and now you're home."

"Now I'm home," she said. He cuddled her against him, kissed her, then got up. In the kitchen, he poured a glass of water, took a sip, and carried it back to the bedroom. Rachel had opened her suitcase and pulled on one of her ribbed cotton T-shirts and the inevitable pajama bottoms, this pair blue-and-white striped.

He handed her the water. She drank, set the glass down, then sat up with her back against the wall, holding her arms out, waiting for his feet.

"Oh, gross," he heard her murmur as she inspected his battered toes, then worked her way up to his calves and his thighs, running her hands lightly over his limbs. "Your body is amazing," she said. "I mean, I thought it was amazing before, but this . . ." She swept her hands from the tops of his thighs to his knees. "I guess I shouldn't be surprised. You basically work out for a living. If someone like you doesn't have an amazing body, nobody does." Rearranging herself until they were side by side again, she asked, "So what do you do all day?"

He told her that he ran, he ate, he lifted, he stretched, he slept, and then he rose to do it all again. He traveled to meets, he raced, he worked on shaving seconds or even fractions of seconds off his best times. Out loud, it sounded silly, the height of self-indulgence. There were people fighting wars and curing diseases, writing great books or, in Rachel's case, helping needy children, and what did he do? He ran around a track, slightly but significantly faster than a small group of other elite runners . . . and got paid more for doing it than she got for helping kids.

"So you got what you always wanted," said Rachel. "Lucky you."

In the darkness, with only the glow of the parking lot lights filtering through his window shade, she looked so pretty and so familiar, like something he'd loved and missed and resigned himself to living without. Her head on his chest, her hand on his side, soothed him in a way that no massage or meditation ever had.

"Lucky me," said Andy, and then, before he'd had a chance to plan or consider—and Andy was a man who planned and considered everything, from the grams of protein in his morning smoothie to how many miles he'd run every afternoon—he rolled onto his side so that he was looking right in her eyes and said, "You should move out here."

" 'Please come to Denver with the snowfall,' " she sang. He cuddled her close. He loved to hear her sing. She had a beautiful voice, he had told her that a hundred times, that she should join a choir or a band or a theater company, but she'd always insisted that she had a range of exactly three notes, that the world was full of people who were a lot better than she was.

"I'm not in Denver," he pointed out, although he'd thought about it. A lot of runners went there, to train at altitude.

"It's a song," she said. "It's actually a country song. You don't know it?" She adjusted herself and sang a little more. " 'Hey, ramblin' boy, why don't you settle down, Denver ain't your kind of town. There ain't no gold, and there ain't nobody like me . . .' "

"It's pretty," he said. "What happens?"

She stretched against him, her arms over her

head, her breasts lifted enticingly, her toes reaching for his shins. "Oh, the guy keeps begging his girlfriend to come here, come there, Los Angeles, Boston, Denver, and she keeps telling him to settle down."

"Do they end up together?"

"I can't remember," she told him.

"Stay with me," he said.

She pulled away, propping her head up on her elbow. In the dark, he could feel her eyes on him. "I'm not sure we know each other well enough for this kind of decision."

"Oh, you," said Andy. Now that she was back, he couldn't imagine being without her again.

"What about grad school?" she asked.

"I bet you can find a program here."

Rachel was quiet for a minute. Then she said, "I have something." She got up, pretty and completely female with her full breasts and round bottom, and padded across the room. He heard her unzip her duffel bag and rummage around. She came back to the bed holding an eight-by-eleven-inch envelope, and leaned across him to turn on a light. Then he was looking at a picture of the two of them as teenagers. Rachel was wearing his hoodie. Andy stood behind her with his arms wrapped around her shoulders.

"Oh my God, my hair," he groaned, turning away from his mullet.

"And look at mine!" Rachel giggled, pointing at

her teased curls. She dipped her hand back into the envelope and pulled out what Andy knew was there, what had to be next: the necklace, with the red paper-clip heart on a chain.

"So," she said, sounding suddenly shy. She rolled onto her back. "So I'd go to school, or work, and you'd run, and then at night we'd have dinner together?"

"Right."

Rachel stared at the ceiling. "We were good together, weren't we?"

Andy looked at the clock. He'd guessed that it was midnight, maybe one in the morning, but it had somehow gotten to be almost 3:00 a.m. He had to be awake in two hours, at the track in three. That should have worried him. In the middle of a six-week course of $V0_2$ max training, he needed his sleep. But he felt too excited to even close his eyes. He could visualize the morning's workout, the feel of the track under his fingers, the sound of the coach counting them down. He could feel his body leaping forward, his legs eating up the yards, erasing space, moving him as fast as they could toward Rachel, his destiny, his one; Rachel, who'd be waiting at the end.

"Has it ever been like it was with us with any-one else?" Rachel asked. "You don't have to be graphic," she said hastily, rolling against him and burying her face in his chest, as if he was going to snap his fingers and force her to watch some videos. "I don't need to know where the rest of those condoms went. I'll just tell myself that the Condom Fairy came and took them. But I just . . ."

She reached up, letting her fingers graze his cheek, then stroke his neck. They both felt it—it was as if she'd struck a match or turned a strong magnet toward iron filings. For Andy, who lived intimately in his body, in tune with every twinge and flutter, the sensation was akin to being shocked.

He heard Rachel laugh, a little ruefully. "Do you remember when I asked you . . ."

". . . if it would always be this way?"

"Maybe," she said, "it's that we're each other's destiny." She'd made her voice deep and jokey, but Andy wasn't in a teasing mood.

"Stay with me," he said. He bent down, kissing her forehead, her cheeks, the tip of her nose, then her lips, at first lightly, then slowly, a lingering kiss, one that told her, in a way his words couldn't, that he adored her, that he always had, that he always would. "Please," he said, and kissed her some more, and when he finally lifted his lips from hers, Rachel raised her head, looking at him as she said, "I will."

Andy

2004

His cell phone hummed on the bedside table, and he reached across Maisie to answer. Maisie slept in the nude, winter or summer, at ease in her body, and justifiably proud . . . but she also slept with her mouth wide open, due to an uncorrected deviated septum that Andy suspected, but had not confirmed, was the result of two separate nose jobs. Also, she snored. But she'd told him that he kicked in his sleep, that his legs churned like he was running at least once a night, which he figured made them even.

He and Maisie had met in a New York Sports Club a little over a year ago. He'd been in New York for the annual USATF Indoor Track & Field Championships, and the hotel's treadmills were broken, so they'd sent him across the street. There, he'd seen Maisie pacing around an elliptical machine, frowning at the blank display board.

"Hey," she'd said, sauntering over in skintight black leggings and a white cotton top that was alluringly sheer where she'd sweated through it. Her smile and her gaze, attentive and intimate, made him feel like they were in a bar at closing time instead of at a gym at nine in the morning. "Sorry to bother you, but I can't figure this out," she said, and lowered her voice. "I think I broke it."

Andy found himself whispering back, "What'd you do?"

"I don't know." Her pretty lips formed a pout. "Can you come look? I'd be very grateful."

As it turned out, the only thing wrong with the elliptical machine was that someone had unplugged it. By the time she'd climbed aboard, Andy had learned that her name was Maisie, that she was a model, and that she actually knew who he was. "I recognized you right away from that feature in *Runner's World*. I used to run track in high school—nothing like you, of course, not even close—but I still run to stay in shape, and I still get all the magazines." She gave him a smile and put her hand, gently and briefly, on his forearm. "I'm rooting for you to make it to Athens."

Andy thanked her. Maisie toyed with the strap of her sports bra and said, "I never, ever do this, but, if you're free tonight, is there any chance you'd want to have dinner with me? Just, you know, as friends." And Andy, who'd been traveling solo for two weeks while Rachel helped set up the Family Aid Society's West Coast office in L.A., surprised himself by telling her, "Sure."

That night, he'd met her in the hotel lobby in

white linen pants and a dark-blue shirt, both borrowed from Mitch, the team's fashion plate. Maisie had been wearing a blue-and-white sundress. "We match!" she'd said, delighted, and took Andy's arm. He noticed how the dress left her shoulders bare, along with lots of cleavage, which Rachel never showed, because of her scar. Maisie smelled of white wine and cigarettes, an alluring bad-girl scent . . . and she was stunning, like God had taken a normal girl, pared her down until she was elegantly slim, given her high cheekbones that made her look mysterious, even dangerous, then softened her face with a sweet smile and beautiful lips, and eyes so big they were almost cartoonish.

The restaurant was a place that even he could tell was fashionable, buzzing with conversation, full of gorgeous women with important-looking men (and important-looking women with average-looking men). He felt people's eyes on them as they walked to their table. Maisie ordered a white-wine spritzer, but when Andy asked for water, she'd asked him, "Is it okay if I drink? It won't bother you? I know you've got a race tomorrow."

"No, it's fine," he'd said. He couldn't help but compare Maisie's attitude with Rachel's. "Oh, I shouldn't," Rachel would say . . . then she'd order some sweet cocktail with maraschino cherries and sometimes an umbrella, eight ounces of booze and liquefied sugar. She'd urge him to take a sip. When he wouldn't, she would roll her eyes and say, "Is one sip really going to hurt you? It's calories. You need those, right?" Maybe she didn't do that all the time—in fact, maybe she'd done it only once or twice—but Andy had to admit that having a girl put his needs so far ahead of her own felt good.

When the menus came, Maisie didn't even open hers. "Grilled swordfish, no sauce, whatever green veggies you've got," she told the waiter . . . which was exactly what Andy was planning on getting.

"I can't tell you how much I admire you," Maisie began.

Andy waved away the compliment. She looked at him, her gaze intent and her drawl entrancingly sweet. "You're being modest, but you don't have to be modest with me. I used to run, remember? I know how it feels, when it's the last lap and every single part of you is burning and it hurts to breathe and you don't think you can even pick your foot up again and you find a way to do it." She reached across the table and gave his hand a little squeeze. "I'd love to see you race sometime."

"You can come tomorrow," he heard himself say. "Madison Square Garden."

"I believe I know where that is," Maisie said, waving away the bread basket and giving him a smile.

He tried asking her about herself. At first she didn't want to say much, leaving him with the impression that her early years hadn't been easy, and that they had left her with a determination to work hard, to scoop up all the prizes the world could offer. She had grown up in a tiny town in Georgia, with a single mother, like him. She, too, had been an only child, the repository of her mother's ambitions, but when he tried to ask her more about her hometown, her modeling, even her high-school track team, she'd turn the conversation back to him. She was a wonderful listener, her eyes always on his face, barely moving, hardly breathing . . . and then when she spoke she would ask some follow-up question that showed how closely she'd been paying attention. It made him feel like the most important person in the world, and he found himself doing some creative editing with his answers. He wasn't leaving Rachel out of his story entirely— that would have been wrong, and probably impossible —but he was definitely downplaying her impor-tance, in a way he knew would have infuriated Rachel if she'd been there.

"You've been dating the same girl since high school?" Maisie's expression was respectful and, Andy thought, a little amused, the same way some of his teammates looked when he told them that Rachel had been his high school sweet-heart. Andy nodded. He couldn't stop looking at

Maisie. It was like she was the next step in female evolution, with her fine bones and tawny skin and long, straight black hair, with a beauty that could have been any kind of ethnic mixture, from Mediterranean to Israeli to Greek to part African American. Eventually, Andy learned that Maisie's father, like his, was black, that her mother was French-Canadian, that her given name was Marie-Suzanne, and that she'd changed it when she'd shown up at Eileen Ford's offices when she turned eighteen and found that they already had three Maries and two Marias on the books.

"When I showed up, I told them that I knew where I want to be in five years."

"Where's that?"

She gave him a sweet smile, a girlish giggle, and then said, "On the cover of the *Sports Illustrated* swimsuit issue."

Andy wondered, briefly, if she thought that dating an athlete would somehow improve her chances. He was deciding that it was paranoid and ridiculous when she said, "I've already done a shoot with them. No cover yet, but I'm on their radar, so it's not completely crazy."

"What's your ten-year plan?" he asked. She looked thoughtful, tapping one finger against her perfect lips.

"By then I probably won't be modeling anymore." She said this without audible disappointment. "Models have a sell-by date, and even if I get all the work done, thirty is thirty. That's why I need to concentrate on building out my brand. Figuring out, 'What does Maisie stand for?'"

Beware of people who talk about themselves in the third person, Rachel liked to say. But Andy was fascinated instead of repelled. Maybe referring to themselves that way was something only really, really attractive women could get away with.

"What does Maisie stand for?" As soon as he'd said it, he realized how flirty it sounded. Oh, well.

"That's the question," she said. "Is it swimwear? Soft goods? Lingerie? Cindy Crawford designs furniture. Kathy Ireland's line for Kmart sells more than Martha Stewart's." Andy, who'd thought that models past their sell-by dates mostly hung on to fame and fortune by marrying rock stars or getting bit parts in movies, was impressed as he listened to Maisie parse her post-modeling future, touching on Christie Brinkley's line of hair extensions, Iman's cosmetics, and Tyra Banks's and Heidi Klum's respective efforts in television. Andy found that he was nodding, mouthing the words *Yes* and *I know* and *I get it* as she spoke, thinking he'd never met anyone so equipped to understand him, to understand that he had two lives to plan for, his current existence and his second life, the one you'd be stuck with after the life that you'd always wanted was over.

Andy learned that Maisie lived in New York,

sharing an apartment with three other girls on the Upper East Side, but wasn't romantic about the city, the way Rachel was. "The truth is, I could be anywhere. It's embarrassing. Everyone from home wants to hear about the museums and the theater, but honestly I just don't have time, and even if I did, I'd never spend two hundred dollars to watch a band or a show. I'd rather just download the music." She tilted her head, smiling, like she was imagining music, or maybe the money she'd saved by not paying for concert tickets.

He nodded, agreeing completely, thinking about how it bugged him the way Rachel went on and on about the city, always comparing Oregon with New York, complaining about how there was no good Indian food and how you couldn't even get a pizza delivered after ten o'clock. "I know it's beautiful here," she'd said, pointing out a particular shade of the sky or describing the way the air tasted, as if air had a taste. He knew she wasn't happy, that she was always trying to convince herself that Oregon was fine, even though she still subscribed to *New York* magazine, and sometimes he'd catch her reading the listings, sighing over some gallery show or performance that she wouldn't be there to see.

As diners came and went, they discussed their workouts, their diets, and which airport of all the ones they'd flown in and out of was the least terrible. When the food arrived, Maisie didn't take a bite and then close her eyes and sigh in ecstasy, as Rachel sometimes did, or demand to know whether his own dinner was good, and glare when he failed to be sufficiently appreciative. Maisie simply cut her swordfish in half and pushed one portion, untouched, off to the side of her plate, then ate the rest in small, methodical bites.

Eventually, Andy got her to tell him a few stories—how she'd taught herself to smile with her lips pressed together because her teeth were terrible until the agency paid for veneers, about how she'd had no friends and no one had asked her to junior or senior prom. Andy nodded and made sympathetic noises, but he wasn't sure he believed her. Her anecdotes had a polished quality, like she had read a book on what could possibly make a beautiful girl sound sympathetic and memorized the answers. When the talent scout had spotted her in a mall's food court when she was seventeen, she said, she'd assumed the guy was playing a trick on her, right up until he'd handed her his business card. She'd been gawky and flat-chested; she'd towered six inches above the tallest boys, and she'd been skeletally thin— an advantage for runway work, but a look that had done her no favors with the guys in Valdosta.

"And none of the girls in school liked me," she said. This at least sounded like it might have been true.

"I bet they just hated you because you're . . . you know," said Andy, unsure of the words to express Maisie's beauty, or whether he was even supposed to mention it explicitly, whether it was somehow gauche or rude. Even though it wasn't fair, he couldn't stop comparing her with Rachel, whose face, in his memory, was pretty but not stunning, whose hair was nice, but nothing like Maisie's shiny mane, and who, if he was being honest, had gained a few pounds since she'd moved in with him. Everyone else in his world was so fitness-minded. Even the civilians he'd meet in the sneaker shop or at the diner were all in training for a sprint-distance triathlon or an ultra-marathon or an Ironman . . . and there was Rachel, content with a two-mile hike followed by a picnic, followed by her complaining all the way back about how she was stuffed and how her boots were giving her blisters and why couldn't they just take a nap.

While Maisie smiled and put her hand on his forearm, he thought about the way Rachel pronounced *NFL* as "Niffle," and then laughed, every single time. He considered how disagreeable she could be at parties. "I'm sorry," she'd say after Andy had asked why she'd change the subject or even walk away every time the conversation swung back to running . . . which, in a room full of runners, was often. "I have limits. There's only so many times I can hear about whether tempo runs with pickups are better than fartlek intervals, or whether it's heat, then ice, or ice, then heat, or why the Kenyans are dominating the mile. Is it so bad to ask someone what they're reading? Except," she sighed, "it's always *Once a Runner*."

At his prompting, Maisie told him about her *Sports Illustrated* shoot, how they'd flown six models to a resort off the coast of Croatia in the middle of March. The call time had been 4:00 a.m., the ocean water, crystalline and turquoise, had been freezing, and the shore was so rocky that three of the girls had cut their feet and they'd had to photoshop out the blood.

"So of course I was so nervous that I forgot to pack a brush. I asked one of the hairdressers if she had one that I could borrow, so she gives me a key to her suite, and I get there, and I scream, because it looks like a mass murder, with, like, twelve scalps laid out on the bed . . ." Eventually she'd learned that the hairdressers had packed multiple sets of extensions for each girl. "*SI* did focus groups. Men are big on hair," she said. "They also like it when the girls touch each other. That's a direct quote from some guy's survey. 'I like it when they're touching each other.' "

Andy had listened, enchanted: by her beauty, by her stories, by the way people looked at them, how every man in the place seemed to regard him with respect bordering on awe. Across the table, smiling from behind long, lowered eyelashes,

Maisie seemed both exotic and familiar, both like him and unlike anyone he'd ever met.

He'd thought that he'd been happy, enjoying the routines of coupled life: simple meals at the little table in the kitchen, the way Rachel's stuff had blended with his—her framed art posters on the wall, her lotion in the bathroom, her books scattered everywhere, the way the apartment would smell like her shampoo for hours after she got out of the shower, the sound of her voice rising and falling as she talked her clients through their crisis of the day. But here in this restaurant, on a cool, clear spring night, with a lovely woman across the table and the city glittering outside, he decided that maybe things with Rachel had gotten a little bit stale. He was only twenty-seven. Was he really ready to settle down? Besides, Rachel took him for granted, hanging around in sweat-pants, spending entire evenings with a mud mask on her face. A few nights before she'd left for Los Angeles, he'd been doing his laundry and she'd been reading on the couch. He'd gone to kiss her and had noticed that, in addition to the garlic and the spices from the vegetarian chili she'd made, there was another smell in the room. With a pair of clean track pants in his hand, he'd said, "Jesus, was that you?"

"A thousand pardons," she'd said. Then she'd started giggling . . . and, eventually, he started laughing, too. But was that what their life was going to be like? Was that what he had to look forward to? Mud masks and unannounced farting?

Maisie reached across the table and took his hand, tracing the lines with the tip of a fingernail. "Your love line. It's very strong." When she looked up, into his eyes, he felt his heart skip. Andy shifted in his seat. He and Rachel hadn't had sex before he left, which was their routine. "My stomach's kind of funny," she'd said, slipping out of bed to get the Pepto-Bismol right after he'd reached for her, and between that and the farting he'd left her alone. "Your life line," said Maisie. He could feel her breath on the palms of his hands. "I see lots of success. Blue ribbons. Gold medals." Andy smiled. Rachel was hundreds of miles away. She'd never find out. And wasn't he entitled? He'd slept with only seven women in his entire life. He was a world-class runner, an Olympic contender, possessor of one of the longest winning streaks in all of American collegiate track history. He should have been getting, as Mitch liked to say, more ass than a toilet seat at a girls' school, and he could still tally his conquests on two hands, with fingers left over. If his teammates ever learned he'd had this chance and failed to close the deal, they'd laugh him right off the track. It was like you'd had TV dinners for a year and someone offered you filet mignon; like you'd been riding a bike— a nice one, but a bike, still—and someone handed you the keys to a sports car, something low-slung and beautiful with a motor that purred when you touched your foot to the pedal.

Andy signaled for the check. Maisie smiled in approval as he pulled out his credit card—between his generous stipend and the bonuses the sneaker company paid him for his wins, he had money to spend. Maisie didn't even try to reach for her wallet, the way Rachel always did. They strolled back to the hotel in an expectant silence. In the lobby, she looked into his eyes.

"Do you think I could come up for a glass of water?"

A voice spoke up in his head. Not Rachel's voice, not his mother's, not a voice belonging to any one of the coaches he'd had through the years, but Mr. Sills's voice, asking him, very seriously, *Is this the kind of man you want to be?*

Feeling like the biggest jackass in the world, Andy took her hand and folded it in his. "You're so beautiful," he said, "and I'm probably going to regret this for the rest of my life. But I'm not exactly single."

Maisie gave a pout that caused Andy to think that whatever she did when she'd finished modeling, it probably wouldn't be acting. "Shit," she said. Andy tried not to flinch. He didn't like cursing, never had; it reminded him of Lori, when she'd been drinking. "Why are all the good ones either taken or gay?"

"Come on," he'd said, giving her a tripod-style hug, careful to keep anything below their shoulders from touching. "You could have any guy in the world."

"But what if you're the guy I want?"

Andy didn't answer. He just wanted to get up to his room, splash some cold water on his face, and call Rachel. But Rachel didn't answer. The cold water didn't work, so Andy took a cold shower and masturbated briskly, like it was the sexual equivalent of clearing his throat. Still, it took him two hours to fall asleep, and when the alarm shrilled, he woke up with a groan, still feeling tired, thinking that if he blew the race Rachel would be to blame.

That afternoon, crouched and waiting for the pistol, exhaustion dragged at him, and he felt frustrated and angry. Poised at the starting line, his body curled and ready to spring, all he wanted to do was go back to the hotel and sleep. Instead of being nervous, the way he usually was, so tense that sometimes he'd throw up right before a race began, he felt tired and calm almost to the point of boredom . . . and then, when he started to run, a weird thing happened. He felt almost airy, like his body was made of something less dense and more durable than flesh and blood. Leaning into the turns, arms swinging smoothly, he knew he was setting up for a PR, maybe even a course record . . . and then what? Would Maisie be waiting at the finish line? Would Rachel call his cell phone, wanting to congratulate him?

Be your body, he thought. It wasn't one of his official mantras—*light and lean,* he'd taught himself to chant, or *no pain*—but, as he finished his first lap, that was what he told himself. He knew what this victory would mean—that Athens was a certainty, that he'd have his shot at the gold. With every step, he put more and more distance between himself and the guy behind him, breathing easily, moving effortlessly, thinking that he could run a marathon if he had to, that he could run forever.

He broke the tape, and then his coach was hugging him, shouting an unbelievable number in his ear. Andy looked up at the Jumbotron to confirm it, and there were TV cameras swinging toward his face, and there was Maisie, Maisie looking lovelier than he remembered, and he reached for her without thinking and pulled her into his arms.

Of course the pictures had ended up on the *Runner's World* website. Of course Rachel saw them. When he picked up his phone he saw that she'd called six times, and when he got back to the hotel to call her back she hadn't wasted a second before she'd started in on him.

"Rachel, it's nothing. It's just some girl. I met her in the gym, she's a runner, too, and she asked if she could come to the race, and I had no idea any of that was going to happen." This was technically mostly true, even if it left out several salient facts, including their dinner together the night before.

"So, what, someone shoved her into your arms and made you hug her?"

Once he'd started running he'd never been interested in ball sports, but he knew what they told the guys on the football team—the best defense is a good offense. "If you're so worried, then why didn't you come out here with me?"

She made a disgusted noise. "So I could sit in a hotel room all day, then watch you run for eight minutes, then spend all night at a party listening to people talk about how their eight minutes of running went?"

Andy was hurt. "I haven't run a three thousand in over eight minutes since my junior year at Oregon."

"Who cares?" Rachel shrieked. "And stop changing the subject! I don't care how fast you can run the three thousand. I care about you hugging random women!"

"Nothing happened," he said, already starting to regret that it was true.

"Do you even know her name?" Rachel demanded.

"Maisie," he'd said. "Maisie Guthrie." And then some impulse he didn't understand made him blurt, "She's a model."

"Oh, a model," she said. "Well, I guess you've hit the big time now."

Andy, who'd expected to at least get some congratulations on his personal record, was getting angry. "Would you let it go? She's someone I met, and she came there to watch me, to cheer for me, which was nice, so I hugged her. End of story."

There was a seething, crackling pause. "Are you saying," Rachel began, "that if I came to cheer for you, you wouldn't have felt the need to embrace models at the finish line?"

"Maybe!" Andy yelled. "I don't know! It's not like I've had a lot of experience with you coming to cheer for me!"

Instead of yelling back, Rachel spoke even more softly. "You want me to be the bad guy, don't you?" she asked. "You want me to be the bitch who won't go to your races so you'll have an excuse to be with Cindy Crawford. Only guess what?" Her voice was a poisonous whisper. "I'm not your mother. I actually do go to your races."

"You come and you sit there with a book. You barely look up. You barely look at me."

Another icy pause ensued. Finally Rachel said, speaking softly, "I am not your cheering squad."

"I know that," he muttered.

"I'm my own person."

If you keep eating the way you do, you'll be

323

your own two people, Andy thought, but all he said was, "I know."

"I think that maybe moving in with you was a mistake."

He felt her words like a hard shove in the chest . . . but, if he was honest, there was also the tiniest undercurrent of relief. "It wasn't a mistake. I want you with me."

"But we're not on equal footing, are we? You're working. Quote-unquote. You're making money. I'm not doing anything."

"But once you get your degree, you'll get a job." Rachel had been taking classes toward a social work degree at Portland State and had just started working at FAS's new West Coast office. "I hate not having my own money," she'd say when he'd buy them dinner or she'd use his credit card to shop for clothes. She did have money— her parents had paid for college, and she'd saved every birthday check and bat mitzvah gift—but it wasn't money she'd earned, and she felt that acutely.

"I think I need to go back to New York. Amy said she's got a job for me. There's work there I should be doing."

"Rachel." This was all happening too fast, like he'd pulled a loose shingle off a roof and now the whole house was falling down. "I don't want you to leave. I'm sorry I got mad."

"I'm sorry, too," she said, in a small voice that

hurt him more than her yelling had. "I shouldn't be surprised. You always wanted the new thing, right? No secondhand coats for you. I'll bet Miss Maisie doesn't have any nasty scars on her chest, right?"

"Rachel." He could hear her crying, and he didn't know how to comfort her, didn't know what to say.

"And she's probably not spoiled. Pulled herself up by her pretty little bootstraps, I bet. Not like snobby Rachel and her snobby sorority friends, right, Andy? Be honest. I was never good enough for you, and no matter what I did, I was never going to be."

She hung up the phone, and wouldn't answer it for the next two hours, at which point his teammates came by, rowdy and shouting and wanting to know why he wasn't at the bar. He went down, thinking that he'd have a few beers and try Rachel again. But there was Maisie, in a short dress that left her long legs bare. This time Andy didn't hesitate. He gulped a Scotch, grabbed Maisie around the waist, pulled her into a hug, and whispered, "Want to see my room?"

They'd started kissing in the elevator. Then they'd raced down the hall, hand in hand, with Andy fumbling for the key card and Maisie whispering, "Hurry, hurry." Once they were in the room, he pushed her back against the wall and kissed her hard, almost angrily, until she wriggled away. "Let me use the little girls' room," she said. Andy lay on the bed, still dressed, waiting, until she came out in nothing but a bathrobe, standing in front of him barefoot. "Hi there," she whispered, letting the robe slip off her shoulders, and stood there naked except for panties that were just a scrap of black lace.

"Like what you see?" she whispered. And oh, God, she was unbelievable. Like something out of a movie or a magazine. Her breasts were small and perfectly shaped, topped by taut nipples big as blackberries. He yanked her toward him, and bent and sucked.

Unreal, he thought, as his hands skimmed the curve of her hips, then cupped her ass. It was like she was a different species from Rachel, her waist so slim, her bottom so perfectly firm and round. Her pubic hair had been trimmed into a triangle that looked like an arrow directing him down. She was wet when he touched her, and she came almost as soon as he'd pushed himself inside, throwing her head back and sighing. "Handsome," she whispered. "Oh, you handsome man."

The next morning, he'd woken up to the sound of running water. He'd rolled onto his side in the fragrant, rumpled sheets, deciding how he should feel, if he was supposed to hate himself or feel like he'd gotten away with something, and who at the bar had seen them leave, and whether everyone knew. The water turned off, and the door opened, sending a puff of steam and the smell of soap into the room. When Maisie, wrapped in a towel, walked toward him, Andy braced for a scene, thinking that she would want promises, assurances that what they'd done had meant something, and that they'd see each other again. Instead, she'd kissed him lightly on his forehead. "Early call time," she'd whispered. "Here's my number." She put a scrap of paper on the nightstand, twisted her wet hair into a bun, pulled her dress on over her head, slipped on her shoes, and sashayed out the door. There had been no talk of fate or destiny or how they were meant to be together. She just gave him a smile, a last look at her perfect body, the beautiful angles of her cheeks and chin, and then she was gone.

When he'd gotten back to Oregon, all he found was the note that Rachel had left him. *I wish you all the best,* it said. By then he did feel guilty —a one-night stand was one thing, a breakup was something else. For two weeks he called her every day, morning, noon, and night. She never answered. He would have flown to see her, but he was in the most rigorous phase of his pretrial training—as Rachel knew. Then one afternoon his phone had rung, and it was Maisie, saying she was out in Vancouver, shooting editorial for a fashion magazine, and could she visit when she was done? Andy had said, "Sounds great."

At his apartment, which he'd carefully purged

of all signs of Rachel, Maisie told him about the shoot. "It's a big spread on some dead lady writer, so they've got, like, a bunch of important male writers being, like, Henry James and diplomats and architects and whatever."

"Who are you supposed to be?"

"Edith Wharton," Maisie said proudly. "Remember that movie Winona Ryder was in? With all the great costumes? Edith Wharton wrote the book that was based on."

"Why didn't they get an important female writer to be Edith Wharton?"

Maisie shrugged. "Dunno. Maybe they're all cows. I think the guy who played Henry James was hitting on me," she giggled, reaching for Andy. "Is that your jealous bone?" she'd whispered, sliding her hand down his pants. She'd stayed for three nights, during which Andy had enjoyed his teammates' approval and envy. At least most of them were approving. "Nice upgrade, man," said James Leonard, a sprinter, and Gary D'Allesandro, who ran the 1500, said, "If she's got a sister, I've got dibs."

Only Mitch had been dubious, Andy could tell. He missed Rachel. He never had much to say to Maisie when she came to watch them practice, and he'd find ways to be elsewhere when Maisie was at Andy's place. "She's beautiful! She's great!" he said when Andy finally asked if he had a problem with her. "Maisie's fantastic. I just . . . you know," he'd said, staring at the ground, "Rachel was great, too."

Andy agreed. He missed her . . . but by then it was too late. She was in New York City, back to what he bet she thought of as her real life, and that knowledge felt like a stone on his chest, something heavy that had fallen and that he'd have to carry for the rest of his life.

Summer came, and he flew to Sacramento for the Olympic tryouts. Even with his life in turmoil, his times kept getting better, as if pain was pushing him around the track, narrowing his focus until he couldn't see anything but the finish line. He wanted to call Rachel when he was named one of the two runners who'd represent the United States in the 5000-meter race in Athens, but Maisie had been there, hugging him, holding his hand, smiling for the photographers, almost like she was trying to make sure that she'd be in every shot. If Rachel saw the news, she probably saw Maisie, too.

He bought plane tickets for his mom and Mr. Sills, sending them to Greece three days early so they could get settled in, see the ruins, treat it like a vacation. Maisie paid her own way. "See you at the finish line," she'd said. He knew the drill—how the athletes would be bused from the airport straight to the Olympic Village, where they'd sleep, eat, and, in the case of the single men and women, hook up. Andy wasn't interested in any of that. When he wasn't eating or sleeping, he was running the race in his head, imagining his competitors, picturing himself powering past them in the first lap and leaving them farther and farther behind.

Thirty-five men ran the two heats for the 5000. Only fifteen of them qualified for the finals. Andy's time, thirteen minutes and twenty seconds, put him right in the middle of the pack, which was perfect—he hadn't burned himself out and run his best race in the qualifiers; he still had something left for the main event.

"Good luck, brother," said Tim Fine, the other American runner who had just missed qualifying for the finals. The rest of the field were Kenyans, Algerians, Moroccans, Ethiopians, guys who were twenty-one or twenty-two, tiny and light and looking like they'd been created specifically for speed. At five-ten and 160 pounds, Andy felt like a giant at the starting line, and was one of only three men in the field who hadn't been born in Africa. Then he'd shut down his mind and focused entirely on his breath. The sunny, slightly breezy day didn't matter, nor did the people in the stands, or his coaches, or his teammates, or all the memories of what had driven him to this place. When the gun went off Andy came charging onto the tracks, and the only thought in his head was *I will not be denied.* Hicham El Guerrouj, the presumptive favorite, hung back in the middle of the pack, biding his time until the last half mile, when his kick took him right to Andy's heels. He stayed with him up until the last two hundred meters, when, with his legs on fire and his body screaming at him to stop, Andy pushed even harder and crossed the line first, a mere fifth of a second before El Guerrouj. The whole race had taken just under ten minutes.

The rest of the day was a blur. His coaches shouted praise in his ear and someone handed him an American flag, which Andy wrapped around his shoulders as he trotted his victory lap. He hugged El Guerrouj, who was crying, and someone led Maisie and Lori and Mr. Sills down to the edge of the track to watch as the winners mounted the rostrum and were crowned with wreaths, and the medals were placed around their necks. Andy touched the medal, running his fingers over the engraving. He still couldn't believe that he'd done it, that he'd gotten what he dreamed of, that he'd won. He felt like he was made of light and air, untethered from all his old shames and sorrows, like he'd been elevated to some plane above other people, with their everyday jobs, their little joys and frustrations, and he'd never have to come down and live in the world again . . . and then, in that moment, a malevolent voice spoke up in his head, in a whisper that sounded like the rattle of old pennies in a beggar's cup. *What if it isn't enough?*

He shuddered as he felt the day suddenly turn cool, and the applause from the crowd turn into a dim, muffled sound, like waves slapping senselessly onto the sand. His body became flesh again, leaden and heavy and pebbled with goose bumps, and the familiar sorrow rose up to engulf him. He had taken every ribbon, won every prize, even this one, the ultimate, the gold medal. He had sacrificed so much—love, friendship, leisure, ownership of his own body and time. And now? What if not even all that was enough to quiet that voice, which sometimes sounded like his mother's and sometimes like the father he'd never known, the voice that said, *You're not worthy, you don't deserve it, nothing you do will ever be enough.*

Then his mother was shrieking in his ear, and he could hear the crowd chanting his name.

Mr. Sills, resplendent in a USA sweatshirt that stretched tight over her belly, kept lifting up his glasses to wipe underneath his eyes. Maisie wouldn't let go of his hand. "You'll need an agent," she said that night, and when Andy had looked at her, still dazed from the win, Maisie had kissed him and said, "You just leave everything to me."

Back at home, the medal went into a velvet-lined box, and Andy began his new life. First came the print ads for the sneakers he'd worn in

Athens. Then came the *Vanity Fair* profile (the sneaker ad ran right next to it, which made Andy wonder about the way those things worked). He and Maisie posed in *People* magazine's Most Beautiful edition. ("I'm not beautiful," Andy had said, to which Maisie had answered, "Sure you are . . . and I am, sugar, and this is publicity that all the money in the world can't buy.") More ads; more endorsement deals; his first pro-am golf tournament, where he played in a foursome with the world's top golfer, a network news anchor, and a basketball star he'd grown up watching. Maisie told him he needed a stylist, and he reluctantly agreed—it was easier than spending hours in stores trying to figure out what looked right. His publicist got him into the *New York Times*, just on the basis of his new look. Maisie had pouted when the photographer told her politely that she just wanted a shot of Andy, but cheered up when the piece on athletes as fashion trendsetters mentioned her by name and called her a supermodel.

Finally came the one thing he'd been hoping for, the call from *Sports Illustrated*. Their track reporter was a guy named Bob Rieper, known to the runners as the Grim Rieper. Bob was lean and tall and stooped, with a narrow rectangle of a face, dark hair that hung past his eyebrows, and a low, sonorous voice that seemed made to deliver bad news.

Bob had been in Athens to watch Andy win his medal. He'd seen him work out in Oregon, where he still stayed and trained at the camp, and in New York, where he'd gotten a place with Maisie. Bob had talked to him about the 2008 games and had accompanied him on a trip back to Philadelphia, where Andy spoke at an elementary school, introducing Bob to Mr. Sills and to Lori. In all that time, Andy had never heard him laugh, never seen him smile.

It was Bob's voice on the phone that morning, waking him up from a dream, where he'd been back in Philadelphia, chasing a woman wearing Rachel's blue cowgirl boots down Frankford Avenue.

"Hey, man, what's up?"

Bob did not believe in small talk. "I need to run something by you."

"What's that?"

"It's about your father."

Andy felt nothing but mild curiosity as he got out of bed and walked to the window, asking, "What about him?"

"You told me that he died in Germany when you were a baby."

"That's right."

"And that you don't remember him at all, and you never tried to find out any of the details."

"Uh-huh." Across the room, Maisie was looking

at him, eyebrows lifted. Andy held up a finger—one minute. Maisie nodded and rolled over as Andy said, "What's up?"

"This is hard," Bob said. "I've never had to tell anyone anything like this before."

"Tell me what?" When he paused, Andy realized that he was bouncing up and down on his toes and drumming his fingers on his thigh.

Across the line, Andy heard him sigh. "The fact-checkers found out that there was a guy named Andrew Landis who went to Roman Catholic, who graduated when your father would have graduated and whose enlistment dates line up with what you've told me."

"Okay . . ."

"But that guy's not dead."

Andy had been pacing, the way he always did when he talked on the phone. When he heard the words *not dead* he stopped, frozen.

"You're kidding," he said, in a voice that didn't sound like his own.

"Not dead," Bob repeated. "He went to prison in 1979. His friend shot someone—a rival drug dealer, it sounds like. That guy gave your dad the gun to get rid of, but the cops caught him with it, which made him an accessory to murder. And because he'd been in trouble before, the judge threw the book at him."

Andy thought later that he must have said something or made some noise, because he felt

Maisie's hand on his shoulder, and her face looked frightened. He shook his head, mouthed, *It's okay,* held up a finger again, and said, "What kind of trouble?"

"Drug dealing, larceny, burglary, grand theft auto . . ."

"Wow," he said, and tried to laugh. "Maybe tell me what he didn't do. Maybe that would take less time."

"I have to put some of this in my story," Bob said. "You understand. If I don't write about this, somebody else is going to, and now that I know about it, I can't not use it. I just wanted to give you a chance to say something, if you want to."

"I get it," Andy said. He walked down the hall of their spacious and still barely furnished apartment, then into the bathroom, where a face he didn't recognize stared from the mirror. *Alive. In prison.* He'd never tried to get in touch. His mom had never said a word. Had she known? How could she not have? "But it wasn't . . . I mean, he wasn't—he was an accessory, but he didn't kill anyone, right?"

"It looks that way. He just got caught holding the gun. Bad luck." Andy couldn't stand the sympathy in the Grim Rieper's voice, thick as frosting on a birthday cake. "Why don't you take some time? Talk to your people. I'll ask you to comment at some point, but don't worry about that now."

A horrifying thought struck him. "Are you going to talk to him?" Andy asked.

"I'll probably reach out. He was paroled eighteen months ago. He's living in Philadelphia now," said Bob. "It's a part of your story."

My story, thought Andy. Is that what he'd become? And if he had to be a story, why couldn't he just be the one he'd crafted, the one he'd been working on since high school, the one *Vanity Fair* and the *Philadelphia Examiner* and all those other places had been content to repeat? *Andy Landis, winner. Andy, who'll push himself to the front of the pack and hang on. He'll pay the price, no matter how high. Andy Landis, who came up from the slums of Philadelphia to win gold in Greece.* Wasn't that a story anyone would want to read? It was simple. Inspiring. American.

He must have said goodbye somehow, because Andy found himself with a phone in his hand buzzing the dial tone, and Maisie looking at him.

"You're not going to believe this," he began . . . and then he found himself wishing, with an intensity that felt like a fever, that he wasn't talking to her; that he was telling Rachel instead.

But Rachel wouldn't take his calls, and Maisie was looking at him, a question on her lovely face.

"It's my dad," he said.

"What do you mean, your dad? Your dad's dead."

"That's what my mom told me," Andy managed. "Except *SI* just found out that he's not. He spent twenty years in jail, and now he's living in Philadelphia."

"Jesus, what'd he do?"

"He was an accessory to murder." Andy punched in his mom's number. When she didn't answer, he said, "Hey, Ma, it's Andy. Can you call me as soon as you get this? It's important." Even as he was hanging up he was realizing that there was nothing that Lori could possibly say to explain this, no way that she could justify that big of a lie.

"Oh, baby," said Maisie. She put her hands on his shoulders and started kneading, a move Andy always found more of an annoyance than a comfort—her hands were so small that she couldn't exert enough pressure for it to feel good—but he'd never said anything. "Oh my God. I can't even . . . Tell me what I can do."

"I don't know," he said. He didn't know how he felt or what he wanted or what the next move should be. He dialed his mother again. No answer. Maisie started in on his neck, and Andy felt like the apartment walls were crushing him, like his clothes were too tight, like his skin was shrinking, and that if he didn't move he would explode.

"Give me a minute." He scrambled into pants, a long-sleeved shirt, and one of the dozens of pairs of sneakers he had, and was out the door without stretching or planning or even telling her where he was going, across the street and into the park, running without a heart monitor or energy gels or the watch that tracked his distance and speed, as fast as he could, until he stopped somewhere along the East River path, pulled out his phone, and punched in the digits he was surprised he still remembered.

She won't answer, Andy thought. *It's not her number anymore. And what can I even say to her? And what will she say to me?*

The phone rang once, then twice, and Andy was about to hang up and put the phone in his pocket, or maybe call a private investigator and try to figure out what had happened and where his dad was now, when a voice said, "Hello," and then, "Andy?"

"Hey, Rachel." Andy stopped and looked around, taking a moment to realize that he'd run far enough to see the Domino Sugar sign across the river.

"What's wrong?"

"How do you know something's wrong?"

"You call me after all this time and you sound awful. Something's wrong." Oh, Rachel. Her voice was so familiar. It all felt so familiar, like they'd picked up a conversation that they'd ended the night before.

"It's my father," Andy said. "He's not dead."

"What?" He heard her talk to someone, then rustling, the sound of a door slamming shut. "Sorry. I thought . . . Did you just say your father's alive?"

"Alive," he repeated. His voice sounded hoarse. His body felt knotted, fists clenched, quads and hamstrings tight. "He didn't die. He got arrested. He's just been in jail for almost my whole life."

"Oh my God." He could picture Rachel thinking, could remember how they would rest together, her head snuggled against his chest; how she'd look at the ceiling and click her tongue against the roof of her mouth. The smell of her hair, the softness of her arms. The way she'd make him laugh. "What are you going to do?" she asked.

"I don't know. Go home, I guess. Talk to my mom. Try to find him. Try to ask him . . ." He lurched backward as a pack of cyclists sped by. "Ask why he didn't want to know me."

"Oh, Andy," she said, her voice so sad, so familiar, so dear, that Andy felt like his body, the finely balanced tool that he'd fueled and coddled and cared for, was crumbling, like it was made of ash or salt. "Oh, Andy."

"Rachel," he croaked . . . and, just as he blurted, "Could you come with me?" he heard her say, "I'm getting married next month."

"Married?" It hit him as if one of the shot-putters had aimed wrong and sent sixteen pounds of iron crashing into his gut. He opened his mouth and the word "Congratulations" hopped out like a toad.

Her voice was tiny. "I was going to call you . . . before it happened, to tell you, but I thought . . ."

How could you? he thought . . . except he had no right to ask that; no claim on her. He'd never tried to get her back, never even tried to tell her that he still thought of her, that he still imagined that somehow they would end up together.

"He's a great guy," she said, and he heard her trying to sound enthusiastic, like she was selling herself on her soon-to-be-husband's greatness . . . and then, in a whispered rush, just before she cut the connection, he thought he heard her say, "Sometimes I wish it had been you."

Rachel

2003

It won't hurt like this forever. That was what I told myself when I was curled on my bed crying, or lying there motionless, feeling stunned and sick and sad, like I couldn't get out of bed, like I couldn't go back and be in the world. *The only way through it is through it.* At least he hadn't pretended that he wanted me with him, hadn't made a big fake effort at getting me to stay. The truth was that I'd been a distraction, poorly suited for a world where the sole focus was on bodies and times, where the party talk was all about lactic acid threshold; where, instead of holding me close and saying that he loved me, Andy's first move every morning was to lie on the floor with a foam roller under his hips, or work his legs with a tool that looked like a plastic windshield wiper designed for myofascial release.

I had packed up my stuff while he was still in New York. I'd thought about going back to Florida, but the picture of my parents' faces, the way that they'd be thinking, if not saying, *I told you so,* made the idea unbearable. Instead, I'd flown to New York, couch-surfed until I'd found a little efficiency on West Eighty-Sixth Street, reenrolled at NYU, and gotten a paying job at the Family Aid Society, where Amy was still my boss and, no big surprise, Brenda was still a client.

"Ooh, girl, what happened to you?" asked Brenda. We'd been scheduled for a nine o'clock meeting, and I'd been waiting on her front steps as she hopped out of a stranger's car, looking perky in knee-high fringed black boots and a cropped black leather jacket. She had cut baby bangs, a quarter-inch fringe. It was a look only girls with perfect features and beautifully shaped skulls could pull off, and Brenda, cute as she was, was not one of them. Andy's new girl probably was. I'd looked her up on the Internet and she was exactly what I'd expected—gorgeous, exotic, with slim hips and small, elegant breasts and a face that seemed flawless from every angle. "Your basic nightmare," I'd told my friends. Amy had asked if I'd wanted to stay with her and Leonard for a while. Pamela had offered to come up from Virginia, and Marissa had volunteered to come down from Vermont. All three of them had told me that I was too good for him, that they'd never trusted him, that world-class runner or not, it was bizarre for any woman to sleep with a guy who had a smaller butt than she did.

"You're late," I told Brenda. It was Monday, mid-March, cold and clear, with trees just starting to show nubs of nascent blossoms. I hated it. I wanted weather like my mood, the skies gray and stormy, ripped by lightning. I had hardly slept for the last month, had barely eaten. The last conversation I'd had with Andy was playing on a loop in my head, illustrated with images of Maisie, leaving me exhausted and with no patience for Brenda's nonsense.

"Yeah. My car broke down, so, um, my friend, um, Lynn, was giving me a ride."

"Your friend Lynn looks exactly like your ex-boyfriend Stephen. You need to be on time for our appointments. No matter what. You know that our help depends on me signing off on your compliance."

"I'll try," said Brenda, sounding unapologetic. She unlocked the front door, leading me up three flights of narrow stairs and into the chaos that she'd managed to re-create in the three different apartments she'd had since I'd known her. A bird in a cage shrilled from a bedroom. Her dog lay farting on the floor. I could hear the frantic beating of the bird's wings, and I could smell cigarette smoke, male sweat, cheap perfume. There were newspapers and magazines layered on the coffee table, shoes and socks on the floor, a coat crumpled in one corner, and the TV remote, backless and emptied of batteries, on the couch. Brenda picked it up, examined it, then held it as she sat. "I had to turn the cable off. Too expensive."

When I didn't answer, she continued. "And then my car broke down, and the guy at the shop won't give me a loaner. 'Go get a rental,' he says."

"Is the car under warranty?"

Brenda looked at me like I'd stopped speaking English, and my sorrow hit me like a sandbag. "You know what?" I said, gathering my bag. I'd stuffed it with a fistful of folders before leaving the office without even making sure they were the right ones. "I'll come back next week."

"Wait, what? You're leaving? But what about my car?"

"What about the subway?"

Her brown eyes widened. "Why are you being so mean?" she whispered. "The whole time I've known you, you've never been mean to me. Never once."

I leaned against the wall. "I owe you an apology," I said, but Brenda wasn't done.

"Everyone else is mean. The people at the OCFS, the people at the school. The supermarket checkers, when I give them my card, everyone else in line, they all look at me like I'm nothing. But you don't make me feel bad."

"I'm sorry," I said. "I've been dealing with some personal issues."

Her expression brightened. "What happened?" she asked, leaning forward, ready to dish. "Why'd you come back, anyhow? You split up with your man?"

"This is not appropriate. I really need to go." A vague memory surfaced. "Did you ever get Dante tested for ADHD?"

Brenda's face fell. "Oh, yeah. That shit. So guess what? No ADHD. He's gifted," she said, her tone making it clear this was not a welcome development.

"Congratulations."

"Yeah, right," she said. "You don't get money for gifted."

"Actually, you can," I said, pulling on my coat, zipping up my bag. "It's a special condition. There's money for enrichment . . ." The zipper caught. I yanked it hard, and it broke off in my hand. My bag burst open, spilling papers all over Brenda's floor. I crouched down to start picking up the mess, and found that I couldn't move. I rocked back on my heels and covered my face with my hands as tears started spilling down my cheeks.

"Oh, now." Tentatively, Brenda touched my shoulder, then wrapped her arm around me, helping me stand. "Hey. Come on. No man's worth all this."

I didn't say a word as she led me to the couch. I just kept crying. Brenda handed me a box of Kleenex (name brand, even though we'd discussed how generic was the exact same thing) and then a cup of instant coffee. "Look at us," she said, and shook her head. "The two saddest girls in New York."

I went to Brenda's bathroom, splashed water on my face, went back to the office, then took the subway home. I made myself behave like I was a normal, functioning person. I set my alarm, savoring the handful of seconds after I woke up and before I remembered what Andy had done, where I was, and that I was alone. I forced myself out of bed and into clothes. I saw my clients, kept my appointments, attended my review session for the licensing exam. At the end of the day, I stopped at the corner grocery, bought a frozen Marie Callender's chicken potpie, put it in the toaster oven, and took a shower while it cooked. By the time the hot water ran out, my dinner was done. I put on a robe, ate my pie with a glass of wine, climbed into bed, took one of the Ambien I'd talked my doctor into prescribing, and fell asleep like I'd been concussed. I wouldn't let myself call him or go near the Internet to look up his race results or see if there were pictures of him, of her, of them together. I tried to remember the bad stuff, how it felt to be the only person in Andy's little enclave who had any visible body fat, the way the female runners looked at me when I'd gone to use the gym; the way I was always the last thing on Andy's mind, behind his workouts, his diet, his training schedule, the race he'd be running the next month or the one he'd run the month before, and how every time I suggested going out to dinner or to a movie or a play or a museum, he was either too busy or too tired. *What kind of a life was that?* I'd asked myself . . . and then I would remember something—having sex in the shower, or how it felt when he'd laugh, and I couldn't lie—despite all the annoyance and embarrassment, it had been the life I'd wanted.

By June, the weather was brutally humid, but Amy insisted that I walk with her to SoHo, then join her for a drink. "Here's to love," she said, lifting her Champagne cocktail. "I signed you up for JDate."

"Oh, no. No. Please no."

"It's not up for discussion," she said, handing me her phone so I could see my profile. At least she'd used a good picture, I thought bleakly, a shot from when I'd been a bridesmaid at Pamela Boudreaux's wedding, my hair drawn back in a chignon, with a single white camellia behind my ear.

"Just go on ten dates," Amy said.

"Five," I bargained.

"Eight," she countered. "Look, if you don't get out there you're just going to spend every Saturday watching *Sleepless in Seattle* and *When Harry Met Sally* on your couch."

"And that's wrong because . . . ?"

"There's a guy out there for you," Amy said. "You have to open yourself up to the universe's possibilities."

"Did your yoga teacher say that?"

"No. I think I read it on a napkin at the new salad place."

"Here's the thing," I said. "What if I already met the guy out there for me? Only he dumped me for a swimsuit model?" As far as I knew, Maisie did not solely model swimwear. Still, whenever I described her, I called her a swimsuit model. It sounded so much worse than just "model."

"Honey," she said, "Andy was not the guy for you."

"How do you know?"

"Because if he was," she said, "he'd be here. Or you'd still be there. You'd be together, and you'd probably be engaged."

It was hard to argue, and easy to log on to the website, sort through the hundreds of guys, like they were entrees on a Love menu. Lots of them looked good and sounded funny and interesting. Then again, I thought, how hard was it to look presentable and sound acceptable online? On the Internet, every guy was a catch.

"It's a numbers game," Amy told me. She counseled me not to get too attached too soon, to develop a thick skin and keep it moving, setting up dates with other guys even while I was waiting to hear from a promising prospect. "Prepare for the worst," she'd said . . . but the worst turned out to be so much worse than I had ever imagined.

My first encounter was with a charmer named Nate, an off-line fix-up and a fraternity brother of Pam's cousin Martin. I arrived at the agreed-upon bar, a place in Midtown near his office, ten minutes early, and was sitting with a glass of chardonnay when Nate showed up, wearing fashionable eyeglasses and carrying a cool canvas bag. He was a little more jowly than he'd appeared in his picture. In repose, his face had a kind of smugness, an expression that said *I have sampled many of life's finer things and expect to enjoy many more.* "Hi there!" he said, his hand extended. The smile on his mouth didn't reach his eyes, which were cool and assessing, moving around the room, possibly scoping for better prospects. "You're Rachel?"

"I'm Rachel." Greek life at our respective campuses would give us a solid ten minutes of conversation, I thought; his job as a speechwriter for the mayor and mine with the Family Aid Society would be good for another ten, at which point we should have finished our beverages and gotten some sense about whether we wanted to see each other again.

The hostess led us to a table. A waiter approached. Nate asked for Scotch as I swallowed a yawn. "You feel like getting food?" he asked.

"I had a late lunch," I lied. I hadn't had lunch at all, had gobbled a granola bar on the subway uptown so my stomach wouldn't grumble during our date. I didn't want food. I wanted to be home, with my boots off and my bra unhooked, a bowl of Cream of Wheat on the table and *Friends* on TV.

"Okay if I order something?"

No. "Sure, that's fine."

"Lunchtime just got away from me. I completely forgot to eat."

I didn't trust people who forgot to eat. Andy, I remembered, didn't trust short men. "They've all got something to prove," he'd said. I pushed Andy out of my mind, wondering how long it would take to permanently evict his voice from my head, and tried to focus on Nate, who was not short, and was Jewish, and reasonably handsome, and perfectly acceptable.

Nate ordered a burger, well-done, with fries. "You sure you don't want anything?" he asked, so I got some soup. Eight dollars for a bowl of watery chicken broth with mealy, limp noodles. I could have made an entire pot of the stuff for eight dollars, and it would have tasted better than what I'd been served. Soup had been one of my go-tos when I'd lived with Andy, healthy enough for him, indulgent enough for me. I'd learned to make three different kinds of lentil soup, split pea, minestrone, Italian wedding soup with tiny meatballs, pungent with garlic and cheese . . .

"So!" Nate had a strand of something green between his two front teeth. Nice hair, I told myself. Nice, thick hair, not a sign of thinning or receding. Focus on the good stuff. Maybe this could work. "Tell me about yourself!"

I'd gotten as far as "born in Florida" when Nate interrupted, launching into the story of his grand-parents, who'd retired in Sarasota, continuing on to the highlights of the spring break he'd spent in St. Pete in 1999 and how, in general, he preferred ski vacations to beaches. "Too much sand in too many places, you know?" Pausing for a bite of burger, he chewed, swallowed, and said, "Do you ski?"

"Never learned. I had a heart condition when I was little, so my parents were really cautious about what they'd let me do."

"Ah." He returned to his burger. Usually,

dropping *heart condition* into a conversation would prompt at least a few questions, a bit of back-and-forth about exactly what was wrong and whether it was better, but Nate seemed more interested in his meal than my health. I stifled another yawn and sneaked a glance at my watch, an inexpensive Timex. Nana had gotten me a Cartier Tank watch, but it caused too much trouble when I wore it to work. Brenda, I remembered, had asked to try it on, had turned her wrist from side to side, then had gotten teary and said, "I'll never have anything this pretty." Andy's watch had monitored his heart rate. Sometimes I'd make him wear it when we were in bed, to see if his heart rate jumped when I kissed him and did other things.

"So tell me about speechwriting," I said.

For five minutes, Nate talked and ate, describing how he'd landed his job (his father had been the mayor's urologist), and how the mayor consistently ruined his best efforts with his high-pitched, nasal voice. Then, somehow, we were back to skiing again. "I learned to ski in Vermont. Didn't ski on powder until I got to college. It was, like, a totally different thing."

Possibly my desperation was starting to create its own gravitational pull, because not one but two waiters came to our table. "We're all set here," said Nate, pushing his last two french fries into his mouth without asking if I wanted anything else. I made the expected gesture toward my purse; he did the obligatory wave-away, saying, "No, no, I got this." In less than two minutes the bill was paid, and we'd collected our coats and bags and were out on the street. "That's me," I said, gesturing toward the subway, trying to decide what I'd do if he went in for the kiss or put me on the spot by asking for another date.

No such luck . . . or no such problem. "Listen, it was great meeting you, but I'll be honest. I'm not sure I'm seeing a future."

"Mmm." I wasn't interested in feedback any more than I was interested in seeing him again, but Nate took my noncommittal noise as a request for explanation.

"You're a great gal, and I'm sure there's a lot of guys who'd be into you, but I mostly date eights and nines."

I'd been slinging my work bag over my shoulder. When he said *eights and nines,* I paused, midsling, positive that I'd heard him wrong. "I beg your pardon?"

"Eights and nines," he repeated, as if it was a normal and inoffensive thing to be rating women like coins in a collection or steaks in the butcher's case—choice, select, prime.

"And I'm a . . ."

He had the nerve to put his glasses on for a closer look. "Did you ever think about straightening your hair?"

I looked past him. The sidewalks were full of people carrying takeout containers and briefcases and shopping bags, people on cell phones, people on bikes, people just walking around like the world was a normal place where everyone obeyed the social contracts and men understood they couldn't go around casually assigning women numbers outside of the privacy of their own heads.

"You're a jerk," I said in a pleasant voice.

"Hey, hey!" He held up his hands, the universal male gesture of *I didn't do it.* "There's plenty of fish in the sea."

"You have bad breath," I said in that same polite voice. I didn't know whether it was true— luckily, I hadn't gotten close enough to smell— but there'd been raw onion on his burger, so it felt like a safe bet. "And you have small, womanish hands." Nate looked at his hands. Then looked at me. "Girlie fingers," I said, and lifted my head, curly hair and all, and walked away.

I didn't cry until I'd made it home, until the door was locked, my work clothes were off, and I was wrapped in my cozy chenille robe, with my unlikable hair in a ponytail. *You're beautiful,* I heard . . . in Andy's voice. *No, you are. You're beautiful.*

Nate, thankfully, was the low point . . . but it didn't get much better. A copywriter for an ad agency spent the whole date complaining about his ex ("I think she was bipolar," he said). A rabbi, funny and charming, spat tiny chunks of food when he talked. A banker rhapsodized about the amazing vacation he'd just taken with his mom. When he showed me pictures of the two of them together, with Mom in a bikini, her arm around his waist, I feigned an appointment and told him that I had to go.

It wasn't always awful. I had a few second and third dates that fizzled out painlessly. I met nice guys to whom I was not attracted; attractive guys who weren't especially nice. No one made me feel passionate, no one even had me wanting to know him better, to hear about his childhood pets and his first girlfriend and what he wanted his life to be like.

Finally, at Amy's insistence, I agreed to meet one of her friends. "He's a little bit older," Amy cautioned.

I raised an eyebrow. "How old?"

"My age."

"Ancient."

Amy threw a packet of paper clips at my head. "You'll like him. He's a do-gooder. Did Teach for America, then the Peace Corps, then AmeriCorps."

"So, lots of America, lots of corps. What's he do now?"

"He went to law school, but he's been working as an editor."

"What's he edit?"

Amy paused. I crossed my arms over my chest. "What is it?"

"The last time we talked, he was editing a magazine for urban farmers."

"Oh, no. Come on. Do I look like someone who wants to be around goats?"

"I don't think he actually has goats, he's just running a magazine for people who do."

"That's not any better! He's probably got a chicken coop in his living room," I said.

"He can't be worse than the Spitting Rabbi."

"If he uses the word *artisanal,* I'm leaving."

"That sounds fair."

"Also 'curated.' None of that. No curation."

"Fine."

"And he's never been married? What's the story there?"

Amy shrugged. "Sometimes there's not a story except 'he just didn't meet the right girl.' "

"Fine," I grumbled. "But I'm oh for eight. If this is a bust, you owe me dinner at Shun Lee."

On Friday night, I did my hair, wriggled into my date dress, and arrived early at my favorite wine bar so I could watch him come through the door. The place served a "grown-up grilled cheese" that I'd decided was the sandwich of the gods, made with homemade sourdough bread and three different cheeses. *Twelve bucks for a sandwich?* I'd heard Andy complaining in my head the first time I'd ordered it. *Nobody's making you pay for it,* I told him. *Now go away.*

The door opened and, maybe because I'd been thinking about him, for one desperate half second I imagined it would be Andy; Andy, come to his senses, Andy, come to rescue me from men who spat or obsessed about their exes or took their mothers to couples' resorts. But of course it wasn't Andy, it was Jay Kravitz, who had shiny brown hair and a generous nose and a nice smile. He held out his hand, saying, "It's Rachel, right?"

"Rachel. Right." He wasn't especially handsome, but his smile improved his looks, and he had a nice firm handshake, and smelled good, like he used just the right amount of some delicious cologne. He pulled out the chair at our table for two, sat down across from me, and looked at me more closely, his expression warm and thoughtful. *Hmm,* I thought to myself as I felt something inside me shifting. At the very least, he'd gotten my attention.

"What would you like? Just drinks, or can I talk you into splitting a sandwich?"

I wanted a grilled cheese so badly I was fighting the urge to snatch one off the plate that had just been set in front of the man at the next table, but I said, "How about we just do drinks? I'm actually meeting someone at seven." A few years ago a book called *The Rules* had become the single girl's bible, and rule number one was

357

never to be too available. If you wanted a man to think of you as a potential wife, you should never okay a last-minute assignation. You had to make him wait, make him chase, let him think that you had suitors lined up and vying for your time. Having no actual plans, I thought that I'd call Amy, who'd be finishing work, to see if she could meet me for a debrief; or I could just have a latte at the Starbucks down the street.

"Is it another guy? It's another guy, isn't it?" Jay pretended to sulk. When I didn't answer, he said, "Tell you what. You meet him, and I'll read my paper, and if it's a no-go you come back here and we'll have dinner."

"What if he's it?" I teased. "What if he's the one?"

"Then I'll let him have you," Jay said, assuming an expression of noble resignation as he spread out his *New York Times*. "Far be it from me to thwart true love's course."

"Did you say 'thwart'?"

"I did," he said, nodding. "I thwarted."

I smiled, ordered a glass of wine from the waitress, and said, "Amy tells me you're an editor."

He shook his head. "An editor no more."

"You gave up on urban farming?"

"There's only so much you can say about how to get around the zoning laws so that you can keep rabbits in Red Hook. So I've gone slinking back to the law."

I fake-applauded. He mock-bowed. "I'm actually an adjunct criminal law professor at NYU. I thought you should know, in case Amy told you all about how I dug latrines in Sierra Leone and you were looking for some kind of Mellors-the-gamekeeper thing."

I smiled and looked away, wondering how he'd known that was exactly what I'd been imagining, and how he knew I'd read *Lady Chatterley's Lover*, which I'd discovered in my parents' bookcase, between *What Color Is Your Parachute?* and a Passover cookbook titled *Let My People Eat*. It would be nice to date a reader. Andy's shelves had featured guides to running, biographies of runners, memoirs by runners, and not one but two copies of *Once a Runner*.

Two white wines and several literary references later, it was time for me to go. Jay stood, walked me out, then said, "Hope to see you soon." I went to a newsstand, bought a tabloid, read half of it in a Starbucks, and then, trying to manage my expectations and prepare for the worst, I went back to the bar.

Jay was reading the Metro section. "No good?" he asked. He looked like he was glad to see me. I found that I was glad to see him.

"I'm starving," I said, and he stood and took my hand, then gave my cheek a kiss.

"Then let's eat."

Over grilled cheese, I learned that Jay was

thirty-four, the oldest of three, with a brother in banking and a sister in grad school. His mother had died of breast cancer when he was twenty-nine. His father did trust and estates law in Greenwich, and expected Jay to join the practice someday.

"Will you?"

"Probably," he said cheerfully. "It's not the most exciting work in the world, but the hours are usually pretty reasonable, and you're hardly ever in court. And it's steady. People are always going to need wills, and rich people are always going to need help figuring out how to keep their greedy kids from snatching their money."

I answered his questions about my job, and the families I was working with, imagining what it would be like to spend time with a guy who was content and comfortable, who wasn't constantly pushing himself, endlessly striving for something that was impossibly hard to attain.

Jay was exactly what my parents would want for me; as perfect as if they'd put him together in some kind of build-a-guy workshop. He'd gone to George Washington and spent his twenties volunteering before law school at Columbia. He'd been in two serious long-term relationships but had been single for the past year. He came from the same kind of background that I did—Jewish, but not super observant, with parents who were comfortably upper-middle-class, but not rich. His passion, he said, was Scrabble, which he played in tournaments. "You shouldn't be too impressed," he told me. "It's not about being a genius. It's more about knowing every two-letter word in the world."

Modest, I thought. A reasonable hobby. A dry, self-deprecating sense of humor, a nice, lived-in face. I could get used to this.

On our second date—*Lost in Translation* at Lincoln Center and noodle soup at a new ramen place afterward—I'd told him stories of how my brother, Jonah, had been so jealous of the attention I'd gotten in the hospital that he'd once tried to feign a brain tumor so he'd get special treats, and Jay told me about his sister's eating disorder, and how weird it had been to visit her in the hospital. "I just kept thinking, 'Eat something! How hard can it be? Have a cheeseburger and you can come home!' " He rode the subway with me, even though he lived uptown, and walked me to my door. "I think you have a beautiful heart," he said, and kissed me. His words didn't move me as much as Andy's once had . . . but I wasn't sixteen anymore, and Andy was gone. I'd spent too many mornings learning that over and over again, waking up hopeful and then feeling the sadness settle into me like a sickness, as soon as I remembered what was starting to feel like the central fact of my existence: *Andy is gone.*

On our third date, Jay and I went out for sushi.

In an enormous, dimly lit room, behind big white plates decorated with curls of white or pinkish flesh, tiny mounds of rice and wasabi, and shreds and flecks of vegetable, we swapped bar and bat mitzvah stories, and Jay told me about the first time he'd had sex, how he and his high school girlfrind had shared a bottle of wine in the room at the Days Inn that they'd gotten, and he'd ejaculated on her thigh and spent five minutes apologizing before he realized that she'd passed out. After the check for a hundred and twenty dollars came we admitted to each other that we were both still starving, and hurried out into the frigid November night, holding hands, mitten to mitten. We race-walked to the Burger Bar, hidden behind heavy velvet curtains in the lobby of Le Parker Meridien, and ordered two cheese-burgers, plus an order of fries and a brownie. Jay had a beer; I had a chocolate malted and licked ketchup off my fingers, saying, "I know it's cool to love sushi, but I just don't."

"Since we're confessing our secrets," Jay began. I sat up straight. So far, Jay had been wonderfully transparent, a what-you-see-is-what-you-get guy. Had that been a lie, or too good to last? He tugged at his sleeves and finally said, "I don't know how you feel about fur, if you're one of those anti-fur people, but I figure that if this"—and here he gestured with one of his hands at the beer, the burgers, the table, and me—

"is going to turn into a thing, I should tell you that there's a fur in the family. My bubbe gave it to my mom, and my mom gave it to me, to give to the girl that I marry."

A flush spread across my face. I wanted to sit for a minute, to cherish the possibility of actually marrying this guy, of someone liking me enough to want to be with me forever. I examined myself, looking for trepidation or anxiety, but all I felt was calm and happy. I was glad I'd found Jay, and thrilled that the hunt would be over, that I could relax into a relationship and stop trying so hard, keeping up with my manicures and my highlights and my leg waxing, making sure my date dresses were dry-cleaned, gobbling Altoids so that my breath would always be sweet, skipping desserts even when I wanted them. "Why wouldn't your sister get it?"

"Robin's a vegan. Hasn't eaten food with a face since she was eight. And she's not one of the quiet, don't-rock-the-boat kind, either. Her ring tone is 'Meat Is Murder.' " Jay leaned back in his chair. Unlike Andy, who was always jigging and tapping, Jay could sit in a chair or lie on my couch as still as a lizard sunning itself on a rock. "I don't know. I think it'd be different if it was a mink, but it's not. Sheared beaver. Doesn't that sound pornographic? My bubbe used to wear it on High Holidays."

"Of course she did," I said. You rarely saw furs

in Florida, but the handful of times I'd been to synagogue when the temperature had dipped below sixty degrees, out they came. The ladies would fan themselves with their announcement brochures, with their coats draped over their tennis-tanned shoulders and their handbags hanging from their golf-muscled forearms.

"So you're fur-tolerant?" He looked so funny and so hopeful that I laughed.

"When I was six I had a rabbit fur coat. In Florida. With a matching muff. Which also sounds pornographic."

"Matching muff," Jay repeated. Underneath the table, his knee bumped mine. It retreated, then returned, pressing firmly, and I could feel myself getting flushed and wobbly.

He leaned across the table and kissed my cheek, then nuzzled the spot just below my earlobe. I shivered, letting my eyes slip shut. "You're a cutie," he whispered in my ear.

"You're a sweetheart," I whispered back.

"Are you busy tomorrow?"

I didn't even try to be coy, to make up some excuse or tell him something about needing to check my calendar. "Busy with you."

Over the spring and the summer, we went to restaurants and movies and plays. We spent afternoons in parks and museums. We strolled across the Brooklyn Bridge—from Brooklyn to Manhattan, so it didn't bring up memories of that terrible, wonderful day—and had falafel at the flea market. We ventured to Jamaica Plain in Boston because Jay had read that a restaurant there had the best samosas in the world; we sampled bulgogi in Queens and arepas in the Bronx and poured liquefied chicken fat on our potatoes at Sammy's Roumanian on the Lower East Side.

Jay was sweet and funny and endlessly solicitous, always offering to carry whatever packages or bags I had, always holding doors. At restaurants, he'd pull out my chair and stand when I left the table; in bars and clubs, he'd stake out someplace comfortable for me to sit. *I could get used to this,* I thought again, on a bench at Rockefeller Center, with Jay kneeling in front of me, lacing up my rented skates. Out on the ice, he held my elbow as I giggled and slid into the wall. My cheeks glowed underneath my wool hat, he looked handsome in his blue plaid scarf, and every time a voice spoke up in my head, whispering *Not Andy,* informing me that while this guy might be a perfect match on paper, he didn't make me feel the way Andy had, I would tell the voice to shut up. Andy had left me, not the other way around. I'd loved him, and he'd left me, and now I had to move on.

Before long, Jay had essentially moved into my apartment. I'd been worried about every-thing my friends and various magazines had told me that living with a guy entailed—socks on the floor, wet towels on the bed, dishes in the sink. It turned out that Jay was neater than I was, though he never criticized when I dumped my bag by the front door or left my sweater on the couch.

When the Olympics began, I ignored them, willing myself to walk past any television set that was tuned to the games, tipping Jay's sports-related magazines directly into the trash. I knew that Andy had won a gold medal—as much as I tried to avoid any news, I couldn't stop myself from finding that out—but I wouldn't permit myself to try to learn where he lived, or send him a note that said *Congratulations*. If I couldn't wish him well, I could at least leave him alone, just as he was leaving me alone, to find the life I was supposed to have . . . one, it seemed, that did not involve being with a star athlete, sanding myself down so that I could fit into the crevices and corners of his life, subsisting on the scraps of his free time and attention, waiting patiently while he ran and stretched and ran and lifted and ran and soaked his touchy left calf in the whirlpool. I would never be the girl in the stands, applauding as he stood on the podium; never be the one thanked in interviews for her support, or named as an inspiration. I would have more ordinary pleasures, a life that was quieter but still fulfilling, and I would be fine.

Six months after Jay had moved his suits and wing tips and loafers into my closet, after his

Scrabble board had taken up residence on my kitchen table and I'd had dinner with his entire family twice, Jay took me ice skating again. We held hands as we glided around the rink, and when we were done, he said, "Let's go get a drink," and walked me to the bar where we'd first met. I wasn't surprised when he pulled a velvet box out of his pocket and presented me with the perfect ring—a round-cut diamond, substantial but not ostentatious, in an ornate Victorian setting. He didn't get down on his knee, didn't make a spectacle or embarrass me in front of a roomful of strangers, or do something cutesy like hide the ring in a dessert, where there was a possibility that I'd eat it. Instead, Jay held my hand, looked into my eyes, and said, "I will love you forever. Will you?"

"Of course I will," I told him, and he slipped the ring on my finger, then kissed me, and said, "Mrs. Kravitz."

This is what I waited for, I thought. This is what all the pain and suffering was about. I'd thought that Andy was my destiny, but maybe he was more of a life lesson, a hurdle I had to keep clearing to show the universe that I was worthy of the life intended for me: this life, with this man.

PART III

LOST TIME

Rachel

2005

"Rachel!" I turned, feeling the muscles in my back tensing, as if for a blow, as I saw Kara and Kelsey and Britt coming at me, walking shoulder to shoulder, like Charlie's Angels, looking almost exactly the way they had in high school.

I'd been on the fence about coming to the reunion. I had worried about what Jay would think, meeting people who probably remembered me as a spoiled, prissy girl who cared more about her hair and her clothes than the world around her. I'd quizzed my ob-gyn about flying at eight months, hoping for an excuse to stay home, and then, when she'd given me the go-ahead, I'd hated myself for still being so shallow while I visited five different stores for a maternity dress that wouldn't make me look like a viscose-clad dirigible.

The night of the reunion, I sat on my bed, with Marissa tugging at her Hervé Léger knockoff in front of the mirror in my childhood bedroom, and made one last attempt to get out of it. "I don't feel so great."

Marissa didn't even bother to look at me. "Rachel—you won. You've got a hot husband, gorgeous ring, a beautiful house, you're knocked up . . ."

"First of all, it's life. You don't win. And Kara and Kelsey and Britt all know about Andy, so if I go, I'll have to talk about him, and I don't want to."

"For God's sake. He was your high school sweetheart. What's the big deal?"

"He won a gold medal. In the Olympics. That's the big deal. People are going to want to know what he's up to, and if we're still in touch." I tugged at my bra, shifting around on the bed, trying to get comfortable, when I hadn't been anything close to comfortable in weeks. Foolishly, I'd envisioned myself sailing through my pregnancy, getting a cute basketball belly and a beautiful glow. Instead, the universe had served up acne, bloated breasts, and an enormous ass, and I'd developed all kinds of odd pains and discomforts. My back ached; my breasts throbbed. Even my vagina hurt. When I complained, my doctor just shrugged and smiled and said, "Well, you're pregnant." *Thanks for that,* I thought.

I was tired all the time. Tired from carrying around the extra weight, tired of the little swimmer inside me, who rolled and kicked all night long, tired just thinking about my reconstructed heart now having to pump for the baby, too. I was also increasingly tired of the conversation Jay and I kept having, one that wasn't quite an argument but was on its way to becoming one. He wanted me to stay home once the baby came. I wanted to go back to work after three months. He said that I'd want to be with our baby once it was born. I said that I'd seen enough newborns on the job to know that I found them as interesting as potted plants that pooped and cried, and that if I was stuck with one I'd go crazy. He said it would be different when it was my own child and not some client's, and we'd finally agreed to table the matter until after the birth, but it was like someone had left the window open in the room that was our marriage, and a chilly wind had blown through. My easygoing, affable husband became almost scary when he didn't get his way, with his lips clamped shut and his nostrils flaring and the condescending, scolding, *Father Knows Best* tone that made me want to clamp my hand over his mouth. I felt like I was getting a preview of what he'd look and sound like in forty years, and the picture did not thrill me.

At least he looked good, I thought, dressed that night in a crisp button-down and khakis, with a confident walk and an easy smile as he introduced himself to my classmates and their dates or spouses, hand extended, saying, "Jay Kravitz," and then cocking his thumb and adding, "I'm with her." Jay had gone to work with his father, and with a little help from his parents and a little more from mine, we'd purchased a beautiful brown-stone in Brooklyn, with fireplaces and a small backyard and enough bedrooms for three or even four kids if we wanted them. He was perfectly comfortable in places like the Clearview Country Club, to which my parents belonged and I would have, too, if I'd stayed in Florida.

"Raaaa-chel!"

Britt's hair was a brighter blond than it had been in high school, and she'd either grown it out or gotten extensions for the occasion. Her dress was short, red, and fringed, her heels impossibly high, and she was doing her makeup the same way she'd done it in high school, heavy on the black eyeliner, flicked out at the corners. "Honey!" she squealed, throwing her tanned arms around me. "Where's your guy?"

"My husband, Jay, is over there," I said.

Britt's head swiveled, along with Kara's and Kelsey's. "Oooh, nice!" she said, like Jay was a handbag I'd bought on sale. "So, okay," said Kelsey, grabbing my arm. "Last summer I was watching the Olympics, and I saw his name, and I screamed . . ." She raised her voice to Olympic-viewing-scream level. Heads turned. "I said, 'Oh my God, I know that guy!' And it was him, wasn't it? The same Andy Landis?"

"The same," I said, resting my hand on my belly and shooting Marissa a look. I'd finally settled on a black jersey tunic with an empire waist, black leggings, a pair of high-heeled boots that I was already regretting, and a statement necklace I'd borrowed from Nana, three strands of amber prayer beads, the first row small as peas and the last big as gumballs. "But how are you guys?"

Britt was teaching fifth grade in Clearview (I wondered what the boys there made of her long blond hair and even longer tanned legs). Kelsey was planning her wedding to a hotel manager named Rick, and Kara had gotten a nursing degree and worked on the labor and delivery floor. "But never mind us. What about you?" Britt grabbed my arm and pulled me close enough to smell the white wine she'd been drinking. "Are you and Andy still in touch?"

"Not really," I said. "Things fizzled out after college." Never mind my years in Portland; never mind that Andy had been living with me when he'd met Maisie. They were still together, I knew. I tried not to care and I tried not to Google, but over the years I'd had a few slips. I decided to try out Marissa's line. "How many people marry their high school sweetheart?"

Grinning, Britt pointed at Patti Cohen, who, per her nametag, was now Patti Cohen Mendelsohn. She'd actually married Larry. I hoped he'd improved as a kisser.

"Not every couple makes it," she said. "But if I had to bet on anyone, I would have bet on you two. You were so . . ." And then she spotted Pete Driscoll by the buffet. Our former quarterback had gained fifty pounds and lost all his hair. Britt shrieked, "Pete, oh my God, you ASSHOLE, you didn't tell me you'd be here!" Giving my arm a final squeeze, she teetered away, with Kara and Kelsey behind her, leaving me limp and tired and wanting desperately to be home.

I looked for Jay. When I didn't see him or Marissa, I got a glass of water at the bar, sat down at a table for ten that had emptied once the music started, and surreptitiously kicked off my boots. I was rubbing my right foot and flexing my left when someone walked up and said, "Hi, Rachel."

It took me a minute to recognize the woman, and when I did, it took a considerable effort not to gasp. Bethie Botts was wearing a dress. Short-sleeved, dark blue, made of jersey that skimmed over her body, showing off her bare arms and creamy skin. Her hair, which wasn't the least bit greasy, was pulled back in a bun. She wore dangly earrings, a beaded comb in her hair . . . and on her left hand, I saw a tiny diamond flash.

"Bethie?"

"It's Elizabeth now." I saw her little teeth, the ones I remembered from high school, like kernels of corn. Hardly anything else was the same. At some point, either she'd swapped her glasses for contacts or she'd gotten the surgery. Her eyes were blue-green, and she had a genuinely pleasant expression on her face.

"You look beautiful," I blurted.

"Thanks," she said, and then looked at my bare feet. "Are they swelling? Mine got so big when I was pregnant I couldn't even lace up my sneakers by the end." She touched her belly with one shapely hand.

"You've got a baby?"

"A little boy. Gabriel. He's six months old. He's with Grandma for the night, so my husband and I could come." From the shyly proud way she said *my husband* I could tell that she, like me, was still getting used to having one.

I stared at her, trying to align the perfectly normal-looking woman with the snot-and-tear-plastered horror show I remembered. I wanted to ask what had happened, how she'd transformed herself, who she was now, but instead, I ended up babbling about random classmates.

"Isn't this crazy? First I think that everyone looks exactly the same or even better, and then I'll see, like, Pete Driscoll, who's entirely bald . . ."

Bethie smiled—a real smile, not the fake, simpering thing she'd worn when I'd known her. It was like seeing an entirely new person, Bethie but not Bethie. Elizabeth now.

"And you!" I said. "You look spectacular!"

"Thanks," she said. "But let's be honest. I looked so awful in high school that all I would've had to do was comb my hair to look about a thousand times better."

I looked at her. "You want to know what happened, right?" I nodded, and she said, "Remember when we went to Atlanta and Melissa Nasser's mom was one of our chaperones?"

"Right."

"Mrs. Nasser—Diane—she's a therapist," Bethie said. "After the trip, she would call me or she'd find me at school or she'd drive to my foster home or she'd corner me at synagogue, and she'd say, 'Let's talk.' I think it was a year before I even spoke to her, and that was just to tell her to go away, until I finally said, 'Okay, fine,' to get her to leave me alone." She twisted her ring. "I didn't think it would work. You know, how was talking about what happened going to help me get over it? But she had some skills that she taught me. Things I could do to distract myself or reframe a situation or break the pattern when I was thinking about the bad times. So it wasn't just talking."

I thought about Dante, Brenda's little boy, and how, in spite of everything that Amy had told me about professionalism and boundaries and not getting too attached, I would think about him more than the rest of my clients' kids combined. Bethie must have been Mrs. Nasser's Dante.

What happened? I wanted to ask. *What were the bad times? What happened to you?* I didn't ask, because I already knew the answer . . . or at least a version of it. What happened to Bethie was the same thing that had happened to so many of the women I'd worked with over the years. Different specifics, same story. Probably if I'd made myself think about it back then, if I'd wanted to think about it, I could have figured it out.

Bethie said, "I aged out of my last foster-care placement when I turned eighteen. I lived with the Nassers for a year, and I got a job at a dog-grooming place and started taking classes at St. Petersburg College, and I just, you know . . ." She lifted her eyebrows. "Cleaned up my act. I'm in rabbinical school, if you can believe that. Paying it forward."

"You'll be great," I said, and Bethie smiled.

"So what are you up to besides growing a person?" she asked.

I told her that I'd become a social worker, and we talked about work for a while, about what the recent federal budget cuts meant for schools and for services to women and children, and whether President Bush's faith-based initiatives would be enough to close the gaps.

"I have to tell you something," I began. This was the reason I'd finally let Marissa talk me into coming. Bethie was the one person I'd hoped to see. But before I could start, she shook her head.

"It's okay," she said quietly.

"I feel so terrible." My eyes were welling. "The way I behaved."

Bethie looked down, one finger tracing lines on

the tablecloth. "At least you never went out of your way, you know? There were people, it was like I was part of their checklist. Drop off their books, sign in at homeroom, make fun of Bethie." I turned my head and wiped my eyes. That was another delightful part of being pregnant—in addition to everything hurting, everything made me cry, from the evening news to novels with plots about babies in peril and commercials for dog food for senior dogs. Now that I was closing in on thirty, it looked like the warnings were right, and I was finally going to turn into my mother.

"Maybe I didn't do that much," I said, even as I remembered the things that I had done or said, the way I'd rolled my eyes and laughed behind her back. Sometimes—more often than I liked—I remembered the scene in the dorm room, Marissa ripping Bethie's bags open, shaking her and calling her names, and the way I'd flicked the eye out of her stuffed elephant. I remembered everything—her unicorn T-shirt, the way her face had looked, the noise the disc of glass had made falling to the floor. "But I didn't try to stop it. Isn't that the saying, about how all it takes for evil to flourish is for good men to do nothing?"

"It was high school. Evil is kind of the name of the game." She patted my hand. "And I really enjoyed your Walkman." I exhaled and smiled back at her, feeling like I'd been granted a forgiveness that I didn't deserve.

"Are you in touch with Andy? Dale—my husband—we were watching the Olympics, and I saw his name, and I said, 'I knew that guy!' "

"I knew him, too."

"So what happened?" she finally asked. "Did you see that *Sports Illustrated* story, about how he thought his father was dead for his whole life, and then it turned out his dad was in prison? I can't imagine what that must have been like."

"Awful," I said. "It must have been awful." If tormenting Bethie was the great regret of my adolescence, then not being able to be there for Andy when he'd learned about his father was surely the great regret of my adulthood.

Maybe I couldn't have been his girlfriend, but I could have been a friend. Someone who'd known him a long time, who knew who he was and how he'd gotten that way.

The day that the *SI* story had come out, I'd been unpacking boxes at the brownstone that Jay and I had closed on the week before. Nana was in the kitchen, hand-washing the dishes that I'd already run through the machine, and my mom was upstairs, having a breakdown on the phone with the owner of the boutique that had sold me my gown, who was now saying that the alterations might not be finished in time for the blessed event. In the midst of all that, I got a call from the fact-checker for the *Times*, who needed to confirm details of our wedding announcement

—where we'd gone to school, whether I was "a daughter" or "the daughter" of Bernard and Helen Blum of Clearview, Florida.

With the phone tucked under my chin, telling the guy that indeed, I had graduated cum laude from Beaumont, I had run down to the mailbox to see if any last-minute RSVPs had arrived, wondering what my mother would do if we needed to change the seating arrangement again. The mailman had left us three bills and Jay's copy of *Sports Illustrated*, with Andy Landis on the cover. It wasn't an action shot or a picture from the Olympics, but a portrait, a tight shot of just his face, his expressive brown eyes and thick, dark brows, the full lips that I'd kissed a thousand times, his teeth just peeking out in a hint of a smile. He looked tentative and guarded and tender underneath, the way he'd look when we'd been talking in bed and he'd finally loosened up enough to use his hands or smile when he got to the funny parts. I wondered who'd taken the picture, and what the photographer had said to Andy to get him to look like that.

"Ma'am?" The fact-checker wanted to know how I spelled my middle name. "Sorry," I said, and spelled out Nicole, and gave him Amy's phone number so he could confirm her role in our how-we'd-met tale. I still needed to check in with the florist and ask if the caterer had vegan meals for my soon-to-be sister-in-law, Robin, and pick up my birth control pills from the pharmacy, but I decided that all of it could wait. I carried the magazine to the park at the end of our block, sat down on a bench in the sun, and started reading.

Running Down a Dream, read the headline, and the first page of the story was a photograph of Andy winning his Olympic race, eyes shut, fists lifted, mouth open, in the instant he crossed the finish line. *How Andy Landis Outraced a Rough Start to Win Olympic Gold.* The piece had gone over everything I'd known about Andy—his life with Lori, the fights he'd gotten into, and how his mother had told him to channel his rage into running. I read about his paper route, his friend, Mr. Sills, his high school career, and the records he'd set. I skimmed, holding my breath, until I got to the new stuff.

Andrew Landis Senior was an athlete, too. A standout basketball player, good-looking, graceful, and fast, with a killer three-point shot, Landis Senior wasn't quite talented enough to attract the attention of college scouts, or strong enough to resist the lure of the streets. Arrested for the first time at seventeen for selling marijuana on a corner of his Philadelphia neighborhood, Landis got in trouble for everything from petty theft and larceny to bar brawls and grand theft auto. When a judge let him choose between jail and the army, Landis enlisted and was posted to Germany. When he came home on a furlough, trouble found him again. Landis was arrested as an accessory to murder after a friend, DeVaughn Sills, shot a twenty-one-year-old former high school classmate and alleged rival drug dealer to death. Landis Senior, who'd been driving the car, was caught trying to dispose of the gun.

DeVaughn Sills. Was that Mr. Sills's son? *Had to be,* I thought. How had Andy felt about that? I read the rest of it, wincing, sometimes gasping in sympathy. The reporter had found Andy's father living in an SRO in Philadelphia. *Landis Senior had watched his son's success from afar, seeing him win his gold medal on a twelve-inch screen in his room. He had papered his walls with pictures and clippings of his son, but hadn't tried to get in touch. "I don't want Andy to think I'm after his money, or that I deserve any credit for his success,"* he'd said. *And if he could send a message to his Olympic-winning son?* the story continued. *Landis Senior doesn't even have to think about it. "I know I wasn't his father, but I'd tell him I was proud."*

Reached by telephone at the Manhattan apartment that he shares with his girlfriend, model Maisie Guthrie, Landis Junior had no comment, I'd read.

Andy. Oh, Andy. I'd rocked back and forth on the bench with my arms wrapped around my shoulders, aching for him. Aching even as I read the rest of the piece, about the endorsement deals, the friendships with the Hollywood stars and the NBA players, and the description of "the ethereally beautiful Guthrie, who has walked the runway for Victoria's Secret and posed in some barely there bikinis for this publication."

How had the ethereally lovely Guthrie handled the revelations? Had Andy gone to Philadelphia to find his father? My phone started buzzing in my lap. "Honey?" said my mother, on the verge of tears again, as always. "They're saying your dress will be there first thing tomorrow, but isn't that when you're getting your nails done?"

Oh, right, I'd thought, getting to my feet. *I'm getting married on Saturday. There is that.* Send him love, I told myself, which was what my yoga instructor always said she did when someone barged in front of her on the stairs to the subway or grabbed the last quart of orange juice at the market. Send him love. He had Maisie, but I had Jay. The universe balanced. Let it be enough.

"It sounds like everything worked out," Bethie said.

"I love living in New York. And Jay is great." I hoped she didn't hear what I was hearing, which was the sound of a woman who'd spent too much on an item of clothing that didn't quite fit and was trying to tell herself that it looked fine. Jay was great. He was calm, he was kind, he was patient, solicitous, devoted . . . and if he was a little dictatorial, the tiniest bit patronizing about the stay-at-home thing, wasn't that understandable? Didn't it mean he would be a wonderful dad; didn't it show that he cared?

"Jay is great," I said again, just as he came into view, carrying two cups of punch.

"I thought you ladies might like some refreshments," he said, and when he smiled, I decided that I couldn't have gotten a better husband, that I couldn't love him more.

"Jay, this is Beth—Elizabeth. Elizabeth Botts . . . Did you change your name?"

"Please. Wouldn't you?" Bethie asked. I heard the faintest hint of the kind of sharp-edged nastiness she'd once used to deliver all of her remarks. *There you are, Bethie,* I thought. "It's Chamberlain now. Elizabeth Chamberlain."

"Elizabeth," said Jay, and held out his hand, before turning to me. "How are you feeling?"

"Just fine."

"Not too warm? And you're staying hydrated?"

I rolled my eyes. "Jay thinks I should have checked into the hospital as soon as the test came back positive."

Bethie pulled out a business card from her beaded clutch. *Elizabeth Chamberlain, Rabbinical*

Student. "Let me know when you have the baby. I want to send you something."

"Oh, you don't have to."

"I want to," she said, as I took her card, and let Jay take my hand and told myself again how lucky I was, how I'd landed in the middle of a life I didn't deserve.

Andy
2009

Lori opened the front door of her dream house, a medium-sized and recently renovated cottage in Bryn Mawr that Andy had bought for her with his first big endorsement-deal check. "The Dream House for Mom," his friend Laurent Dillard, who'd been a first-round draft pick for the 'Sixers, had said. "Gotta get that Dream House for Mom."

Standing in the entryway, her bare feet on the terra-cotta tiles, she looked at him. "Andy," she said. "Welcome home."

"It's the place they have to take you in, right?"

Lori tried to smile, but he could see concern etched into the lines around her eyes and mouth.

"I'm sorry," he told her. "I'm sorry for everything."

"Oh, honey," she said . . . and for the first time

since the Olympics, his mother pulled him into her arms and held him tight.

He remembered the night back in 2006 that Mitch had shown up at the door of the two-bedroom apartment he'd bought with Maisie, in a new high-rise in Carnegie Hill. Sometimes, riding up in the elevator, he imagined, or thought he could, the white guys in suits staring at him, and he told himself it was because they recognized him from Athens. Not because he was the only nonwhite guy in the building who wasn't delivering someone's dinner.

He and Mitch were both spending half the year training at a newly constructed facility in Westchester, with a bunch of new guys, most of them a year or two out of college, fast and strong and getting almost magically faster and stronger. Andy had watched in frustration and fear as his times failed to improve, telling himself that he'd work harder, work smarter, train more efficiently, suffer more than he ever had . . . but even when he did all of those things, he wasn't able to make any meaningful improvements. In fact, his times had started slipping. The young pups were not only coming up behind him; they'd run right past.

"You know what they're doing, right?" Mitch asked. He was dressed in street clothes, jeans and a dark-blue pullover, with a backpack over one shoulder, a weariness around his eyes, and an angry scowl on his face. Short and wiry, Mitch was looking almost gaunt these days—he'd been doing some kind of low-carb thing, Andy knew, hoping that if he cut three or four pounds he'd see his times improve.

"Being younger than we are," Andy said morosely. He'd already made up his mind that the Penn Relays in May would be his test. If things didn't improve by then—if he got trounced as thoroughly as the times he'd been putting up suggested that he would—then he'd have no hope of making the 2008 Olympic team, and he'd need to think about retiring. He'd be thirty-two by then, old for a runner, and there was no shame in quitting while you were ahead, and a gold medal certainly meant that he'd be going out on top, but he'd hoped for one more season, one more whack at the piñata . . . because he loved it and also because whenever he tried to think of what would come next his mind felt like a big, empty whiteboard that some zealous kid had wiped perfectly clean. What would he do when that voice spoke up, the one that said he was undeserving of everything he had, if he couldn't run it into submission on his way toward even more prizes, more affirmations that yes, he'd proven his worth, he'd earned his right to be?

He and Rachel had sometimes talked about a post-racing life—maybe he could be a coach or a teacher; maybe he could help boys who needed someone in their lives, the same way Mr. Sills had helped him. "Picture a little love nest," Rachel would sing, and Andy could see it—a cozy house, a yard that he'd mow, a swimming pool with a hot tub where he could soak. Maisie talked endlessly about her post-modeling plans, but they never discussed his future—because, he knew, it scared her, too. There was also an element of superstition involved. To talk about what came next was to signal to God or the universe or whatever forces were out there that you knew that what you had wouldn't last . . . which might, of course, invite those forces to sweep down and take it away.

"We're just getting older," Andy said. "All that training can't make us twenty-seven again."

"It's not that. How about Matt Parker?"

Andy sighed. Parker was a year older than he was. He ran the mile, and unlike Andy, his times had gotten faster in the past year, improving at an almost unheard-of rate.

Mitch reached into his backpack and pulled out a stainless-steel tube, the kind they sold toothpaste and hand cream in . . . except this tube had no label, no writing. It was perfectly blank.

"What is it?" Andy asked.

"What do you think it is?"

They stared at each other in silence. Mitch looked exasperated. Andy had no idea what was showing up on his face. He felt shocked, and then he felt stupid for being shocked. He'd always known about doping. There'd always been talk about this team or that guy, and, even among his own team-mates, conversations that ended abruptly when he walked into the showers or the trainers' room. He'd heard talk about certain trainers, whispers about doctors who'd hook you up with anything you needed. Andy had never listened, because he had never needed anything. But now . . .

"Everyone's doing it," said Mitch. Andy recognized the speech for what it was: the same talk boys in junior high gave to get each other to sneak beers or try cigarettes.

"The French, the Finns, the Kenyans. Not to mention our own so-called teammates. If we don't keep up we're going to be standing at the starting line looking like our legs are tied together."

So there it was. Right out in the open. In his apartment. In his friend's hand.

"Where'd you get this?" Andy's voice sounded hoarse. "Who's handing it out?"

"John Mahoney, for one. Les Carter." Andy got to his feet and started pacing. John Mahoney was the team manager, a man he'd known since college. Les was one of the trainers, always with a smile and a guy-walks-into-a-bar joke, who'd sit with you while you were in the ice baths or the whirlpool and ask about your girlfriend or wife or kids. "Other guys, but John's the one you want to talk to about the rest of it."

391

"There's more?" Of course there was more, Mitch told him. Creams and pills and shots, transfusions of your own stored blood. *Everyone's doing it,* he said again, and then went home, leaving the tube behind him.

Andy had carried it to the bathroom and looked at himself in the mirror. He understood that if he went along with this, if he chose to do what Mitch and, ostensibly, most of the other runners were doing, his life would be divided by a bright line—before and after. The races he'd won, the times he'd put up honestly, and what he'd do with this stuff in his system. It was cheating . . . but was it really something he could refuse and still hope to compete? And was it really unfair if he did it to even the playing field, so that he wasn't starting his races half a lap behind everyone else?

He'd pulled his pants down to his ankles and stood in his briefs, feeling undignified and welcoming the feeling. There was nothing dignified, nothing honorable or admirable about this. Uncapping the bottle, he squirted some of the clear ointment into his hands and rubbed it first on his left quad, then on his right, as if it were the arnica gel some of the trainers used. His thighs ached. Everything ached. It used to be that he was in pain only while he was running, and then immediately after, when the acid would flood his muscles, making everything burn. Now there was something hurting almost all the time.

He was stiff when he got out of bed, he walked to the bathroom as if his bones were made of glass, and it took a solid ten minutes of stretching and foam rolling before things loosened up. With all the pounding he'd given his limbs and his joints, it shouldn't have come as a surprise.

Once this new phase of his career had begun, he had hoped that the injections and the creams and the spun blood would help him feel better, stronger; and for a while he imagined that they did. He'd tied his personal best at the Penn Relays, then run a 5K in Central Park just for fun and creamed it, beating the second-place finisher by almost a minute. At the Middle Distance Classic in Pasadena, he'd come within four-tenths of a second of the winner, and then, back in Oregon, at the Nike Prefontaine Classic, he'd honored his hero by winning not only the 5000 but the 10,000, prompting ESPN to do a feature on him and other mid-career runners getting a surprising second wind.

He could see his body changing, his thighs getting bigger, his shoulders broader. He could hear his voice deepening and could feel the acne on his back. "You're fine," Maisie would tell him, going through his closet and pulling out his suit jackets to have them altered. "You just look like you've been lifting." Maisie knew what he was doing. Some of the stuff had to be kept on hand and refrigerated. In their place in New York, where, often, the only things in her refrigerator were Champagne and fancy mustard, they stored it in the crisper drawer, and Maisie started calling it the lettuce, as in "Are we out of lettuce yet?" A few times, she'd even rendezvoused with whichever intern or trainee John Mahoney was using as a delivery boy, and she'd booked his appoint-ments with the doctor in Miami who wrote his prescriptions and Mitch's. They'd fly down together, play some golf, then drive their rented car to an office in a grimy strip mall and sit in the scuffed plastic chairs in the waiting room before the receptionist called their names —first names only, Andy noticed. There was a mirror on the back door of the doctor's exam rooms. Andy wondered about that. Did the doctor want his patients to see themselves, to see what they were doing to their bodies? Were he and Mitch meant to look with approval and gratitude? By then, Andy had gotten good at avoiding his own face in the mirror. He was used to scrutinizing his body, always looking out for any injury, any change. Since the night that Mitch had come over, though, he found that he couldn't look at his own reflection, couldn't stand to meet his own eyes.

The Adidas Grand Prix was in New York that June, and Andy was scheduled to compete in both the 5000 and the 10,000. The day before the heats, he'd run an easy three miles in Central

Park, then came back to the apartment and saw reporters and a news van with a satellite dish blooming on its roof. He knew, even before he got close enough to hear them shouting his name, what had happened and why they were there. It was like the nuns had told him, "Be sure your sin will find you out."

He kept his head down as he made his way through the throng, ignoring the questions— "How long have you been doping?" "Have you been subpoenaed?" "Will they make you give your medal back?" He heard cameras clicking and saw, across the street, a perfectly groomed woman in a yellow dress and high heels standing in front of a camera with a microphone raised to her lips. He was almost to the front door when he saw Bob Rieper from *Sports Illustrated*, the Grim Rieper, who'd written that profile of him, who'd found out about his father.

"Hey, man," said Bob. He put his hand on Andy's shoulder, and with that touch, those two words, Andy knew that his life as a runner was done, that his second life had started, whether he was ready or not.

Up in the apartment, he found his cell phone and called John Mahoney, who answered on the first ring.

"Andy," he said, in his familiar rasp. "Did you hear?"

"I haven't heard anything, but there's a bunch

of reporters outside of my building." Instead of being panicked, he felt a weird, shocked kind of calm. His pulse felt almost sluggish, and his heartbeat seemed to slow.

"Don't say a word," Mahoney instructed. "If they call, just hang up, and if they catch you, say 'No comment.' "

"No comment," Andy practiced, pacing the living room, then walking back to the bedroom to see if Maisie was there. He heard the shower running, and saw the TV tuned to ESPN, which seemed to be showing a loop—runners on a track, followed by a banner reading DOPING SCANDAL and a serious-looking white guy with an incongruously orange face saying something that Andy couldn't hear because Maisie had turned the volume down. Her suitcase was already open on the bed. He wondered what she'd say, what excuses she'd make, what last-minute photo shoot or family crisis she'd invent to get herself out of here, away from him.

He barely had to wait to find out. Maisie came out of the bathroom with one towel wrapped around her, another around her hair, and looked at him like he was a burglar who'd made it past the doorman and up to the thirty-third floor.

"Hey," Andy began.

Her expression was a mixture of sorrow and embarrassment. Underneath that, like the primer she smoothed on beneath her makeup in the morning, Andy glimpsed a familiar cool calculation. This was what Maisie did when she met someone new—a teammate's new wife, a photographer's new assistant—and was trying to decide who that person was, what he or she represented, and how he or she could be of any use to Maisie or Andy, individually or together. She'd turned them into a pair of beautiful people, featured in all the magazines, invited to all the parties. Now, Andy saw, she was figuring out how to turn herself into someone new, a woman betrayed by a boyfriend who was a criminal and a cheat.

"Mitch called for you. And Alex." Alex was Alejandro Pérez-Peña, Andy's new coach.

"What'd they say?"

"Call Alex back. There's going to be a conference call at three. They hired a crisis management firm. And lawyers."

"Lawyers?" Andy felt his legs, those world-beating, record-setting, medal-winning legs, start trembling underneath him. Could he go to jail for this? Was that even possible? Was it fair? Who had he hurt, except himself?

The fans, his mind whispered. All those people who believed in you, who thought you were winning fair and square. Not to mention the companies who'd paid for him to speak, the manufacturers who'd paid for him to endorse their goods, the publisher with whom he'd just signed a contract to write his story. *"Andy*

Landis," his publicist, chic in a fitted suit with gold buttons, had announced, at a luncheon with his new publicity and marketing team. *"An American Story."*

Some story, he thought as Maisie looked at him, eyebrows arched in a parody of surprise. "Yes, you need lawyers. The stuff you were doing was against the law." She gave a small, theatrical shudder. Her fake shudders, Andy observed from his bubble of detachment, had improved over the years. The acting lessons were paying off. "Some of it's only been approved for use on animals."

"How do you know all this?"

Instead of answering, Maisie flipped open the laptop she'd left next to the bed. *Nine Olympians Indicted in Drug Probe. Records, Medals in Jeopardy. No Response Yet from Team USA.* And pictures. His pictures. The ones they'd run in *Sports Illustrated,* of him in Athens, edging out the runner from Morocco, his arms raised in triumph. Maisie scrolled down just far enough for Andy to read the quote and recognize his own words: *"I'd never take shortcuts, or do anything illegal. Everything I got, I earned."*

"Oh," he said, and shut his eyes, feeling numb and hollow, the way he had when he'd been ten and the policeman caught him—like he'd lost everything, like he'd never feel good or proud or happy ever again.

Maisie didn't say anything . . . but then, what could she say that would help? He watched as she went to the closet, came back with an armful of clothing, and folded it into the suitcase.

"Where are you going?"

"Tenerife. Remember?"

"That's next week."

Without turning to face him, she said, "I'm going to go stay with Bethany for the night. We'll leave together in the morning. I know you've got a lot to deal with, and I didn't want to be in your way."

"I need you here," he told her.

"Oh, Andy," she said with a sigh. He watched with a sense of déjà vu as she raised her perfect chin a fraction of an inch, like she was responding to a photographer's command. *Give me just a teeny bit of profile, babydoll . . . that's it. Right there. Perfection.* "You knew the risks. You knew this could happen."

"I didn't have a choice!" he yelled.

She just looked at him.

"What?" he asked. "What choice did I have? What else can I do? I'm not good at anything else except this. If I wanted to compete, I had to take that stuff. I didn't have a choice."

She didn't answer. She zipped up the suitcase. *Answer enough,* Andy thought.

"If someone told you that you needed breast implants to be a model, are you saying you wouldn't get them?"

"Implants aren't illegal," she said, and slung her purse over her shoulder. Andy stood, his arms dangling at his sides, legs weak and wobbling, watching the red soles of her shoes flashing as she wheeled her suitcase out the door.

For a minute he stood there, feeling sick and shaky and terrified, hoping she'd come back, willing her to return, if only to tell him that she loved him. Knowing that she wouldn't. Maisie looked out for Maisie. At night, sometimes, lying awake, he'd tried to imagine her staying with him if they lost everything; tried to picture the two of them scratching out a living in some anonymous town in Middle America. He couldn't do it. Maisie was made for cities, for late nights, for glamorous clubs, for Champagne and sushi, not small towns, fish sticks, and generic ginger ale. Nor would she sacrifice a second of the time she had left to work as a model. He was convinced that was the reason she hadn't agreed to get married or have a baby. She'd said all the right things about how happy they were and why rock the boat and that they had plenty of time. When he pushed her, she talked about not being able to take a year off from work and what would happen if she couldn't get her body back. She'd told him the story of a stunning girl from Iceland who'd given birth to twins and found it impossible to shed the last ten pounds of baby weight. Poor Karine had gotten liposuction, and there were filters that could erase her stretch marks. Still, Maisie had told him, eyes wide and horrified, poor Karine had never . . . worked . . . again.

"At least, not in Manhattan," Maisie had said with a final shudder. "I heard she was doing, like, catalog work for Dillard's."

"A fate worse than death," Andy had deadpanned, and Maisie, not getting it, had nodded so vigorously that she'd almost lost a hair extension and had said, "I know! I know!" Then she'd kissed him, purring, "We can wait. For now, let's just enjoy our freedom." He'd agreed, all the while thinking that it wasn't about work or freedom or stretch marks or how good things were between them, but about the way a baby would link them, inextricably and forever, uniting them in a bond that would be harder to break than even marriage.

He knew she'd rather die than lose her spot on the ladder. If her boyfriend became a liability, she'd do exactly what she'd done—take ten minutes to cram some stuff in a suitcase, call her agent, and change her ticket and move on to the next thing.

For the next few weeks, Andy stayed in the apartment, wondering if it was possible to die of shame. Whenever he thought about going outside, usually after he'd been pacing for a few hours and was desperate for fresh air and open space, he would hear the words *Everything I've got, I earned* and decide it wasn't worth it. Valerie, his personal assistant of five years, gave her notice, saying that she'd loved working for him but she couldn't handle the volume of calls and e-mails, not to mention the questions from her friends and family about whether she'd known what was going on. His calls to his agent went straight to voice mail; his publicist handed him off to a different firm, one that handled oil companies who'd dumped thousands of gallons into the ocean and right-wing senators who'd been paying off their same-sex, underage lovers.

If he'd earned his previous life—the endorsement deals, the perks, the famous friends—then surely he'd earned this one, too. He'd earned the barista at Starbucks who'd refused to take his order, the waitress who'd turned on her heel when Andy and his old friend Miles Stratton sat down for lunch to discuss his finances in light of what Miles called "these new developments." He'd earned the ten-year-old girl who'd mailed him a poster depicting his Olympic win with a note that read *You used to be my hero but you aren't anymore.*

Still in his bubble of numbed disbelief, Andy went to the hearings, the meetings, the conferences with the publicists and the ones with the lawyers. He sat at long tables in offices on high floors with stunning views of Central Park and tried to pay attention as attorneys for the USATF and the runners who were being called the Athens Nine tried to work out a deal. Eventually, they decided that if Andy and his teammates would testify about how they'd gotten the drugs and who else they knew was using, they could keep the medals and the prizes they'd won up to 2006 . . . but none of them would be able to run competitively ever again.

The sneaker company that had underwritten his running life since college sent a certified letter explaining that, given his current circumstances, they could no longer continue their association. They wished him well. So did the watch company he'd done ads for, and the sports drink he'd endorsed. He moved his stuff out of his place in Oregon, downsized from two bedrooms in Carnegie Hill to a studio in a not-great neighbor-hood in Brooklyn. Those moves, plus his savings, gave him a nest egg he could live off for a while. He would need to do something eventually, but for now, there was vodka and premium cable for binge-watching old shows. He'd learned to avoid live TV after flipping through the channels and seeing a late-night wit urging the public, "Give blood. Our Olympic runners might need extra."

He ate delivery pizza or Chinese food, bagels for breakfast, bags of pretzels in between, for once not caring about calories or carbs or sodium or nutrients or any of it. He'd wash it all down with PowerUp, the sports drink that he'd spike with vodka after the sun went down. He had cases and cases of the stuff—he'd been the face of PowerUp, and part of his deal included free drinks for life. Only now, he noted with sour amusement, they sent him boxes full of discontinued flavors, something called Red Rage that tasted like fermented cough syrup, and Blue Crush, which tasted like chalk.

For the first time in a long time, Andy was faced with empty days to fill, hours and hours when he had nowhere to be and nothing to do. The *Sports Illustrated* with his face on the cover was in one of the boxes he'd brought over, along with his tax returns and copies of the contracts he'd signed. In the years since it had been published, he'd never been able to bring himself to read Bob Rieper's profile. One day he found it, flipped it open to the page with his picture, and began scanning the text for his father's name.

At fifty-one, Andrew Landis Senior bears little resemblance to his son, or to the teenage basketball star that he was once. Tall and lanky in his youth, he is stooped now, heavier through the chest and belly, with rounded shoulders and a mostly bald head. His walk is a head-down, shoulders-hunched shuffle. The only trace of the son that Landis Senior and his wife, Lori, named after him are his feet, size fourteen, big as flippers in heavy brown work boots. "I was always fast," Landis Senior says.

After getting out of prison he moved to an SRO hotel. His tiny, windowless room in a no-name neighborhood in Philadelphia has the feel of a cell, the single bed neatly made, books and magazines arranged in perfect stacks, posters and pictures taped to his cinder-block wall. The posters and pictures are all of his son; the magazines all feature stories about him. In a scrapbook, Landis has newspaper clippings charting Andy Landis's history as a runner, beginning in high school. Over the years, Landis Senior says, friends sent them to him in prison. He is proud of his son, but has, he says, no desire to get in touch. "It's too many men who come out of the woodwork when their children make something of themselves," he said, mentioning Shaquille O'Neal's father, who'd abandoned his son as a six-month-old baby, who'd disappeared into addiction, then prison, only to finally come forward, brandishing a birth certificate, looking to be taken into O'Neal's fold after his son became a star.

"I don't want Andy to think I'm after his money, or that I deserve any credit for his success. Everything he did, that's all him."

And if he could send a message to his Olympic-winning son? Landis Senior doesn't even have to think about it. "I know I wasn't his father, but I'd tell him I was proud."

Andy stared at the words. He wondered which friends had sent his father clippings about him, and then pictured Mr. Sills, carefully cutting out each story. Maybe writing a note. Had his old friend felt guilty, that it was his own son's fault, and maybe somehow his, too, that Andy's dad was in prison?

Inside the magazine's pages was an envelope from the Grim Rieper. *This is your father's address and phone number. He asked me to pass them along.* Andy studied the note for a minute, trying to imagine the reunion, the ex-con father meeting his infamous, tainted son. He looked at his phone, but instead of reaching for it he grabbed the vodka, adding another dollop to his Red Rage. That night, for the first time in his life, he drank until he passed out.

He might have stayed in that room forever, eating, drinking, sleeping, then waking to do it all again, except one day his cell phone had started ringing. He'd seen 215, the area code for Philadelphia, and, on a whim, he'd answered it.

"No comment," he'd said instead of *hello*. The words sounded a little slushy. Oh, well.

Instead of a volley of questions, his opening

sally earned him a wheezy laugh. "Andy Landis," said a familiar voice that had gotten fainter over time. "Is that any way to say hello to your old friend?"

Andy, who'd been lounging on the couch with a go-cup full of Blue Crush and vodka balanced on his chest, sat up so fast that the drink spilled all over his shirt.

"Mr. Sills?"

Another wheezy laugh. "You can call me Clement now, remember? I make it a policy for all my friends who've won gold medals."

The familiar searing, scalding shame rose through his body, making him flush and squirm with the desperate desire to outrun what could never be outrun. Disgrace was now his shadow, and he couldn't ever leave it behind.

"Your friend who cheated."

Mr. Sills sighed. "Now, I'm not saying you didn't do wrong. But name me someone who goes through life without making mistakes. I know you," he continued. "You're probably sitting in the dark, not talking to anyone, beating yourself up." Looking around, Andy realized that he hadn't turned any lights on that night or, he suspected, most nights. "You've still got a long time to live, and there's plenty of good you could be doing. Lots of boys out there could use a helping hand. Maybe even a coach."

"Who'd hire me?" Andy hated that he sounded

whiny, in addition to drunk. "Nobody'd want a cheater coaching their kids."

Mr. Sills was relentless. "Do you know that for sure? Have you asked anyone? I'd bet you a whole stack of *National Geographic*s that if you went back to Roman Catholic, went to the coach, said, 'I'd like to help out,' he'd have you doing it in a minute."

Andy, who wasn't so sure, said nothing.

"But that's not why I called," his friend continued. "Truth is, I haven't been doing so well lately. I've got that emphysema, you know."

Andy hadn't known.

"I'd sure like a visit," Mr. Sills had said. "Maybe you could come down here, we'd have some breakfast, maybe visit a few junk shops." *Junk shops,* Andy remembered, had been Mr. Sills's name for the antiques shops and the vintage and resale stores that they'd frequented. "I don't drive anymore . . ."

"What happened?"

"Ah, well, you know, I never could parallel park, and then it just seemed like everyone on the road was so angry, honking all the time. I got friends who take me places now, and I get Meals on Wheels for lunch and dinner."

"I'll come," Andy heard himself say. He was moving through the kitchen by then, pulling out a trash bag from the box on the counter, scooping up pizza boxes and half-full Chinese food containers and dozens of empty plastic Red Rage bottles and sweeping them inside. It was unendurable, the thought of Mr. Sills stuck home alone, eating Meals on Wheels, while he sat here like a petulant prince with more money than he needed. "I'll come tomorrow."

"No need to rush," said Mr. Sills. Then he started coughing again.

"Tomorrow," Andy had repeated, pouring the rest of the vodka down the kitchen sink. He'd spent the night cleaning, doing laundry, packing what he needed. He was waiting at the car dealership when it opened, grabbing the first salesman he saw, pointing at a car, cutting off the other man's speech with a curt "Just give me the keys and I'll write you a check." By noon, he was pulling off the exit for Allegheny Avenue.

He'd gone straight to see Mr. Sills, whose apartment had grown, if anything, even more crammed with the collages of pictures and paintings now covering the walls entirely. After Athens, Andy had offered to buy him a house, a condo, something in Center City, so he could walk to the museums and the restaurants, but Mr. Sills had shaken his head and told him, "I lived here with Mrs. Sills. This is home."

"Son," Mr. Sills had said, struggling to his feet. The man who'd once seemed like a giant to Andy was smaller all over; shorter and thinner, with a clear tube running across his cheek and up into his nose. Beside the corduroy-covered armchair that Andy remembered sat an oxygen tank, like a small, faithful dog.

It made him think of Rachel, and all the mistakes he'd made, all the bad choices, and he wanted to bang his head against a wall until the shame subsided. Instead, he made himself hold still as Mr. Sills said, "It's good to see you," and gave him a hug. In that instant, he hated himself more than he ever had; hated himself for all the people he'd disappointed, all the ones he'd hurt or left behind.

I'm sorry, he thought. He knew that if he tried to talk he wouldn't be able to get the words out . . . but it seemed, somehow, that Mr. Sills had heard them anyhow. "There, there," he said, patting Andy's back, the way a mother might have soothed a crying baby. "There, there."

They'd visited all afternoon. Mr. Sills showed Andy his latest treasures—an oil painting of a parrot ("It really brightens up the place," he'd said), a Spode tea service, and a real silver tray. "A genuine antique!" he'd pronounced, and told Andy how many times he'd had to go over all the vines and curlicues to clear away the tarnish. He asked after Maisie, and Andy told him briefly that Maisie was gone. As the day wound down and the sky began to darken, Mr. Sills asked, "Did you ever think to look up your daddy?"

Andy shook his head. Mr. Sills smiled.

"Talkative as ever. You suppose that's something you might want to undertake?"

Andy shrugged. "Maybe someday."

"Maybe someday," Mr. Sills repeated. He settled into his chair, glanced at the tank beside him, and said, "I know that you are hurting. Only thing I'd say is, don't wait too long." He'd smiled, crinkling his cheeks, making his glasses rise. "None of us live forever."

He'd given Mr. Sills a long hug goodbye. Then he had gone home to his mother.

"You can stay as long as you want to," Lori told him, leading him up the stairs to where the guest room sat in readiness for a visit that, so far, had never come. The queen-size bed had a blue-and-red bedspread; the dresser displayed a dozen photographs of Andy through the years. Fresh towels sat at the foot of the bed, and there was a new toothbrush in the bathroom. That was Lori. She'd hardly hug, she'd never kiss, she'd rarely say *I love you,* but when you showed up at her door unannounced, the bed was made, the freezer was full of Stouffer's French bread pizzas, and there was a fresh tube of the kind of Crest he'd used when he was a boy.

Andy walked into the room and set his bag on the dresser. Lori stood in the doorway, playing with her hair.

"Andy."

He looked at her.

411

"When you told me you were sorry—you should know that I am, too. If I ever made you feel like you weren't good enough . . ." She paused, then gave a rueful, shamed laugh. "If I always made you feel like you weren't good enough . . ."

"Mom," he said, but Lori kept talking, her face pale, and her hands gripping each other. "That's why you did it, right? That's why you wanted to keep running. You had a gold medal—you beat the whole world—and you still couldn't let yourself stop. And it's my fault," she said. "I should have made you feel like I loved you, like I loved you no matter what, and I didn't do it."

"Mom," he said again, or tried to say, because he could hardly talk and she was crying.

"All I thought of was myself, and just getting through the day, and how lonely I felt, and I put too much on you, and I didn't give you enough, and I'm sorry, Andy. I can't tell you how sorry . . ." Andy crossed the room to take her hands and she grabbed his and squeezed them hard.

"I was never ashamed of you. I was never anything but proud. You're my boy," she said, still crying. "And I'm proud to be your mom."

Rachel

2014

"Rachel?" There was a hand on my shoulder, and a sweet, well-meaning voice in my ear. I groaned. "Tired," I said.

"Rachel, honey." The hand jiggled me. I let my body wobble bonelessly on the mattress. Today was . . . I thought. A school day. Maybe a Wednesday. I could detect a Wednesday feel, a middle-of-the-week lassitude, the good intentions of Monday faded, the excitement of the weekend yet to come.

"Rachel." The hand was not moving. The voice was getting more insistent. Not Brenda, this time, but Nana, who'd come all the way from Florida, the way she had after each of my daughters was born. "Come on, honey. The girls are going to be home soon."

"Send 'em in," I sighed, and forced myself to sit up and open my eyes.

If Jay had cheated, that would have been one thing. If he'd cheated and left me for his mistress, it would have been humiliating and sad, but I might not have been knocked down as hard as this. But what happened was so much worse. I'd lost everything—my job, my husband, what felt like my whole life—all in one terrible night.

I was at my desk in the office on a Friday morning when a reminder from OpenTable popped up on my calendar. "Don't forget your reservation at Eleven Madison Park tonight." I rocked back in my chair, frowning. That morning, in the midst of the usual scramble to get the girls washed and brushed and backpacked, Jay had been talking about something, and I thought he'd said *Don't forget about tonight*—but I hadn't caught the part about what I needed to remember, because I'd been staring into the freezer, hoping that more coffee beans would magically appear, while thinking about a client who needed a new phone so she could put a number on the résumés that she needed to start handing out to potential employers. With a minute left before they needed to go, Adele had gone running up the stairs in search of her recorder and Delaney had used the delay to start going through her lunch— "Mommy, why do you keep giving me wasabi seaweed? I only like sesame!" Jay had given me his usual businesslike kiss and herded the girls out the door.

On my way to the subway, I'd scrolled through my calendar, trying to see if we had plans for the evening. Adele had a recorder concert, but that wasn't until Thursday, and Delaney's move-up night at school, which parents were required to attend, wasn't for weeks. The only thing I'd been intending to do that night was a five o'clock yoga class, until the reservation reminder arrived.

At work, I continued to stare at the screen. Our anniversary wasn't for three months. It wasn't his birthday or mine. When Eleven Madison Park had been written up in the *Times* a few months ago, with a foie-gras-stuffed chicken earning special praise, I'd sighed and said, "I'd love to get dressed up and go somewhere fancy." Had Jay actually listened?

I texted our sitter to see if she could stay late, thanking whatever gods looked out for working mothers that Meredith had broken up with her girlfriend a few months before and now had most nights free. At lunchtime I took a cab up to Bloomingdale's and found a flattering fit-and-flare dress on sale, which let me justify the purchase of some Kate Spade heels, which were not. The Drybar at my gym took care of my hair— I'd been planning on pretending that I'd worked out, but my stylist had been deep in conversation with the guy working at the next station and hadn't even asked. Back at work, I popped into Amy's office to ask if I could head out early for a special romantic evening that I'd somehow managed to not know about, or know about and then forget, but she'd left early, too.

No matter. At seven o'clock I Uber'd a town car, gave the address, and scrolled through the review on my phone. I had figured out which appetizer and main course I wanted when I reached the maître d's stand, five minutes before our seven-thirty reservation. "Party of two? Kravitz?" I said. The hostess looked at her book, frowning.

"I'm so sorry, ma'am. The reservation was for two, and both parties have already arrived."

Huh. "Let me see if I can figure out what's going on. It's my husband," I said, giving her a conspiratorial, you-know-how-men-are look. She smiled politely and led me to the table, and there was Jay, in one of the sharp new suits he'd bought the month before and a dark-blue shirt that picked up on its pinstripes. He didn't see me coming. He was leaning forward, speaking intently to the woman in the other chair, who was petite and shapely, in a black dress with lacy black sleeves, with jet-black hair pinned up in a twist. Rage and terror rose inside of me. My knees started to shake so that I wasn't sure I'd be able to close the distance, but I made myself keep walking. I was almost at the table when Jay finally looked up.

"Sorry if I'm interrupting," I said. Then I looked down and saw that his dinner companion was Amy, unrecognizable out of her work uniform of a crisp white shirt and trousers.

"Oh, thank God!" Weak with relief, I almost collapsed into the third chair that a waiter had whisked over. "Do you know that for ten seconds I thought Jay was having an affair?"

Jay just stared at me, mouth open, eyes bulging slightly, like a fish. Amy bent her head, staring down at the gold-rimmed charger. And then I knew. "Oh," I said, feeling so faint that if I hadn't been sitting I would have collapsed. "Oh, no."

I should have noticed, I told myself when I was in a cab, heading home alone. In September, when Delaney had started full-day kindergarten, we'd cut back our sitter's hours, and had a little more money and a little more free time. Jay joined a gym and began exercising five days a week, after he'd walked the girls to school. In a depressingly short amount of time he'd shed twenty pounds and an absurd percentage of his body fat. He bought a fancy bike with a titanium frame and joined a cycling club, coming home late three nights a week freshly showered, glowing with exertion and good cheer. He'd hoist Delaney up over his head as she shrieked in mock terror, and listen patiently to Adele's lengthy recounting of her day at school, and who'd snubbed her in the lunchroom. I hadn't paid much attention when he'd bought new suits and shirts and even new underpants—boxer-briefs, Calvin Klein, not the stodgy baggy cotton boxer shorts that I'd been getting him for years. He was thinner; of course he'd needed new clothes, and if he wanted to buy them instead of texting me a shopping list, that was just fine.

Three months went by; three months of me

noticing nothing. Three months of doing the laundry and helping with homework and making beds and making dinner; three months of doing the dishes and sweeping the floors, so busy that it didn't seem to matter that Jay and I hadn't really kissed, let alone said "I love you," in a long time and that when we had sex it was predictable and fast. We'd send each other texts during the day, mostly about the girls' schedules or whether we'd left money for the cleaning lady, and adding an *ILY* to the message seemed meaningless, like a waste of time. When we finally did get to bed, we were both too exhausted to even touch each other. Sleep was all we longed for; the voluptuous embrace of linen and down the only touch we craved.

Amy and Jay. Of course we'd all spent time together over the years—Amy and her husband had been guests at the girls' naming ceremonies, and at every one of their birthday parties, and we'd gone to their house for the elaborate feasts that Leonard would prepare after he took up cooking as a hobby. There'd been impromptu get-togethers, summer afternoons in our little backyard, where we'd downed pitchers of sangria and watched the girls run through the sprinklers as Jay tried manfully to light the grill—but, as far as I knew, Jay and Amy had never had much of a connection. They'd dated for just six weeks in college, and Jay had been typically vague when I'd asked why they'd ended things. "She's a little pushy," he'd say, and all my boss ever said about my husband was "He's a great guy."

"We never meant for this to happen," Amy finally managed.

"Few do," I said. Then Jay had stammered out some nonsense about how now he finally knew what people meant when they talked about soul mates, the *coup de foudre*, except his French accent was so terrible that I didn't know what he was talking about and made him repeat it twice. Soul mates! Had I ever imagined my sensible, lawyerly husband, with his monogrammed brief-case and receding hairline, using a phrase like that?

"Could you excuse us for a moment?" I asked Amy politely. "I need to speak to my husband alone."

She'd at least had the grace to look pained by the word *husband* as she'd slunk toward the door. I took the seat she'd left empty—metaphor!—and stared at my husband, whose brow was furrowed and eyes were soft, like some director had told him, "Do contrition," and he was trying his very hardest to look sorry.

"Why?" I asked him. Waiters passed the table, bearing trays of delicious-smelling dinners. Somewhere in the restaurant, I could hear people singing "Happy Birthday." Outside, it had started to rain.

Jay sighed. It was the same sigh I'd heard thousands of times during our marriage, a sigh as familiar to me as my own. Then I watched his face transform, lighting up like someone had lit a match inside a carved pumpkin. His eyes were shining as he described his beloved. "I'm not saying this to hurt you, but I want to be honest. What I feel with Amy, that's what love is supposed to be. Real love."

"So what do we have? Fake love? Ten years of nothing?" My voice was grating, probably too loud. I was furious at him, for cheating, and for doing it for such dopey, predictable reasons.

"I haven't been happy for a long time."

I rocked back in the chair like he'd shoved me. "You might have mentioned it. You know, just a little clue or two, during your years and years of misery."

"When would I have mentioned it? You're never home! And when you are home, you're on the phone with one of your clients, and there's always some kind of crisis. You don't know me anymore."

"I love you," I whispered . . . even though at that moment I was not entirely sure that it was true.

He shook his head, a patient teacher instructing a slow learner. "No, Rachel, you don't. You admire me. You need me. You like the things I do. But you don't love me. You don't know me. You don't . . ."

"How about I don't cheat?" I hissed. "How about when I promised to love you, in sickness and health, forsaking all others, I wasn't kidding? How about I'd never fuck your boss?" Which was especially true, given that Jay's boss was his father, a kind, avuncular man of seventy-six. "Oh, and also, how about if I did cheat, I wouldn't be enough of a dumbass to use my wife's OpenTable account to make my reservations!"

Jay sighed again. "I'm prepared to be fair," he said.

"Oh, yeah? Well, maybe you'd better prepare to be broke, because I'm going to find the biggest shark in the tank and I'm going to take you to the cleaners." *Biggest shark in the tank. Take you to the cleaners.* Where had I gotten these lines? Probably from one of the reality shows I loved, the ones Jay called *my programs. Oh, no, we can't go out on Monday, Rachel needs to be home for her programs.* I'd believed he was just being playful. Only now I thought maybe his dislike hadn't been feigned. There'd been things that had annoyed me about him, too, but I'd picked my battles strategically, refusing to fight about the petty irritations that went with living with another adult. I'd thought I'd been so smart, managing my marriage like it was another case at work, and what had it gotten me? My husband with another woman, looking forward to a long, happy life with my ex–best friend.

"Are you coming home?" I asked. My voice cracked on the last word, and finally, I could feel the tears, a scalding tide of them, waiting to wash through my numbness. "No, you know what? You're not. You're not welcome. You can stay somewhere else." Then, with my back straight and my head held high and my gait a little strange because I was locking my knees to keep them from shaking, I'd walked out of the restaurant and then all the way downtown. The rain had tapered off to a light mist, and the smell rising up from the pavement was a blend of filth and urine and that wet, wormy scent that came from the ground after a storm. The urge to cry had receded; the rage had returned. My jaw was clenched, my feet came down hard with each step, stomping the wet pavement, and I glared at any pedestrian who blocked my path or tried to edge me out with their umbrella. I was furious at Jay for what he'd done, furious at myself for having missed all the signs, furious at Amy, who'd set me up with Jay in the first place and then decided she wanted him back.

But that wasn't the worst part. For years, I'd told myself that Andy was my big mistake; that he, along with all the surgeries and everything that had gone with them, were the tests I had to pass so that I could meet the man I was meant to be with, and live the life I was supposed to live. But if my husband, that promised gold at the end of the rainbow, was leaving, then clearly I'd been wrong. What story could I tell myself now?

I'd found out about the affair on a Friday night, the start of one of the many long weekends that sending your children to private school guaranteed. The girls would be home Monday while their teachers attended some kind of enrichment. Jay texted me to say that he'd arranged for Adele and Delaney to spend the weekend with his father in Long Island. His brother, Ben, and his wife and their three-year-old daughter would be there, too, and there was nothing Adele and Delaney loved better than being the big girls when their little cousin was around. That weekend, before Brenda's arrival, I only left the bed to pee and scoop the occasional swallow of water out of the sink. I couldn't stop hearing the crap Jay had said, about soul mates and the thunderclap and how he finally knew how love was supposed to feel.

I could have told you, is what I should have said. *I felt that way, once, but not about you. About Andy.*

I'd planned on staying in bed indefinitely, but now Nana was here, ushering the girls into my bedroom, where they found me showered, in a clean nightgown, on clean sheets.

"Mommy!" cried Delaney, racing across the room to vault onto the mattress and into my arms. Her hair was done in a fancy French braid

—courtesy of Aunt Katie, I assumed—and she was wearing strawberry-scented lip gloss and her favorite maxi-dress.

"Why are you in here?" asked Adele, whose book-crammed backpack was still hanging from her skinny shoulders.

"I have taken to my bed. It's like an in-service day."

"Yay!" Delaney whooped, and went dashing to her bedroom. Delaney was a pistol. Older people said she looked like Shirley Temple; people my age saw a brunette Annie. She was delightfully plump, with light-brown ringlets and a constant smile, the adorableness of which was only enhanced by the gap where her front teeth used to be.

"You want us to wear our nightgowns in the daytime?" asked Adele. She had the same light-brown hair as her younger sister, only hers was thick and straight, cut, at her insistence, in an old-fashioned ear-length bob. She'd been sober, reserved, thoughtful, and cautious ever since she was an infant, when she'd squirm away from hugs and cuddles in order to gaze at dust motes in a beam of sunshine, or a bug batting itself against a window, or her own baby fingers wiggling in the air. Some days I thought she'd be a scientist, because of the way she'd assess every situation, considering every potential outcome before committing, whether the action in question was jumping into a swimming pool or blowing out the candles on a birthday cake.

Some days I wondered what had made her such a pessimist, perpetually braced for disappointments: the wrong kind of sandwich in her lunchbox, the wrong color tights laid out on her bed, the scary sixty-year-old first-grade teacher instead of the pretty Miss Rose, who had a tiny, glittery stud in her nose and a tattoo of birds on her shoulder. Delaney loved sweets; Adele had been known to dismiss desserts as "too rich." Delaney left a litter of toys and shoes and clothing wherever she went. Adele kept her room hospital-neat, and had told me more than once that we didn't need to spend money on a cleaning lady when we could just clean up after ourselves. On vacation, Delaney adored ordering room service, and would watch eagerly while the waiter wheeled the white-draped cart into our room, then opened up its wings, turning it into a table. Adele, meanwhile, would scrutinize the bill, purse her lips at the 18 percent delivery surcharge, and tell her sister that it would be much less expensive to just eat in the restaurant. "Or we could just bring food from home!"

Once, after a five-year-old classmate's birthday party where Adele had refused to play in the ball pit—"because there are germs in there," she'd earnestly explained, "and because also, what if somebody pees?"—I'd been so concerned that

I'd taken her to a therapist, who reassured me that children were different, that to a large degree their personalities were hardwired, and that I should love Adele the way she was while doing my best to show her that the world was not a terrible place full of bad things just waiting to happen. I wondered how I could get her to believe that now.

"Why do we need our nightgowns?" she asked.

"We are taking to our beds," I repeated. "Well, my bed, technically."

"I have homework," Adele protested.

"You are lying," I said. "I know for a fact that your teachers didn't give you anything over the weekend."

Adele fidgeted, frowning. "I want to read ahead."

"Can I watch *Victorious*?" Delaney wheedled, skipping back into the bedroom in her flannel Lanz nightgown with the iPad already in her hand. I shut my eyes. I couldn't remember if that was a show we let her see or something we'd decided was too mature, but I knew that Jay and I had discussed it, probably in this very bed. Probably I hadn't been paying attention. More likely than not, I'd had my phone on and my earpiece tucked into my ear and I'd been solving some other mother's problems.

"You're in charge of the entertainment," I told Delaney, ignoring her big sister's gasp. Then I pointed at Adele. "You're in charge of dinner. You can pick what we're having. There's money in the cookie jar." "Seriously?" Amy had once asked when I'd told her I kept my money in the cookie jar. "That is so 1950s."

When Delaney was engrossed in her program and Adele was sorting through menus, her straight hair obscuring her cheeks and the tip of her tongue poking out, I found Nana in the living room. She was dressed in one of what I'd always thought of as her New York outfits—tailored tweed pants, low-heeled leather boots, a cream-colored pullover, clothes she'd bought at Saks Fifth Avenue when she came to the city (there were, of course, Saks stores in Florida, but Nana said they didn't have the inventory of New York City). I looked at myself, in my stretched-out ten-year-old nightgown and my hair that I'd washed and combed but hadn't dried or styled.

"I have a suggestion," she said. "When is their school year over?"

"The first Thursday in June." The date—ridiculously early, in my opinion—had been on my mind for weeks as I'd scrambled to find day camps that started before July.

"Why don't you take some time off and come to Florida?" she asked. "I'm sure your boss will let you take a few weeks' leave, all things considered."

"All things considered," I repeated, and struggled to push the words through my brain. It was like shoving clumps of Delaney's Play-Doh through the plastic extruder, hoping they'd yield some meaning.

"I will help Delaney pack," said Adele, who'd come into the room with a pad and a pen, ready to take dinner orders. A judgmental tone crept into her voice. "Last time all she put in her suitcase was stuffed animals and glitter glue and three princess costumes."

"I remember." Last time had been in November, when we'd made a pilgrimage to Disney World to celebrate Delaney's fifth birthday. While Jay tried to coax Adele to ride at least one of the roller coasters, I'd taken Delaney for her big present, a session with a stylist at the Bibbidi Bobbidi Boutique. Her "fairy godmother in training," a heavyset teenager in a blue-and-white gown and apron combination, had asked, "Did you make your list for Santa yet, princess?" Delaney's nose wrinkled as she considered the question. "I did NOT make a list for Santa," Delaney finally said, in her sweetly piping voice, "because I am a Jewish princess." I'd laughed so hard that I'd inhaled some of my soda and Delaney had stared at me in alarm and irritation, demanding to know what was so funny. Later, in our suite at the Polynesian Village, with fire-works blooming outside in the dark and the girls asleep on the bed, Delaney still dressed as

Cinderella, with glitter in her hair, and Adele clutching her Mickey Mouse ears, Jay had put his arm around my waist and said, "This is so great."

Had he been with Amy even then? And what would I do about work? There was only room for one of us at FAS, and I hoped it would be me. I loved my job. Maybe that had been the problem. Defying Jay's wishes, I'd gone back to work after six weeks at home with each of my girls, leaving them with an extremely capable nanny for eight hours a day, and unlike my husband, I'd never learned the trick of leaving my work at the door. Jay would set his briefcase down in the entryway and not utter a word—or, as best I could tell, entertain a thought—about his clients or cases, or his annual performance evaluation, whereas I was always dragging messy stacks of folders into the living room, and leaving my cell phone on in case my clients needed to reach me. I thought that Jay's nonchalance was the byproduct of working at his father's firm. Even if he failed to meet the benchmark for billable hours, even if he screwed up spectacularly and got himself accused of malpractice, as one of the partners once had, he'd never lose his job. I didn't think I'd ever lose mine, either, but I knew that my clients needed me available and at my best. Maybe a son had been arrested; maybe the gas had been shut off; maybe a woman who'd already put in a twelve-hour day needed help finishing her homework for the class she was taking at night. *A woman of valor,* I would think sometimes . . . and when Jay chided me for staying up late or texting one of my ladies when I could have been joining him in whatever he was currently watching, I would tell him that it was important for the girls to see me do my job, to know what I did, to know who I worked with and that not everyone was as privileged as they were.

"What about after?" I asked Nana, who patted my hand reassuringly.

"You'll get through it," she said, leaving out the part I already knew—*because you're a mother now. Because mothers don't have a choice.*

Andy

2014

New York

"Mr. Landis?" Andy's latest hire, a kid named Paul Martindale, was standing in front of him looking even more nervous than he normally did. Paul was nineteen, a part-time student at CCNY, tall, pimply, and terrified. If a woman asked him where to find the lightbulbs or the paint display or the gardening mulch, he'd look at her like she'd pulled a knife out of her diaper bag, and if a man asked him anything, he'd stammer, "Let me get the manager," and run.

"Yes, Paul," Andy said patiently, and wondered, again, whether moving him from the overnight shift to days had been a mistake.

"Phone call for you."

"I'll be right there," said Andy, and walked toward his office at the back of the store.

Andy had come to Wallen Home Goods five years ago, not hoping for much but telling himself that he had to start somewhere. Years ago, the home-goods chain had announced a policy of hiring Olympic hopefuls, giving them flexible schedules so they could keep up with their training. Andy hadn't known how they would feel about hiring a disgraced ex-Olympian, but he'd decided it wouldn't be a bad place to try.

His interview had been scheduled for 8:00 in the morning. He'd been in the parking lot at 7:00 a.m., sweating behind the wheel of the sedan that he'd bought for its trunk space and the easy access it offered to the front seats. On weekends he went to Philadelphia and drove Mr. Sills wherever he wanted to go—to junk shops, to bookstores, to church, to visit family and friends. It was Mr. Sills who'd encouraged him to get a job —because, he said, Andy needed purpose, and structure to his days. Routine, respectability, the first step on the road back to not hating himself quite so much. Andy's first thought had been coaching, but after he'd written to Roman Catholic and gotten a form-letter rejection, he'd decided that if his alma mater didn't want him, no one would.

"You always were handy," Mr. Sills had said. Andy had wondered if he could be a superintendent for an apartment complex or even work as a handyman, but then he'd thought of Wallen and imagined a big, anonymous store, different faces every day, not the same small handful of people in a neighborhood or apartment building, who'd have too many questions, and decided to try. They offered benefits, he vaguely remem-bered, and they had classes there, in plumbing and painting and basic repairs. Maybe someday he'd teach them.

He remembered how hot it had been that morning, the air almost liquid, a heavy soup you had to push through to get anywhere. As he sat behind the wheel, his muscles clenched in a familiar knot, as if he was waiting for a starter's gun that would never go off. His right leg jiggled and jumped; his toes flexed and curled; his fingers were rattling on the dashboard. In spite of the air-conditioning and the liberal application of deodorant, he'd already sweated through his undershirt.

That was just one of the post-scandal adjustments—the new clothes he'd had to buy. Khakis and jeans, shoes that weren't sneakers, shirts that had long sleeves and weren't made of wickable, odor-fighting fabric. On Interview Day, he'd worn Dockers, a white button-down, and the only tie that he'd kept, a heavy red-and-gold silk one from Hermès that Maisie had bought him for a birthday. With the fifteen pounds he'd put on since he had made what would be his final magazine appearance—*Newsweek*, six weeks after the revelations, had put the runners on the cover, beneath the single word DISGRACE—he no longer had an athlete's leanness. He looked like every other clock-bound couch rider, like a guy who put in maybe three halfhearted days a week at the gym, and who'd get winded after a single turn around a track.

How do you act when you've lost everything? he'd wondered, walking through the parking lot to the front door. He'd kept his medal, but all of the prizes were gone: the endorsement deals, the pricey restaurants, the fine wines and fancy friends, actors and politicians who liked to collect athletes the same way they collected vintage cars and Impressionist paintings. And Maisie, of course. Maisie used to laugh and roll her eyes at the phrase *trophy girlfriend. So I'm just another one of your things,* she would tease, usually while she was naked, lying on the bed, long, smooth legs stretched out on the duvet cover, hips angled just so. She would act offended, but Andy thought that she enjoyed being the female equivalent of a gold medal.

He wondered what Maisie would make of his Brooklyn apartment, which could fit, in its entirety, into their Manhattan living room; what she'd say about his new clothes, not to mention his new body. He wondered, too, about Rachel—if she'd gotten married, if she was still doing social work, if she'd ever had kids. He'd wanted to see if she would call or write in the wake of the scandal—maybe to sympathize, maybe to gloat—but she hadn't, and he'd never tried to find her, never hunted her down on Facebook or punched her name into Google. He imagined her husband, probably a guy with the right kind of background, upper-middle-class and Jewish, someone who'd make her parents happy. He thought that she would have had children and be good with them, her social-worker training combined with her good instincts and big heart. A happy, normal life. That's what she deserved, and he hoped it was what she'd gotten.

He'd walked into the manager's office holding his résumé, sad thing that it was, trying not to sweat on the paper. In a perverse way, he was proud of it. The résumé was a triumph of creativity, the first fiction he'd ever written. Describing his years as a paperboy, Andy had promoted himself to an "employee of the distribution department of a major news organization." He had written that he'd been "self-employed as an independent contractor working around the world" for the last ten years, without saying that he'd been a runner, and if the manager asked him about the years between losing that job and applying for this one, Andy would simply say that he'd been a free-lance consultant and then shut his mouth and hope that the follow-up question wasn't "Consulting about what?" He'd also have to hope that the manager wouldn't instantly know who he was.

Short answers, he'd told himself as he walked into the air-conditioning, down an aisle of lawn mowers and hedge trimmers. If Andy was hired, he'd be working the midnight-to-eight shift. Night stocker. The thought made him smile, and think, as jokes sometimes did, of Rachel, who would have laughed.

He found a door labeled EMPLOYEES ONLY, pushed through it, found another door with a strip of plastic reading JACK KINCAID, STORE MANAGER, and knocked. A voice yelled, "Come on in!" Andy walked into the office and saw a man struggling to get up from an ergonomic desk chair. Jack Kincaid wore steel-rimmed glasses, a dark-blue shirt, pleated khaki pants, and work boots. A pocket protector held half a dozen ball-point pens, and a cell phone was holstered to his brown leather belt. Toothpick legs floated inside of his pants; spindly arms poked out of the short sleeves of his shirt. Between them was what looked like a giant inflatable sphere, perfectly round and looking as hard as a basketball, bulging at the buttons of the shirt (the bottom two, Andy noted, were unbuttoned, the cloth gaping to reveal a white undershirt).

Mr. Kincaid finally made it to his feet. "Andrew Landis?"

Andy had offered his hand. Jack Kincaid shook it once, gripping hard as he looked at him more closely. Andy tensed his muscles and braced for the inevitable.

"Not *the* Andy Landis, are you? Andy Landis the runner?"

"Yessir," he said. He hated the servility in his voice, the fresh sweat underneath his arms, the way his body was still wound tight, desperate for motion. "Andy Landis," he said. "That's me."

"Well," said Jack Kincaid. "Well, well, well." He rocked back on his heels. Given the belly, Andy half expected him to tip onto his back, but Mr. Kincaid, like a Weeble, wobbled but did not fall down. He took a seat, laced his fingers across that formidable gut, and looked Andy over, from the top of his head to his feet, encased in blameless brown loafers from the Hecht's in Cherry Hill, where he'd taken Mr. Sills to buy clothes for his newest grandnephew.

Andy waited for *Lo, how the mighty have fallen.* He waited for *Crime doesn't pay* or *Actions have consequences* or *Serves you right.* He waited for the man to tell him to get the hell out of his office and never darken the door of a Wallen Home Goods ever again.

Jack Kincaid finally spoke. "Need a job, huh?"

Andy nodded and sweated.

"Didn't save any of that PowerUp money?"

"I paid my sponsors back, as much as I could."

Jack Kincaid went quiet, pausing for what felt like forever. The office was small and airless, a concrete cube lit by fluorescent tubes, with a metal desk, cinder-block walls, and a plain office calendar thumbtacked to a bulletin board on one wall. On the desk, Andy saw family photographs—Jack Kincaid with his wife, adults who Andy supposed were his children, and little kids who had to be grandchildren.

"You have a beautiful family," Andy said.

"Got any kids?" the other man asked.

Andy shook his head.

"You and your wife break up?"

Another nod. No sense correcting the man, telling him that Maisie had never been his wife. The news of their split had appeared in *People* magazine. Maisie had posed for a picture, barefoot in a lacy white sundress. *Running Free*, read the headline. The piece had been a roundup about the wives and families of the Athens Nine. The quote that Maisie had given, printed in big letters, read, *Andy Landis wasn't the man I thought he was.*

Kincaid picked up Andy's résumé and flapped

it in the air a few times. "You're overqualified."
He gave a dry, chuffing laugh. "Hell, probably a
monkey would be overqualified for this. It's
midnight to eight in the morning. You'll run a
flat-loader and a forklift. Break down boxes,
build endcaps, get contractors' orders ready to go.
Dust the stuff on the high shelves, dry-mop the
floors, recycle the cardboard, clean the rest-
rooms, make sure everything's shipshape in the
morning. No customers." He considered, giving
the hard mound of his belly an affectionate pat.
"Probably that's for the best. It's minimum wage,
and I can't offer more, so don't ask. You don't
have any injuries, do you? Back's okay?"

Andy shook his head. "No injuries." His back
was fine. He'd had three operations on his right
knee, but that, too, was fine, at least for work like
this.

"We drug test, you know. Probably not for the
stuff you were doing—we don't have many
clerks on steroids—but everything else. Booze,
too. Don't even think about showing up loaded."

"I don't drink." This was another part of the
mythology that the publicists had cultivated:
Andy Landis as a clean-cut, square-jawed, all-
American boy who wouldn't celebrate a victory
with so much as a beer. That, of course, had only
added to the irony when it turned out the all-
American boy was a doper. Kincaid gave him a
dubious look before folding the résumé in half,

then in quarters, and setting it in the middle of the empty blotter at the center of his desk.

"I believe in second chances," he said. "Show up on time, do your work, don't make any trouble."

"I can do all that," said Andy, and backed out of the office before Jack Kincaid could change his mind.

On his first night, Andy met the two men whom he'd go on to work with for years. There was Martin, a skinny black guy in his twenties who talked nonstop, and Arturo, who was middle-aged and Mexican and barely spoke at all. Martin had a carefully tended puff of an Afro and wore jeans that drooped low enough to display six inches of blinding-white boxer-briefs. Arturo wore jeans, too, only his were stiff and new-looking, cinched with a leather belt with a giant buckle that, per its engraving, he'd won riding bulls.

"Hey, man, welcome," said Martin, and Arturo lifted a hand and gave a quiet "Hello." Andy had introduced himself, and they'd gone right to work restocking the garden center, two hours of lifting fifty-pound sacks of mulch and peat moss. Martin plugged in his earbuds, bobbed his head, and chanted rap lyrics under his breath. Arturo, too, had an iPod, but he hadn't turned the volume up enough so that Andy could hear what he was playing. They didn't talk much, other than the necessary exchanges about when it was time to wheel over another pallet of bags, until 3:00 a.m., when they stopped to eat.

There was, as Mr. Kincaid had promised, a break room in the back of the cavernous store, with a microwave, a machine that sold sodas and another that sold snacks, four round tables with folding chairs, and a refrigerator where they could keep what they'd brought from home. Martin went to the fridge and pulled out a plastic bag from 7-Eleven filled with half a dozen Slim Jims, a box of Nutter Butter cookies, a quart of Pepsi, and a bag of Funyuns, which Andy hadn't seen since the 1980s and didn't realize people were still eating. Arturo walked to the front of the store, unlocked the doors, and came back with a thermos full of steaming coffee and two cardboard trays loaded with enough food for half a dozen men. "Please," he said, offering Andy the trays. Andy saw stacks of foil-wrapped tortillas, con-tainers of beans and rice and garlicky pork and chicken in a rich-smelling brown sauce, guacamole and salsa with chunks of pineapple and cilantro. It all smelled amazing, but he had packed himself a pair of clumsy peanut-butter-and-banana sandwiches, a bag of baby carrots, an apple, and two bottles of PowerUp. "I'm okay," he said.

Arturo then offered the trays to Martin.

"You know this stuff gonna give me the runs." Martin shook his head, then selected a tortilla and layered on cheese and beans and spicy pork.

440

Arturo didn't seem to hear, or at least he didn't respond as he took a seat. Martin ate the burrito he'd claimed not to want almost daintily, using a scrap of tortilla to scoop up every bit of cheese and sauce. Then he plugged some crumpled bills into the vending machine and came back with another bottle of Pepsi. He took a long swallow, belched, recapped the bottle, then said, "You ever notice that white people never drink Pepsi? Just Coke. No Pepsi."

Andy, who hadn't noticed, shook his head. When Arturo offered the trays again, Andy helped himself to arroz con pollo, beans, and tortillas.

"Arturo's wife runs a food truck," Martin said. Andy took a bite of the beans, piping hot and perfectly seasoned.

"This is delicious. Thanks."

"What's your deal?" asked Martin, pronouncing the word like *dill,* as in pickle. "Where'd you come from? How'd you end up here?"

"I grew up near Philadelphia, but I've been living in New York for a while."

"What'd you do before this?"

"I was a freelance consultant," Andy answered. Over the years, he'd collected meaningless job descriptions—the woman at one of the parties Maisie had taken him to who'd said, "I'm in the art world" ("I bet that means she's a seventh-grade art teacher," Maisie had sniffed); a guy at a photo shoot who'd said he was a stylist, then looked at Andy like Andy had just crapped on the floor after he asked, "So, like, hair?"

"I style everything," the man had answered, and stalked off to join the rest of his whispering, black-clad crew. Worst of all was one of Mitch's college friends, a guy Andy had met on a golf course in Florida, who'd said he was a freelance consultant, without telling them anything else. Freelance consultant, Andy had decided, was what he'd say if anyone had questions about his work that he didn't want to answer . . . and if they kept asking, he'd just throw in the word *finance*.

"So you went from 'consulting' "—Martin hooked his fingers into air quotes—"to working the night shift here at Wallen."

"I'm taking some time to regroup," Andy said. "I went through a pretty bad breakup."

"Ah-HAH," said Martin. "Now we are getting somewhere." He leaned toward Andy like a TV reporter who specialized in getting his subjects to cry. "What happened with you and the missus?" he asked. "Was she cheating? Were you cheating? You guys have any kids?"

"Leave him alone," Arturo said. Martin ignored him.

"Things had run their course," said Andy— another answer he'd prepared during his days on the couch. He got to his feet, dropped his paper plate in the trash, and pulled out the apple he'd packed for dessert.

"Aw, no, man. No way. Give it up! If we're going to spend forty hours a week together, I'm gonna need some actual information. *Ran its course*," he repeated, giving the words a nasal white-guy-with-an-overbite rendering. "What does that mean? It means nothing. You feel me?" *Feel* sounded like *fill*.

Andy shrugged, hoping the subject would stay changed. No such luck. "Lemme see a picture," Martin demanded.

"Don't have one," said Andy.

"Now I know that's not true," Martin said. "You look like you're pining over her. Piiiiining," he repeated. "Plus, you got your phone."

Andy wondered what would happen if he did a Google search for images of Maisie. Maybe Martin would think he was kidding . . . and maybe that would be the end of it. Mentally crossing his fingers, he took his phone from his pocket, tapped her name into the search bar, then clicked on a picture of her in a bikini bottom, with her right arm crossed over her breasts and swim-suit top dangling coyly from her fingertips. "Here."

Martin looked, then grinned, shaking his head. "Oh, sure, man," he said. "Ha fuckin' ha. Who's she, the number-one girl in your spank bank?"

"We can all dream," said Andy, and held his hand out for the phone. Instead of giving it back, though, Martin stared at the picture more closely. Then he looked up at Andy. Then down at the picture again.

"Hold up, hold up," he said, lifting one hand into the air.

Andy's stomach was churning. "Shouldn't we get back to work?" he asked.

"Fifteen more minutes," said Arturo. His face was expressionless, but Andy had the distinct impression that he was enjoying this.

"Aw, shit," Martin said, and did a little leap of delight. "You're that guy! You're, you're . . ." He snapped his fingers, then pointed at Andy. "The runner! Marathon man! With the drugs! And that's your wife!"

"Girlfriend. Ex-girlfriend." Andy looked at the clock. His anonymity had lasted less than three hours. "And it wasn't the marathon, it was—"

"You're Andy Landis!" Martin said. "That's your name! Holy shit! Is that why you're here? Because Wallen hires ath-a-letes? Are you still a runner? You in training for something new?"

"Retired," Andy said. He threw out his apple and looked at Arturo. "What's next?"

"Ten minutes of break left," said Arturo. No question at all, he was enjoying the show.

"I got more questions!" said Martin.

"No comment," Andy said. He walked to the back of the store, hoping to find something to lift or stack or maybe even hit. Martin followed him, jabbering queries and opinions. "Damn, man. You gonna do drugs, why not do the ones that make you feel good? That crap you was on, you don't even get high off it. Plus, it shrinks your nuts." He gave his own crotch a check-in squeeze through jeans baggy enough to contain another person, then looked at Andy sideways. "Your nuts get shrunk?"

Andy gave a single headshake. Martin's cackles rose to the ceiling and seemed to gather volume as they echoed through the empty store. "Yeah, you say. But if your nuts were shrunk, would you really tell anyone?" Andy bent his head and grabbed three bags of mulch, hoping that work would end the chatter. No such luck. Martin picked up two bags of his own, talking about Maisie, about running, about his own skill on the basketball court and how he, too, could have had a shot at the Olympics, could have been a contender.

Feeling desperate, Andy tried to change the subject. "Do you like working here?"

Martin made a noise somewhere between a grunt and a laugh. "It ain't bad. Kincaid a'ight. Long as the work gets done, we can use headsets, talk on the phone, whatever." Martin plugged in his ear-buds but didn't start his music. "So she left you?"

Andy nodded.

Martin's face grew comically somber. "She dump you 'cause of the dope?"

"That's right." Andy didn't feel like going into specifics. They made one trip to the greenhouse in silence, with Martin sneaking looks at Andy.

"Must be rough," Martin said as they set down

their load. He didn't say anything else on the subject, and Arturo, who'd been up on the ladder, restocking the shelves of plant food, hadn't spoken, either, but the next night when they'd had their break Arturo had carried back three trays instead of two, and at the end of the night Martin had mentioned a Saturday-morning pickup game on the high school basketball courts, open to anyone, including ex-marathon-running, gold-medal-winning pretty boys with shrunken testicles. Andy thought that was when he'd felt things start to turn, when he'd sensed the possibility that someday he could be reasonably happy again.

On Saturday morning, Martin and his friends, who ranged in age from eighteen to forty, had more or less mopped the court with Andy, who discovered that he was disgustingly, terrifyingly out of shape, that he had no shot at all and no way to defend himself against the bigger, brawnier guys who'd come for him under the boards. Early the next morning, bruised in a dozen places and aching all over, he'd started driving toward Philadelphia . . . but then, instead of taking the exit that would have brought him to his mother's house, he'd decided to keep going, over the Walt Whitman Bridge and onto the Atlantic City Expressway, following the signs reading BEACHES until he found a parking spot. It was just after seven in the morning. The sun was turning the sky the color of orange sherbet, glinting off the water, making each ripple shine. Lifeguards with zinc-coated noses were climbing up into their chairs; waves were spending themselves gently, leaving lacy foam on the sand; walkers and joggers were making their way along the boardwalk.

After everything that had happened, Andy had privately sworn that he would never run again, not even to catch a bus. But that had been years ago. Who would know? More important, why should he deny himself the pleasure of something he'd once loved? Running had once taken him to a place beyond thought, a place where there were no questions, no conversations, no debates about right or wrong, fate and destiny. Would it still work?

Andy unlaced his work boots and peeled off his socks. His feet had the unhealthy pallor of mushrooms that had sprouted during a rainstorm, and there was a basketball-induced blister on his left heel. His jeans would chafe if he went too far, and he hadn't brought sunscreen. He rolled up his cuffs and walked down to the water, feeling the sand, cool and firm, underneath his feet. First he started walking, swinging his arms, getting a feel for the sand. Then he eased into a slow trot. It felt, for a few hundred yards, like he was relearning something basic, like he'd somehow managed to forget to breathe and had to figure it out again. His legs felt clumsy; his arms were as stiff as sticks shoved into a snowman's side; his breath burned in his throat. He veered toward the water and stumbled as the sand shifted, almost bumping into a pair of optimistic surfers, chatting as they zipped up their wet suits. Then it started coming back to him, the rhythm and the flow. His stride smoothed out; his arms began swinging with a purpose; his heart and lungs took up their assignments. His skin tingled as he sped up. The sun shone down on his head and his shoulders, and sweat sprang up on his face and back, good, cleansing sweat, not the acrid excretions of a man who felt trapped. The air had a salty tang, the sky was suddenly full of birds, wheeling and squawking overhead. He didn't feel trapped anymore. For the first time in a long time, as he jogged, then ran, then sprinted along the water, Andy Landis felt like he was right where he should be, doing the thing he was meant to be doing, like the constant chatter of criticism in his mind had finally stilled. For the first time in a long time, he felt free.

That had been five years ago. He'd gotten merit raises, promotions; he'd become a section manager and had eventually started teaching those classes he'd once wondered about, instructing stressed-out dads and blissed-out newlyweds on how to paint a bedroom, how to install tile, repair drywall, stain a deck, build a grilling cart. When

Mr. Kincaid had retired, the regional supervisor had offered Andy his job, and Andy, who'd never imagined his life after running at all and had certainly never imagined spending it in charge of a cavernous, concrete-floored megastore, had agreed.

He walked into the office that had once been Jack Kincaid's, picked up the telephone that Paul had remembered to place on hold, and braced himself for the news he'd been expecting, and dreading, for the past six months, ever since Mr. Sills's pulmonary disease had gotten worse.

"Hello?"

"Andrew Landis?" It was an unfamiliar man's voice, hoarse and soft. "This is DeVaughn Sills. I'm Clement Sills's son."

"Hello," said Andy, setting his free hand on the desk, surprised and yet not surprised to hear from the son whom his friend so rarely mentioned, a son he'd never met, even as Mr. Sills's health had declined.

"My daddy passed last night."

"Oh, no," Andy said. He and Mr. Sills had talked it over—the death, and what would happen next—when he'd visited the previous weekend. Mr. Sills, whom Andy had never been able to call by his first name, had been in his bedroom. The room had been cleared of all the stacks, the books and magazines, the collections of teapots and ceramic roosters, the thick scrapbooks about

Andy. There was only a hospital bed, and two white plastic chairs for visitors. "I'm ready to go," Mr. Sills told him. "I lived a good long while."

"You have so many friends," Andy said. This was true. There'd been the boys whom Mr. Sills had met and befriended and helped over the years, many of whom had found their way into one of those white plastic chairs over the last weeks. They had left tokens, too: photographs of themselves with Mr. Sills, at basketball games and graduations, at weddings and christenings and First Communions and commencements. Pride of place had been saved for a framed photograph from Athens, of Mr. Sills, beaming, with his arm around Andy and the two of them wrapped in the American flag, with Andy in his laurel wreath and Mr. Sills wearing Andy's gold medal.

"I've made my peace," Mr. Sills wheezed. A tear slipped down his cheek. "I'm not afraid." But his hand was trembling when Andy took it. "I will miss this world," he said. His chest labored upward, paused, and sank down. "Andy," he said, reaching for Andy's hand. Andy leaned close. Mr. Sills's eyes were closed, and his voice was faint, but each word was clear and deliberate. "You can stop running now." Andy sat with him, waiting for more, but his friend's eyes stayed closed, and he didn't wake up again for the rest of the afternoon.

"Visitation's Wednesday and Thursday, and the

funeral's Friday at noon, at Mother Bethel on Sixth and South," DeVaughn Sills said.

Andy knew the church. Mr. Sills had brought him there for years on the day before Christmas, to hear the choir sing Handel's *Messiah.* Once, he'd gone to Midnight Mass on Christmas Eve.

"I'll be there," Andy promised.

"Then I'll see you," said DeVaughn.

On Friday morning, the church was packed with people, hushed and dim, with the sunshine filtered through stained glass, and it smelled like dusty carpet, old paper, and the lilies in the flower arrangement that decorated the handsome brass-trimmed casket that stood in the front of the room. It was closed, per Mr. Sills's request. "Let 'em remember me living, not dead," he'd told Andy, and Andy had been the one to bring the clothes his friend had chosen to the funeral parlor and tell the director there to skip the cosmetics.

He spotted DeVaughn right away, standing in the back of the church and looking so much like his father that Andy's heart almost stopped. DeVaughn wore a black suit, a white shirt, and a dark-gray tie. His hands were free, but when he walked, Andy saw the shackles around his ankles, and then he spotted the corrections officer who stood by the door. He felt his eyes welling, and wondered if DeVaughn even had gotten a chance to say goodbye.

The first row was filled with boys and young men, some in suits and some in collared blue shirts and khakis. A few of them were crying. Lori had left him at the doorway and had gone to sit beside a tall man in a dark suit. Andy looked at him, then looked away.

After Mr. Sills's favorite hymn, "What a Friend We Have in Jesus," the preacher stepped up to the lectern. He bowed his head for a long moment, then began. "Our friend is gone," he said.

"Yes, Lord," said one of the ladies Andy recognized from Mr. Sills's house, an older lady in a pink suit and matching hat.

"Whose lives did our friend Clement Sills not touch?"

"That's right," called another woman.

"Our friend was a humble man. A man who knew how to fix what was broken. He came into our homes with his box of tools and the young man he'd taken under his wing, and he fixed things. Fixed broken windows, leaky faucets, furnaces that didn't want to heat and air conditioners that didn't want to cool. But more than that, he fixed those young men. He saw what was broken in each of them, and he fixed it."

"Praise Jesus!"

"He was kind."

"Yes, God!"

"He was a father figure to the young men whose daddies couldn't or wouldn't be there for them.

By example, our friend Clement showed each and every one of them what it was to be a man." The preacher lowered his head again, as if lost in thought. Then he raised it and looked at the crowd.

"There's a young man here who's a lawyer. Another two go to Temple on scholarship. Up front, we got Terrance Parker, who's a vice president at Comcast. You got a problem with your cable bill, go talk to him." Laughter rippled through the audience. "In the back, I see a young friend of Clement's who became an Olympic runner." Andy froze, mortified, as he felt every eye turn toward him. He hung his head.

"All these men learned how to live their lives, how to make their way in the world, but more than that, even more than that, every single one of them learned how to love."

The room exploded with shouts of praise, to God, to Jesus, with cries of "Tell it!" and "Preach!"

"They learned how to love," called the preacher. He raised his hands and, immediately, the din dropped away. "And that, my brothers and sisters, is the true measure of a man. Not money."

"No, sir!"

"Not success."

"That's right!"

"Not job titles. Not degrees. Not even gold medals." The preacher's voice dropped to a whisper. "The measure of a man is, does he know how to love. Clement Sills knew how to love. That's what he did. That's what he taught every single one of us who were lucky enough to know him."

In the back of the room DeVaughn was crying. Andy saw the corrections officer hand him a handkerchief, as the pastor invited anyone who wanted to speak to come to the podium and send their friend on.

The young man who'd become a lawyer thanked Mr. Sills for showing him another path, "because I so easily could have walked down the wrong one." The Comcast vice president talked about how he'd been so shy as a little boy he'd barely opened his mouth in the classroom, and that his teachers thought he was slow until Mr. Sills started bringing him around to antiques stores and restaurants, making him talk to the salesladies and the waitresses until he could speak up a little better.

"When things got noisy in my house, Mr. Sills let me come over and study, as long as I could find room for my books," one of the Temple students said, to smiles and laughter, as the audience members recalled Mr. Sills's hobbit warren of a house. A single mom remembered how when her young daughter had broken her leg, Mr. Sills had been there, morning and night, to carry the girl down the stairs, and then carry her back up for bedtime.

Then the preacher called Andy up to the

podium, introducing him as "Andy Landis, the gold-medal-winning Olympic runner," and asked if he wanted to speak.

Andy had gripped the edges of the lectern. He thought about how long it had been since people had looked at him with anything but disdain. Enough time had passed so that, at least in some places, sometimes, he could just be what he'd become—the manager of a home-goods store, a so-so basketball player, a son, a coworker, a friend. "I grew up without a father," Andy began, "and I wasn't the greatest kid. I got in fights at school. Threw a brick through someone's windshield. I almost got sent to juvenile hall for that one," he said as some of the boys up front nodded. "Mr. Sills saved me. He made me feel like I was worth something. Nothing I did, nothing I had . . ." His voice caught, but he made himself push through it. "Nothing I achieved would have been possible without him."

Afterward, a few of the attendees came to introduce themselves. More than one told him how Mr. Sills had always talked about Andy, the way he'd run his paper route, how he'd been such a quiet boy, and how he'd flown Mr. Sills first class all the way to Athens, Greece, so he'd be there to watch Andy win his gold medal. "I think it was the highlight of his life," said the young man who'd gone to law school, and Terrance Parker had nodded and said, "He told me that, too."

Finally, Lori's aisle-mate, a tall, stooped man with a bald head and glasses, came over. He stood shyly a few feet away from Andy, the way autograph-seekers once had when they were waiting for a signal or permission to approach him.

Andy knew who he was; knew in his bones, knew from the way the other man was looking at him, and the shape of his face, and his hands.

"Hello," said Andy. He held out his hand to the man who he'd seen only in pictures and carefully his father shook it.

In the car, on the way home, his mother was quiet. It wasn't until they pulled into the driveway of the house she shared with her new husband, a retired police officer named Tony Lucrezi, that she said, "He wants to get to know you. He's sorry for everything."

"What's everything?" Andy felt furious, and he welcomed the feeling that pushed aside the sorrow. It felt good, he thought, to be angry at someone other than himself. "Which part is he ashamed of? The drugs, or the being an accessory to murder, or the part about lying to me for my entire life?"

Lori looked into her lap. "I'm not saying that the way he handled it was right, but we did it for the best reasons."

Andy just stared at her, not trying to disguise his skepticism or his disgust, and, instead of meeting his anger with her own, Lori continued to talk, her eyes on her lap as she stumbled through an explanation.

"Your father and DeVaughn were friends. They grew up together; they played sports together; they were high school basketball stars, the big men on campus." She smiled a little, remembering.

"So how'd they get from there to jail?" Andy asked.

Lori shut her eyes. "Once high school was over, and I was pregnant, there were a lot of temptations in the neighborhood. A lot of ways to make easy, quick money. Your dad wanted a house for us. He thought if he could just do one big thing, just one time, we'd move to Haddonfield, near my parents, and he'd learn a trade. He was doing okay in the army. They were training him to be a mechanic. He figured he'd stay a few years, learn how to do it, and when he got out he'd get a job. But he came home on a furlough, and DeVaughn had this idea, this great idea about how they were going to each get ten thousand dollars . . ."

"By robbing a friend," Andy supplied.

Lori shook her head. "It was stupid. They thought it was a Robin Hood thing, stealing from the rich, giving to the poor. Which was the three of us." She looked at him, her eyes wide and beseeching, an unfamiliar pleading tone in her voice. "They never meant to hurt David. They weren't like that. They just thought they'd roll up, stick the gun out the window, and he'd give them the money, and that would be the end of it."

"You're kidding."

"Andy, they were teenagers. They weren't criminal masterminds."

Andy shook his head. He was trying to make sense of it, to put it all together, his father and DeVaughn Sills, who'd driven the car, who'd used the gun.

"Mr. Sills lied to me," he said slowly. "He said he didn't know my father that well. And he sure never told me that my dad was alive."

"He didn't know your father that well. He only knew him as DeVaughn's friend. And he wanted to tell you. He thought that even having a father in jail was better than no father at all. He only kept quiet because Andy and I—your father and I—had asked him to. He was always looking out for us," Lori said. "He felt responsible. He thought that if he'd been a better father to DeVaughn none of it would have happened. It was stupid," said Lori, her voice catching. "It was stupid and awful, and it ruined so many lives, but, Andy, it's over. It's in the past. It was a long time ago, and you've got a chance to get to know your father now." She touched his hand. Her voice was gentle. Maybe her new marriage had softened her. Maybe it was just time. "If you can find it in your heart. But he'll understand if you can't."

"I'll think about it," Andy said . . . and he had, for months, considering each piece of the story, the new facts, trying to understand why they'd done what they'd done, and how their choices had shaped his own life. He had been so lonely as a kid. No friends, because his mother had wanted his strongest—his only—connection to be to her. When he was being charitable, he thought that she'd lied because she'd wanted to keep him safe, away from the influences and the kinds of people who had caused his father to make such bad choices. When he was angry, he thought that she'd kept him so close because other people in the neighborhood had to have known the truth . . . and that she hadn't noticed, or hadn't cared, about the way he was always on the outside; how he'd never really had friends.

A dozen times he sat behind the wheel of his car or climbed the steps to the El with a token in his hand. But he never turned the key, never boarded the train. He wished he could have done it all differently. Maybe he would never have agreed to the doping. Maybe he'd never have met Maisie. Maybe he could have had the life he'd imagined with Rachel, a quiet, happy Act Two, with his medal on the mantel of some cozy little home, kids playing in the yard, Lori visiting, and his father, too. Rachel would have known how to navigate the situation; she'd have made arrangements and made jokes and helped him figure out how to talk to a ghost that was now flesh and blood. But now he'd have to figure it out alone.

Rachel

2015

Jay had called me at the end of March, on a Thursday afternoon almost a year after I'd found out about Amy. On Thursdays, the girls had dance lessons. Delaney was enthusiastically attempting ballet—mostly because she loved the pink leotard and white tights, and she knew that if she made it to the recital, she'd get a pink tulle tutu—while Adele was the least energetic hip-hop dancer in the history of hip-hop. "I was wondering if I could come to the Seder."

I tamped down my first instinct, which was to ask why he and Amy hadn't been invited to celebrate with anyone. He'd moved into her place in Brooklyn Heights, just a few subway stops away from where we lived. I had seen the outside of their building but had never stepped inside. I hadn't seen Amy, either, since the night she and Jay had made their confession. She'd left FAS, and I'd never found out where she'd landed. The girls would mention her occasionally—as in "Amy came with us to see *The Nutcracker*," they'd say, or "Amy bought us sparkly shoes"— but I curbed my curiosity and never permitted myself to ask about her, or about them.

Per our divorce agreement, Jay got the girls for two nights during the week, plus the twenty-four hours from dinnertime Friday until dinnertime Saturday. Even after her departure, Amy must have put in a good word for me, because they'd approved my request to trim my hours from nine to three Monday through Friday, then work a long day every other weekend. Every weekday afternoon I'd dash to the subway to arrive at the girls' school by the time the dismissal bell rang. Together, the three of us would go to the park or shop for dinner or pick up our clothes at the laundry. We'd go to the shoe store or the bookstore or to dance class, to Adele's oboe lessons or Delaney's playdates. I would make them dinner, and on Tuesdays and Wednesdays Jay would arrive at seven, and I'd send the girls out the door, each with their backpacks and a school lunch in their hands.

I thought that it was working as well as arrangements like these could work. Half the time, Delaney would cry on the way out the door, wailing, "I will miss my bedroom!" or, worse, "I will miss my mom!" Meanwhile, my super-organized Adele began forgetting things —her math binder, her sheet music—at Dad's house, maybe, I suspected, in an effort to get the two of us in the same place as often as she could. I held it together for the hand-offs, but it had taken me a few months to stop being a wreck once they were gone. These days, I felt guilty about how much I enjoyed my kid-free hours. I could watch what-ever I wanted, read a book uninterrupted, even go out for an eight o'clock yoga class, or to sit in a coffee shop if I liked.

I tried to make it painless, to assure the girls that Daddy and I might not live together but would always be their parents . . . but every time Jay took them, it felt like pulling a bandage off a half-healed wound, making everything bleed again. It hurt, sometimes in a way that felt unendurable. I blamed Jay. I blamed Amy. I blamed myself, too, sometimes, thinking if I'd only paid more attention to him, if I'd only worked less, if we'd only made love more. *It should have been Andy,* a voice in my mind would whisper when I'd think that way. *You shouldn't have settled*—even though I'd never thought of marrying Jay as settling at the time. *You should have waited for him.*

"So, just you?" I asked my ex.

"Just me," he said. "I already mentioned to the girls that I'd be asking. Just a heads-up." Which meant, of course, that it was a fait accompli. As soon as school ended and Delaney came running toward me with her curls and backpack bouncing and her big sister following, walking and reading her book at the same time, the assault began.

"Mommy, Mommy!" Delaney said. "Daddy

462

wants to know if he can come for Passover. Can he? Can he please? I want him to hear me do the Four Questions."

"We were going to do them together," said Adele, closing her book. She'd discovered *Little Women*, one of my favorites at her age, and was reading it for what had to be the third or fourth time.

"What do you guys think?" I asked.

"It would be great!" said Delaney.

"You're only saying that because Daddy gives you ten dollars if you find the *afikomen* and Mom only gives us five," said Adele.

"Ten dollars?" This was the first I'd heard of it.

"I am not!" Delaney said. "I am not saying it because I'm greedy! I just want Daddy to be here!"

I reviewed the guest list. My parents and Nana were flying up, as they did every other year, alternating New York with Los Angeles, where Jonah, who'd astonished everyone by excelling in law school, had passed the California bar on his first attempt, becoming a successful entertainment lawyer and marrying one of his law-school classmates, a coolly pretty and extremely business-like woman named Suzanne. Brenda, who'd become a Seder regular, would be attending, along with Dante, one of my professional victories, who was getting ready to graduate from Cornell.

"You know you always tell, like, everyone in the world to come," said Adele. "Remember the

463

year we left the door open for Elijah and Mr. Hammerschmidt from across the street wandered in?"

"*Wandered* is kind of judgmental. How about we go with *came in?*" Mr. Hammerschmidt had gotten a little forgetful since his wife had died, and one of the things he sometimes forgot was which front door was his.

"And that creepy little kid from two years ago. What was his name? Jason?"

"Jared." Jared was the five-year-old son of that rarity in my line of work, a single father. After we'd explained about the *afikomen*—how a grown-up would hide it, and how the first kid to find it would get a prize—Jared had, very solemnly, followed Jay out of the room and refused to return to the table, even when we explained to him that witnessing the hiding made the finding sort of beside the point. "And he isn't creepy, just little."

My eldest gave me a very adult expression, a little incredulity, a twist of disdain. I suspected I'd be seeing a lot of that look as she entered her teenage years.

"So if you let anyone in the neighborhood just show up, why can't Dad come?"

"Let Daddy come! Let Daddy come!" Delaney chanted.

"The Haggadah says you're supposed to welcome the stranger," Adele pointed out. "It says, 'Let all who are hungry come eat.' "

"Let me think about it," I said. Once we were home I retreated to the little room right beside our bedroom. It had been the nursery, but once Delaney was out of diapers, I'd moved her into a bigger bedroom and turned it into a small office, with a little antique desk and a pink-and-green rug on the floor, and on the walls, the pictures I'd had a photographer friend take of a three-year-old Adele holding her newborn sister in her arms.

I talked with Marissa, who now ran a bakery in Burlington, Vermont. I spoke with Sharon, a colleague at FAS, who'd become my yoga buddy and post-Amy New York City best friend. The verdict: can't hurt. "You should at least find out what's on his mind," Marissa said. "It's good for the girls to see you as a team," was Sharon's take.

So, grudgingly, feeling conflicted in direct proportion to which Delaney and even Adele were excited, I draped the rented tables in the lacy white tablecloths Nana had given me for my wedding, and set them with the china that Jay and I had gotten for our wedding that he'd graciously agreed to let me keep. The girls helped me prepare the Seder plate—bitter herbs for sadness, salt water for tears, a mixture of apples and nuts and honey and wine to represent the mortar with which the Jews had built pyramids for the pharaoh, matzoh for the bread that hadn't had time to rise. Nana was in the kitchen, tasting her brisket, my mother was stirring the chicken soup that I'd made and frozen the weekend before, and my father was setting out napkins and silverware and sneaking peeks at the score of the basketball game on his iPhone when the guests began to arrive. Brenda and Dante, who now towered over his mom, came first, then Jared and his father, Ron, and Taneisha and her daughter, Sondra, a poised and elegant twelve-year-old in a belted white dress and matching sandals. Delaney's eyes lit up when she saw a big girl. "I will show you around," she said, grabbing Sondra and, I suspected, dragging her to her room to show her each of the dozens of stuffed animals that she'd collected and named.

Nana untied her apron as I looked for serving pieces. "You look lovely," she said. I thanked her, hoping it was true. I hadn't agonized over my outfit, but I had spent some time thinking about it, determined not to wear anything more special than usual just because Jay would be there, but wanting to look good, to show him what he was missing. Ten minutes before the doorbell started ringing, I'd settled on a dress I'd bought on sale at Saks, a tube of coral jersey, and a pair of sand-colored sandals with a little bit of a heel. The dress had three-quarter-length sleeves and my preferred high neckline, but it was clingier than the things I normally wore, tight enough to show my shape. I had finally shed the last few pounds of baby weight after Jay had left when, for the first time in my life, I'd become a woman who forgot to eat.

"Hello, ladies!" Enter the ex. My mother kissed his cheek and my dad looked up from his phone long enough to deliver a baleful, albeit brief, glare. The girls mobbed him, Delaney sprinting down the stairs to throw herself against him, Adele permitting her father a single hug and kiss. Once Jay had greeted them, he approached me, with flowers in one hand, candy in the other. "You look beautiful," he said.

"You look nice, too."

It was true. Jay wore a slim-cut single-breasted suit of fine gray wool, a tie in alternating stripes of burnt-orange and gold, and lace-up wing tips polished to a high gloss. In our year apart he'd become significantly balder, a development that had revealed the rectangular shape of his skull, making him look a little Frankensteiny. He'd also gained the seven or eight pounds I'd lost. When we'd met, I'd been struck by his smile, his expressive mouth, the way he'd use his hands when he told stories, and I couldn't wait to feel those hands on me. Maybe it was love that had made him look more attractive than he was. The man standing in front of me now was just another well-dressed guy with good taste, not anyone I would have taken special notice of if I'd seen him in a subway car or in line for a latte at one of the six sustainable coffee shops that had arrived in our neighborhood. Now Jay resembled his father, kind but phlegmatic, without much of a sense of humor, a man you'd want probating your will but not at your table during the last round on Trivia Night at the bar. Not in bed, either.

"These are for you." The flowers were peonies, my favorite, and the candy was dark-chocolate-dipped orange peel. "Why'd you get that?" Delaney complained. "Nobody eats it but Mommy."

"Maybe Mommy deserved a treat, after working so hard to get everything ready," said Jay. He wore the look he always gave me since we'd split, soft-eyed and apologetic, only now I thought I saw something else in his expression . . . Was it hope? Desperation? Actual sadness?

I gave him a polite smile and thanked him, and instructed the girls to put coats in my bedroom, relishing the way Jay stiffened when I said *my*. Delaney, who loved dressing up, was arrayed in a pink party dress with crinolines under the skirt, white tights, and pink patent-leather Mary Janes and a pink bow in her hair. Adele detested waist-bands and collars, and had avoided pants with zippers ever since she was five and had an accident because she couldn't get out of her snow-suit fast enough, but I'd managed to get her to agree to a pair of black leggings and a long, silky white tunic. She'd even consented to a sparkly black band in her hair. Delaney, of course, had begged for a fancy 'do, and I'd watched YouTube tutorials until I could approximate the fishtail braid she'd requested.

With so many children at the meal, and, usually, at least a few adults who weren't familiar with the Passover rituals, I'd condensed the Haggadah to a twenty-minute highlight reel. Wine was sipped (grape juice, in the kids' cases), the Four Questions were asked, all the foods on the Seder plate were explained, and the story of the Exodus was read, round-robin-style, with everyone at the table who could read taking a turn. This year, Dante got the conclusion. " 'Once we were slaves, now we are free,' " Dante read, looking meaning-fully at his mother, who smiled proudly—which meant, I thought, that she'd dumped yet another loser boyfriend. " 'This year we are here, next year in Jerusalem.' " We sang "Dayenu," and I was reminded that Jay's voice was surprisingly tuneful, and that the song was annoyingly long.

As soon as the final verse of "Chad Gadya" had been completed, Nana and my mother and I went to the kitchen to serve the gefilte fish and chopped liver. Delaney took orders, and she and Adele delivered the plates to the table. "Delicious!" Jay exclaimed, even though I'd never known him to be a gefilte fan. "These are just as good as I remember them," he said of Nana's matzoh balls. "Bernie, can I give you a hand?" he asked my dad, taking over the turkey-carving duties.

When I announced I was going to hide the

afikomen, Jay gave me a private eyebrow waggle, the same one he'd done ever since I'd told him I thought that "hide the *afikomen*" sounded like a euphemism for sex. When the meal was over, Jay helped pack the leftovers into Tupperware to-go containers and bundle them into bags for everyone to bring home. He stayed until the last salad fork and soup spoon had been put in the dishwasher, and the Seder plate, the one Adele had made in Hebrew school, was washed and dried and restored to its spot in the cabinet. After my parents and Nana went back to their hotel in Manhattan and Brenda, my last guest, had hugged me goodbye, Jay was still there.

"Let me help you put the girls to bed," he said. Adele had already brushed and flossed, hung up her party clothes, and put on her pajamas and was in bed, scrutinizing *The Popularity Papers* as if the book contained an actual blueprint for popularity, and Delaney was asleep on the couch with her shoes kicked off and the soles of her white tights grimy. "Come on, party girl," he said, lifting her into his arms. With her eyes still shut, Delaney settled her head against his shoulder. I felt the familiar tearing sensation, the same pain I felt every time I heard the girls refer, with increasing nonchalance, to "Daddy's house," or whenever I watched them follow him out the door. I had never wanted this divided life for Adele and Delaney. I could have forgiven Jay for an affair, could maybe even have forgiven him for an affair with one of my best friends, if he hadn't hurt his daughters this way.

"Here's your coat," I said.

"Here's your hat, what's your hurry," said Jay. "Is this what they call the bum's rush?" He draped his coat over his arm and stood facing me at the base of the stairs. "It felt good to be here," he said.

"Passover's always nice." My matter-of-fact, blandly polite tone had to be hurting him more than screaming and shouting.

"Your grandmother's looking well."

"Being single has always agreed with her," I said. "She told me once that she never got to travel when she was married. She never got to have the life she wanted until she was alone."

"Zing," said Jay, and followed me into the dining room, where I started zipping the good china into its padded containers, where the bowls and plates would stay until the next occasion. Jay picked up a container and started zipping like nothing had happened, like everything was fine.

"How have you been feeling?" he'd asked. "You had your appointment with Dr. Adelman last month, right?"

Oh, that was a mean trick, remembering my annual check-in with the cardiologist, acting like he cared. When I'd been pregnant with each of the girls, he had accompanied me to every single doctor's visit, even the early ones when all they did was weigh me and check my blood pressure. He'd framed both girls' ultrasounds, and, when they'd each been delivered, the cord cut and the goop wiped off, he had cradled them in his arms and sung "You Are My Sunshine."

"What are you doing here?" I asked, finally letting an edge creep into my voice. "What do you want?"

Jay treated me to a Jay-ish sigh—an audible inhale, a meaningful pause, then the noisy rush of air that telegraphed the extent of his frustration or his pain. "I guess the girls told you about Amy."

"The girls didn't tell me anything." I saw his eyes widen. "I don't ask. What you do is your business."

"They don't say anything?" He sounded incredulous.

"They tell me when you take them to the amusement park or the zoo. Or out to dinner—Delaney tells me about that. But as far as your personal life . . ." I shrugged, and then glanced at the door, already imagining what would happen when he'd left, how I would take off my dress and my shoes, pull on my most worn and comfortable white cotton pajamas, and climb into the bed that we'd once shared and I had since claimed as my own.

Jay assumed a somber aspect. "Amy went back to Leonard."

"I'm sorry," I said, while not feeling particularly sorry. Not feeling much of anything, really. Was it possible that I'd finally stopped caring?

Jay reached for my hands, which I immediately filled with more plates. Undeterred, he performed another one of those three-part sighs, and then said in a low voice, "I made a mistake."

For so long I had prayed for this moment. I had dragged out the divorce proceedings longer than I needed to, hoping he would change his mind. I had thought that time would make him miss us, make him appreciate what he'd thrown away. With a strange woman sleeping beside him (and snoring, I hoped), he would recall Delaney's high, sweet voice and how she'd slip into our bed on Sunday mornings, while forgetting her tantrums, or how the bed invasions had curtailed our sex life. He'd remember Adele's good grades, and he wouldn't think about how every year our parent-teacher conferences had included a long talk about Adele's inability to make friends, or the cost of the therapist she was now seeing. He would picture me like this, with my hair styled, in lipstick that matched my dress, with the house clean and a home-cooked meal on the table, and forget whatever it was about me that he'd found so wearying or unlovely, whatever it was that had sent him to my former best friend. He would miss us, and he'd want us back, and I, obviously, would want the same thing.

But now? I looked at him—pursed lips, bent chin, hands in his pockets as he gazed at the floor, the very picture of contrition. I should have been moved. I wasn't. It was as if I'd been frozen, as if I was now a woman made of ice, and he'd come at me not with a torch or even a candle, but with a toothpick, and was *plink plink plink*ing against the smooth impenetrability of my body. I couldn't feel a thing.

Courtly as ever, Jay didn't make me say it. "See you soon," he said quietly, and turned toward the door.

"Wait." He turned around. The hope was so bright on his face that it wrenched at me to blot it out.

"I heard someone say that people who were married are never really unmarried," I said. "When you have kids together, you don't get to really untie the knot. We're family."

He shook his head. "That isn't what I want."

"I'll always care about you," I said, knowing how limp and wan the words sounded, how they were the opposite of what he'd wanted to hear. Even rage, even fury was passion. Now he didn't matter enough for me to be angry.

"You'll find someone." I made a face. "You found me, didn't you?"

He shook his head without answering, and walked to the door. I remembered listening to him packing and leaving a week after I'd con-fronted him at the restaurant, the sound of his suitcase bumping down each stair. I still felt frozen, like all of this was happening in a movie that I was watching; like it was hurting, but it was hurting someone else.

In my bedroom, I took off my makeup and smoothed expensive and allegedly restorative cream on my face. The pajamas felt as good as I'd hoped that they would, and my hair, unpinned, fell in a luxuriant tumble, the curls still dark-brown and glossy. Standing in front of the mirror, I unbuttoned the two top buttons of my shirt and looked at my scar. It had faded some over the years, the livid pink softening, the raised, corded knot of it so familiar that I hardly even noticed it.

Now I touched it gently. *You should have something pretty, right there,* I remembered Andy saying. Did any love ever feel as sweet as first love? Were we all just damaged goods now, battered cans in the grocery-store sale bin, day-old bread, marked down at the register, hoping that someone would look past the obvious flaws and love us enough to take us home?

You could find him, the voice in my head whispered. My laptop was in my office, one room over. I could punch his name into the search bar and read a hundred magazine pieces about the doping and the disgrace. Maybe I'd find a "Where Are They Now" story, and maybe it would say where he lived, what he was doing. Did he ever think of me?

Probably not, I decided. He certainly had other things to occupy his mind. "Hello, young lovers," I sang as I put a glass of water on the bedside table, plucked a few dead blooms out of the bouquet on top of my bookshelf, and tucked myself into bed. *All of my mem'ries are happy tonight. I've had a love of my own.*

Andy
2015

Because there seemed to be no one else available or interested in the job, Andy took the first week of May off from work, went to Philadelphia, and began the process of sifting through Mr. Sills's belongings. He divided it into piles, sorting things into trash cans and crates—toss, recycle, donate, see if anyone wants. The old newspapers and magazines went to a used-book store, after Andy called the Free Library to make sure there wasn't a demand for stacks of *National Geographic*s from the 1970s. The antique teapots and china plates, the hand-painted gold-rimmed teacups, all got wrapped, boxed, and driven back to the shops from which some of them had surely come. The mirrors went to Goodwill, along with the paintings, although Andy kept the picture of the yellow parrot for himself. "It really brightens up the place," he said when he hung it above his television set in Brooklyn. Andy found a charity that sent a moving van and three glum-looking men to collect the TV set and the furniture (he later learned that the men were doing community service after they'd each received their third DUI).

After four days, the apartment was almost empty, except for the corduroy chair that had been Mr. Sills's favorite, the photo albums and the scrapbooks, and a few boxes that still needed sorting. Andy settled in with a contractor-sized trash can beside him, and started to page through the books. Some of them were family albums that began generations ago. Andy recognized Mr. Sills as a little boy only after he began wearing glasses. He watched his friend grow from a smiling kid in old-fashioned knee-length shorts that became long pants, to a young man in an army uniform, to a groom wearing a dark suit and a serious expres-sion, to a new father, with his arm wrapped protectively around a pretty, slim woman who cradled a wrapped bundle in her arms.

There were hundreds of pictures of the family of three throughout the years, at a dozen different occasions, church picnics and parties and trips to the shore. Andy wondered if there'd ever been an attempt at other children, but Mrs. Sills hadn't appeared pregnant in any of the shots, so maybe she'd never conceived again, or maybe they'd decided that one was enough. Within the jumble of images of a small family enjoying the pleasures of a happy life in the city—block parties and fireworks viewings, boys in drooping swimsuits splashing in the kiddie pools or, later, graduating to the deep end and cannonballing from a diving board—there was one shot that was always the same. Every April 14, Mr. Sills and his wife would pose with DeVaughn on his birthday.

Andy watched DeVaughn grow from a baby cradled in his mother's arms to a toddler who stood, holding her hand and looking up with adoration, to a little boy with a Wiffle bat, to a bigger boy with a bike. He saw the pictures go from black-and-white to Polaroids to color. Mr. Sills grew an Afro, and wore a succession of eye-glasses, each pair more enormous than the last, while his wife traded her ironed dresses for bell-bottoms and turtlenecks. The pictures all had the same thing written underneath them— *DeVaughn Anthony Sills, April 14, our "pride and joy."* They went all the way through 1978, when the pattern broke. There was the April shot, with DeVaughn smiling as he put one large hand on his father's shoulders and the other one on his mother's back. Then there was another picture, taken only a couple of months later. Same spot on the street, in front of the house where Andy was now sitting, same arrangement—son standing between mom and dad—only this time, DeVaughn was in a cap and gown. The cap seemed to float on top of his cloud of hair, and the robe was dark-purple with gold accents, Roman Catholic's colors. Mr. Sills was smiling so broadly that his glasses had been lifted to eyebrow level, and Mrs. Sills, in a brightly colored patterned shirt that Andy thought was called a dashiki, held a white handkerchief in one hand. "High school graduation, 1978," Mr. Sills had written.

There were no more pictures after that one, just a blank page, followed by a single clipping from the *Examiner*: *Arrest Made in Murder Case.*

A 19-year-old man has been charged with murder in the wake of a shooting in Kensington. DeVaughn Anthony Sills was arrested Monday in connection with the October slaying of David Cassady, who was found mortally wounded on the 200 block of East Indiana Street at 4:29 a.m., police said. Cassady, 19, had been shot once in the abdomen, and was pronounced dead at Temple University Hospital later that morning. Eye-witnesses say they saw a dark-colored sedan drive up Indiana. The driver then rolled down his window and shot Cassady, police said. They are now searching for the car's passenger and the murder weapon.

My father, Andy thought. His knee was bouncing, faster and faster, causing the plastic-topped pages of the album to bounce against his other leg.

He turned the page. On November 26, 1980, a Common Pleas Court jury convicted DeVaughn Anthony Sills and Andrew Raymond Landis in the 1978 slaying of Kensington native David Cassady.

Andy stilled his leg and his drumming fingers and made himself get up, go to the kitchen, find a glass, and drink some water. *Change the setting, change the mood,* his therapist, the one he'd seen for a year, used to say. When he got stuck in the spiral of feeling insurmountably embarrassed, she'd taught him to make himself go outside if he was in, or inside if he was out, to interrupt the plummet with something as simple as making a cup of tea or spending a few minutes working on a crossword puzzle. He'd downloaded apps for Sudoku and Whirly Word on his phone and had stocked his cabinets back in Brooklyn with a dozen different varieties of herbal tea.

Back in Mr. Sills's living room, he sat, thinking. The windowsills were lined with potted plants, a half-dozen orchids with white and pink and purple blooms, succulents and aloe plants and cacti that Andy hoped he could convince some of the neighbors to take. He imagined his old friend cutting these stories out of the newspaper, centering them on the page, annotating them in his own handwriting—*DeVaughn* was all he'd put beneath the article. How had it felt to write his son's name there, the way he had for each of the birthday shots, and the pictures of DeVaughn on his bike, at his T-ball and softball games, at a dozen birthday parties and Christmases? What had it cost him, to put those letters down on paper, underneath the stories about the awful things his "pride and joy" had done?

For years following DeVaughn's conviction there were no pictures at all. Mr. Sills had left a few blank pages, as if he and his wife and his imprisoned son had disappeared, had fallen down into the hole of their grief and pulled the manhole cover up over the top. Andy wondered if he'd gone to visit his son and what that had been like, and whether anyone had thought to bring a camera.

When the pages started to fill again, Mrs. Sills's hair had been cut very short and was starting to go gray. Mr. Sills had put on perhaps twenty pounds, and had shaved off the extravagant mustache he'd worn during DeVaughn's high school years. Andy noticed the way Mrs. Sills's mouth always turned down at the corners, where previously she'd greeted the camera with a sunny smile, and the way Mr. Sills's eyes looked weary behind the lenses of his glasses, as he and his wife posed, arm in arm, at picnics and weddings and family reunions in Fairmount Park, at anniversaries and retirement parties and christenings.

Midway through 1982, there was a picture of a niece's Sweet Sixteen. Then another blank page. Andy's fingers began drumming as he flipped and saw, under the plastic, not a photograph but, instead, a black-bordered program. *Lavonia Rita Sills. 1942–1983.* There was a picture, a black-and-white shot of just her face in profile, centered beneath the dates, and then the words *Who can find a virtuous woman, for her price is far above rubies. Strength and honor are her clothing; and she shall rejoice in time to come.*

Forty-one, Andy thought, flipping past another blank page. The next picture he saw was his own. It was wintertime, judging from his coat and hat, and there was a skinny twelve-year-old Andy, with two canvas bags looped, Indiana Jones–style, across his chest, grinning at the camera.

He didn't remember Mr. Sills ever taking his picture, but here was the evidence. Andy turned the pages and watched himself grow up. High school cross-country, the first race he'd ever won, the first time he'd made the All-State team. Mr. Sills seemed to have a record of every race, and he had an entire album devoted to the Olympics, where news stories and professional photographs alternated with the snapshots he'd taken of the Acropolis and the Parthenon and Hadrian's Arch.

Andy flipped back to the first picture, that big, hopeful smile, how skinny his chest had been, how big the bags of papers were. He'd been so lonely. He wasn't black; he wasn't white; he wasn't allowed to have friends. He hadn't had a father; he'd barely had a mother. One pair of grandparents had been evicted from his life, the other two he'd never met. What would things have been like if his father had been there? Would he have pushed himself as hard as he'd pushed, would he have made it as far? Maybe not. Or maybe he would have ended up a championship runner, only one with the good sense to have retired after Athens. He knew that he couldn't blame an absent father for his bad choices—taking steroids, letting Rachel go. What would have happened if he'd gone to her, that terrible day that Bob Rieper had told him that his father was alive? What if he'd gone to her and asked her to call off her wedding and told her *We belong together?*

He found that he was pacing, and probably had been for a while, walking back and forth in Mr. Sills's almost empty living room, imagining impossible futures. He had a life now, just a different kind of life; one where he made sure the top shelves got dusted and the bathrooms were cleaned, that Paul didn't forget to punch his time card and that Martin, who now ran the paint department, didn't curse in front of the customers. In this life, he'd been a good friend and a good worker and, now, a good boss. Maybe it wasn't much, but it wasn't nothing . . . and he could look in the mirror again.

He flipped through the albums one more time, to see if he'd missed anything . . . and, sure enough, after he'd pried two blank pages apart, he found it—a single picture with two words underneath. In the shot, his father stood beside DeVaughn, the two of them looking at the bundle in Andy Senior's arms. Andy could just see the top of his bald, newborn head, and his little clenched fist waving like he was giving the world the black power salute. His father's gaze was tender, his mouth open, like he'd been saying something to his friend. Mr. Sills stood beside them, one of his hands on DeVaughn's shoulder, the other on Andy Senior's back.

My Boys, Mr. Sills had written.

Andy's car keys were on the spindly legged black table that was still standing by Mr. Sills's front door. Andy took them, carried a pair of boxes out to the car, and drove as if he'd made the trip a hundred times before, from I-95 to Vine Street to Spring Garden. It took just fifteen minutes to cross the borders that divided the gentrifying neighborhoods from the edge of Center City. He parked and looked around, seeing the kind of neighborhood that was politely called "in transition," with treatment centers and halfway houses for drunks and addicts, and then a diner that had gotten a great review in the *Examiner* and hosted a DJ and dancing on the weekends. There were gas stations and quick-lube spots, a little Colombian restaurant with its front painted bright red and orange advertising gourmet hot chocolate, a Spaghetti Warehouse, and a tired-looking church where people were lined up for free lunch.

Maybe he's not home, he thought. It was a Sunday in May, a few puffy clouds drifting in the bright-blue sky, people pedaling along the bike lanes, the weather warm but not humid; a perfect day to take in a ball game or go for a stroll by the river. With his throat constricted and heavy and his heart pounding hard, Andy checked the directory and walked up two flights, then down a hallway with worn tanned carpet and walls painted institutional beige. He smelled canned soup and Bengay, and heard the sounds of televisions coming from underneath the doors, the Phillies' play-by-play announcer, and then Marvin Gaye. "You know, we've got to find a way, to bring some lovin' here today." *Your father always loved that song,* his mother had once told him. *Tell me,* Andy had asked. *Tell me what else he liked, tell me who did he love, tell me who he was.* But her face had closed up, and she'd turned away and hadn't told him anything. Not then. Not ever.

He held his breath and knocked. He won't be home, he thought. He isn't here. Then the door swung open, and there was his dad.

He wore a plaid shirt and khaki pants and bright white athletic socks. It was the socks that undid him, that untied the knot that had bound his heart forever. He could imagine his father, who, clearly, didn't have much, walking to one of the stores on Chestnut Street or maybe even more than one of them, looking carefully through the merchandise, carrying his selection to the cash register, counting out exact change with dollar bills and pennies.

You can stop running now, he imagined he heard Mr. Sills saying.

"Andy," said his father, and held out his hand.

Rachel and Andy

2015

The telephone rang, jolting me out of a dream about college, where I'd signed up for a class that I hated but had forgotten to go to the registrar's to drop, and now it was the day of the final and I hadn't even bought the books. Next to me was Delaney, who'd fallen asleep in what she called "the big bed" wearing nothing but a rhinestone tiara and a pair of Hello Kitty underpants, with Moochie, the little terrier we'd adopted for her birthday, asleep in the crook of her arm.

"Hello?"

"Rachel?" I sat up, with the last shreds of the dream evaporating.

"Brenda? What's wrong?"

"Nothing's wrong," she said indignantly. "Jesus. If I hadn't known you for so long I'd be insulted."

"Well, it is . . ." I glanced at the clock, preparing to scold her for how early she'd called, except it was almost nine, which was a long way from ridiculous. "Saturday!" I finally remembered.

"I know it's Saturday. But I just got off the phone with Dante, and he wants me to come up for parents' weekend, except I already told Laurel that I'd babysit for her, and also . . ." Her voice took on a familiar, good-natured wheedling tone. "That's a long-ass bus ride up there."

"That it is." With the phone against my ear I slipped out of bed. Moochie opened one eye, considered her options, then recurled herself and went back to sleep. I walked downstairs in my white cotton nightgown, which covered me right down to my toes and had pockets. Now that I was officially man-less, I could wear whatever I wanted to bed, and cover up anything that I didn't feel like shaving or waxing. "But it's a pretty drive, especially when the leaves are changing."

"Don't give me 'pretty drive,' " Brenda said. "Isn't there some kind of fund for poor single mothers whose kids got into Ivy League colleges, and they want to go visit them, only they don't want to take the bus?"

"I believe we call that fund 'my credit card.' " I used my shoulder to keep the phone in place while I started a pot of coffee, put four slices of bread into the toaster, and wondered, again, whether it was time to repaint the first floor. I'd done the bedroom over the summer, going from the light blue that Jay had chosen to a creamy ivory, with new curtains and a new bedspread to match. New pillows, on which he'd never slept, and new sheets. Bit by bit, I was reclaiming the house for myself and the girls, turning it into an increasingly girlie little nest.

While Brenda complained about Laurel's lax attitude toward her children—"She lets them drink that energy stuff, where it says right on the can it's not for kids!"—I emptied the dishwasher and looked at the calendar. Delaney had a birthday party that afternoon. Adele had a makeup oboe lesson, and then, as was all too commonly the case, nothing. Maybe I'd take Adele out for dim sum and then to the library, and then we'd pick up Delaney and grab something to cook for dinner.

"So listen." Brenda paused in her litany of complaints. "What if," she said, then stopped.

After over a decade on the job, I knew the steps to this dance. "What if what?"

"What if, just for example, if you knew that a mom with little kids was doing something bad, but you didn't want to, you know, tell anyone about it because they'd start a file on her and she'd lose her babies."

"What would I do?" I asked. "What do you

488

mean by *something bad?* Are the kids in danger?"
She was talking about Laurel, I thought, and there
was already a file on Laurel, one that had been
started after she'd told her pediatrician that she
gave her three-year-old daughter, Olivia, a
Tylenol PM so she'd stop getting up in the
middle of the night.

Brenda sighed. "It's my daughter," she said.
"My baby, you know? I don't want to get her in
any trouble. I love her, and I know that the way
she turned out is 'cause I wasn't around enough
and I wasn't the best mom myself."

"I know how much you love her, but I know
you love Olivia and Tyler, too."

Brenda sighed. "When I was over there last
night I saw stuff in her bathroom."

"What kind of stuff?"

"Needles."

Shit. Shit shit shit. Laurel had been through
rehab three times already, and had been clean for
almost six months.

"It's that boyfriend," Brenda said. "That Jason.
Maybe it's his stuff. He's a bad influence, I've
been telling Laurel that he is. Maybe they're his
needles."

"Do you think she's using?"

Silence.

"Do you think the kids are safe?"

Silence, and then another sigh. "Maybe I could
just take them for a while. I've got an empty

room, with Dante away. Maybe it's just a slip, and I can call her therapist and some of her friends, and she can get it together and I'll watch the babies."

While we worked out a plan for Laurel and Olivia and Marcus, Moochie traipsed down the stairs, with Delaney behind her, both of them probably drawn by the scent of toast. Upstairs, I heard the shower go on. Ever since she'd turned ten, Adele, who'd always been fastidiously neat, had gotten even more neurotic about possibly smelling bad and was bathing twice a day.

"Can I have bacon?" Delaney wore a long-sleeved white shirt with a pink star in the center and capri-length polka-dotted pink leggings, an ensemble that would be joined by slip-on sneakers covered in multicolored sparkly sequins. *Understated* was not a word you'd apply to my little one's sense of style.

I pointed at the refrigerator, then at the cupboard. Delaney took the bacon out of the fridge, then rummaged for the frying pan. When I pointed to the table she frowned and pointed upstairs, letting me know that it was Adele's turn to set, but when I pointed again, she gave a noisy, Jay-influenced sigh and started pulling out place mats and napkins. I was just hanging up and starting to boil a pot of water for poached eggs when Adele came downstairs in her bathrobe with an angry expression and her hair full of suds.

"The showerhead fell off," she said, and pulled it out of her pocket to show me.

"Oh, shit."

"Language!" said Delaney, through a mouthful of toast.

"Okay, you go rinse off in my shower, and then I've got a quick call to make after breakfast, so I need both of you to walk the dog and be ready to go by ten. There's a present for Maria Cristina in the closet, Delaney. You just need to wrap it. Adele, help your sister."

"Don't I always?" grumbled Adele, who was turning the corner from the charming path of girlhood to the freeway of adolescence. She gave me a withering look, dropped the showerhead on the counter, and stalked back up the stairs.

Okay, I thought, as I scrolled through my phone, looking for the number for Laurel's therapist. I could take Adele to her lesson, run to the home-goods store, buy another showerhead and maybe even get someone to explain to me how to install it, before picking up Adele and taking Delaney to her party. And if that didn't work I'd call a plumber. "Thirty minutes!" I called. The water boiled, the coffee dripped, the bacon spat in the pan, and the house was warm, full of good smells and comfortable couches and music and two relatively happy girls. *All will be well,* I told myself, and dashed upstairs to take a shower of my own.

• • •

Two hours later, after dropping off a sulky Adele, appeasing Delaney with a package of Jolly Ranchers, and getting lost twice, I found a parking spot at Wallen Home Goods and carried the amputated showerhead inside. I peered at the signs, thinking that I'd need to get my eyes checked soon, and led Delaney through paint and toward plumbing. "Ooh!" she said, spying the strips of paint chips in their revolving displays. "Can I take some?" she asked as she spun one of the racks to the pinks and purples.

"Just a few. We have to hurry." I watched as she considered each strip, sounding out the names of the colors. "Come on, cookie," I said, and she sighed, filling her hands and following me deeper into the store. In the plumbing section I cornered a tall, pimply kid in a Wallen shirt.

"Excuse me," I said, pulling the showerhead out of my purse. "This fell off. Do I need a whole new one, or is there a way to put it back on?"

"Let me find someone who knows," he squawked, and practically ran down the aisle.

Delaney sighed. "This is boring," she said, staring at the wall of bathroom fixtures.

"Someday I will tell you about the week I spent building houses."

She eyed me with a mixture of skepticism and respect. "You built houses?"

"I surely did."

A plumbing specialist arrived, and we discussed my situation, eventually choosing a new shower-head and the tools I could use to try to install it. The clerk also gave me the number of a reliable plumber. I suspected I'd be calling him before long.

"Delaney!" I turned around, but she was gone. Shit. I looked at my phone and dialed Adele's oboe instructor while jogging back to the paint section. "Hi, Marcia, I'm running a little late. . . . She's got a book, right? Just tell her I'm on my way."

Marcia said that Adele was fine and could fill the extra time by practicing. Delaney wasn't in the paint aisle. "Excuse me," I called, raising my voice so the shoppers could hear me in the huge, echoing store. "Has anyone seen a little girl with curly hair? Pink and white shirt, sparkly sneakers?" People shook their heads as the PA system crackled, and I heard, "Would Rachel Pearl Kravitz please come to the service desk up front?"

Smiling, I raced to the front of the store. Delaney's middle name was Pearl, so, of course, she'd assumed that mine was, too. I saw my daughter perched on the counter, her paint samples fanned out in her hand, talking intently to a man with close-cropped dark curls.

"Mommy!" she squealed. I saw that somehow she'd also glommed on to a balloon and a Hershey bar. "I got lost!"

"I'm so sorry, honey. I turned around and you weren't there, and I was so worried!"

She handed me her pile of paint chips and hopped nimbly to the ground. "A lady asked if I was lost and took me up here, and this man says I can have a free sample of any color paint I want! And I can take it home and paint it on my wall and if I don't like how it looks, then I can come back and get another one and it is also free! And look what he made me!" She opened her palm and showed me the letter D, made out of a straightened and rebent paper clip. "D for Delaney! And I can keep it! Can I have the candy bar?"

"No more candy, and we don't have time right now, but . . ." My voice died in my throat as the man turned and I could see him. The manager. The paper-clip man.

"Andy."

"Rachel," he said. "I didn't know your married name."

"Oh, she isn't married," Delaney said smartly. "We are divorced. That means Mommy and Daddy don't live together anymore, they live three subway stops apart, and in my daddy's house I have to share a room with my big sister."

He kept looking at me, his dark eyes, his smile, all of it so familiar, so welcoming. "Andy," I said again, in a voice that I could barely hear.

Delaney frowned. "His name tag says An-DREW."

494

"Andy is a nickname," he told her. He was looking at me, and I felt like I was going to faint. My heart was beating so hard I felt myself shaking.

"Honey, can you go wait for Mommy on that bench right there?"

"Can I have the Hershey bar?"

"Yes."

Delaney skipped away with her prize before I could change my mind. Andy came out from around the desk and stood close enough to touch me. When I'd known him he'd always been in motion, but now he was still, motionless, waiting.

"I should have known," he said. "She looks just like you."

I put my hands on the desk, turning away. I couldn't look at him. I was so sad, so mad at him, and my heart was in my throat, and I had so many questions: *Why didn't you come for me?* and *How did you live through what happened?* and *Who are you? Who are you now?*

Instead, I pulled the showerhead out of my purse. "It broke," I said, and then I started to cry.

"Then I'll fix it," he said.

"I missed you," I said. "I thought you'd come back for me, but you didn't."

"I should have," he said. "I wanted to, so many times, but I thought you didn't want me, and then I made such a mess out of everything."

"So now you're here?" I tried to make myself

look at him. He was bigger than he'd been as a runner, that almost scary whippet-lean look gone. He looked like a man now, broad-shouldered and solid, with a nametag that said "Manager" and glasses with gold rims.

"Now I'm here," he confirmed. I looked at his hands. No rings. He was close enough for me to feel the warmth from his body, to smell his familiar smell, and I realized, as he touched my cheek, then my hair, that I had never stopped hoping for this, not in all the years we'd been apart.

My phone buzzed. WHERE R U? Adele had texted, and I knew that if I didn't leave soon Delaney would be late for her party. "I have to go," I said. My voice sounded gaspy. "I'm late . . . I have to . . ." The showerhead and the paint samples I'd been holding spilled onto the floor. I bent down, still crying, not knowing what I was doing, with no idea of what I wanted to happen next.

Andy put his hands on my shoulders and pulled me gently to my feet. "Do you remember the night we met? Do you remember what I asked you?"

I nodded, thinking of why I'd gone down to the emergency room that night, how I'd meant to collect a story for Alice, and how, if it was a good one, she'd answer my question and tell me what I needed to know. *Will it hurt?*

"You asked me, 'Does it hurt?' " I told him, crying harder. I'd lived long enough now to know the answer. *It hurts more than you think you can stand,* I would tell our little-girl and little-boy selves, two children lost in different dark woods, *and no one escapes it . . . but it's going to be better than you can believe.*

"I love you," I said, not caring that my face was wet and that I couldn't stop crying, not caring that I'd said it first. "You always had my heart."

"Rachel," said Andy, "I will love you forever." Then he wrapped me in his arms, and I buried my face in the soft spot just beneath his shoulder, until he put his fingers under my chin and tilted my face up to his and kissed me.

Acknowledgments

First, I want to acknowledge my agent, Joanna Pulcini, and my editor, Greer Hendricks, with whom I've worked for many years, on many books, and whose fingerprints are on every scene and every sentence of this one. Both of them put in endless hours reading countless drafts and turning *Who Do You Love* into a story they thought readers would want (here's hoping they were right!).

My brilliant, funny, and unflappably patient and kind assistant, Meghan Burnett, worked overtime on this one to make sure that Rachel and Andy could inhabit their respective worlds fully. Thank you, Meghan, for never blinking, no matter what weird thing I told you I needed to know about, for never complaining, no matter what impossible feats I was asking you to perform. You're the best.

I am very grateful to Katherine Compitus, who helped with background about MSW programs in New York City; Chris Chmielewski and Patrick Donnelly, who gave me insight into the runner's life; and Laura Hoagland, for sharing her own story about life with tricuspid atresia. Apologies for the liberties I took with the 2004 Olympics, and for demoting Hicham El Guerrouj, the real gold medalist, to second place.

Sarah Cantin stepped up to bat in the ninth

inning and hit it out of the ballpark. Also at Atria, I am grateful for the help and support of Haley Weaver, Kitt Reckord-Mabicka, Suzanne Donahue, Lisa Sciambra, Lisa Keim, Hillary Tisman, Elisa Shokoff, Kathleen Rizzo, and Lisa Silverman. Jin Yu, who does online marketing, might be the only person in the world who loves Twitter as much as I do. Judith Curr, publisher of Atria Books, and Carolyn Reidy, CEO and president of Simon & Schuster, continue to be powerhouses and role models whom I want to be when I grow up. I'm also grateful to Joanna's assistant, Haley Heidemann. Finally, big love to copyeditor extraordinaire Nancy Inglis, who came out of retirement and saved me from myself another dozen times, and to my friend Carol Williams for her thoughtful advice.

At Simon & Schuster UK, I'm grateful to Suzanne Baboneau, Ian Chapman, and Jo Dickinson. Marcy Engelman is a PR miracle worker and a true friend who has never once made me feel bad for being completely obsessed with *The Bachelor*. Thanks to Simone Swink and Patty Neger at *Good Morning America* for giving me a platform on which to dissect the Most Dramatic Rose Ceremony Ever, and to Trish Hall and Jessica Lustig at the *New York Times* for letting me get back to my opinionating roots and write about Passover traditions, personal grooming, and mean girls in assisted living.

At Engelman & Co., Emily Gambir helps to tell the world about my books. At Greater Talent Network, my lecture agent, Jessica Fee, lets me travel the country and tell my stories. Tamara Staples took my author photograph and Albert Tang and Chin-Yee Lai made this book, and the rest of my backlist, look fresh and enticing.

On the home front, I am, as ever, grateful to Terri Gottlieb for tending to my girls and my garden. Thanks to my mom, Frances Frumin Weiner; her partner, Clair Kaplan; Clair's son, David; and my siblings, Jake, Molly, and Joe Weiner and David Reek. Adam Bonin's love and support go above and beyond. He is a first-rate father and a great friend. Susan Abrams will always be my BFF. Lucy Jane and Phoebe Pearl are the lights of my life. I am proud to be their mother every day.

A very special shout-out to my Berkshires breakfast club—Tom O'Reilly, Tim Swain, Charles Cohen, Pat Donnelly, Emma Hart, Elizabeth Ekeblad, Lesley Carter, and Franklin Mattei. I will always say "hi" to you in the halls.

To Bill Syken, whose father once saw me unexpectedly appear in his house early one morning and grumbled, "You again?" Thank you for being with me through the hard times, for always making me laugh, and for showing me, through your patience and kindness, what love looks like. Me, again. Me, forever.

And to my readers, for coming with me this far.

Permissions

Center Point Large Print
600 Brooks Road / PO Box 1
Thorndike, ME 04986-0001 USA

(207) 568-3717

US & Canada:
1 800 929-9108
www.centerpointlargeprint.com

11-15